"Do you somehow imagine, Cecilia, that I have been suffering from unrequited love these last six years?"

Delacourt threw back his head and forced himself to laugh. "Unrequited lust, perhaps."

Suddenly, their gazes locked. He stepped nearer, studying her. And then, hidden deeply in her wide blue eyes, he saw it. Anger, yes. And loathing. But there was something else. *Desire.* The merest hint. But Delacourt was a master of seduction. He could sense its keen edge tormenting her. Delacourt slipped his finger beneath her chin, tilting up her face. One red-gold curl brushed the back of his wrist, like silken fire. Her breath had sped up to short, desperate pants. She was afraid. And enthralled.

Good God, he wanted her.

And she wanted him.

He was not perfectly sure which truth frightened him more.

A WOMAN OF VIRTUE

A WOMAN SCORNED

MY FALSE HEART

Books by Liz Carlyle

A Deal With the Devil
The Devil You Know
No True Gentleman
A Woman of Virtue
Beauty Like the Night
A Woman Scorned
My False Heart

Tea for Two (anthology with Cathy Maxwell)

LIZ CARLYLE

A Woman of Virtue

POCKET BOOKS

New York   London   Toronto   Sydney

An *Original* Publication of POCKET BOOKS

POCKET BOOKS, a division of Simon & Schuster, Inc.
1230 Avenue of the Americas, New York, NY 10020

Copyright © 2001 by S. T. Woodhouse

ISBN -13: 978-0-7434-1055-7
ISBN -10: 0-7434-1055-6

First Pocket Books printing March 2001

10 9 8 7 6 5

POCKET and colophon are registered trademarks of Simon & Schuster, Inc.

Original Hand lettering by Iskra Design

Manufactured in the United States of America

For information regarding special discounts for bulk purchases, please contact Simon & Schuster Special Sales at 1-800-456-6798 or business@simonandschuster.com

To my three sisters,
who looketh well to the ways
of their households,
and eateth not the bread of idleness.

Open thy mouth, judge righteously,
and plead the cause of the poor and needy.
Who can find a virtuous woman?
for her price is far above rubies.
The heart of her husband doth safely trust
*   in her,*
so that he shall have no need of spoil.
She will do him good and not evil all the
*   days of her life.*

—Proverbs 31:9–12

A
Woman
of
Virtue

PROLOGUE

~

Who can find a virtuous woman?

June 1818

Lord Delacourt thought he'd finally found her. God's most perfect creation. And she had breasts like plump summer peaches. Bathed in gold and brushed with pink by a shaft of late-day sun which streamed almost celestially through the open barn loft, her high, perfectly sculpted orbs bounced and glimmered as she moved, tempting a man's mouth to unrepentant sin.

As he leaned precariously forward to better peer over the door, the peaches bounced yet again, and Delacourt found himself unexpectedly eager to be led astray. Rather shocking, that—both his lust and old Wally Waldron's taste in women.

Initially, he'd not been at all sure that he wanted to take a tumble inside a dusty horse stall with a local strumpet, especially not one of another man's choosing. The jaded and discriminating viscount preferred a different sort of woman altogether, one who took no one's shilling but his and slaked no one's need but his.

Nonetheless, this woman—with her bare breasts and her pile of flame-gold hair—was far too fine to leave unattended. And until now, it had been a dull day at Newmarket. The first four races had been both uneventful and unprofitable. Then in the fifth, Sands' Setting Star had come in first with twelve-to-one odds while David's horse had brought up the rear, draining his carefully allotted racing purse along with their last bottle of decent brandy.

But Waldron had watched Setting Star fly over the finish line with a frustrated devilment in his eye. His lips had quirked into a wry grin, and at once he'd turned to Delacourt to extend his generous offer. He had a luscious little armful cooling her heels in the stables, he'd glibly explained, but Waldron had decided Lady Luck was too hot to abandon.

Bored and bad-tempered, the viscount had decided to take a peek. "Just remember, old boy," Waldron had cautioned with a knowing wink. "She's a rowdy piece! A pretty cat with pretty claws likes a little tussle."

"Ah, like that, is it?" Delacourt had responded, but with little concern. He had yet to meet the kitten that wouldn't purr for him.

Still, this one did look like a handful—and in more ways than one. Balanced precariously atop an up-turned feedbox, the viscount watched in fascination as the woman slithered back into her cotton shift with a motion so sinuous it sobered him. When she jiggled her peaches into place and reached for her stockings, his mouth went dry, his breath caught, and the roar of the Newmarket racetrack faded into sensual oblivion.

Oh, yes. Delacourt would gladly take Waldron's place with this little *fille de joie*. Then, suddenly, insight dawned. "Peaches" was putting her clothes *back on!* And he was late. Before he could reconsider, Delacourt was off the feedbox and through the door, sliding it shut behind him.

At once, a mop of red-gold curls jerked up and a pair of stockings went gliding to the floor. One hand

flew to her mouth as if she'd not expected anyone.
Deep blue eyes popped wide as saucers. And in confusion, Delacourt yanked her against his chest and
pressed his lips fervently to her ear.

"Hush, sweet!" he coaxed. "Wally sends his regrets.
But I'll gladly ease your disappointment."

But the pretty thing seemed to have her heart set
on Waldron. She pressed the heels of her hands into
Delacourt's shoulders and shoved him back. "Who are
you?" she hissed. "Get out! Are you mad?"

But even half drunk, Delacourt had already seen
that she was a sterling example of feminine pulchri-
tude. "Oh, come now," he coaxed, easing one hand
down to cup her lusciously round bottom. "I'll pleasure you far better than old Wally—and pay twice as
well." He yanked her hips into his, thrust one knee
between her unsteady legs, and gently urged her
backward.

With a gasp, Peaches jerked, stumbling back
against the wall. Eyes widening further, she opened
her mouth and drew breath as if to scream.

Vaguely alarmed, Delacourt clapped one hand over
her lips. Something seemed amiss. But the blood was
already rushing from his head to his loins. Her eyes
were wide and lovely. Her scent was entrancing. All
rational thought was fleeing. And before he could
gather his wits, Delacourt shifted clumsily, catching
his boot in her hems.

Together, they went sprawling into the hay. Delacourt fell half on top. Her shift ripped open with an
awful sound. Still writhing like a wildcat, she sucked in
a second breath. Delacourt's lust fought his confusion.

"For pity's sake, Peaches!" he whispered, suddenly
desperate to have her. "I'll pay twice your price." By
way of persuasion, he slid what he hoped was a

soothing hand down her leg while starting to un-
clamp her mouth.

In response, the redhead clamped down and bit
him. Hard. Then her claws raked down his neck.

The pain was wildly arousing. Delacourt jerked his
hand away and felt his gaze heat as it swept over her.
"So that's how it's to be?" he whispered silkily, mar-
veling at staid old Wally's taste in women. *Rowdy
piece, indeed!*

Beneath him, Peaches shifted as Delacourt's
mouth sought and captured hers. For a moment, her
motions stilled. Fleetingly, she responded, her mouth
almost parting beneath his, her hips arching delicately against him.

Well! It seemed Waldron was on to something.
Persuasion was bloody exhilarating! He kissed her
hard, surging inside her mouth with wild abandon. At
once, Peaches moaned sweetly. And then she kissed
him back. Unmistakably. With a deep shudder of
pleasure, she lightly touched her tongue to his, and
her hands slid from his shoulders, down his arms,
and almost around his waist. Her right leg began to
slide enticingly up his own.

And in the next instant, she regained herself. Up
jerked her left knee, with every intention of unman-
ning him.

She missed. But it was ever so close.

Suddenly, a grave misgiving seized him. Then
Peaches seized a fistful of his hair. It was altogether
too much seizing for Delacourt. He had to get out.
Enough was enough.

But before he could flee, the chit yanked at his
scalp for all she was worth, then drove a solid fist into
the side of his ribcage. *Bloody hell!* Delacourt was beginning to doubt there was enough liquor in all of

England to give him the ballocks to bed this red-haired hellion. Devil fly away with Wally. And his rowdy piece. "Point taken, madam," he growled, bracing his weight to lift himself off her.

But just then, hinges squalled alarmingly. Delacourt's head jerked toward the door. The woman went limp, as if relieved, and at once, a small, sickly look-ing fellow clad only in his small-clothes jerked open the lower door and darted into the stall.

Abruptly, he jerked to a halt. "Gor blimey, m'lady!" he gasped, whirling about to avert his eyes.

Gracelessly, Delacourt staggered to his feet, only to find himself staring at a second man. A young gentle-man whose name completely escaped him. But through the haze of thwarted lust, he realized some-thing had gone horribly awry. The wrong stall, per-haps? The wrong woman, certainly.

"Oh, Jed!" cried the girl in a rich, throaty voice. "And Harry! Oh, thank God!" She scrambled up from the floor, her torn shift clutched awkwardly in one fist.

Harry? Yes, that was the name! Young Harold Markham-Somebody. Impoverished Earl of . . . Some-thing. Manfully, Delacourt shook himself off and ex-tended a hand.

But no one moved to take it. Harold Markham-Whoever just stood there blinking in stupefaction.

"Beg pardon, Harry!" Delacourt muttered sheep-ishly. "Thought the girl was Waldron's. Damned ill-mannered of me, to be sure."

To his shock, however, the woman collapsed back against the stall, arms crossed over her chest in a pa-thetically protective gesture. And then, she exhaled deeply, a ragged, tremulous sigh which racked her delicate ribs, shook her narrow shoulders, and sounded as if it had been wrenched from her soul.

Unease pierced him. *Oh, God. Oh, God, no. Don't let her cry.*

He felt panic begin to churn. His hands began to tremble. What was wrong? What in God's name had he done?

Delacourt felt suddenly sick. Worse than sick. It was as if his life had come full circle. For the briefest of moments, the flame-haired girl was another young woman altogether. In another dark and lonely place. Another time. Frightened. Violated.

Delacourt clutched his stomach.

Good Lord, he was going to disgrace himself. Right here in the middle of a Newmarket box stall. He fought for control, willing a day's worth of drink and dissolution to settle back into the pit of his belly. And then, slowly, he lifted his eyes to stare at the girl, who was still shaking against the wall.

She was so beautiful. And for the briefest of moments, she looked so alone, so desperately in need of protection. And without his understanding how or why, Delacourt felt all his hidden rage, his carefully crafted arrogance, and a decade's worth of bitterness surge, and then drain away, as if it were his very blood being spilt upon the stable floor.

On a rare rush of compassion, he turned to gather the young woman into his arms, frantically wanting—no, needing—to pull her against his chest.

Then he froze.

No. Innocent or not, she clearly belonged to Harry. Still, the chit hadn't bolted for Harry's arms as one would have expected. Instead, she merely stiffened her spine, came away from the wall, and bent down to snatch up her stockings.

She looked fine now. Angry. But perfectly fine.

Whatever he thought he'd seen had been but a figment of his imagination.

The viscount struggled to regain his composure and his devil-may-care expression. "Well," he lightly interjected. "No harm done, it seems. I'll just get out of your way."

At last, Harry's mouth dropped gracelessly open. "Ahh, L-l-lord Delacourt?" he finally managed to wheeze. "B-b-before you go—I daresay I'm supposed to ask—why were you forcing yourself on m'sister?"

The Reverend Mr. Cole Amherst was enjoying an afternoon of divine intervention inside his lady wife when the butler knocked upon his dressing-room door to announce that Lord Delacourt, his rakehell of a brother-in-law, had come a-visiting again.

With a long-suffering sigh and a few finely calculated motions, her ladyship discreetly finished what she'd started, then retied her husband's cravat, patted him on the rump, and sent him off to see what new misfortune had occasioned this particular visit.

Never a paragon of patience, Jonet, Lady Kildermore, lingered for a few more minutes, willing her notorious temper under control. Of late, she had been a bit out of charity with her brother. And sadly, David was really just her half-brother—and a secret, illegitimate brother at that, if one wished to be strictly technical.

But Jonet did not wish to be technical. She loved David dearly, and kept his secrets willingly. But heaven above! His temper and his timing were dreadful. And now he was back at Elmwood to beleaguer her again.

And yet, David had not asked for her, had he? He had asked for Cole. How very strange! Her husband and her brother took great pleasure in pretending not to like one another. Or perhaps it was better said that they enjoyed tormenting one another. And in truth, never were two men more different.

So what on earth could her brother want with Cole? It was now almost dark, and David was to have spent the week at Newmarket. And yet, here he was in the middle of Cambridgeshire, almost thirty miles away!

Suddenly, her brother's angry voice boomed up the stairs and down the corridor. Curiosity got the better of Jonet, as it always did. Stabbing one last pin into her hair, then smoothing a hand over her slight belly, she turned from the pier glass and bolted downstairs at a pace which was most inappropriate for a lady in her delicate condition.

The actual tenor of the argument was made plain before she had hit the first-floor landing.

"And I say she damned well will wed me!" Jonet heard her brother bellow from behind the drawing-room door. "And I want you, Amherst, to send to the archbishop right this instant! Use your influence, man! Fetch me a bloody special license! And fetch it now!"

Jonet heard the high, feminine shriek which followed. "Good God, you really are mad!" the unknown woman yelled. "Not just an ordinary rapist—a *deranged* rapist! A *drunken* and deranged rapist! And you may well fetch yourself a dozen such licenses—be they special or regular or tattooed upon your backside—but I'll die a dried-up old spinster before I'll take a lunatic to my bed!"

Over the din, Jonet could hear her husband murmuring, his gentle voice grappling for control.

But David was having none of it. "Yes, I'll grant you I may well be mad—after all, I've just spent three hours trapped in a barouche with a mean-mouthed, red-haired shrew!" he boomed.

"Oh! *Oh—!*" she screeched. "And just whose fault was that?"

At that moment, Mrs. Birtwhistle poked her head through the kitchen door. Cook stood right behind, peering over the diminutive housekeeper's head. With a withering glance at them, Jonet strode across the hall and through the drawing-room door.

"My!" she said brightly, pushing it shut again. "This sounds like a most stimulating debate! Certainly all of the servants find it so."

Three sets of wide eyes swiveled toward the door to stare at her. Her husband's face had gone utterly pale. Her brother's gaze burned with a hard, bitter mockery. But it was the delicate, flame-haired woman who ultimately caught Jonet's attention. And her sympathy.

The girl—for she was really little more than that— stood rigidly by the hearth in a shabby pelisse and a blue gros de Naples carriage dress which had obviously seen better days. But atop her head sat a rakish little bonnet, and upon her tear-stained face was a look of grim, implacable resolve.

Jonet's husband turned to look at her. "My dear, you will take Lord Delacourt into my library, if you please. Ring for coffee. Heaven knows he needs it."

"I damned well do not!" insisted David, his voice hoarse and more strained than ever she had heard it.

"Coffee, of course," answered Jonet smoothly. "But pray introduce our guest."

"Good heavens, where are my manners!" Cole ran a hand wearily through his hair. "Lady Cecilia, this is my wife, Jonet Amherst, Lady Kildermore. My dear, this is Lady Cecilia Markham-Sands."

"Soon to be Lady Delacourt!" growled David.

Tossing a disparaging glance at David, Lady Cecilia turned and made Jonet a very pretty curtsy.

Despite her shabby clothing, the girl seemed a well-bred little thing. Well! There was quite a story here, Jonet did not doubt. But it would keep. Laying one hand upon the doorknob, Jonet turned to her brother and extended the other. "David?"

"No!" Her brother's scowl deepened, and he crossed his arms over his chest stubbornly. "I shan't leave this room, do you hear? I have been accused, abused, and, I do not doubt, well nigh swindled. But I am nonetheless here to see this dreadful mistake rectified."

"A mistake—?" Lady Cecilia Markham-Sands set one hand on her hip and glared at him. "Your *mistake* was made when you forced your attentions on me! I'm not some spineless idiot to be debauched at your whim!"

With a glittering challenge in his eye, David lifted his chin. "You seemed willing to be debauched for a moment there, Cecilia. You kissed me back. Rather passionately, too. Indeed, I think you wanted me."

Cecilia stamped her foot. "Your reputation precedes you, sir! I could never want a man of your ilk!"

"Apparently, my ilk wasn't so readily apparent when your tongue was in my mouth," snarled David.

"You wretch!" She jerked as if she might leap at him and claw out his eyes, but Cole laid a gentle hand upon her arm.

David drew back a pace and turned a desperate face toward Cole. "You see! She's a madwoman! A shrew! And I shan't leave merely to permit her"—he jerked his head disdainfully in the girl's direction—"to further impugn my honor."

Arms going rigid at his side, Cole's hands balled into eager, un-Christian fists. "Oh, for pity's sake, David! Your own admissions have impugned your character a vast deal too much for my taste! Now, you will go with

Jonet, or you and I shall set about something far more bruising than our usual silly squabbles."

A ghost of some painful emotion passed over David's face. Abruptly, his stance shifted. His arms fell, and to Cole's surprise, he strode through the room, past his sister, and into the hall.

Cole listened as the door softly closed behind them. Muttering a low, uncharacteristic curse beneath his breath, he crossed to a small table beneath the double windows and unsteadily sloshed out two glasses of wine.

He returned to the girl, pressing one of them into her hand. "My dear child," he said softly. "I think you must drink this. Or if you will have it, I'll pour you a tot of brandy."

The girl drew herself up regally. "Thank you," she said very stiffly. "But I shan't require any spirits."

Cole said no more but merely gestured toward a chair. Reluctantly, the girl took it, neatly folding her skirts about her knees with one hand. Cole put down his glass and went to the fireplace. Drawing out the poker, he jabbed it viciously into the coals and stirred.

Damn David to hell and back!

No, no! Assuredly, he did not mean that. But *David!* Oh, the man had a way of stirring up the very worst sort of trouble. And this time, Cole very much feared his brother-in-law had stirred up something which could not now be set to rights.

Lady Cecilia Markham-Sands was unknown to him. But then, much of England's nobility and gentry was unknown to him. Cole simply did not care to trouble his mind with remembering the finer points of something so unimportant. He was a scholar, and a simple man of God, and so he confined himself to the things he understood.

But this! Even Cole could see that this was a scandal which would set all the *ton* on its ear, were it to become known. And at this point, all he could pray for was that he might somehow mitigate the damage.

Abruptly, he shoved the poker back into its stand with a harsh ringing sound and turned to take the seat opposite Lady Cecilia. "You know, do you not," he softly began, "that Lord Delacourt is a particular friend of mine, all appearances to the contrary?"

"So he has said," replied the lady with a sniff.

Slowly, Cole extended his hand. "But I am foremost a clergyman, and so you may be sure that I will do all within my power to help you—*if* you can bring yourself to trust me?"

Lady Cecilia looked at the proffered hand suspiciously, and then, with a second little snuffle, she slid her small, cold fingers into it.

Cole was vaguely alarmed. Despite the warm spring air, the girl was frozen. In shock, no doubt. He'd struck a tinder to the fire as soon as he'd seen her, pale, trembling, and looking so desperately alone in the middle of his drawing room. But it had done little to warm her.

Gently, he squeezed her fingers. "My dear, you must tell me—who is responsible for you?"

The girl's deep blue eyes flared, wide and angry. "When last I checked, sir, I was responsible for myself."

Inwardly, Cole smiled. "What I mean, Lady Cecilia, is have you a family? A father?"

Lady Cecilia's eyes narrowed knowingly. "A man to look after me? Is that what you mean?" She gave a ladylike snort of disgust. "The answer is no. My father has been dead these twelve months past. I have only my elder brother, Harry, Lord Sands. But I am more apt to be looking after him, than he me."

Cole felt a wave of relief. Good. At least there was

someone. "Then I daresay we ought to fetch him, ma'am," said Cole calmly. "This is, you know, a very serious business."

"A very serious business?" echoed Lady Cecilia tremulously, jerking her hand from Cole's. "You hardly need tell me that, sir! I was present when your friend Lord Delacourt so ruthlessly assaulted my—my person! And my brother is well aware of it, you may be sure. It was he who permitted me to be carted away from Newmarket in such a high-handed fashion."

Cole let his shoulders sag. Pensively, he rubbed his finger up and down the side of his nose. This was very bad indeed. "But why, ma'am, would your brother allow such a thing?"

Lady Cecilia bristled. "Perhaps because he is a spineless idiot—?" she retorted. Then she, too, let her shoulders sag. "No, forgive me," she said softly, pressing her fingertips to her temple as if her head ached. "That really is not true. It was just that Harry had no notion what ought to be done."

"What ought to be done?"

"Well, it isn't every day a young man sees his sister being pawed by a drunken and notoriously dissolute lord. And when Delacourt exploded, and accused Harry of attempting to ensnare him—"

"Ensnare him?" interjected Cole sharply. "Whatever do you mean?"

Lady Cecilia lifted her chin haughtily. "It would seem your friend Delacourt thinks himself worthy of being trapped into marriage by a pair of near penniless orphans. For my part, I have never been so insulted." She waved a hand wildly about the room. "Indeed, there I was, simply enjoying a day at the track with my brother, when I was viciously and relentlessly assaulted by a man I have scarce heard tell of."

Cole took a long, slow sip of his sherry, steeling himself for a difficult question. "You must forgive me, ma'am," he finally said, "but I feel compelled to ask—just what were you doing in the Newmarket stables? And in a state of . . . what I understand to have been . . ." He strove to look very grave. "Well, suffice it to say that the track stables are no place for a young lady in any state of dress."

Lady Cecilia looked momentarily contrite. "Oh, it was Harry, you see. The debts. Our estate." Her huge blue eyes fluttered up at Cole, but he did not understand. So he kept staring at her rather pointedly, forcing her to continue. He was afraid he had to get at the truth, even at the cost of a few tears.

Lady Cecilia sighed and began again. "I mean to say, Mr. Amherst, that my brother is very young. And possessed of the worst sort of luck, too—not that it's his fault!" She shook her head full of burnished curls emphatically. "Indeed, it runs in our family. And of course, both Harry and I are underage, as it happens."

"Both underage?" Worse and worse, thought Cole.

"Yes, I fear so. For I am just turned eighteen, and my brother not quite twenty-one. And our trustee—our Uncle Reggie—is very hard on Harry. Often justifiably, to be sure. But this time, it was a game of hazard with that horrid Mr. Waldron. Harry was quite sick with desperation. And so, I did the only thing I knew to do, the only thing I thought might make some money—"

Cole gave a horrified gasp. "Oh, my dear!"

Suddenly, Lady Cecilia laughed, a rich, gorgeous, bubbly sound. "Oh, heavens no, Mr. Amherst! It was our horse! Sands' Setting Star—a sure-fire winner in the fifth." She leaned intently forward in her chair. "Papa bred her himself, at Holly Hill—that's our estate near Upper Brayfield—and she's the only stroke of good fortune my father ever had. She runs like a bolt of lightning, and the winnings would have cleared all Harry's gaming losses and kept that awful Mr. Waldron from calling upon Uncle Reggie, as he had threatened to do."

Cole leaned incrementally nearer, resting his elbows on his knees. "I confess, Lady Cecilia, you have captured the whole of my attention. Pray continue."

The girl began to pick nervously at the skirts of her carriage dress. "Well, sir, you see, it was like this. Poor Jed—that's Papa's jockey—ate a sliver of smoked mackerel at a very disreputable-looking inn at Bottisham last night."

"In Bottisham—?" Cole encouraged.

"Yes, you see, the outlying villages are considerably cheaper, if one wants a room or a meal. Anyway, I told Jed to have the mutton pie, as Harry and I did. But he eats like a bird before a race, and—"

Cole cleared his throat sharply. It was dreadfully clear where this was going. "And so your jockey was taken ill, was he not? And when your brother could not find another, he came to you? And because you are very short . . ." Cole let his words trail away.

Lady Cecilia lowered her eyes in embarrassment. "Yes—but I'm a bruising rider, sir. Indeed, we're a little short of staff at Holly Hill just now, so I work with Jed. He says my touch is almost as good as his, and we are nearly of a size." Suddenly, she jerked her head up again, tossing the flame-gold curls back off her face, her eyes at last brightening. "And I won, too! No one even noticed that it was not Jed who crossed the finish line."

Doubtingly, Cole let his eyes drift over her milky skin and distinctive hair. One little curl exposed, and a discerning eye would have known. "My dear child—are you sure?"

"Yes." She paused, her dark, angular brows

abruptly drawing together. "At least, I *hope* they did not. I daresay I could be disqualified. And I should hate above all things for Harry to be unable to collect his vowels, after all the trouble I've been put to."

After all the trouble she'd been put to—? Cole wanted to rail at her until the rafters rattled. She had been compromised! Probably ruined! And still, it seemed she was more concerned for her brother than for herself.

Ruthlessly, Cole tamped down his frustration. "Your concern for your brother is admirable, ma'am, but I believe we have a more pressing concern. You have been compromised, and Lord Delacourt has offered to make things right. He wishes to marry you. Indeed, he seems rather intent upon it."

When she drew breath to argue, he held up a staying hand. "Please, hear me out. Delacourt shall soon realize—indeed, I daresay he already does—that there was no . . . no *ensnarement* at all. In his heart, he is a good man. As a member of the clergy, I feel morally bound to suggest you set aside your distress and accept his offer."

Resolutely, she shook her head. "No, Mr. Amherst, I will not. And as to being compromised, I was not precisely . . . that is to say, not completely . . ."

Discreetly, Cole gave a little cough. He understood, but he was deeply uncomfortable. "Lady Cecilia, I must ask, did you really . . . that is to say, when Lord Delacourt kissed you, were you at all . . . I mean, David is generally thought a very striking man, and if you found him in any way . . ." At last, Cole surrendered, unable to get the question out.

It hardly mattered. Lady Cecilia's face was flaming with humiliation. "Very striking, indeed," she bitterly admitted. "But his faults are legendary. As to mine, I should rather we not speak of them. I shan't wed Lord Delacourt. Can we not leave it at that? Please?"

Slowly, Cole nodded. And in truth, he was almost glad she had refused to marry. Despite David's rather shocking alacrity to wed this poor child, Cole was not at all sure that Jonet's brother would make any woman a good husband, let alone under these circumstances.

But one thing was all too clear. Could they but see past their righteous indignation, these two were at least a little attracted to each other. And perhaps it was something more. *Or something worse.* A strange, obsessive light had burned in David's eyes. Moreover, Lady Cecilia was as angry with herself as she was with David, though she was probably too inexperienced to understand why.

Cole wondered what to make of it all. Perhaps nothing. Perhaps, as she said, this was simply a matter best not pursued. He put his glass aside and pensively steepled his fingers. "Very well, ma'am, I must bow to your wishes. But you must understand, when rumor of this debacle leaks out, you *will* have been compromised, regardless of how you see it."

Again, Lady Cecilia shook her head, even more vigorously. "No one shall hear of it! Harry certainly shan't say a word, and I would trust Jed with my very life. Moreover, if Delacourt is the gentleman you seem to think him, then he certainly will keep quiet, too, will he not?" Her eyes full of questions, she lifted her gaze to his.

"I can personally guarantee that not one word will ever pass his lips," said Cole grimly. "But are you sure, ma'am? Are you *perfectly* sure that you were seen by no one else?"

Lady Cecilia looked away, catching her bottom lip between her teeth. "Well, no doubt I was observed leaving with Lord Delacourt in his barouche," she finally answered. "But is that so very bad, do you think? After all, it was broad daylight, and we were alone for just a few hours."

For long, uncertain moments, Cole tapped one finger against the bowl of his wine glass. Perhaps, had they taken but a short journey through her home village, under the auspices of her parents . . . Yes, perhaps then she might have a point. But they had not been with her parents. She was an orphan. And her brother apparently hadn't sense enough to come along.

Finally, Cole spoke. "Perhaps there is a way to mitigate the risk. Tomorrow, David will announce your engagement." At her squawk of outrage, he held up one hand. "No, no, dear girl! Do let me finish. My wife will say that you are a particular friend of hers—and by the end of the day, you no doubt will be. Moreover, if your father was a gamester—" Cole looked at her for confirmation.

Grimly, Lady Cecilia nodded, still biting hard at her lip.

"Then undoubtedly my wife's late husband knew him well. It will surprise no one to learn that the two of you are acquainted. With a few careful hints on Jonet's part, the gossips will assume that you and David met here at Elmwood as our guests and fell at once in love."

Lady Cecilia looked doubtful. "Really, Mr. Amherst—!"

Cole cut her off. "But of course, David being David, you will soon see the error of your ways and give him the jilting he so richly deserves. And since society loves to cast Lord Delacourt in the role of scorned suitor, the gossips will seize upon it with relish."

Carefully, he studied Lady Cecilia's expression. "Will that do, ma'am, do you think?" he asked softly.

Slowly, the girl nodded, but she did not look at all pleased. In truth, for all her brave words, she still looked terrified. And dreadfully alone.

Inwardly, Cole sighed. It was the best of a bad bargain. Abruptly, he stood and extended her his hand. "Then come, my dear. Let us go find David and Jonet. We have a betrothal to announce."

1

The incorrigible Henrietta Healy

February 1824

The Countess of Walrafen—who in a long-ago life had been known as Cecilia Markham-Sands—was newly possessed of a most fashionable villa in Park Crescent. Mr. Nash's latest spurt of architectural genious boasted every modern convenience, including flushing lavatories, an elegantly stuccoed façade, and pale yellow paint so sumptuously applied it looked like butter running down the walls.

There was nothing of the old or the venerated about Park Crescent, though the earldom of Walrafen was both. In fact, to her ladyship's way of thinking, the Walrafen title was so old and stuffy it was well nigh to moldering. She could smell the musty self-righteousness drifting all the way across Marylebone.

The official London address of the earldom was situated deep in the heart of Mayfair, in an imposing brick town house in Hill Street, from which her ladyship had taken her congé as soon as her elderly husband had breathed his last at the ripe old age of seven-and-fifty. Her stepson Giles, two years her senior, lived there alone now and was very welcome to do so.

For her part, the Countess of Walrafen was the un-

pretentious descendant of a title even older than that of
her late husband, a fact which had always needled him
a bit, and for no good reason that her ladyship could
see. What good was a coronet, she often asked herself,
when the generations of Markham-Sands men had
been—and still were—such a luckless and clueless lot?

Indeed, the first Earl of Sands had been ennobled
by old William the Red himself. In a reign pock-
marked by avariciousness, arrogance, and atheism,
the Sands family had been one of the few Saxon dy-
nasties that had not only survived but also prospered
in the Norman yoke.

And that circumstance had, so far as Lady Walrafen
could determine, been the last bit of fortuity to befall
her ancestors. After the War of the Roses, most of their
land had been seized. During the Dissolution, they had
been faithful papists, and following the rise of Bloody
Mary, they had somehow become staunch Protestants.
Sometime in the seventeenth century, they had spread
their ill luck to the moneyed Markham family, by
means of a financially motivated marriage.

And following that, the succeeding noblemen of
the Markham-Sands dynasty had managed to situate
themselves on the wrong side of every political con-
flict, civil disturbance, cockfight, dog scrap, horse
race, and bear baiting which came their way, all of it
culminating with the Divine Right of Kings debacle,
which they had assiduously supported, and the
Restoration, which they had not.

Cecilia sighed aloud. She had never understood
that bit of perversity.

All she had understood, and from a very young
age, was that it fell to her to look out for both herself
and her misbegotten elder brother, the current Earl of
Sands. Until her sister-in-law Julia had joined their

household and taken that little job off her hands. Cecilia still wasn't sure how she felt about that, but at least Julia's subtle pressure had propelled her out of the family brick pile and into a wedding dress.

At that recollection, Cecilia sighed and leaned a little closer to her dressing mirror. Oh, was that a wrinkle at the corner of her right eye? Indeed it was. And was that another on the left? Well. At least her life held some consistency. At least her wrinkles matched.

She took up her hairbrush, then thumped it back down again, staring pensively across the dressing table full of bottles and vials. Cecilia simply could not escape the dreadful feeling that her life had ended even before it had begun. The first anniversary of her husband's death was now six months gone. Yet here she was, at the grand old age of four-and-twenty, unable to shake the sensation of being in deep mourning. And why? Had she loved him?

No, not as a husband.

Did she miss him?

No, not greatly, but—

Suddenly, a piercing shriek rang out from her dressing room. *Etta!*

Cecilia let her face fall forward into her hands. Lord, what had the girl done now?

At that moment, Etta emerged from the dressing room holding a length of emerald green sarcenet before her face, peering straight through the big brown hole in the middle of it. Even through the hole, Lady Walrafen could see that tears were already rolling down Etta's narrow face.

"Oh lor, Lady Walrafen!" the maid squalled, rolling her damp eyes dramatically. "Look 'ere what I've done! Yer ortter 'ave me whipped, and that's a fact. Yer ortter 'ave me skinned, that's what—then ship me right back to the King's Arms t'make a livin' on me tail."

Cecilia managed a smile. "It's perfectly all right, Etta. I shall wear the blue silk."

But as usual, the maid did not listen. "I just put the iron down for the veriest wee second, and now look!" Etta shook the scorched sarcenet for emphasis. "*Look!* And what you'd be wantin' with a dresser the likes of me, mum, is more'n I'll ever know. I'm too witless to iron a little bit of fluff like this—" Again, she rolled her watery eyes and shook the ruined shawl. "And I reckon I'm not apt to learn, neither."

At that, Cecilia rose from her stool and snatched the green sarcenet from her maid's hands. "Now, just hush, Etta!" she commanded with an impatient stamp of her foot. "I'll not have such talk, do you hear? It's a silk shawl, for pity's sake! I've a dozen just like it. Now, stop crying and stand up straight! Who will believe in you, if you don't believe in yourself?"

"Oh, very well!" Etta gave a last dramatic sniff. "I'll fetch the blue. But I'm telling you straight out now, it don't look near so good as this green. And I mean for you to look your best when you go to that Mrs. Rowland's sore-ay tonight, since you know bloody well—"

"*Perfectly* well," corrected her ladyship gently.

"*Perfectly* well," echoed Etta without missing a beat, "that old high-in-the-instep Giles'll be watchin' your every twitch."

Cecilia watched as Etta, still chattering, hastened into the dressing room, pitched the ruined shawl into one corner, and began to shake out the blue silk evening gown, all without pausing for breath. "And d'ye know, Lady Walrafen, I sometimes suspicion but what 'e ain't got it a little hot for you, stepson or no.

Don't mean to say 'e likes it none too good—but there! A fellow don't always get to pick what pricks his—er, his *fancy,* if yer takes my meaning."

"Why, I daresay I do," murmured Cecilia a bit unsteadily, lifting the back of one hand to her forehead. Good Lord! After three weeks, Etta still seemed incorrigible. "But Giles simply feels responsible for me, that's all. Now, pray talk of something else. How shall we dress my hair for tonight?"

It was as if she had not spoken. "And what about that Mrs. Rowland?" continued Etta, picking through a handful of lawn undergarments. "Coo! Ain't she a downy one? Mean looking, too, with all them sharp bones and high eyebrows. And her husband a cousin to that nice Mr. Amherst! It don't figure."

"Like the rest of us, the Reverend Mr. Amherst did not get to choose his relatives," murmured Cecilia dryly. "And as to Edmund and Anne Rowland, I daresay even they have their uses. If they are so shallow as to crave fine society above all else, then very well! But there is a price to be paid for folly, and I'll gladly extract a pound of flesh on Mr. Amherst's behalf."

From the dressing room, Etta hooted with laughter. "Now 'oo's the downy one, I arst you, mum? That hoity-toity Mrs. Rowland'll soon be buying new mattresses for the good vicar's mission house, or my name ain't 'Enrietta 'Ealy."

"*H*enriettà *H*ealy!"

"Right, mum!" The maid stuck her head through the dressing-room door long enough to flash a wicked grin. "Won't Mr. Amherst get a laugh out 'er that! And bless me if that wouldn't be a sight to fair heat up a room, 'cause that smile o' his has melted gamer gals 'n me. It don't seem quite right for a parson to be so purely 'andsome, do it?"

Cecilia had risen from her dressing table and had begun to pick through her jewel chest for something to wear with the blue silk. "Oh, to be sure, he is most striking," she wryly admitted, pulling out a heavy topaz pendant and laying it across her palm. "But do not mistake him, Etta. He's deeply devout, though perhaps not in the conventional way. His mission has done a great deal of good in east London."

Etta, now with pins stuck in her mouth, nodded and rattled on. "Aye, there's many an uprighter what wants savin' from them petticoat merchants, and he's just the gent to—"

Her ladyship dropped the necklace with a *ker-thunk!* "An . . . *an uprighter?*" she interjected sharply.

"A whore, mum," came Etta's garbled explanation around her mouthful of pins. "Beggin' your pardon 'n all. And speaking of that 'andsome Mr. Amherst, I knows one a sight prettier. That friend of 'is—or friend of the wife's, more like—that fancy Lord Delacourt. Coo! 'Ave ye ever laid eyes on 'im?"

"Really, Etta!" chided Cecilia uncomfortably. "Do stop dropping your *h*'s! And we need to know nothing about Lord Delacourt!" Cecilia felt the heat flush up her cheeks.

"Aye, well," said Etta with an amiable shrug. "*He's* a right *h*andsome swell, that's wot I knows of *h*im," she announced, leaning heavily on her *h*'s. "Now, mum, you've 'eard me talk o' me Aunt Mercy, the one 'oo owned a flash house orf the Ratcliffe Highway?"

"Yes," agreed Cecilia hesitantly. Etta's family was legion, and none of them above the law.

"Well," announced Etta, "she knew a gal 'oo'd been in the theater, very fine in 'er ways, and this Lord Delacourt took a liking to 'er, see? Set 'er up in a grand style, 'e did. Two servants, a carriage, and a lit-

tle trained monkey with a red waistcoat and bells
'round its neck. Went everywhere with 'er, that little
monkey did—"

"Really, Etta!" interjected Cecilia for the fifth time,
hurling herself onto her bed in despair. "I have no interest whatsoever in Lord Delacourt's trained monkey!"

Indeed, Delacourt was the last man on earth
Cecilia wished to think about. She had made a deliberate effort these last six years to *not* think of that self-
indulgent libertine. It didn't matter that his lips were
as sinfully full as a woman's. Or that his sleepy green
eyes were as unfathomable as the ocean at dusk. And
that hair! As heavy and rich as burnished mahogany.

Yes, even superficial elements—the low, mocking
sound of his laugh in a crowded ballroom, the reflection of candlelight in his eye as he whirled across the
dance floor—any of these things could awaken a
wrath she did not understand. And that was before
one even considered his sadly lacking morals.

But in a society as limited as London's, it had been
impossible *not* to see him. And to her acute discomfort,
he'd grown leaner, harder, and harsher with the passage of time. And certainly more dissolute. Lord
Delacourt's intrigues made for most common sort of
gossip. When he passed through a room, the less discerning ladies of the *ton* would draw a collective
breath, strike simpering smiles, and snap open their
fans, fluttering them back and forth as if kindling a fire.

But no decent woman would let a man like that
cross her mind. Certainly, she had no wish to remember him. None at all. Oh, but how often in her dreams
she had felt his hand skimming up her thigh, his
mouth hot against her throat, only to wake up burning with lust and shame? Delacourt had awakened in
her the baser side of her nature long before she had

even realized she *had* one. Still, Cecilia had never been a fool. She knew lust for what it was.

"Righty-ho," agreed Etta cheerfully as she tugged out a pair of new silk stockings. "Got orf me subject again, didn't I? What I meant to be telling you was that I seen 'im meself once. With Aunt Mercy in the Haymarket, it was, and Gawd bless me!" The maid's eyes rolled back in her head. "A finer set of shoulders and a snugger rump I never did see on a gent! And they do say Lord Delacourt is about the best thing a gal can get between 'er legs on a cold ni—"

"Etta!" screeched Cecilia. "That will do. Really! It's excessively vulgar! Moreover, I have seen Lord Delacourt and his—his *fine shoulders*. I see nothing in him at all. Nothing but a handsome debauchee. And where is your aunt's friend now, Etta, I ask you?"

Etta shrugged. "Couldn't say, mum."

"Well, I can!" Cecilia's fervor ratcheted sharply upward. "She's starving in some workhouse, old before her time and riddled with the pox, I do not doubt. Whilst his lordship and his *snug rump* are being cosseted by a bevy of expensive servants down in Curzon Street."

It was precisely half-past six when Lord Delacourt and his aforementioned rump arrived at his sister's imposing brick town house in Brook Street, just as he did at least four times a week. Lifting his gold-knobbed stick, he rapped his customary brisk tattoo upon the door, and, as always, it was immediately flung open by Charles Donaldson, her ladyship's butler.

"Ah, good evening, Charlie," said the viscount, just as usual. Smiling widely, he slid out of his elegant black greatcoat. "How the devil are you?"

Donaldson lifted the coat from Delacourt's fine

shoulders and gave his standard reply. "Weel enough, m'lord. Yerself?"

The viscount forced a bland expression. "Ah, Charlie," he routinely replied, "you know there's not a fellow in all of England more content than I! Now, where might I find her ladyship? Not, you understand, that I am fully certain that I wish to." He flashed the butler a dry smile.

Donaldson nodded knowingly and draped the coat over his arm. Of late, one small aspect of their age-old routine had altered—uncomfortably so. "Aye, my lord, she's a wee bit fashed t'day," Donaldson warned. "And wearin' out the rug in the book room."

"A bad sign, that," muttered Delacourt. "Is there brandy, Charlie?" He really didn't know why he asked. There was always brandy. And always his brand, the very best cognac money could buy. Donaldson made sure of it.

"Aye, m'lord. I've set a bottle o' your favorite atop the sideboard."

Then, very discreetly, the butler cut a glance up and down the corridor and bent his head to Delacourt's. "And if ye dinna mind a word o' warning, m'lord, she's scratching out anither o' those lists. It does'na look too gude for you."

"Hmph!" Delacourt's dark brows drew together. "Has Mother's footman been 'round today?"

Grimly, Donaldson nodded. "Brought anither note."

Delacourt's jaw hardened. "Plaguey, conspiring women," he grumbled. "Where's Amherst? Out saving more harlots from a life of sin and degradation?"

"Aye, gone off tae the mission 'til dinner. Ye'll have tae manage her w'out 'im."

* * *

But in the end, all Delacourt managed was his thirst. He'd downed but half a snifter of his sister's fine cognac before she set about her business. Watching her brother out of the corner of one eye, Lady Kildermore paced thoughtfully back and forth along the rich Turkey carpet of her book room, pencil and paper in hand. Outside, the early evening traffic rumbled up and down Brook Street. Impatiently, she sighed.

It was very hard to concentrate amidst all the racket of town when one had grown so used to the country. But her husband's work here was pressing. Nonetheless, he had faithfully sworn that they would soon return to Elmwood. And her husband was a man who always kept his promises.

Comforted by that thought, she paused to bite the tip of her pencil. "Very well, David. Here's one I think shall do quite nicely," she announced, turning the paper a little to the candlelight. "Miss Mary Ayers. She's young, biddable, and has very large—"

Suddenly, Lord Delacourt set his cognac down with a clatter. "I don't want *large* anythings, Jonet!" he interjected, shoving back his armchair with a vengeance. "You need say no more! I do not want a wife. Not Miss Mary Ayers. Not Lady Caroline Kirk. Not—*good God!* Not anyone. Stop bedeviling me!"

Jonet tossed her paper down with a huff, slid one hand beneath her stomach, and eased herself gingerly down into the chair opposite. With a resigned sigh, she settled one hand atop the baby to feel it kick. Arabella, Davinia, and Baby Fiona were already in the nursery, and this one certainly seemed eager to join them. She did not remember ever having been so tired. And now, her brother meant to drive her mad.

"David, my dear," she began, her voice exasperated, "Lady Delacourt is seven-and-sixty! She wishes to see her grandchildren before she dies! If you cannot marry out of choice—out of love—as I have done, then marry for her, and for the sake of the title."

David tossed off the rest of his glass, eyeing her swollen belly and weary countenance. "You look as if you've had a shade too much love in your life, my dear," he said dryly. "Moreover, I do not give one bloody damn about the title, Jonet. And you know why."

Jonet refused to be baited. "Perhaps, but what of your sister Charlotte? Someone must retain the viscountcy and take care of her."

"I have provided for Charlotte," he insisted hotly. "And not out of the Delacourt coffers, but with my own money. I do have a little, you know!"

Jonet shifted uncomfortably in her chair. "Yes, I know. You're rich as Croesus. But that does not make a man happy."

David looked at her derisively. "Oh? And you and Mama—with your damned lists and smuggled missives and your Miss Marys and Lady Carolines—*that* will make me happy? I swear, I wish I'd never introduced you two meddling women."

Jonet's angular brows snapped together. "Lady Delacourt wants what's best for you, yes. And Cole says that a man cannot be truly fulfilled until—"

"Oh, no!" David cut her off at once. "No, no, no, Jonet! You'll not drag your husband into this! Cole does not concern himself with my affairs, nor I with his. Men, my dear, do not meddle. Which is as it should be."

Jonet threw back her head with laughter. "Oh, David! For such a clever man, you can be shockingly naïve! Do you really imagine *men* do not *meddle?*"

"Indeed not! They have better things to do."

Again, she laughed. "Oh, my dear! Women are cast

utterly into the shade by men when it comes to manipulation. Indeed, do not men always think they know best?"

"And they often do!"

"Yes, sometimes," she graciously admitted. "But I know my husband. And of the two of us, he's by far the more devious."

David let his eyes drift down her length. "Really, Jonet. You say the most outlandish things when you're increasing."

Smugly, Jonet smiled. "What you need, David, are children of your own. I see the desire in those wicked green eyes of yours every time one of my girls crawls into your lap. You'll get nowhere playing the hardened rake with me."

David cast her a disparaging glance and bent forward to refill his snifter from the round crystal decanter. "Come, darling! Have done tormenting me. Let us speak of something else."

"Very well," said Jonet silkily.

Her voice settled over David with an uncomfortable chill. It was frightening when his sister feigned surrender. Absently, he picked a bit of imaginary lint from his fine wool trousers. "Speaking of the girls, how do they go on? Has my Bella stopped biting her governess?"

Jonet's gaze was drifting aimlessly about the room. "Oh, yes. Almost."

"Good! Good! And by the by, I wish to give Davinia a pony for her birthday. I trust you have no objection?"

"No, no. None whatsoever." Jonet made an impatient little gesture with her hands, then clasped them tightly in her lap.

David lifted his brows inquiringly. "And what of you, my dear? How do you feel?"

"Fine, David, I feel fine." Nervously, her thumbs began to play with each other.

"And Cole? The . . . the Daughters of Nazareth Society—he is pleased?"

"Oh, yes! Donations are picking up."

"Ah! Capital. Just capital."

The hands twitched again. Jonet could obviously bear no more. "Listen, David—just tell me this. Are you happy? Truly happy? That is all I wish to know. I wish only for you to be content, as I am content. I know it makes no sense, but I cannot bear thinking that you might be lonely or sad."

Jonet watched as her brother pushed his glass disdainfully away and jerked from his chair. "You simply cannot leave it, can you, Jonet?" he answered, striding toward the window. With one hand sliding through his thick, dark hair, he pulled open the underdrapes with the other and stared out into the cold winter night.

"You've already cast off that red-haired dasher I saw you with in Bond Street last week, have you not?" she said softly.

"I'll likely find another soon enough," he returned, speaking to the windowpanes.

"Will she again possess masses of red-gold curls?"

"Perhaps," he lightly admitted. "I hope you do not worry, dear sister, that I lack for feminine attention."

"Not at all," agreed Jonet easily. "Indeed, there seems to be an overabundance of it. She was the second you've broken with this year, and it is but February."

"Your point?" he sharply returned. "I'm not sure I take it."

"And there were eight last year. Darling, that's a new mistress every six weeks."

"Not quite—but what of it? I see to their every

comfort whilst they're under my protection, Jonet. And I provide for them well enough when it is over. No one suffers." He laughed a little bitterly. "Indeed, many have profited quite handsomely."

"And what of you, my dear?" she asked softly. "What have you profited? Have you gained the whole world yet lost a little bit of your soul?"

Jonet had risen from her chair to join him at the window, and she shivered at the chill which pervaded the glass. She leaned closer to David's warmth, and in the murky light of a street lamp below, she could see that a silvery fog had settled over Mayfair, riming the cobblestones with a dull sheen of ice and shrouding the scene in a cold, depthless beauty. It made her think of her brother's heart, and for a moment, she wanted to cry.

Lightly, she laid one hand against his back, feeling the tension which thrummed inside him, and slowly, David turned from the window, his face suddenly stripped of all pretense. For one brief instant, Jonet feared he might truly lash out at her this time. But then, almost reluctantly, he opened his arms and drew her hard against his chest. "Ah, Jonet!" he sighed into her hair. "Have we no secrets from one another?"

"No," she softly admitted. And, indeed, they had not. Few siblings were as close, even those who shared both parents instead of just one dissolute father.

They were much alike, she and David. Too proud, too unyielding, and often far too alone. Before Cole had come to change her life, she and David had had no one but each other. Well, she had had a husband, but that marriage had not been a good one. And of course, David had a widowed mother, as well as his elder sibling, Charlotte—a sister of the heart but not the blood.

But Jonet was both. For to be coldly precise, David was Jonet's father's bastard. It was the appalling family secret. Her father's blackest sin. The result of an innocent young woman's rape.

In her brother's arms, Jonet shuddered, unable to imagine the horror of rape. Certainly, David thought of it often enough, though he hid it well. His mother, well bred but impoverished, had served the late Lord Delacourt as governess to young Charlotte. During a raucous party at the Delacourt country house, she had been violated by the dissolute Earl of Kildermore when she'd crept innocently down the back stairs to fetch a cup of milk.

Jonet had been but a toddler, living quietly with her mother at Kildermore Castle. The secret had never reached them, or anyone else for that matter. Lord Delacourt, appalled, had seen to that. But when it became apparent that there was to be a child, the elderly Delacourt had married his servant to give the babe a name.

Perhaps he had thought it just restitution for having befriended a scoundrel like the Earl of Kildermore and for allowing him into a home where an innocent young woman lived.

Cole knew it all, of course. And on their fourteenth birthdays, David and Jonet had told each of her two sons in turn. But knowing was not the same as understanding, and Jonet would never understand. And oh, how she wished that David knew nothing of it. She would have given up David's companionship a thousand times over, could she but snatch back her father's deathbed confession.

Had her father believed that God would forgive him if he sent such a letter to his only son? No, Kildermore had helped no one but himself by his actions. He had gone on to his great reward with his conscience unburdened, leaving David with an awful knowledge: that the tainted blood of a dissolute Scottish rogue pulsed through his veins, instead of the noble Norman blood of the man who had raised him.

But life was not fair, and one wasted time grieving over it. Abruptly, she pulled back from her brother's embrace. "Was there ever a time, David, when you felt yourself on the verge of true happiness? What would it take? Can you tell me?"

He jerked her back to his chest and let his chin rest atop her head. It was as if he refused to look her in the eyes. "Ah, Jonet," he said, the words soft and fraught with despair. "I hardly think I know."

For long moments, the book room fell silent as David listened to his sister's low, rhythmic breathing. Against his chest, Jonet felt warm and comforting. But it was not enough. In truth, it never had been.

Why did she torture him so? Jonet knew better than anyone why he ought not wed. His estates, his titles, and yes, even his very blood, felt alien to him. He was not *Delacourt*. He was nothing. Not noble, not titled, and barely even respectable. Though, admittedly, the latter was his own fault.

Still, how did a man properly explain such an unfortunate bloodline to a prospective bride? What if she then refused him? Or betrayed the confidence? But the alternative was worse. For how could a man wed a woman without being honest about who and what he was?

There had been an extraordinary situation once—a situation in which he'd been almost compelled to marry because of a dreadful misunderstanding. But as dreadful as that misunderstanding had been, and as shoddily as he had behaved, his actions had not been as intentionally wrong as courting a bride while willfully misrepresenting the blood which coursed through his veins. Not when it was the blood her children would share.

But in the end, he had not been compelled to marry, despite his willingness to make reparation. He had misunderstood, it seemed. They had been victims of a tasteless prank. The lady had not wanted him at all. So he'd silenced Wally Waldron by thrashing him within an inch of his life—a rare, bare-knuckled brawl it had been—and continued his efforts to make amends to the girl.

And yet, he'd been a fool, perhaps, to persist when all reason was past. She had turned out to be colder and less forgiving than he had hoped. Arrogant, really. She had insulted him, belittled his efforts, and, ultimately, she'd made him a laughingstock.

But at least he had escaped a leg shackle. And of course, he was grateful. Certainly, he would not now seek another one. It was a risk he had no wish to take.

Oh, he knew—yes, he *knew* that something was missing from his life. But it most assuredly wasn't marital bliss. Still, he was thirty-two years old, and the years since Jonet's second marriage had been hard ones, for he'd somehow lost his grounding.

Tucked away in the country with her beloved second husband, Jonet had found true happiness and had begun a wonderful new family. But David, deprived of his best friend—indeed, his moral compass and the only person whom he'd ever really taken care of—had found himself painfully alone. David had somehow let himself run to dissolution. And he had done it quite deliberately, too, in some futile hope of outrunning the darkness which chased him ever more intently with every passing year.

He was glad for Jonet. Truly happy. And she was right. It really was time to stop wasting his life. The certainty of it was dawning on him. A man could not spend the whole of his life flitting from one elegant drawing room to the next—as well as a few less reputable places—without becoming jaded and useless.

And yet, he felt thwarted, as if an invisible wall had been thrown up in his face by forces he could neither see nor understand. But to whom could he turn for advice? Certainly not Jonet, for she already felt irrationally responsible for the whole bloody mess.

Certainly not his mother; it would crush her to realize the depth and breadth of the hatred he felt for his circumstances. Cole? Perhaps. Though in his more honest moments, David could admit that he was deeply jealous of his brother-in-law.

Yes, he envied the man his quiet confidence and steadfast restraint. And yet, David often found himself aching to talk with Cole—and about something less mundane than horses, hounds, and the weather. But he could never quite get out the words, for they always caught on his damnable pride before they left his mouth.

Inwardly, David sighed and set Jonet a little away from him. There was no point in all this introspection. Nothing good ever came of it.

Suddenly, Nanna threw open the door and presented him with a reprieve. A tide of little girls burst in, surging about David's feet in a froth of white nightclothes.

"David, David!" Six-year-old Arabella threw one arm about his thigh and looked up at him. "My toof fewel out!" she announced, pointing inside her gaping mouth. "Can I have a guinea for it?"

Arabella was the very picture of her mother with her slick raven tresses and flashing eyes. "Heavens, what a greedy little Scot you are!" proclaimed David, grabbing her up and lifting her high in the air. In response, Davinia tried to clamber up his leg. She looked very like her father, with a wild mane of blonde hair and brilliant golden eyes. David fell back into the nearest chair, taking both girls with him.

"Bella cried when it came out," tattled four-year-old Davinia, grunting as she scrabbled onto his left thigh.

"Did not!" protested Arabella, scowling across David's lap.

"Did too!" challenged Davinia, turning her warmest smile on David and raising her lips to his ear. "Have you brought my pony?"

Alone on the floor, and clearly feeling neglected, little Fiona fell back on her rump and burst into tears.

"Davinia!" Jonet chided, leaning down to pick up Fiona. "Don't carry tales! And don't wheedle gifts from your godfather!"

"Hush, goose!" David whispered to Davinia. "You weren't to say a word yet. Now! Why do we not move to the sofa, where we may all sit together? Your mother wishes to tell a new bedtime story."

"Do I?" asked Jonet archly, bouncing Fiona on her hip. "Which one would that be?"

David scooped up Davinia in one arm and Arabella in the other. "Oh, surely you must remember my dear—? It is the one about the little girl who kept poking her nose into other people's business, until it somehow got chopped off."

"Eeeew!" said Arabella appreciatively. "That sounds like a good one!"

Lord Walrafen's equipage rolled up Portland Place and made the sharp turn into Park Crescent at precisely two minutes before the appointed hour. With her hair perfectly coifed and the blue silk neatly pressed, Cecilia stood in her foyer and watched Giles's footman put down the steps.

She felt a strange, sinking sensation as her stepson alit from the carriage. She had almost hoped he would be unable to accompany her to the Rowlands' tonight. After all, she was a widow, was she not? Did she really require an escort? Oh, she cared very deeply for Giles. Beneath all his cool formality, he was kind. He took great pains to oversee her welfare. Giles was the sort of man who made a woman feel *safe*. So why, then, did Cecilia sometimes feel stifled?

But it was too late. Giles was coming up her steps, looking resplendent in his flowing black evening cloak. His heavy black locks were still damp from his bath, his evening attire severe yet elegant. Cecilia sighed. At least Giles was willing to help her with her charity work—when he wasn't busy chiding her for traveling into the East End. Tonight, they would have much to discuss en route to the Rowlands'.

Her butler let him in, and swiftly Giles bent to kiss her cheek. "My dear, how lovely you look!" He gave her his usual smooth smile and carefully veiled appraisal. "Surely I shall have the loveliest step-mama at tonight's affair."

And then they were off into the chilly February night, rolling toward Regent Street and into Mayfair. The Rowland residence was but a short distance away—a regrettable circumstance, Cecilia soon decided. Within an hour of their arrival, she had greeted all of those few friends whom she shared with Anne Rowland. Then true boredom settled in.

For better than an hour, she moved from one dull circle of people she did not like to an equally dull cir-

cle of people she did not know. And thus went the
evening, for there were a great many such circles. The
air was stale, the food tasted like sawdust, and Cecilia
wanted desperately to go home. But she could not.
Not until she had seen what might yet be had from
the Rowlands. She had not risked Etta's hapless iron-
ing to go home empty-handed.

But at present, Edmund Rowland appeared to be
deep in conversation with a tall, balding gentleman
who leaned heavily onto a carved walking stick inlaid
with silver. They stood just beyond the wide, arched entrance which gave onto the main corridor, seemingly
oblivious to those within the drawing room. Amongst
the guests inside, Anne Rowland was nowhere to be
seen. Discreetly, Cecilia slipped through the crowd into
the corridor, brushing behind Edmund and making her
way into the shadows in search of a moment's peace.

She paused on the threshold, looking just beyond
Edmund's shoulder toward the front door where two
somnolent footmen awaited any departing guests. In
the other direction, however, were the stairs to the
ladies' retiring room. Hastily, Cecilia picked up her
skirts and started in that direction, but as she swept
past a tall mahogany *secretaire* which stood against
the wall, she very nearly tripped on a length of red
silk which trailed from its shadows. Had someone
dropped a scarf?

Abruptly, she bent to retrieve it, but with a soft rustle, the fabric slithered from her grasp. "Why, good
evening, Lady Walrafen," drawled a refined feminine
voice from beyond the *secretaire*.

Cecilia jumped.

With a bemused smile, Anne Rowland stepped out,
her red skirts gathered into one hand as she drew up
the scarf in the other. "Heavens, I did not intend to star-

tle you," she said softly, giving Cecilia a quizzical smile. "How good of you to join our little entertainment."

Cecilia quickly regained her aplomb. "It's my pleasure, Mrs. Rowland," she glibly lied. "I collect we have a great many acquaintances in common."

"Indeed," returned Anne. "Then we must become better acquainted, my lady. Will you take a turn down the hall with me? I've just come out for some fresh air."

But at that moment, Edmund Rowland turned to stare over his shoulder at his wife. Mrs. Rowland held his gaze for a long, steady moment. "Your pardon," she finally said, lowering her eyelashes with a sweeping gesture. "I must rescind my offer. I perceive that I am needed elsewhere."

Suddenly, Cecilia felt terribly awkward. Had Anne Rowland been eavesdropping on her husband? And if so, why? For once, his behavior looked innocuous.

But Edmund had not looked precisely surprised to see Anne there. Nor had he looked at Cecilia, but given the furniture and the shadows, it was possible he did not know to whom his wife spoke. Still, it mattered little, for Edmund had turned away to stroll toward the front door with his guest, while Mrs. Rowland's long red skirts were already swishing down the hall and around the corner.

Hastily, Cecilia rushed up the steps to the ladies' retiring room, only to find it too busy. Pausing just long enough to fix her face into the relentlessly poised smile she'd perfected during her come-out, she hastened back down the stairs and plunged into the crowded withdrawing room. It was time either to make her move or go home.

At that very moment, however, she saw Edmund yet again. His elderly friend with the walking stick was gone, and her host was now wading through the room toward her. Good. It was as she had expected.

A waiter brushed past her shoulder, and in a tiny act of desperation, Cecilia snatched another glass of champagne and discreetly pitched back a big swallow. It was her third glass, but she was very much afraid she would have need of it. Men like Edmund Rowland made her nervous. But at least she had a great deal of experience in fending them off.

Since her entrée into society four years ago, Cecilia had often felt the heat of Edmund's eyes sliding up and down her length. Her marriage had merely worsened his efforts. While he apparently thought himself a very dashing blade, she found Edmund to be little more than a vain popinjay who possessed—if rumor could be believed—some exceedingly nasty habits.

Nonetheless, upon his father's recent death, Edmund had come into what was accounted a moderate inheritance, along with a lovely home in Mayfair, and it seemed that his occasional brushes with the insolvency court were a thing of the past. Now, with her staid old papa-in-law laid to rest, Anne had set about entertaining in high style and wanted nothing so much as a guest list littered with old titles and wealthy nabobs. And Cecilia was among the former.

Edmund swept into an elegant bow, almost brushing her glove with his lips. "Lady Walrafen," he warmly purred. "Such an honor! Mrs. Rowland is almost beside herself."

Forcing a smile, Cecilia baited her hook. "Indeed?" she returned, sipping more delicately at her champagne. "One would hardly think your wife the excitable sort."

Edmund's thin mouth twitched with some indefinable emotion, and then he smartly offered his arm.

"Will you take a turn about the room with me, ma'am?" he oozed. "All of London is pleased that you've put off your black and can again give us the pleasure of your company."

Just then, a second waiter passed and Rowland snagged his own glass from the tray. "Now, tell me, my dear lady, however do you occupy your time now that you are . . . *all alone?*"

Cecilia could not miss his silky undertone. She cast her line for all she was worth. "How kind you are, Mr. Rowland, to think of us lonely widows!" she answered, lowering her lashes and cutting a glance up at him. "But I can scarce imagine your having any interest in hearing about or—*oh, dare I say it?*—joining in any of my little pursuits . . . ?"

Slowing to a near halt, Edmund Rowland gave her a wide, wolfish grin. "I believe you very much mistake me, ma'am. I have always found everything about you inordinately interesting. And I am always looking for a pursuit worthy of joining."

Cecilia lifted her glass and stared languidly across the crystal rim. "Oh, my!" she said softly, deliberately holding Edmund's gaze. "I am so *very* glad to hear it. So many men, you know, merely feign an interest in a poor widow's most intimate concerns."

"Indeed?" Edmund lowered his gaze suggestively.

"Oh, yes," breathed Cecilia. She decided to jiggle the worm a bit. "And yet, they seem incapable of, er, following through any *measure* of *satisfaction*. It's simply crushing when a man fails to uphold his—ah, his promise."

Cecilia watched his eyes light up. Rowland steered her toward a potted palm in one corner of the room. "Oh, it would take a worthless sort of fellow indeed to fail a woman of your enduring charms, Lady

Walrafen," he returned, swallowing the hook in one greedy gulp.

"My charms?"

"Oh, yes," he said, leaning a little nearer. "And for my part, I can pledge myself most assiduously—and most *vigorously*—to your long-neglected interests."

"Indeed?" she whispered, mentally setting the hook into his flesh.

"Of course! In a more private moment, you need only tell me precisely what you wish of me, and I shall make all the appropriate efforts."

"Oh, how wonderful!" she said breathlessly, tapping the rim of her glass against his in salute. "Though I'm not too concerned with the privacy of the thing, you've greatly relieved my mind, sir! It's embarrassing to confess that I came here with the express hope of capturing your attention."

"Did you?" Edmund sounded momentarily flattered. Then he looked into her eyes and seemed to choke ever so slightly. "I—I would never have guessed."

Yes, the slick, shiny fellow felt something in his throat, didn't he? It had been too easy, and he was just beginning to wonder . . .

Cecilia tossed off the rest of her champagne, flashed him her brightest smile, then tapped him teasingly on the arm with the empty bowl. "Oh, Mr. Rowland!" she effused. "I knew I could count on you as soon as I learned that you were the Reverend Mr. Amherst's cousin!"

Some of the color drained from Edmund's face at that. "My cousin, do you say?" He laughed a little nervously. "I suppose I must remember to thank dear Cole."

"Oh, we all should, do not you think?" Cecilia cast her eyes heavenward and tried to look suddenly pious, but it was a stretch. "And I must be doubly grateful, for I have no notion how I would have survived dear Walrafen's death had I not devoted myself to Mr. Amherst's mission."

"M-m-mission?"

"Oh, yes." Cecilia shot him another blinding smile and gave her rod one last jerk. "Now! Precisely what might you be able to do for me, Mr. Rowland? Don't be shy! I need to know your preferences, you see."

"*Preferences?*" Edmund's eyes began to dart about the room as if searching for an open door, or perhaps some opportune hole in the floor which might swallow him up. Sharply, he gave a strangled little cough.

Lightly, Cecilia laid her hand upon his sleeve. "My dear Mr. Rowland! Are you perfectly all right? I say, I do hope there's nothing irritating your throat. After all, it is February. The slightest inflammation might turn to quinsy!"

Edmund coughed again. "No," he rasped. "Throat's fine."

"No swelling, then? Excellent! Now, as I was saying," Cecilia continued, slowly reeling in her fish, "I daresay that a man of your importance must be exceedingly busy, so perhaps one big cash donation would be best? Of course, we always have need of volunteers—if, that is, you do not mind venturing in into the East End slums? In truth, the stench is not all that bad."

"The—the East End?"

Cecilia dropped her voice to a confessional tone. "Yes, some people, you know, do not care for it at all! It is one thing to wish to *help* the lower orders, and another thing altogether to actually *associate* with them, is it not?"

Edmund lost the rest of his color. "Associate with?"

"Indeed!" answered Cecilia, nodding more fervently.

She studied Edmund's face. On second thought, he wasn't exactly a fish. More of an eel, really. "Why, just last week, I attended a soiree very like this one—at the home of a very dear friend of the Duke of York. Oh, but I should not name names, should I? Anyway, the gentleman in question was very like yourself."

"Like me—?"

"That is to say, well placed in good society and very desirous of helping our cause. But he just gave me a bank draft for five thousand pounds. I daresay you might find it expedient simply to do the same? And to be sure, you needn't feel one bit ashamed of it."

Cecilia's fish fell metaphorically at her feet, flopping about and gasping for breath.

Suddenly, someone touched her lightly on the arm. It was Giles, bringing a death cudgel in the form of a rotund, purple-turbaned matron who wheezed and creaked on his arm. How fortuitous!

"Oh, look," Cecilia squealed. "Here is Giles! And dear Lady William! Giles, my dear, you shall never guess! Mr. Rowland wishes to make a donation to the mission! Indeed, he wishes to donate—?" Cecilia arched one eyebrow and looked at Edmund delicately.

Edmund looked witheringly at the matron, Lady William Heath, a notorious gossip and inveterate blowhard. Again, he cleared his throat with an agonizing *harumph*. "F-f-five thousand pounds, I believe it was."

Giles sucked in his breath. "Good God!"

"Indeed!" exclaimed Lady William Heath appreciatively.

"Oh!" chirped Cecilia, reverently clutching her empty glass to her bosom. "How very good you are, sir! Your generosity warms my heart! That is by far our largest contribution to date."

Her fish gave another little twitch and flop. "B-b-but the Duke of York," Edmund stuttered. "Did you not say . . . did not his friend . . . give five thousand pounds?"

Cecilia let her eyes roll back down from heaven to catch his gaze. "Oh, dear!" she innocently exclaimed. "How silly I am! Did I misspeak? It was five hundred pounds. Of course, if I have confused you—that is to say, if you wish to reconsider . . ."

Lady William lifted her lorgnette to peer at Edmund, leaning forward until her stays creaked and her purple-feathered turban protruded into the midst of the conversation. The timing could not have been better.

Edmund's eyes widened in alarm. "Do you mean *renege?*" he asked haughtily. "Certainly not!"

With a pained expression, Giles watched Edmund Rowland walk away. At that moment, Lady William turned to snatch another dollop of the goose liver pâté.

"Really, Cecilia!" Giles whispered disapprovingly. "I tell you, I won't be a party to this sort of thing again. Unlike you, I cannot call it Christian duty. I daresay I ought simply to write you a bloody bank draft myself and be done with it!"

Cecilia flashed him her most radiant smile. "Oh, Giles! That wouldn't be nearly as much fun. And by the way, your timing was sheer perfection. And Lady William! A true touch of genius."

"I beg your pardon?" Lady William turned back to face them as she swallowed her pâté. "Did I hear my name?"

Again, Cecilia beamed. "Oh, indeed, ma'am. I was just telling Giles that I have not had the pleasure of seeing you in ever so long. You must come up to Park

Crescent for tea soon. And in truth, I have been wondering—"

Lady William threw up a staying hand as she swallowed one last lump of goose liver. "No, no, my dear! You'll not suck me in with those pretty blue eyes!" She paused introspectively. "Though I must say, I was rather proud of the way you handled Edmund Rowland. That man is not known for his charitable nature, to say the least!"

But Cecilia did not cut bait quite so easily. "Oh, Lady William! How can you not support the Reverend Mr. Amherst's efforts when he is working so diligently to save the souls of innocent women who have been compromised and mistreated by men? Wealthy, well-placed men, for the most part."

Sardonically, Lady William chuckled, the purple plumes of her turban bouncing merrily. "Oh, my dear—indeed, my very *naïve* Lady Walrafen! Decent women do not end up in *compromising* situations unless they are morally deficient! Everyone knows that!"

There but by the grace of God, thought Cecilia as an unsettling memory stirred. "*Everyone* knows?" she challenged, clutching her empty wine glass until she feared the stem might snap. "And just who among us might constitute this omniscient *everyone*, Lady William? For in my experience, I have found that decent women are often put upon very much against their will and that—"

"Cecilia, my dear!" Giles interrupted with a firm tug on her arm. "You must forgive my forgetfulness. I sent for my carriage a quarter-hour past. You look terribly wan. It is time I saw you home."

Cecilia looked about the room just as the clock struck eleven. Giles was right. Lady William was hopelessly narrow-minded, and it was time to go home. A few of Edmund's guests had already left, and at an hour which was rather early, even for London's off-season.

Forcing a bright smile, Cecilia looked up at her stepson and lightly laid her hand upon his arm. "Why, how attentive you are, Giles! I am perfectly drained. Do let us go."

2

In which Delacourt falls victim to a Captain Sharp

The Reverend Mr. Amherst had come home bone-weary and more than a little disheartened from a day spent trudging about in the bitter environs of Lower Shadwell. And then, much to his disappointment, he had been able to steal but a moment alone with his beloved wife and daughters before being required to go back downstairs to join his stepsons in playing the congenial host to his troublesome brother-in-law.

But one moment alone with Jonet was enough to renew his worst fears. She was fretting herself sick over Delacourt again—and at a time when it was most unwise to do so. Indeed, Cole had resisted the impulse to scold her soundly, to tell her that the child she carried had to be foremost in both their minds. Nonetheless, he, too, was deeply concerned about his brother-in-law.

In Cole's estimation, Delacourt had been pissing away his life for far too long. He was among the most haughty, extravagant, and indolent gentlemen in all of London. But that was not what bothered Cole. No, what bothered Cole was just how miserable Delacourt was about it. Misery was a complicated thing for a vicar to deal with.

If a man reveled in a life of sloth and sin, it was a simple enough matter for a clergyman to appeal to his sense of remorse. Only the most hardened and hell-bound of scoundrels felt no guilt over a life of iniquity. But when a man felt nothing—or near to it—that limited what anyone might do to help him. And Delacourt's deadened emotions were of long duration.

There had been a time, not so many years ago, when Cole had begun to believe that the very thing Delacourt needed had finally arrived, but it had come on the wings of an appalling misunderstanding.

But soon, he had begun to believe that Cecilia Markham-Sands was just what was required to jolt the arrogant young viscount out of his discontent and lethargy. For weeks after Lord Delacourt's sham betrothal to Lady Cecilia had been announced, Cole had watched his brother-in-law pace nervously up and down the corridors of Elmwood like an expectant father. Surprisingly, Delacourt had tried to push the marriage forward. And then, when Lady Cecilia had refused to see him, Delacourt had gone so far as to call upon both her uncle and her brother in Buckinghamshire, in the hope that they might persuade her to make the betrothal more than just a charade.

But Lady Cecilia had seemed insulted by his interest.

When asked, Delacourt had hotly insisted that he was simply attempting to do the honorable thing and that Lady Cecilia was too young to know what was best. But it had hardly required a soothsayer to see that the haughty young viscount's perseverance had been far more rooted in his own obsession than in any wish to respect the conventions of society.

No, Lord Delacourt was notorious for flaunting convention, and for enjoying the doing of it. But Cecilia Markham-Sands had been his first—and his last—obsession. And there was nothing about that which had ever given Delacourt a moment's pleasure.

Well, perhaps one or two. Before he'd known just whom he'd got hold of.

After crying off her mock engagement, it had been almost two years before Lady Cecilia had deigned to leave her home and make her belated London debut—and Jonet had always theorized that that circumstance had had more to do with Harry Markham-Sands's sudden marriage than any desire to wed.

But by then, the vivacious girl had blossomed into an extraordinarily beautiful woman, the very embodiment of restrained feminine elegance. Despite her lack of fortune, many of the *ton*'s young rogues and all of its more staid suitors had fallen at Cecilia's feet. The brilliant young MP, Giles Lorimer, had tumbled first. Oddly, his widowed father had followed shortly thereafter, with a string of others in between.

Yes, Lady Cecilia's suitors had given Delacourt some stiff competition, and he'd been the only confirmed ne'er-do-well amongst them. But again, he'd done his best, apparently believing that her reappearance in society meant that perhaps Lady Cecilia, all grown up, might be willing to receive his attentions.

She had not been willing.

Indeed, she had spurned him to the point of embarrassment. And at the end of the season, she had quietly married Giles Lorimer's father, the widowed Lord Walrafen, a man more than twice her age, who possessed less than half Delacourt's wealth.

So much for painting the chit a fortune hunter.

Delacourt had hidden his disappointment with better success the second time around. If he had been a hardened rakehell before, he was twice as bad after.

So far as Cole or Jonet knew, Delacourt had not

spoken one word to Lady Walrafen during the whole of her marriage. Indeed, they had once seen him walk a circle around a receiving line—a dreadful breach of etiquette—merely to avoid acknowledging her. Others had seen it, too, and while they might have quietly laughed about it, no one was apparently bold enough or foolish enough to tease the volatile viscount openly.

And then, when Lord Walrafen had died less than three years into the marriage, Delacourt had refused to send so much as a letter of condolence. And he seemed incapable of admitting just what the problem was. Or perhaps he knew it and simply did not know how to go forward with his life.

And just what *was* the problem?

Was Delacourt in love with Cecilia Markham-Sands? Even Cole did not have the answer to that one. Probably not. Delacourt's obsession seemed even deeper than that, and rooted in a kind of remorse so caustic and so cancerous that even Cole could barely understand it.

Yes, Delacourt had very nearly forced himself upon Cecilia—an act so heinous and so horribly close to Delacourt's own soul that Cole believed it still tormented him. And she had coolly refused to allow him to assuage so much as a twinge of his guilt. Though her actions had been more self-preserving than deliberately punitive, Cole wondered if there was a more merciless punishment a person could mete out to another human being.

Well! Perhaps there was a lesson there? Cole shook his head and dressed for dinner.

But despite Cole's fatigue and Jonet's delightful dinner conversation, he continued to find himself obsessed with the problem of his brother-in-law all through the meal. Indeed, he kept on turning it over in his mind, even as port was being served to David, himself, and his elder stepson, Stuart, Lord Mercer. Moreover, by the time he had found himself reseated with his family in the withdrawing room, he was still thinking about it.

In the book room next door, the longcase clock struck eleven. At once, Jonet stood, pressing one hand to the small of her back and stifling a yawn with the other. "Gentlemen, I must say good night, or at least two of you will be required to carry me up to bed."

Lovingly, Cole gazed at his wife. "Any one of us could carry you, my dear, for you are the merest sprite," he said gently, but he turned to his younger stepson, Lord Robert Rowland. "Robin, you will give your mother your arm and see her safely up the stairs, if you please."

Lord Robert leapt up to do as he was bid.

David's eyes followed Jonet as she left the room. As soon as the two had vanished down the hall, he turned his narrow gaze upon his brother-in-law. "Really, Amherst!" he complained. "This is to be her fourth confinement in eight years! It certainly appears you men of the cloth are a little more—how shall I put it?—more *zealous* than one might suppose."

Cole merely settled himself back into his chair. "Have you a point, David?" he asked softly. "For in truth, I cannot imagine my marriage is any of your concern, so long as I take good care of your sister."

David cut a swift glance in Stuart's direction. "Do you call it *care* to keep a woman with child six months out of every twelve?" he demanded in a cold undertone.

Clearly uncomfortable, Stuart rose and went to the sideboard to pour himself a glass of sherry.

Cole studied his brother-in-law. "Your concern for Jonet, while admirable, leads you to exaggerate."

"Does it?" replied his brother-in-law.

Cole ignored the question, rising abruptly from his chair. "For the nonce, why do we not occupy ourselves in a sport which is a little less apt to bring us all to fisticuffs? What do you fellows say to a few hands of whist?"

Just then, the ever ebullient Robin reentered the room. "By gad, a card game!" he interjected enthusiastically. "That would be famous."

"What sort of stakes?" asked David, looking perfectly bored as he neatened the cuffs of his shirt.

Cole bent down to the table and calmly refilled his brandy. For a long moment, he said nothing. "How does this strike you, David?" he finally replied, settling the decanter back onto its tray. "We shall play five games at twenty guineas a point—"

"Ouch!" exclaimed Robin. "That's a bit rich, Papa."

"—the winnings to be donated to the Daughters of Nazareth Society," continued Cole. "And Robin, I'm painfully aware that you've been supplementing your quarterly allowance down at the Bucket of Blood—or whatever you choose to call that Covent Garden hellhole—in ways which we will discuss at a more private moment. Nonetheless, I'm persuaded that your losing tonight would scarce put a dent in your ill-gotten gains."

Robin's chin promptly dropped into his cravat.

David struck a thoughtful pose. "That is all very well," he finally answered. "But dashed dull, you must admit."

"Assuredly, we are not up to snuff with the sort of gamesters you normally sport with," agreed Cole with equanimity. "But of course, a good host would not wish his more worldly guests to suffer any sort of *ennui*. Perhaps we ought to propose something a little more challenging?"

"Such as?" asked David suspiciously.

"Something just between the two of us. If you'll

consent to take the seat opposite me, I will make you a private wager."

"Of what sort?" David coolly returned, reluctant to admit how loath he was to return home alone. He wanted desperately to stay here with his nephews. And with Cole.

"A favor," answered Cole thoughtfully. "A personal favor. If you can take three of five games, I shall grant you one of your choosing. Perhaps I can do something to ease your concerns about your sister's welfare? But of course, you may choose anything you like, as long as it is relatively legal and completely moral."

David smiled grimly. "Ah!" he whispered, cutting a sharp glance toward Robin. "A favor of my choosing! But would you be so obliging, I wonder, as to promise that my sister shall have a long—perhaps even an in-definite—period of rest after this next child? I collect you take my meaning here."

"That, sir, is a very hard bargain!" Cole looked grave. "Moreover, your sister has a mind of her own, lest you've forgotten. But, yes—I can pledge that after this confinement, I shall do all within my power to do as you ask."

"Excellent!" proclaimed David. "Come, Stuart! Let us pull that marquetry table a little nearer to the fire. Robin, you will find us two fresh packs of cards, if you please."

But the vicar still stood by his chair, his snifter held loosely in one hand. "David," he said softly, "do you not wish to know what I shall ask of you?"

By now, David and Stuart had already taken hold of the table. "It scarce matters," David grunted as they hefted the furniture. "I've not lost a game of whist in fifteen years."

"Really?" returned Cole, sounding singularly un-

impressed. "Nonetheless, I should feel that I had un-
fairly advantaged myself had I not fully explained
what it is I wish you to do."

"Then by all means," said David arrogantly as they
moved the table across the room.

"I've promised to take your sister back to Elmwood
for her confinement. We're to leave in ten days' time
and stay three months. I want you to take over my duties at the mission until I return."

David dropped the table on his nephew's toe.

"Bloody hell!" screeched Stuart, clutching one foot
while hopping about on the other.

Both men ignored him. Robin pulled a chair toward the table and shoved his elder brother into it.

Finally, David spoke. "Very well," he answered
calmly. "What do you do there, anyway? Keep a few
ledgers? Badger the Home Office? Write a few bank
drafts, perhaps?"

"I fancy you'll find it rather more than that."

David tossed his hand dismissively. "Well, it doesn't
signify, for I shan't lose. I never lose." He turned his attention to his nephews. "Break the first pack, Robin.
Cole and I shall draw for partners between you."

Chairs were pulled to the table. Cards were drawn
pairing David with Stuart and passing the first deal to
Robin. Play commenced at a brisk pace. Cole and
Robin were defeated in the first game when David effortlessly racked the requisite points and went out in
three hands.

The second game dragged on interminably, and
the luck had clearly shifted. Eight hands in, David
began to sweat. He sent Charlie Donaldson after another bottle of cognac. When Cole finally took the last
trick to win seven to six, it was clear that the four of
them had settled in for a long night.

The third went soundly to Cole's team. David muttered a curse beneath his breath and totted up the score. He had a very grim feeling.

Yet it was unthinkable that he might be beaten by a man who'd never seen the inside of a gaming hell and a whelp who'd yet to see his majority. He vowed it would not happen and ruthlessly tightened his concentration.

Robin opened the deal for the fourth and turned up diamonds as trumps. David held nothing but a handful of black. He poured out another dram of courage and hunkered down to play as if the devil himself sat across the table. Indeed, it was beginning to feel just that way, despite Cole's clerical garb.

For his part, Robin played inexpertly, often tossing out trumps when there was no call and surrendering face cards with little logic. And yet, Cole seemed to be able to recoup. Ten arduous deals later, David and Stuart managed to triumph, but never in his life had he seen a fellow with luck like Cole's. Had he been pitted against anyone other than his pious brother-in-law, David would probably have called the fellow for a sharp.

The opening of the fifth was blessedly swift, like the blade of a guillotine being drawn to its height. It took but two deals before Cole pushed his score precariously close to the edge. The clock struck one just as the last deal fell to Cole, who snapped out the cards with his usual military precision and flicked up the queen of spades to set trumps.

David swallowed hard and looked at the fan of blood-red cards he clutched in his fist. *What damnable luck!* An ominous chill settled over him as he looked again at the black queen, who lay upon the table like a prophetess.

Three months of penal servitude at the Daughters

of Nazareth Society stared back at him. *Good God!* Absently, David reached for the bottle at his elbow at the same moment as Cole.

Somehow—afterward, David could never quite understand how—the bottle tipped over and went rolling across the table, spattering cognac over the fine marquetry, then tumbling onto the floor. Play was suspended for a moment as he and Stuart mopped up the table with their handkerchiefs and righted the bottle.

David cast a final eye over the table to see that it was clean and that cards and tally sheet had been spared any mess. Just then, Robin leaned urgently across the table, his cards held loosely in his right hand. "Papa—?"

"Shh!" hissed his stepfather with uncharacteristic intensity. "No discussion across the table while the hand is in play."

"But Papa!" the boy hotly persisted.

"Hush, son!" Cole reprimanded, his voice sharp. "I'm studying my hand. We shall discuss it later."

Stuart opened play, and it soon appeared that Cole held nearly every spade in the pack. Even Robin, who tossed out his cards with sulky, halfhearted motions, managed well enough.

The last hand was like a death knell. Having briefly snared the lead, David opened it, but Cole trumped in with the ace of spades.

David felt the blade come slicing down upon his neck.

Long moments later, after Robin had gathered up the cards and put them away, Cole looked up from his tally sheet. "Well, gentlemen, it was a near-run thing, was it not? Just three points difference." He gave them all a light smile. "Stuart, you owe the mission precisely thirty guineas. You may give it to me tomorrow."

"Yes, sir."

Cole turned his steady gaze on his brother-in-law. "David, you may deliver yours in person on Friday. That's a four-day reprieve. You look as though you need it."

David slid an unsteady hand down his face. "What time?" he mumbled through his fingers, as if they might shield him from reality.

"Oh, around eleven. Just drop in, introduce yourself to the matron and the patroness on duty, that sort of thing. Afterward, I shall review the files with you and answer your questions. The board of governors meets next week, so you will wish to be prepared."

"Prepared." David's voice was hollow.

For a moment, Cole stared at him. "And David, if it's any consolation to you, I do mean to care for Jonet's welfare in the way which you asked. Our lives are full now, and I have persuaded her that her health must come first." Abruptly, Cole slapped his hands down upon the tabletop. "And that, sirs, must conclude our evening. I'm soon for bed."

Staring blindly into the dark depths of the room, David slowly slid his chair from the table. "I think perhaps I ought to go down to the club now," he muttered to himself. "I think perhaps I need something more to drink."

Stuart jerked from his seat. "I shall come with you, then," he said decisively.

Cole looked at his elder stepson as if he meant to refuse, for the young Lord Mercer was but eighteen and only recently admitted inside Brooks's exalted portals. Then Cole looked back at David's pale face and seemed to reconsider. "Yes, well, good night to you both, then. Robin, you will remain behind, please. We must talk."

With steps that were slow and heavy, Lord Delacourt quit the room, trailed by his elder nephew. Robin observed their departure with a measured gaze. "You trounced David rather badly tonight, sir," challenged the young man as soon as the drawing-room door clicked shut.

Cole left the card table and crossed the room to the long leather sofa beneath the windows. He settled himself onto it and motioned for Robin to take the chair opposite. "I daresay I know what you are thinking," he said, giving his stepson a weak smile.

Robin hurled himself into the chair and let his long legs stretch indifferently across the floor. "Tell me, Papa—just how *did* David and Stuart manage to lose that card game?"

"You may well ask!" Cole gave Robin a knowing wink. "Can I persuade you it was God's will—?"

"Oh? Did God tell you to swap the packs of cards beneath the table? Or to palm those three spades before the deal?"

Cole flashed the boy a rueful grin. "Ah! The Lord does indeed work in mysterious ways, my son. And I see you've learned to spot a few tricks down at the Bucket—an edification I've taken pains to keep from your mama, not that I'm expecting your gratitude, mind."

Robin threw his arms across his chest. "It just don't seem a'tall like you to cheat, sir," he said, clearly more interested in focusing on his stepfather's sins than on his own. "I daresay you have your reasons for such a thing, but I think I deserve to be made privy to 'em!"

Cole leaned across to close the space between them and lightly patted the boy on his knee. "Look, Robin, I know on its face my actions seem patently wrong. But what if I wasn't precisely cheating? What if I were trying to right an old wrong? Just trust me. Can you do that?"

His expression only slightly more lenient, Robin finally nodded. Then, together, they stood, put out the lamps, and went upstairs to bed.

Sir William Blackstone once wrote that "man was formed for society," and surely that learned jurist would never have disputed that the most critical element of a gentleman's society was the sheltering portal of his club. Be it situated in Jermyn Street or St. James's, within such a bastion of masculinity, a fellow could take shelter from whatever new misfortune life had dealt him, whether it was a careless tailor, a petulant mistress, or a bad week at Epsom.

And so it should have been for Lord Delacourt.

Unfortunately, there appeared to be a great many men about town who were in need of such solace on this particular night. Indeed, he had barely flung himself into his favorite chair in the Great Subscription Room and sent an anxious waiter scurrying off for a bottle of their best port, when Edmund Rowland strolled through the door.

At first, Delacourt paid him little heed. They were not friends. In fact, they were just one step removed from being outright enemies, albeit an ever-so-civil step.

Edmund had the dubious honor of being a nephew of Jonet's late husband, and thus he was Stuart's first cousin. And on his mother's side, Edmund was also related to Cole, in a tangle of bloodlines so convoluted that Delacourt simply ignored it.

Indeed, the whole damned Rowland family—in Delacourt's opinion—was little better than an incestuous snake pit, and it was his intention to keep young Stuart out of it. Delacourt's kinship to the inexperienced Marquis of Mercer might be a secret, but at least he had Stuart's best interests at heart.

The wine was brought, the young marquis sat down with his uncle, and a masculine sort of silence fell across the table. A few passing gentlemen nodded or spoke to the pair, but the expression on Delacourt's face did not invite them to linger. Between the two, no word was spoken of what had just occurred at Mercer House.

And really, Delacourt inwardly considered, what was there that one might say? He'd done an exceedingly foolish thing. Yet he was still uncertain as to how it had occurred. *Beaten by Cole?* Unthinkable! And now, for the next three bloody months, he was to be little more than his brother-in-law's indentured servant. There was no gentlemanly way out of it, and David would be damned if he'd even give Cole the satisfaction of watching him look for one.

Yes, publicly, he would do what he'd agreed to do, and hang the embarrassment. But privately, he was wishing Cole to perdition. Blister it, the fellow was no sort of card player at all!

"Cards—?" interjected Lord Mercer abruptly.

David put his glass down with a clatter. "Good God, Stuart! Is that your idea of a joke?"

"N-no, sir!" stammered the young marquis. "I just thought . . . well, we cannot very well just sit here all night looking daggers at everyone who dares walk past."

"Oh?" David shot him a darkly humorous expression. "Have you come to nursemaid me?"

"Not precisely," averred Stuart. "I just thought . . . well, sir, your mood looked very black. I don't think any fellow ought to be left alone in that sort of humor. I'm awfully sorry Papa whipped us."

Lightly, David smiled at his nephew and stood. "Well, come along, then. Get up! I dare not try my luck any further tonight, but there's no harm in our watching the dicing for a bit."

David carefully selected the most promising of several games of hazard. He was an aggressive but skilled gamester. When he gambled, David prided himself on knowing his limits, and in the long run, he never, ever lost. Tonight, the table he chose was surrounded by the very best and the very richest of England's society. Stuart's stepfather's virtuous career notwithstanding, this was the real world, in all its obnoxious glory. The world in which the young peer was destined to live. And David had taken it upon himself to introduce the boy into it, while keeping one watchful eye upon him at all times.

When play paused for the banker to take a count, David leaned discreetly into the table and cleared his throat. "Gentlemen, I wonder, have you had the pleasure of meeting my friend, Stuart Rowland, Lord Mercer?"

Most had, but two had not, and so a pair of players stepped from behind the table to be introduced to the young marquis. At once, David felt someone brush against his shoulder. He turned just as Edmund Rowland strolled up to join the four of them.

"Why, look here!" Edmund smoothly interjected. "If it isn't my young cousin Stuart, looking all grown up. And Sir Lester. Mr. Reed." He nodded at the two gentlemen who had just stepped forward. "And of course, my Lord Delacourt! I give you all good evening."

"Good evening, Cousin Edmund," said Stuart coolly.

Edmund shot an appraising look at David. "My dear boy," he said, turning toward Stuart, "if you mean to make your way into society, you really ought

to allow *family* to make your introductions. Call upon
me next week. We shall chat." Deftly, he snapped
open a delicately enameled snuffbox and dropped a
pinch onto the back of his hand. "Now, I wonder,
might I join this game?"

"Yes, of course," said Mr. Reed graciously. "I'm
done for, so you may as well have my place."

Edmund cocked a dark, angular brow at David.
"Will you hazard a throw, Delacourt?" he asked softly.

Mr. Reed hooted with laughter. "By gad, Rowland,
you'd better hope that he won't!"

Sir Lester Blake raised an unsteady glass, as if he
were just a little drunk. "No, Rowland, you dare not
play with the likes of Delacourt tonight," he agreed,
"for I've heard it said that you're newly in need of five
thousand pounds."

Edmund cut a dark glance in the direction of Giles
Lorimer, Lord Walrafen, who was observing a game
at the next table. "I see that rumor travels rapidly," he
said quietly. "But I find it an honor to contribute any
small amount of money to benefit my cousin's worthy
mission."

Sir Lester laughed richly. "Are you sure it was the
mission you wished to benefit, Rowland? Or might it
have been one of Mr. Amherst's lovely patronesses?"

Edmund's eyes narrowed. "What balderdash! Why,
I find Lady Walrafen to be as cold as a woman can
be—at least when it comes to men. And none of us
knows that better than poor Delacourt here."

Suddenly uneasy, Delacourt let his gaze shift back
and forth between the two men. "Look here,
Rowland," he interjected very quietly. "I neither appreciate nor understand that remark. What has Lady
Walrafen to do with Cole Amherst's work?"

Edmund's eyes mocked. "Why, it seems the good

lady has devoted her worthy efforts to the Daughters of Nazareth Society! Do you mean to say that you were unaware?"

Delacourt wanted to give Edmund a brutal cut, but he was suddenly too alarmed to do so. And his fear had nothing to do with Edmund and everything to do with the dreaded name which had slipped so smoothly from his lips.

"The Daughters of Nazareth Society?" interjected Stuart abruptly. "Isn't that the organization you're to run when Papa goes back to Cambridgeshire?"

At once, Mr. Reed and Sir Lester exchanged glances, then burst into peals of laughter. Edmund's mouth gaped gracelessly. David turned his darkest glower upon his nephew. But it was too late.

"Surely you cannot be serious, Lord Mercer?" Sir Lester managed to ask Stuart between gasps.

Mr. Reed was wiping a tear from his eye. Stuart looked dreadfully ill at ease. "Well, it's not as though he volunteered," the young marquis added helpfully. "He just lost a bet to Papa at whist, that's all."

But the laughter merely increased, and this time Edmund joined in. "Oh, please! The notorious Lord Delacourt trumped by my saintly cousin? That is too rich! Too rich indeed!"

Abruptly, David took his nephew by the arm. "Excuse me," he snapped. "But I think my young friend and I must have a word."

He propelled his earnest nephew back toward their table, where the pair remained for the next quarter-hour, while Stuart profusely apologized. But it was no use. David's humiliation was deep, and his evening could not be salvaged. Soon, he jerked Stuart from his chair and urged him toward the cloakroom.

But as they passed from the Subscription Room,

he caught sight of Sir Lester and Mr. Reed darting away from the betting book, both giggling like tippling schoolgirls. Abruptly, he changed directions, dragging Lord Mercer with him.

The damning evidence of his own humiliation leapt up at him in thick, black ink:

> *Sir Lester wagers fifty guineas to Mr. Reed that Lord D. shall bed a certain widowed countess before May Day has passed.*

David cringed. *Good God!* There was no doubt as to whom they referred. Cecilia Markham-Sands. Cecilia Lorimer. Lady Walrafen. And no matter what one called her, Edmund was right. That spiteful bitch had ice water in her veins.

Pennington Street in the parish of St. George Middlesex was a place of dark despair, both literally and figuratively. The figurative darkness of Pennington resulted primarily from its neighbors: the crime-riddled City of London to one side and Shadwell, teeming with its whoremongering and thievery and general degradation, to the other. And far, far to the west lay London's more exclusive neighborhoods, filled with people who thought the parish of St. George's to be more foreign than France and darker than darkest Africa.

But along the south side of Pennington, that darkness was literal indeed. It slapped Cecilia right in the face every time she drew open the draperies of the mission's upstairs office, for along the lower edge of the street rose the twenty-foot-high wall of the London Docks. The soaring fortification of soot-stained masonry cut Pennington Street off from most of the light, some of the noise, but none of the stench which drifted up from the Thames.

Cecilia dropped the drapery she'd just drawn and returned to her scarred wooden desk, one of three which, along with a collection of mismatched chairs, two storage cabinets, and a small worktable, filled the long, lofty room. The light was marginally better now, but the carpet runner beneath the window was still worse than threadbare, and the air was still filled with the odor of boiling cabbage, which would no doubt constitute the main course of today's midday meal.

But things could be worse, Cecilia carefully reminded herself. The mission house of the Daughters of Nazareth Society was clean and warm, a haven of security and kindness in a world which rarely provided either. Below, she could hear the foot traffic which went in and out of the mission's storefronts, jangling the bells and rattling the big bow windows.

Architecturally, the mission was little more than a series of five early Georgian row houses which had been linked by knocking out walls and adding doors until the place resembled a brick and mortar rabbit warren. One floor below, she could hear the occasional creak of the mangling machines as the laundry workers went about their daily chores. On the floor above, broganed feet trammeled to and fro, scrubbing and dusting the vast women's dormitory which was filled with row upon row of reasonably clean cots and blankets.

It was rough, yet it was a far better life than most of its residents had ever known. Still, the price they paid for it was accounted by many to be simply too steep. Women who chose to enter the mission were required to forswear lives of prostitution and thievery, to study the Bible daily, and to learn a self-supporting trade such as sewing, laundressing, or even leatherworking.

Many of their products were then sold to seamen, stevedores, and the like, thus plowing much needed revenue back into the organization. Unlike many of her class, Cecilia harbored no misconceptions. While the mission was far from being a workhouse, the denizens of the Daughters of Nazareth had no easy life.

Cecilia pulled up her chair and flipped open the first of the week's account books. This had become her specialty, and Mr. Amherst had been more than happy to leave it to her. Cecilia's head for numbers, combined with her shameless ability to wheedle money from the vain and unsuspecting *ton*, made her ideally suited for the task.

She had expected some resistance when she'd first volunteered for duty at the mission. Oh, of course, members of the *ton* willingly sat on the board of governors or hosted the occasional posh fundraiser. And yes, many of them were women of rank and wealth like herself. But when Cecilia had approached Cole Amherst to offer her services, she had had a little more than another fancy dinner party in mind.

At the time, her husband had scarcely been cold in his grave, and her life, which had never been very full, had been completely drained of all meaning. She had long remembered Mr. Amherst's kindness to her, given at a time when she had felt young and frightened and very much at the mercy of men. And perhaps because of it, she had watched with admiration his quiet work in the slums and rookeries of Middlesex.

Quickly, Cecilia began to tally the columns across the ledger, lightly penciling the totals at the bottom of each column and carrying the balance forward to the appropriate place. But she was scarcely three pages into her task when an abrupt knock sounded at the office door.

Cecilia looked up to see that Etta—who absolutely refused to permit her mistress to travel beyond Mayfair alone—stood in the doorway. Oddly, her face was drained of all color. Beyond the girl's narrow shoulders, Cecilia could see the shadowy presence of a tall, rangy man who lingered in the darkness of the hallway.

"A visitor, mum," she announced with an unusual degree of solemnity.

The man pushed forward rather aggressively, but he held his hat in his hands. He wore a nondescript suit of dark wool worsted and, over it, a swirling black greatcoat, which made him look like some lean, black-eyed bird of prey. His clothing was neither expensive nor fashionable, and the hat had clearly suffered from the effects of the weather.

Overall, his mien was intimidating, yet not malevolent, could one but look beyond the hard, mesmerizing eyes which flicked about the room, taking in Cecilia, her attire, and every stick of furniture in about two seconds.

Cecilia was walking forward to greet him before she realized she had left her seat. There was something in the man's expression which both drew her and gave her pause. "I am Lady Walrafen," she announced. "You wished to see me?"

Etta pulled shut the door, leaving them alone. A very grave sign indeed. Abruptly, the man cleared his throat. "I asked to see the Reverend Mr. Amherst, but the shopgirl belowstairs said that he was unavailable. Your . . ." He searched for the right word, his expression troubled. "Your Miss Healy brought me here."

Cecilia motioned toward a chair before the desk. "Then do come in, Mr. . . . ?"

"De Rohan," he said, stepping hesitantly toward the chair. "Maximilian de Rohan, Chief Inspector with the Thames Marine Police."

"P-police?" Cecilia sat down rather gracelessly behind the desk. "What could the police possibly want here? Our women cause no trouble."

Inspector de Rohan did not sit. "You took in an Irish girl some three weeks past, I believe? Miss Mary O'Gavin? She may have had a friend or a younger sister with her."

"Yes, you must mean Kitty," said Cecilia, trying to calm her sudden unease. "Mary and Kathleen O'Gavin. They've been here above a fortnight."

"Kitty O'Gavin may indeed be here, my lady, but her sister assuredly is not," de Rohan answered, finally settling into the proffered chair. He looked very much as if he did not wish to be there, either.

No doubt he was uncomfortable speaking with her, not only because of her gender but also because of her class. There was also just a hint of a Continental accent underlying his low, gruff voice, so perhaps he was an immigrant, too. But Mr. de Rohan's social unease was obviously not her most pressing problem.

"What do you mean, Mary is *not* here?" Cecilia asked.

Mr. de Rohan twisted uncomfortably in the hard chair. "I should really prefer to discuss this with Mr. Amherst first," he said miserably. "But I suppose I must see the sister. One of our snitches—a river police informant—was watching a suspicious warehouse last night. He found Mary O'Gavin's body in an alley off Pearl Street this morning."

"Body—?" Cecilia dropped the pencil she had been

toying with. It hit the desk with a clatter. "Do you mean—*dead?*"

De Rohan's mouth twisted bitterly. "That is the inevitable result of having one's throat slit from ear to ear, yes."

Cecilia tried to rise from her chair and faltered. De Rohan started to stand, as if uncertain as to whether he should offer some assistance, but Cecilia held up a hand. "No, please! I am . . . perfectly all right."

"My apologies," he said gruffly, his gaze sweeping over her expensive clothes again. "I forgot myself. I ought not be speaking to you at all. Indeed, I am quite certain you should not be exposed to any of this atrocity."

"Not exposed?" echoed Cecilia in frustration. "Sir, I appreciate your concern for my delicate sensibilities, but I can assure you I am *exposed* to this every day I come here. One must only pass over Fleet Street to see all manner of inhumanity. I do not visit the docklands to take the fine morning air."

Mr. de Rohan's mouth quirked with wry humor, and he looked suddenly handsome. "No, ma'am. I am sure you do not."

Cecilia ignored him. "Have you a suspect, sir?"

De Rohan gave a harsh bark of laughter. "No, and not apt to find one. The poor girl could have been done in by anybody."

"But why?" asked Cecilia. "Why should anyone wish to attack a poor Irish girl without a penny in her pocket?"

The policeman looked at her patronizingly. "It is a hazard of her trade, ma'am. Prostitutes die in the Middlesex boroughs with a rather startling frequency."

Cecilia slammed her hands down onto the desk. "Oh, no!" she protested. "No, Mr. de Rohan, that simply will not do! Mary O'Gavin was not prostituting herself. If she meant to continue with that sort of life, then she had no reason to remain here at all."

De Rohan's chin jerked up. "So you think you have no backsliders here, ma'am?" he asked rather coldly. "Instead, every soiled dove who crosses your doorstep has her immortal soul saved, and goes on to live a life of unblemished respectability? Is that what you imagine?"

"Oh, good heavens, no!" Cecilia looked at him in bitter amusement. "Of course we have backsliders! Some of our women have been here two or three times. How can we turn them away when God has not yet done so? But the very nature of sin is the reason for our pass system. Mary could not possibly earn any meaningful income by trolling for flats one night out of seven."

"Trolling for flats?" he echoed weakly.

Cecilia was suddenly rather pleased at having listened to Etta's earthy cant with such diligence. "Streetwalking," she returned, trying hard to keep up a brave front.

"I know what it means, Lady Walrafen." But just the same, he was rather obviously appalled to learn that she did.

Inwardly, Cecilia shrugged. Well, one could hardly be expected to cling to one's innocence in a place like this.

"Lady Walrafen?" De Rohan's voice was suddenly tentative. "These girls, were they professionals?"

"Professionals?" she asked.

Cecilia was surprised to see a flush of faint color rise up his hard face. "Did they work in a brothel?" he clarified. "Or did they simply walk the streets when they needed extra money? Or do you know?"

Cecilia frowned in concentration. "I don't know. Does it matter?"

De Rohan settled back into his chair. "It might," he mused, his fleeting embarrassment gone. "The girls who work in houses generally have protectors. Fancy men, bawds, someone who has a vested interest in keeping them alive. They also guard their territory rather aggressively."

Cecilia felt herself grow cold. How dreadful it all sounded! Poor Mary. To push away the threat of tears, Cecilia took up her pencil again and began to slide it absently through her fingers. "Mary was found near Pearl Street, did you say? That's very near the Middlesex Foundling Home, is it not?"

"Yes." De Rohan frowned. "Is there some significance which escapes me?"

Slowly, Cecilia shook her head. "I doubt it. But it is possible that she had left a child there, although it is our policy never to inquire into a woman's past. Nonetheless, every Monday, Mary has asked Mrs. Quince for a pass to go to the orphanage on Tuesday evening. And she always seemed . . . rather subdued on Wednesdays."

"You are here every day?" he asked in some surprise.

"Just three days a week, and only for a few hours. Lady Kirton takes the other two." Cecilia smiled lamely. "We are here—and I shall endeavor to say this with a straight face—to set an example of our sterling upper-class morality. On weekends, Mrs. Quince, the mission's matron, is fully in charge." Abjectly, she lifted her gaze to his. "So what do you mean to do now, sir?"

He shifted uncomfortably again. "I hardly know. I'm with the River Police, and this is a parish matter. However, this mission is a great favorite amongst some of our more vociferous MPs." He shrugged. "I'm told the local magistrates wish everything properly done, and it seems that Bow Street is overwhelmed just now."

"What a pity every girl found dead in St. George's does not warrant such attention to duty," answered Cecilia dryly.

Abruptly, the policeman stood. If she'd insulted him, one could not discern it. "Thank you, Lady Walrafen. Would you be so obliging as to send for the sister? I suppose I must inform her."

"No!" Cecilia interjected. Inspector de Rohan did not look like the sympathetic sort. "I should rather tell her myself."

De Rohan nodded. "But I must have a word with her."

"To be sure, if she's well enough." Briefly, Cecilia hesitated. "Mr. de Rohan, did you know there was a third young woman—Margaret McNamara? I believe she's called Meg, and she came here with the two sisters. Perhaps you ought to speak with her as well?"

Something which looked like respect flared in de Rohan's pitch-black eyes. "Thank you," he responded. "Perhaps one of them can tell us something helpful."

Cecilia nodded and pulled the bell for Etta. At this time of day, the younger Miss O'Gavin should be busy sewing seaman's trousers, for they had a huge shipment on order for the crew of a merchantman which was due to put out next week.

For Cecilia's part, she vowed to stay by Kitty O'Gavin's side until the worst was over. It was the least she could do. And then, she would have to send word to Mr. Amherst. How horrible that would be! He would be crushed, of course. And illogically, Cecilia felt as if she were somehow responsible, as if she had failed to protect those whom he'd entrusted to her care.

It took but a moment before Kitty was found and the sorrowful news broken. Cecilia thought it the hardest thing she'd ever done, worse even than telling

Giles that his father was dead. Kitty asked no questions. Indeed, she seemed beyond it, for her color drained to a dead white, and she very nearly swooned. Gently, Mrs. Quince escorted her out and up to her room. It was apparent, even to de Rohan, that the girl was not able to answer anyone's questions.

At once, Cecilia sent Etta to fetch Meg McNamara. It was immediately clear she was frightened to learn of her friend's murder. And yet, her demeanor was altogether different from Kitty's. Clearly, she did not like the sight of Maximilian de Rohan, and Cecilia got the very distinct impression that she was far more hardened than either of the O'Gavin girls had been.

At first, she answered de Rohan's questions in monosyllables. No, she didn't know where Mary O'Gavin had gone. No, she knew no one with whom Mary might have quarreled. No, Mary had confided nothing in her. But when de Rohan pressed rather stridently on the issue of whether or not Mary had given birth to a child, Meg's voice softened a little.

"Aye, she did, some two years past. No way to keep it, though." Meg shrugged weakly. "Give it over to the foundling 'ome, and accounted 'erself lucky they took it. A girl, it was. But it died just a few months ago, right afore Christmas."

"But why—?" interjected Cecilia, feeling yet another swell of unexpected grief.

Blankly, Meg looked up at them, her gaze passing from de Rohan to Cecilia. "D'ye mean why'd she keep goin' to that school every week like there weren't nothin' amiss? Mary was just soft, she was. The burying ground was out back, and she liked to go to the grave. And she'd got 'erself attached to all them other brats, too." Finally, her voice choked a bit. "And

maybe she didn't really understand 'ers was gone.
There's some that don't, you know."

"Do you know who fathered the child?" de Rohan
gently pressed.

At that, Meg laughed harshly, showing teeth which
were broken and yellow. "Oh, that's a rum 'un, that
is." She chuckled, and then her face fell again, as if
she could not keep up the pretense. "Truth is, Mary
had a man as what kept 'er back then. But 'e up and
disappeared afore she knew of the babe."

Cecilia felt a cold anger burn through her. "Why
did she not demand that the father support the child?"

Meg sneered derisively. "It don't work that way, my
lady. But yeah, she carried a note 'round to his hotel.
The man at the desk run 'er orf. Said he didn't live
there anymore. Might 'ave been the truth, too. We
don't get the society rags down 'ere."

"What was his name?" De Rohan prodded, leaning
forward. "Where was he from?"

"Save yer snappish tongue," returned Meg wearily.
"For I don't know 'is name. Mary never said—in our
kind o' game it don't pay ter yap. But he 'ad a house in
the country where 'e stayed sometimes—and 'e took
'er there once. She said it was pretty, rose gardens all
around." Again, the girl snorted in disdain. "A right
proper fool she was, dreamin' o' such things. But 'e
didn't kill 'er. I mean, why should 'e? 'Oo cares when a
gentry cove gets a bastard on some two-penny whore?
An' since when d'the bleedin' magistrates care that
one got done for?"

"Why indeed?" De Rohan asked very softly, his
expression bleak. He shifted in his chair as if he
might stand. "I'll come back in a day or two and
speak with the sister. Perhaps she'll be feeling more
herself."

"Won't do yer no good," Meg interjected. "Kitty knows nothing of it. Mary was too ashamed. And Kitty lived with her da over in St. Giles 'til the fever carried 'im off last spring. She ain't but fifteen."

De Rohan eyed Meg coolly. "And how long had you worked with Mary?"

Meg looked as though she was regretting her loose tongue. "Met 'er not long after 'er babe come."

"And you worked out of a house?" de Rohan guessed, obviously trying to keep her talking. "All three of you?"

Meg's eyes shied away for the first time. "Aye, a place off Black Horse Lane. Mother Derbin's it's called." Suddenly, her gaze cut toward Cecilia. "Can I go now, mum? I don't 'ave ter answer 'is questions if I don't want, do I? Bereaved as I am 'n all, I'd like some time alone."

Cecilia turned to de Rohan, whose black eyes glittered with frustration. "I have no authority to force her to speak with me, no," he said tightly.

Cecilia knew the limits of the law as well as de Rohan did. Succinctly, she nodded, and Meg fled the room. Abruptly, de Rohan jerked to his feet and made Cecilia a stiff, formal bow. "Your servant, Lady Walrafen. I shall return in a few days' time."

And then he was gone, leaving Cecilia alone in an office which seemed colder and more empty than ever before. No longer able to restrain herself, Cecilia let the tears begin to fall silently. But even as she did so, she pulled open the desk drawer and with slow, precise motions, withdrew a sheet of paper. It was time to begin the dreadful missive which must be carried straightaway to Mr. Amherst in Brook Street.

Life in east London was hard, yes. And the shadow

of death lurked around every corner. But the truth did little to assuage Cecilia's grief. Today, she felt as though they had lost not just one of their own but a child as well. And Cecilia could not escape the awful feeling that life at the mission would never be the same.

3

*In which Lady Walrafen tumbles Headfirst
into Trouble*

 $\mathcal{M}$ r. Hiram Pringle was that most revered of personages, a stately gentleman's gentleman of the old school,
with unerringly conservative taste and the good sense
never to bother urging it upon his employer. And for
forty of his sixty-five years, his employer had been one
of the successive Viscounts Delacourt, all of whom had
been frequently temperamental, often vain, and occasionally ostentatious. And all of whom he had served
with perfect grace and practiced patience.

But on this particular Friday morning, even a casual
observer could have seen that Pringle was on the verge
of asking to be pensioned. With a withering glance, his
eyes followed yet another perfectly starched cravat as it
went sailing onto his lordship's dressing-room floor. By
anyone's count, that made seven. Staring into the
cheval glass before him, Lord Delacourt reached out
his hand, impatiently snapping his fingers. Pringle
grudgingly thrust forward the eighth.

For his part, Lord Delacourt was uncertain as to
precisely why his bloody cravat had chosen today of
all days to refuse to fall into its normally flawless folds.
He did not understand why his favorite waistcoat felt

too tight and his brand-new top boots looked dull as ditch water. Nor was he perfectly sure why he was even going to Cole's bloody mission, whether immaculately dressed, badly dressed, or bare-arsed naked.

But it seemed that he was, in fact, going. Oh, it occurred to him that he could stride right back to Brook Street and cry foul. But inwardly, David convinced himself that he was too much the gentleman. Besides, what the devil did he care that he was suddenly the laughingstock of his club? He'd never given a ha'penny what anyone thought of him—and *anyone* certainly included Edmund Rowland.

Moreover, it was highly unlikely that he would actually *see* Cecilia Markham-Sands at the Daughters of Nazareth Society. Certainly, he had no wish to speak another word to her again for as long as he lived. And indeed, as long as he continued to avoid her discreetly within the narrow circles of society, he probably wouldn't have to. He rather doubted she ever darkened the door of such a mean, miserable place.

A patroness indeed! David knew the type. Prim and upright, they went swishing about at garden parties, cattily remarking on one another's wardrobes and boasting of their charitable do-goodings. And all the while, they were busy exchanging spiteful gossip and meddling in other people's business.

No, women of that ilk did not sully their lily-white hands with the likes of the lower orders. Indeed, the fine Lady Walrafen had not deigned to sully her hands with even the likes of him.

Feeling unexpectedly weary—perhaps even a little old—David studied his reflection in the long mirror, realizing as he did so that the knot of neck cloth number eight looked as limp and shapeless as its predecessors. With a low, violent curse, he stripped the damn thing loose and let it slither to the floor.

In Park Crescent, Friday morning dawned cold but unusually sunny for February. It did little to warm Lady Walrafen, for today was to be the day of Mary O'Gavin's funeral. Cecilia departed for Pennington Street an hour early in hope of catching up the ledgers. Lady Kirton, a well-intentioned but flighty sort, always preferred to content herself with lectures on cleanliness, godliness, deadly sins, and such. All very worthwhile efforts, to be sure. But Cecilia preferred a more hands-on effort.

And so the household accounts would want posting. Otherwise Mr. Amherst would have no idea how much money had been cleared in the stores, no clue as to how much mangling had been taken in by the laundresses, and therefore no assurance of the mission's ability to house and feed fifty homeless women for another month.

Nonetheless, Cecilia was determined to attend the funeral, and propriety be damned. Poor Mary had been possessed of few friends in London, but she'd been a cheerful soul, and so it seemed a grave injustice to have her final words said to a church filled with nothing but two mourners and an empty echo.

Cecilia alit from her carriage and pushed through the front doors to find that a quiet despondency had settled over the mission. As she strode beyond the shop and up the narrow stairs, everyone she passed looked subdued. Along the row of sewing rooms, she heard no singing, no jesting, not even a good cat fight in the corridor—something she normally would not have welcomed. But today, a little cursing and clawing would not have gone amiss.

There was no question that Mary's death had dis-

turbed the fragile well-being of the women who had
come to depend upon the shelter for safety. The fact
that the murder had occurred elsewhere was of small
comfort. With a sigh, Cecilia sent Etta belowstairs to
help out in the shop and, in preparation for the morning's work, carefully laid out the account books.

But she had just finished sharpening her half-
dozen new pencils when Etta pounded perfunctorily
on the door and came flying back in, her face flushed
with color, her bony arms flailing with excitement.
"You'll never guess, mum!" she squeaked. "No, no,
not in a month o' Sundays, you'll not!"

Carefully, Cecilia laid her penknife to one side. "I
daresay you're right," she agreed. "What am I to
guess, pray tell?"

Etta seemed almost to bounce on her toes, her lips
tightly pursed. "Oh, mum! 'E's right here! Right 'ere at
the Daughters of Nazareth Society! Ain't that a joke?
And listen 'ere—he says that nice Mr. Amherst sent
him. Reckon I ought'er show 'im up? 'E's arstin' for
the person in charge."

Cecilia stood, frowning in confusion as she leaned
over the desk. "Upon my word, Etta, you make no
sense at all! *Who* is asking? And for what?"

"That 'andsome Lord Delacourt!" Etta cast her
eyes heavenward. " 'E's right downstairs, or my name
ain't Henrietta Healy! Him and 'is tight little rump, all
togged out in a high silk crumpler and blue coat what
looks to be spun of angel's hair!"

Abruptly, Cecilia sat back down. "Lord Delacourt?"
she squeaked. "What in heaven's name?" With a
strange sense of doom, she lifted her eyes to look at
Etta. Her mind whirled with possibilities, and she
thought of the trick she'd played on Edmund
Rowland. "Do you think—could it possibly be—that

perhaps he's been persuaded to make some sort of donation?"

Etta screwed up her face. "P'raps."

Cecilia let out her breath sharply. Yes, that was the only notion which made any sense. Mr. Amherst would not have sent him otherwise. Delacourt was known to be a dear friend of Mr. Amherst's wife—and had once been a great deal more, some whispered. But Amherst had befriended him, which meant that, given her role here, Cecilia had little choice but to see him. And to be as polite as was humanly possible. She merely hoped she wouldn't choke on her own civility.

Anxiously, Cecilia bounced from her chair and ran her palms down her skirts, uncomfortably aware that they were damp with perspiration.

Suddenly, Etta leaned across the desk. "Look 'ere, m'lady—are you all right? You've gone pale as new-bleached linen!"

Cecilia hardened her gaze. "I'm perfectly fine. Please show him up."

Etta eyed her suspiciously. "Now, why do I wonder if you know 'is 'andsome lordship a little better than you've said, mum?" the maid asked. "D'you 'ave some reason to expect trouble out'er the bounder? 'Cause I'll 'ave 'im out on 'is ear, viscount or no."

Cecilia jerked her chin up and fisted her hands at her sides. "Don't be ridiculous, Etta. I can more than handle someone as vain and transparent as Delacourt. Now, go and fetch him if you please! I have serious work to attend to, and he certainly does not fall into that category."

But the thought of seeing him again did make her uncomfortable. Cecilia inwardly admitted it as she watched Etta go flying back out the door. With her nerves too unsteady to permit her to sit down again,

Cecilia began to pace back and forth along the carpet runner which stretched beneath the windows. Delacourt. *Delacourt.* What on earth?

Cecilia remembered with perfect clarity the moment when last she'd seen him. It had been but two months past, at a country house party, the first invitation she'd accepted since her mourning had ended. She had not really wanted to go. Certainly, she would not have done so had she expected to see him there. However, the affair had been littered with the *crème de la crème* of society, the only people Delacourt knew. In hindsight, she realized she should have expected it.

He had arrived late on the second night, during an evening of dancing. Cecilia had gone reluctantly downstairs unaccompanied, attired in her favorite green silk evening dress. Even swathed in the now-ruined sarcenet shawl, she had been left feeling horribly naked after two years of marriage and a third spent in black.

The awful shock had come just as she had waded innocently into the crowd in search of her hostess. Suddenly, almost as if it had been timed thus, a formation of dancers had rolled back like the Red Sea. And across the room, she had seen him, framed beneath a pair of scarlet window hangings as he bent low over the hand of Lady Snelling, the *ton*'s raciest widow.

For the briefest of moments, Cecilia had found herself unable to look away. As always, he had been dressed with opulent but flawless elegance; rich black evening attire with an ivory silk waistcoat embroidered in gold and an impossibly high neckcloth embellished with a glittering emerald stickpin.

His hair, she remembered, had always been his glory. It was a heavy dark chestnut, with just a hint of a deep red sheen. "Claret brown," she'd once heard it called by some admiring ladies of the *ton*—ladies who looked as if they knew about such things. But on that night, beneath the hundreds of blazing candles, Delacourt's hair had looked as rich and as black as a starless night.

Abruptly, Cecilia had managed to grab hold of herself. She had remembered that she did not give one whit what he wore. That it did not matter to her what one called the color of the scoundrel's hair. But it was already too late.

Something in the crowd—a gasp, a titter—must have alerted him to her presence. With Lady Snelling's hand still held lightly in his, and with the other positioned gracefully at the small of his back, Lord Delacourt had turned his head ever so slightly and stared at Cecilia, allowing his eyes to slide languidly down her length.

Cecilia's sensation of nakedness had heightened, flushing her cheeks with warmth.

Then, with a few whispered words and a devastatingly handsome smile, Lord Delacourt had released Lady Snelling's hand and strolled right out of the room, never to be seen at the house party again.

"Good God!" The voice from the door sliced through her memories.

Abruptly, Cecilia jerked to a halt and whirled about.

And there he stood, nose in the air, his glossy black top boots seemingly fixed to the threshold.

Cecilia swallowed hard, then somehow managed to step forward without tripping. "My lord?" she managed to say, her voice almost steady.

But Delacourt was having none of it. "What the devil are you doing here?" he demanded. "I asked to see the—the—"

"The person in charge?" Cecilia finished, lifting her chin. "Regrettably, that would be me, since this is Friday."

Lord Delacourt's harsh black brows snapped together. "I'm sure I don't know what you mean," he insisted irritably. "I wish to see the person in charge. What has Friday to do with anything?"

Cecilia crossed the room to stand behind her desk. The position made her feel only slightly less vulnerable. "I am a patroness of the Daughters of Nazareth Society," she answered stiffly. "I am one of two ladies who sit on the board of governors, and I serve here for a few hours three days a week."

A skeptical, almost snide expression passed over his face. "And just what is it, Lady Walrafen, that you do here, pray tell?"

Cecilia felt her ire leap into flame. "Why, you will no doubt say I exploit the value of my husband's good name, I suppose," she snapped.

"Will I—?" Lord Delacourt lifted his brows elegantly. "I can certainly think of no higher use for it."

"You are very impertinent, sir."

"And you are very unwelcoming," he returned.

"My presence here lends countenance to the Society's moral objectives," she insisted, forgetting her vow to be civil. "I shudder to think what yours might do."

"I see," he responded, his voice almost seductive in its sweetness. Cecilia had the strangest sense that he was deliberately goading her.

"Well, I do not *see*," she hotly returned. "Why on earth have you come?"

Lord Delacourt's boots, as it turned out, were not nailed to the threshold. Almost effortlessly, he stirred himself and crossed the room with a lazy masculine grace. His expression was one of bitter amusement. "Might I sit?"

Cecilia realized her extraordinarily bad manners.

"By all means." She tossed a hand toward the chair opposite hers and then sat down behind the desk.

He was tall, long-legged, and lean, more elegant than large. And yet, Delacourt somehow managed to dwarf the cavernous room, even as his fashionable clothing made a joke of its shabby furnishings. He relaxed into the chair, lightly steepled his fingers together, then spoke without preamble. "As it happens, I am here to assume directorship of the Society."

Cecilia's mouth fell open. She had the manners to snap it quickly shut again. "I do not perfectly understand."

"Then let me try again," said Delacourt with unerring civility. "For the next three months, I am to administer this godly and charitable institution on behalf of the Reverend Mr. Amherst. He has asked it of me, and I have agreed."

"Asked *you?*"

"Hoodwinked me, perhaps, is more accurate."

"Then he must be very desperate indeed."

"Yes, if one takes a charitable view of his actions," agreed Delacourt dryly. But despite his studied grace and languid motions, the viscount was clearly not in a charitable frame of mind. "Amherst's wife is unwell. It seems he wishes her to rest at home in Cambridgeshire until the late spring. And I am to remain here until then."

"Remain *here?*" Cecilia leapt up from the desk. "I cannot believe you mean it!"

Lord Delacourt looked faintly amused as he stretched across her desk to take up the first in her stack of ledgers. "You may believe me or not as you wish, my lady," he replied, flipping it open in a most proprietary manner. "But assuredly, I mean it."

Cecilia set one hand at her hip as she paced behind

the desk. "What in heaven's name can Amherst have
been thinking?"

"It wants answering, does it not?" he mused, his
eyes scanning a column of numbers. "Now, this debit
entry for soap last month—is that a seven? Or a two?"

"But—but this is wholly inappropriate, sir! Indeed,
you are inappropriate!"

Abruptly, Delacourt's hand stilled, hovering over the
ledger like a serpent. "Now it is I," he said very quietly,
"who does not perfectly understand you, madam."

Cecilia was incensed by his arrogance. She whirled
fully toward him, narrowing her gaze. "Then let me
be blunt. You, sir, are a devil-may-care fribble," she
announced, undaunted when his steely gaze locked
onto hers. "You have the morals of an alley cat. If your
reputation were a rag, it would be too foul to wipe the
floors. And with what you spend in a month on waistcoats alone, we could house a dozen women."

"Dear me!" he spat. "I hope you won't hold back."

"I shan't!" Cecilia returned, burning with righteous
indignation. "Our director must be a responsible
man—accountable not only for the ethical leadership
of this organization but for our fiscal well-being, too.
He cannot run willy-nilly from one gaming hell to the
next, flinging money like cattle fodder."

At last, she saw his body stiffen with anger.
Strangely, it satisfied her.

"That, madam," he snapped, "is an unspeakable insult. I have never in the whole of my life been careless
with money."

"Oh? But you offer no argument on behalf of your
careless morals?"

Delacourt jerked from his chair and hurled the
ledger back onto the desk. It went skidding across
the waxed surface, taking Cecilia's new pencils to the

floor with it. "By the grace of God, Cecilia, I am not accountable to you!" he growled, pencils clattering all about them. "Not for my morals. Not for my finances. And not for one infinitesimal element of my character. You had an opportunity to make my life a living hell, and you gave it up. Do not you dare presume to lecture me now."

Cecilia began to shudder uncontrollably. "*You bastard!*" she hissed.

At that, Lord Delacourt's face went white. Cecilia knew she'd gone too far. His hand tightened into an implacable fist and crashed down upon the desk. "I do not have to stand for this," he thundered. "Indeed, I have grown quite weary of your incessant insults these past many years. Damn you, Cecilia, I once tried to be civil—more than civil—yet you rebuked me at every turn."

Abruptly, Cecilia paced toward him, ignoring the pencils which were scattered across the hard, planked floor. "Why, I never!" she whispered.

Delacourt gave a bitter laugh. "That, madam, I do not doubt, given the old goat you married!"

Cecilia felt her face go blood-red. "You insufferable pig! How dare you speak to me in such a manner! Particularly when it was you who—who—" Suddenly choked by rage and embarrassment, Cecilia was unable to finish.

Delacourt's arms went rigid at his sides. "Who what—?" he bellowed. "I was the one who *did* what? What eternally unforgivable sin did I commit? Yes, I found you attractive! Yes, I made an unutterable error in judgment! And in so doing, I distressed you most appallingly. But, by God, you cannot say I did not try to make it right! And you cannot say that we both have not suffered."

The depth of his anger was compelling. But determined to hold her moral high ground, Cecilia shut it out. "You, my Lord Delacourt, have never suffered a day in your life. You have no notion of what the word means."

"And you, madam, are unendurable in your high-handed arrogance," he gritted out. "You know nothing whatsoever about me."

Cecilia started toward the door. "I know rather more than I should wish," she snapped, with every intention of jerking it open and shoving him through it. "And I tell you plainly, sir, that one of us is about to leave this very inst—"

Cecilia never completed her sentence.

Instead, Delacourt watched in horror as her head snapped back and her arms began to flail wildly. Too late, just as the pencil shot from beneath her feet, comprehension dawned. But before he could reach her, Cecilia toppled backward, striking her head on the hard oak planking with a reverberating crack.

Delacourt had no memory of flying toward her, nor of falling to his knees on the floor. Anger instantly evaporated on a rush of blind terror. "Cecilia—!" he cried. With one arm beneath her narrow shoulders, he was already pulling her to him when Henrietta Healy burst into the room.

Ignoring her, he bent over Cecilia's limp body, cradling her in one arm as his opposite hand lightly patted her cheek. "Cecilia!" he whispered. "Oh, my God! What have I done to you this time?"

Just then, Cecilia's eyes began to flutter. "Ooow," she whispered.

Suddenly, Cecilia's maidservant was on the floor beside him. "Lawks-a-mercy!" said Etta, fingering Cecilia's scalp with rough, capable hands. "Lorst yer balance, mum? No 'arm done, but that'll be one devil of a goose-egg!"

Cecilia's dazed eyes shifted from Etta's face to Delacourt's, then back again. Unsteadily, she raised one hand to the back of her head. "Ooh!" she managed to say. "Delacourt, wh-what happened?"

"Just be still, Cecilia," he whispered, sliding his other arm beneath her knees and lifting her easily from the floor. Black bombazine flowed over his arm like a somber waterfall as Cecilia's warm fragrance drifted up to tease at his nostrils.

Abruptly, he turned to the maidservant. "Fetch some ice and a cloth, if you please," he ordered.

Etta shot him an assessing look, then snapped to attention. "Straightaway, m'lord!" She bobbed a slap-dash curtsy and darted out the door.

Swiftly, he crossed the room to settle Cecilia onto the long, leather sofa beneath the windows. When the back of her head touched the arm, she winced. "Damnation!" She jerked her head up again.

"That's my girl," muttered Delacourt, feeling a weak smile tug at his mouth. At once, he stripped off his angel-hair coat and rolled it into a ball, placing it gingerly behind her shoulders. "There. Better?"

Very carefully, Cecilia leaned back again. "Y-yes," she answered, wincing as she lightly touched her fingertips to her temple. "Thank you. Did I step on a pencil?"

Still kneeling by the sofa, Delacourt began to tug at her skirts. "I fear so," he admitted, giving a neat jerk on her hems so that they covered her ankles. "And I am to blame. It was quite careless of me to pitch that ledger on your desk."

"Oh, I'm just clumsy," she responded, her vision beginning to refocus. It was only then that she realized just how close Lord Delacourt was. He now knelt beside her on the floor, discreetly rearranging her skirts.

It should have made her anxious. Indeed, there had been a time when the words *Delacourt* and *skirts* in the same sentence would have made her squirm with discomfort. But absent his elegant coat, and with his cravat and hair askew, he looked harmless, almost boyish.

Delacourt's face had gone white, and Cecilia had the startling impression that her fall really had frightened him. She loathed him, yes. But she had no wish to alarm him. Abruptly, she extended her hand. "Honestly, I'm not hurt," she said. "If you could just help me sit up, I daresay I'll regain my balance."

Lord Delacourt shot her a reproving glance. "Really, Lady Walrafen, I must insist you lie down."

His tone brooked no opposition, and Cecilia knew she should snap back with some cold retort. But her head hurt, and her heart was no longer steeled for battle.

Suddenly, she felt very fragile. And Delacourt seemed infallibly strong. At that precise moment, however, Cecilia realized she was staring at him.

Abruptly, he tore his gaze from hers and bent his head, staring down at the folds of her skirt. His heavy dark hair fell forward and again, despite her dizziness, Cecilia found herself unexpectedly captivated. It fell thick, straight, and just a little too long, emphasizing the aristocratic bones of his face.

Still kneeling, he absently smoothed the back of his hand across the dark bombazine. She watched the odd motion until his hand fell to his knee. For a long moment, he simply stared at the fabric of her dress. Finally, he spoke, but his words were very quiet. "Did you indeed love him, Cecilia?"

"I beg your pardon?" she asked uncertainly.

Lord Delacourt gave a wintry smile. "Walrafen," he said quietly, returning his gaze to hers. "I thought you'd put off your widow's weeds."

Suddenly, comprehension dawned. "Oh, the dress!" she whispered. "No, no, my lord. I am going to the funeral."

The veiled emotion in Delacourt's eyes shifted to confusion. "The funeral?"

And then Cecilia remembered. "Good heavens! I shall be late!" Awkwardly, she struggled to a sitting position. What was she doing here, gaping at Delacourt like some moon calf?

Delacourt made a disapproving sound in the back of his throat, but he gave her his arm for balance. "Thank you," she said. "Now I must have my carriage at once."

Before Delacourt could refuse her, Cecilia's maid returned bearing a small, damp bundle. "No, no," protested Cecilia, waving Etta away when the maid attempted to place it against the back of her head. "I don't want ice. I want my coach."

Still kneeling beside Cecilia, Delacourt cut a swift glance up at Etta. "What funeral? What does she mean?"

Cecilia answered in Etta's stead. "Good heavens! Did Amherst not tell you of my letter? One of our girls was found dead, horribly murdered."

Delacourt's eyes flared with alarm. "Good God! Not here?"

Cecilia managed to shake her head. "No, in Pearl Street. Two nights past." Quickly, she looked up at Etta. "Has Kitty gone?"

Etta nodded. "Went orf w' Meg McNamara 'alf an hour ago."

Cecilia braced one hand on the sofa and stood. At once, Delacourt slid his arm smoothly beneath hers, and instinctively she leaned on it. "I was told nothing of any murder," he protested anxiously. "And any note to Amherst likely went unread. Lady Kildermore sprained her ankle yesterday, and he's been dogging her like a mother hen."

Suddenly, Cecilia wanted to laugh—from the blow to her head, she did not doubt. "Isn't that a mixed metaphor?" she asked, steadying herself on Delacourt's arm. "Dogs and hens?"

Delacourt scowled. "Do not change the subject. You are unwell. I must insist upon seeing you safely home."

Cecilia caught the arrogance which had returned to his voice, and it sobered her. Really, what was she doing making a jest with Lord Delacourt? The man was nothing more than the fribble she'd called him. "Well, if you wish to see me home, then you'll do it by way of Moorfields," she calmly returned. "For I am most assuredly going to the service, whether you like it or not."

"A funeral is no place for a lady,". he calmly insisted. "And certainly not in that neighborhood."

"The neighborhood is not an issue, and no one will know I've gone."

Delacourt's eyes narrowed. "You cannot be sure of that, Cecilia."

Cecilia laughed out loud. "It is a Catholic mass for an East End prostitute, Delacourt," she cynically retorted. "I rather doubt your *beau monde* dandies will mistake it for a musicale."

And so it was that within the hour, Lord Delacourt found himself in a dank, empty church situated near one of the bleakest squares in London. He looked about the vaulted chamber and wondered what had possessed him to come. Cecilia did indeed seem recovered from the blow to her head. Had assistance been required, her maid could have accompanied her. No doubt she had planned on doing precisely that, had he not insisted upon acting the gentleman.

She was an interesting one, that saucy lady's maid, and Delacourt did not doubt for one moment just where Cecilia had found her, either. A Covent Garden nunnery, or he'd eat his next cheroot with one end still smoldering.

Before leaving the mission on Pennington Street, the girl had awkwardly redressed Lady Walrafen's heavy hair, fluffed it just a bit, then repositioned her hat and veil just a little to the back. Strangely, Delacourt had found himself caught up in—no, *mesmerized* by the process. And for the briefest of moments, he'd wished that the fingers which slid through that mass of flame-gold curls had been his.

The bizarre thought had maddened him, coming as it did on the heels of that extraordinary rush of fear which had nearly choked him when he'd seen her fall. He had been compelled to remind himself of just why he did not like her. Of why he had so assiduously avoided her all these years.

Abruptly, he had jerked to his feet, muttered his excuses, and gone downstairs for a smoke on the pavement while he waited for Cecilia's carriage.

And now, here he stood. In the middle of Saint Mary Moorfields, with Cecilia Lorimer—a woman he deeply despised—at his elbow. Through the high, arched windows, weak shafts of wintry sunlight seeped in, and to his grave discomfort, one of them shone directly on Cecilia's open, angelic face. Discreetly, he looked down to study her.

He had forgotten how short she was. And how delicately lovely. It had been a very long time since he had looked—truly looked—at her face. Certainly, he

had not been looking at her face the first time he'd
seen her. No, Delacourt had been captivated by something just a little bit lower.

Yes, he was sorry it had happened. The guilt he still
suffered far outweighed the pleasure he'd taken in
gazing upon her nakedness. But the pleasure had been
great indeed. Sweet heaven, what a lithe little body
she'd possessed. A body which had only improved
with time, if the lush curves beneath her plain jet-
black dress could be trusted. What he wouldn't give to
get his hands on those fine, full mounds one more . . .

Oh, no. He tried to jerk himself up short. Delacourt
knew all too well that a man did not have to like a
woman to lust after her. And he did not like Cecilia
Lorimer. She was a coldblooded, sharp-tongued
shrew. But sometimes, it was hard to forget how perfect she'd felt in his arms. Yes, it galled him to admit,
even to himself, that in the past six years, there had
been more than a few occasions when he'd honestly
found himself wondering. Wondering if it mightn't
have been worth the torment.

Yet, to his surprise, he had escaped that fate. She
really had not wanted him. The truth of what he'd
done had never leaked out. And two years later,
Cecilia had been able to make a highly respectable
match with nothing worse than "jilt" whispered behind her back.

Delacourt questioned—not for the first time—
what she had seen in old Lord Walrafen, a man more
than twice her age. And now, did the beautiful Cecilia
find her widowhood lonely? Did she seek any masculine comfort at all? What about Giles? She was often
seen in his company, and it was no secret that he'd
once hoped to offer for her. But Giles had missed his
chance. Old Walrafen had stolen a march on his heir.

Perhaps she and Giles were lovers? Still, it was said Cecilia spurned all offers. It was—on a purely physical level, of course—a shame to watch such exquisite femininity go to waste.

Yes, perhaps he ought to insist upon completing this foolish task of Amherst's. In truth, there was no gentlemanly way out of it. Not unless Cecilia cut up enough fuss to convince Cole to release him. And she might. But if he stayed—if he had no choice but to put up with her—perhaps he might at least find some way to amuse himself. She was still skittish as a colt, yes. But the lady was no longer an innocent. Perhaps the right amount of heat might melt that ice water of hers to a hissing, hot steam.

His hand, which rested upon the pew in front of him, clenched visibly at the thought. Still standing rigidly, Delacourt drew in a deep, unsteady breath and stared into the shadows of the chancel. What a challenge she would be. But Delacourt had never failed to seduce any woman. Not once he'd set his mind to it.

Suddenly, he realized the horrible direction his thoughts were taking. And he realized, too, just where he was. Delacourt was by no means as pious as his annoyingly perfect brother-in-law, but even he did not wish to tempt God's thunderbolts by reveling in lascivious thoughts amidst a funeral mass. He paused to send up a little prayer for forgiveness. At that very moment, however, the priest waddled out of the vestry, crossed the chancel, and with a sonorous rumble, cleared his throat. Delacourt sighed with relief.

Following the graveside prayers, Cecilia lingered just long enough to slip the priest a generous donation then, with Lord Delacourt still at her side, she walked out of the graveyard's cold shadows and into the brilliance of day. It seemed somehow inappropriate that the sun shone so brightly on such a dreadful afternoon. She only hoped that poor Mary had found such a light at the end of her journey.

Standing pensively by the wrought-iron gate, she looked down the length of Bunhill Row to see that both Kitty and Meg had vanished. Somehow, Delacourt had already managed to send for her carriage, which had been left behind at Finsbury Square. It now awaited her in the street beyond.

Gently, he urged her along the pavement, and without waiting for her footman, he opened the door himself. The creaking of the door hinges brought her back to reality, and to the truth of just who it was standing at her elbow.

As her skirts brushed past him, Delacourt turned to look at her, his expression inscrutable. "You will return straightaway to Marylebone, will you not, Lady Walrafen?" he asked forcefully, as if he did not mean to accompany her.

Cecilia drew her cloak a little nearer and looked up—quite far up—to stare at him. How had she managed to forget how incredibly tall the viscount was? "No, I fear I cannot," she finally responded. "I must go back down to Pennington Street. I have things yet to do."

Lord Delacourt looked displeased. "You have taken a nasty blow to the head, ma'am, and suffered a most trying afternoon," he firmly asserted. "You would be well advised to rest."

Cecilia mounted the steps into her carriage. "But you have left your equipage at the mission," she returned, settling herself onto the seat. She looked back at him with an exasperated sigh. "Oh, look here,

Delacourt—you may as well get in. I mean to go, whether you like it or not."

With a grim expression, Delacourt hauled himself up. "You seem to possess an extraordinary fondness for that particular expression. Indeed, you *mean to do* a great many things which are ill advised."

Cecilia merely stared into the depths of the carriage. She was acutely aware that her anger had irrationally surged forth again, but she felt powerless to stop it. Really, what was her problem? His manner was no more high-handed than that of any other man of her acquaintance, and yet, she seemed unable to ignore Delacourt as she did them. He seemed too large, too close. In his proximity, her heartbeat skipped and her temperature climbed, and Cecilia found herself wishing to punish *him* for it.

Abruptly, Delacourt rapped the gold knob of his stick impatiently against the roof. "Walk on!" he commanded, and the vehicle lurched into motion.

She snapped her gaze back to his. "I'll thank you not to order my coachman about, if you please."

Delacourt lifted his brows haughtily. "You wished to return to Pennington Street, I believe," he coldly responded. "To do that, someone must give the command."

"Then do it in a more civil tone."

Delacourt ripped off his very elegant hat and tossed it onto the bench. "You really do mean to quarrel, do you not, Cecilia? You really must insist upon it."

Cecilia jerked loose the frog which closed her cloak. "I did not invite you to accompany me here, Delacourt," she said, shoving the cloak off her shoulders with a sharp, impatient motion. "That was your decision."

"And what choice did you leave me, madam? You

were clearly unwell. And I think my reputation has suffered enough at your hands—"

"*Your* reputation?" she interjected.

Coldly, Delacourt cut her off. "And I will not be thought less than a gentleman for permitting an injured, unaccompanied woman to go haring back along a cesspit like Whitechapel."

"My maid would have come, had you not done so!"

"But you failed to mention that, did you not?" His voice was low and rough. "Indeed, Cecilia, I sometimes think you wish to torment me quite deliberately."

Cecilia drew back into the shadows so that he could not see the color which flamed in her cheeks. Good heavens, why must she be cursed with such a complexion? And with such a companion! "I did not give you leave to use my Christian name," she answered in a cold, quiet voice.

Delacourt slid forward on the carriage seat and leaned very intently forward, right into her face. "Oh, but you must have, my dear," he said, his voice lethally soft. "Recollect, if you will, that to all the world, we were once betrothed. A love match, it was said, until you came to your senses and saw me for the blackguard that I am."

Smoothly, Delacourt lifted his long, elegant fingers and brushed them ever so lightly around the turn of her jaw, skimming her flesh like silk.

The caress was brief but not quite gentle. And though he sat cloaked in shadows, Cecilia could see the wicked green light which flared in his eyes. Delacourt's mouth was a hard line, the skin drawn tight across the lean lines of his face.

Cecilia shuddered, a bone-deep tremor of lust, loathing, and confusion. "Just leave me alone, Delacourt," she whispered.

Delacourt saw right through her. "Why should I? Why should I leave you alone, Cecilia, when I could do things to you that no decent man ought? I could make you scream and scratch and claw at me like a madwoman. If I wished to. That's what you think, isn't it?"

"I said *leave me alone.*"

But he would not be silenced so easily. "Remember, Cecilia?" he whispered silkily. "Remember the first time I kissed you? Put my tongue deep into your mouth? I remember. Oh, yes. For I still have the scar down the back of my neck to prove it."

She could almost smell the surge of antagonism, deeper than anything she might have expected from him. And why? In the past six years, Delacourt had never shown her anything but cool disdain.

Alarmed by his proximity, she drew further into her corner. With a look of disgust, he moved his hand again, apparently intending to retrieve his hat. But in the shifting light, she foolishly mistook the motion. "Do not touch me again!" she hissed, recoiling.

The intensity in Delacourt's expression flared, then suddenly burned down to simple disdain. "Not if you were the last woman on earth," he whispered, his eyes narrow. "I'd sooner cut it off and pickle it in a cask of ha'penny gin than offer it to you again."

Suddenly, the carriage lurched hard to the right, making the turn onto Bishopsgate. Unprepared, Cecilia was tossed gracelessly against the wall, almost losing her bonnet. Grabbing at the door with one hand, she threw up the other to grasp her hat, somehow managing to whack the lump on her head.

"Ouch!" she yelped. With the bonnet slid over one eye, she must have looked ridiculous. Delacourt's mouth twitched suspiciously, and pressing one knuckle to his sinful lips, he cut his eyes toward the window.

A sharp retort sprang to her mouth. But just then, Cecilia caught sight of Kitty O'Gavin trudging along the pavement beyond. An ill-fitting gray cloak hung off her narrow shoulders. But beneath it, she wore a decent dress of plain black serge, supplied by the resourceful Mrs. Quince. The hems swept the rough cobblestones as Kitty walked south toward the river, her head low, her posture sagging.

Abruptly, Cecilia stopped her coachman then put down her window. "My dear, are you alone?" she asked. "I thought Miss McNamara was with you."

A guilty look passed over Kitty's face. Her gaze darted across Bishopsgate to the shadowy entrance to Artillery Lane. "Meg was keen to see her ma," she explained, rubbing the back of her hand across her reddened nose. "We're to 'ave a pass 'til dusk, so she thought as how t'would be all right."

Delacourt all but forgotten, Cecilia felt a chill run down her spine. But then again, this neighborhood was familiar ground to girls like Meg and Kitty. Cecilia forced a smile. "Perfectly all right, as long as she is back before dark. But what of you? May we take you up?"

Kitty shook her head. "No, m'lady," she said miserably. "I'd sooner be to meself."

Cecilia nodded, and the coach lurched forward, sending light and shadow flickering across Delacourt's face.

"Ah, alone again," he remarked in a silky voice. "You are stuck with me, my dear."

"Not for long," vowed Cecilia, jerking her gaze from his.

"For three whole months," he whispered, grinning at her. "Three . . . long . . . months."

Darkly, Cecilia turned a challenging gaze upon him. "Then I wish you joy of it, you arrogant devil.

Perhaps we will find it improving upon your character."

And then Delacourt did the strangest thing. He threw back his head and laughed. He laughed with a rich, unrestrained resonance she'd never dreamed he possessed.

And he continued laughing—to himself, like some sort of Bedlamite—all the way down Bishopsgate, all along Houndsditch, and into the environs of the docklands.

That evening, Cecilia ate a solitary meal of cold ham and asparagus in her small breakfast parlor. She could have asked Giles to dine with her. Since his father's death, he often did so. But tonight, she had a great deal weighing on her mind. Still, she felt restless, anxious, and inexplicably lonely.

Why? She was accustomed to being by herself. Even during her marriage, her husband's political obligations had often kept him from home. Cecilia had not objected, for theirs had been no love match. Lord Walrafen had wed her, so far as she could tell, simply to have a young wife to hang upon his arm. And she had married because she had yearned to have a family.

Well. At least one of them had gotten what he wanted out of the marriage. And now, how strange it was to find that tonight, her elegant new house—the very symbol of her independence—had become vast and empty, yet confining in a way which she could scarce explain. After dinner, Cecilia paced from room to room, telling herself that her restlessness was caused by grief for Mary O'Gavin. But that was, she knew, just a small part of it.

Cecilia was naïve but not witless. She was beginning to fear that she could put a name to what she felt for Delacourt. And when wasted on a man like that, such an emotion became distasteful. Good Lord, why him? Why did she blush wildly over a rogue like Delacourt, when her own husband—a good man, a man whom she'd *wanted* to please—had held no fascination for her at all?

During her one and only season, Cecilia had been courted by a bevy of young men whom many would have called handsome, and yet she'd felt nothing for any of them. Nonetheless, she had only to look across a crowded ballroom and catch Delacourt staring at her with that burning green-eyed gaze, and every inch of Cecilia's skin would flush with heat.

At first, he tormented her deliberately. But ever so discreetly. In the midst of a waltz, he would come gliding past with his fluid grace, cut a glance over his partner's shoulder, and give Cecilia his lazy, enigmatic half-smile. It was a look which beckoned, teased, and promised a woman a wealth of wicked pleasure would she but throw caution to the wind.

And under such an onslaught of masculine charm, she *had* felt wicked. Wanton, as if she were someone else—someone wild and undisciplined—a stranger trapped in her own fiery skin, with needs and emotions she dared not understand. When she ignored him, he pressed further. Soon, he was there at every turn, sliding his hand beneath her elbow, whispering in her ear, asking her to dance, his low, sultry voice sounding as if he were proposing something altogether more tempting.

At the time, she had believed he pursued her merely to assuage some affront to his pride. Such presumption had made her angry. And she had relished that anger, fed it like a fire, stoking it with righteous indignation. But why?

Cecilia hung her head. Because she had been still young and so horribly inexperienced. And because anger was much easier to face than the truth. So coldly, perhaps even cruelly, Cecilia had refused his every overture, until at last she had succeeded in driving him away. Only then did the beating of her heart slow. Only then had she felt normal again.

When Lord Walrafen had come along, it had almost been a relief. He seemed neutral, benign, almost dull. *Safe.* A mature, dependable man, unlike her father, her brother, or Delacourt. A man who could guide her through a world which she found intimidating. A man who could give the children she yearned for an honorable name. And so she had accepted him.

But in so doing, had she perhaps robbed Delacourt of a measure of his pride? Perhaps he had not meant to torment her. Perhaps—just perhaps—he'd merely meant to offer up an olive branch? She remembered the rage she had sensed inside him, and the thought did not seem so inconceivable now. Oh, it was true that David had once wronged her. But in her immaturity, had she unknowingly exacted a revenge which exceeded the sin?

How lowering it was to realize he could still inflame her with just a look, just a touch. And worse, that he was well aware of his power. Oh, yes. He knew. And to her shame, he could still make her wonder about that wealth of wicked pleasure he seemed to offer. He could still make her consider throwing caution to the wind. And what, she wondered, would it feel like to . . .

Oh, no. Not even alone, in the privacy of her home, would she entertain such thoughts.

Suddenly, Cecilia found herself standing in the middle of the drawing room and wondering how she'd gotten there. By choice, Cecilia kept few servants, and tonight she'd sent all but the butler up to bed early. And so there was no one to question her aimless wandering as she strolled silently over the carpets, tugging books from shelves, shoving them back again, and then moving on to rearrange her collections of porcelain bric-a-brac, none of which needed rearrangement. Finally, she paused at her writing table to shuffle through the day's post. There was nothing but an outrageous bill from her dressmaker and a note from Harry's wife saying they meant to come to town for the season.

Poor old Harry! *Marry in haste, repent at leisure,* Cecilia thought, tossing the letter onto the desk. The union was a miserable one, but Cecilia could muster little sympathy for her sister-in-law. Julia had been willing enough to push her out of Holly Hill and into a marriage—and any sort of marriage would have done. Julia had been persuaded that, having once jilted the infamous Lord Delacourt, Cecilia could not hope for much. But following Walrafen's unexpected offer, Julia had quickly reconsidered her haste.

Well, let them come if they wished. It mattered little. Almost without realizing that she did so, Cecilia resumed her pacing. And so it was that she came to be standing on the drawing-room threshold when someone seized her door knocker and plied it almost viciously. Noiselessly, Shaw slid from the shadows and crossed the foyer.

Still cloaked in darkness, Cecilia watched as the strange policeman, Mr. de Rohan, swept inside. Withdrawing his hat, he turned and spoke a harsh command to someone yet outside, and a huge, black dog—mostly mastiff, she thought—flopped down beside Cecilia's doorstep, sighing through his heavy jowls.

De Rohan wore essentially the same clothing as before, and Cecilia could see Shaw effortlessly taking his measure. The policeman may have been tall, striking, and confident, but he was obviously not to the manor born. He certainly would not be permitted to breach her ladyship's exalted portals.

Impelled by fretful curiosity, Cecilia stepped forward to intervene. "I will see Mr. de Rohan, Shaw. Thank you."

With a diplomatic bow, her butler smoothly withdrew. Cecilia studied her unexpected guest for a moment. "I cannot imagine, sir," she said quietly, "that you bring me any good news. Will you come into my drawing room?"

"No, thank you." De Rohan looked dreadfully ill at ease. "I regret disturbing your evening, but I called at the mission tonight to further question Meg McNamara and Kitty O'Gavin, but it seems Miss McNamara has gone missing."

"Missing?" echoed Cecilia sharply. "Meg was to visit her mother. Perhaps she has simply been delayed?"

De Rohan shook his head. "Her mother works out of a Whitechapel alehouse, yes. But Meg's not been there in above a month." Sharply, he sighed. "Really, Lady Walrafen, a missing prostitute is hardly a matter for the River Police. Nor is it a matter for you to be troubled with, but Mrs. Quince was beside herself. She hoped you'd know something of where the girl might have gone."

Her concern rapidly escalating, Cecilia studied him. "I fear I know nothing that would be of help, sir, though it's true I did see Meg last. But what is wrong? You seem inordinately worried."

"And you are perceptive," he returned with a dry smile. "When last we spoke with Meg, I felt as if she were hiding something."

"Hiding something?"

"Underneath all that Cockney brass, Meg McNamara was *afraid*. And yet, she would tell us so little." A cool draft passed through the foyer, chilling Cecilia to the bone. De Rohan's eyes were bleak, his expression grim.

"What do you mean to do next, Mr. de Rohan?" she asked softly. "And what am I to do? Tell me, and I shall surely do it."

De Rohan shook his head and turned to place his hand on the doorknob. "Nothing," he said softly. "At this point, there is little anyone can do. But do let me know at once if she returns."

"Yes, of course," Cecilia agreed.

And then, de Rohan opened the door and stepped back into the night. At once, the big black beast on the doorstep uncurled himself and rose.

"What a handsome dog," Cecilia remarked. "Really, you needn't have left him outside."

As if he understood her words, the mastiff thumped his tail. De Rohan lifted one brow in what looked like surprise, then faintly smiled. "You're very kind." And then he snapped his fingers at the mastiff. "Lucifer!" he quietly commanded. "*Vieni qui!*"

4

~

In which Lord Delacourt performs heroically

"*O*ooh!" she breathed. "David—! Harder. Harder! Yes—just like that. Right there. Oh, yessss! Oh, you are sooo good!"

Lord Delacourt let his sister's stockinged foot drop gracelessly onto her chaise longue. "Blister it, Jonnie, you aren't listening to a word I say!"

Jonet lifted her head from a heap of pillows and stared down her swollen belly at her brother. "Oh, but I am!" she wheedled. "Just keep rubbing my feet, David. I hear better that way."

Delacourt leaned back into his chair, the one she'd instructed her footman to position at the foot of her chaise longue. "You have a husband, Jonet," he groused. "Let him rub your feet. After all, he is responsible for your misery, not I."

Jonet made a moue with her lips and flopped back down into the puff of feather pillows.

Delacourt shoved one hand rather ruthlessly through his hair. "Anyway, as I was saying, Jonet, I really cannot think it proper she be exposed to such a place." He leaned intently forward, gesturing plaintively. "Only think of it! A lady of her station, wading daily through the filth and rabble of the docklands! I think Cole must be out of his mind!"

Stubbornly, Jonet lifted up the other foot and thrust it at him. With a long-suffering sigh, Delacourt dragged it across his knee. "Get the swollen ankle, too, if you please," she insisted, goosing him ever so gently with her toes.

Reflexively, Delacourt jerked. "Ow, Jonet! I hate that!"

"Then rub!" she commanded.

"Fine! Let your servants barge in!"

"After bearing five children, I'm quite beyond modesty," Jonet insisted. "Now, let us return to this situation at the mission. Are you not distressed, my dear, that Cole sent you? I should have thought those to be the first words from your lips." She lifted her dark brows and looked at him inquiringly. "You are dreadfully angry, are you not?"

Delacourt blinked for a moment, then his expression shifted. "Yes, of course," he agreed irritably. "I cannot think what possessed him. I mean, I know he's rather eccentric and intellectual . . . but how the devil could he forget what I went through with that red-haired hellion?"

Jonet pulled a mockingly sympathetic face. "Indeed! How *could* Cole be so thoughtless?"

Delacourt jerked his gaze from hers and resumed rubbing, sliding his fingers expertly around the arch of her foot. "And that's hardly the worst of it," he muttered quietly. "You would not believe, Jonnie, the insults that spiteful cat spit at me."

"My poor boy!" Jonet made a little clucking sound. "Shall I insist that Cole release you from this bargain?"

Delacourt's head snapped up. "Absolutely not! It would be ungentlemanly."

"Even if I should ask on your behalf?" she responded, cocking her head to one side to study him.

"Particularly so!" Suddenly, his intelligent green eyes narrowed, and he began to massage her foot more thoughtfully. "Do you know, Jonet, I still believe Cole did this out of spite. I cannot think of anyone less appropriate to such a duty. Though I'll be damned if I'll admit it to Cecilia Markham-Sands. Or Lorimer. Or whatever the hell her name is."

"Oh, it is Lorimer," said Jonet softly. "She married Lord Walrafen, you'll recall." Suddenly, Delacourt rubbed too deeply. "Ouch!" Jonet jerked back her foot.

Inexplicably, her brother blushed. "Sorry!" he exclaimed, sounding like Robin caught in an indiscretion.

Jonet struggled into a seated position, then leaned intently toward her brother. "Look, David, why do you not simply tell me what troubles you? I think it's something more than an empty insult from an old lover—"

"She was never that, Jonet," he interjected. "Indeed, she has made it rather plain that I am far beneath her touch."

"And that does not trouble you?" Jonet asked slyly. When her brother merely glowered at her, she answered her own question. "No, of course not. But something does. Will you not tell me? As you said last week, we have no secrets."

"I'm just worried," he insisted roughly. "My dislike of Lady Walrafen aside, I am now responsible for her welfare. The East End—indeed, all of Middlesex—is perilous. And it might as well be Afghanistan for all I know of it. Already, there has been a murder. A poor girl who came to the mission for shelter was knifed to death in Pearl Street, and for no good reason."

Lightly, Jonet lifted her brows. "You seem to know a vast deal about *that*."

"Well, someone must, if your husband means to leave!" Delacourt's mouth tightened. "After the funeral, I went down to the High Street Public Office to call upon the chief magistrate—a blithering idiot who started whining that he hadn't the staff to investigate a prostitute's death. He seemed to feel that since it was a River Police informant who'd found her, they should deal with it!"

"Indeed?"

"Yes, and to be sure, we'd all be better off if they did," fumed Delacourt. "At least they are said to be competent—and more vicious even than Bow Street. Still, I made it plain that if he wished to keep his situation, he'd best stay on top of it, or I'd set a few rabid hounds from the Home Office on him. Peel would be happy to oblige me, since it is just this sort of confusion and understaffing which he rails against."

"Really, David!" exclaimed Jonet, well aware that her brother's threat was not an idle one. His influence was great, when he troubled himself to use it. "Perhaps my husband has not made such a grave error after all."

"Good heavens, Jonet." Delacourt looked astonished. "I have no notion what you mean."

Jonet merely smiled. "First you tell me how worried you are for Lady Walrafen, a woman who, by your own complaint, you dislike inordinately. And now I find you concerned for a young prostitute whom you do not even know, and lecturing on behalf of the Home Secretary!"

Delacourt gave her a piercing look. "Jonet, what manner of man do you take me for? That conniving husband of yours may have rooked me into this miserable job, but I'll bloody well see it properly done."

Jonet heard an uncharacteristic chill in his tone.

"You think this girl's death could be other than random violence?" she asked.

Delacourt looked uncharacteristically pensive. "I think it highly unlikely." His voice was suddenly quiet. "But I'm sure there are people—very unpleasant people—who do not want the flesh markets interfered with. It is remotely possible someone wishes to cast a pall over Cole's work. Has he considered that, Jonet? Has he?"

"I don't know, my dear," she said soothingly.

"Then someone must." Abruptly, he stopped and ran a hand wearily down his handsome face. "But in truth, I can scarce find my way past Bloomsbury! I begin to see just how little I know of life beyond Westminster."

"You do have a point." Jonet felt more than a little worried. "Listen, when you meet with Cole this afternoon, you must tell him all that you have told me."

"Of course," he agreed, as if sorry to have distressed her.

Absently, Jonet leaned forward and began to neaten the folds of his neck cloth. "And do you know, darling," she said thoughtfully, giving the cambric a perfecting twitch, "I fancy that valet of yours is falling down upon his duty. Indeed, I believe I shall find you a new one. You may send Pringle on a long holiday tomorrow."

"A new valet?" asked Delacourt sourly. "Really, Jonet! What need have I of a new one, when Pringle has been with me for a dozen years?"

"And never had a holiday in the whole of it, I do not doubt." Jonet gave a mocking frown. "How selfish you are! Pringle must go away at once. He must go to Brighton! Or to the Lakes, perhaps?"

"But I cannot do without him!"

Jonet shrugged. "As it happens, Lord Rannoch owes me a small favor. Elliot has gone home to

Scotland—he was a distant relation of Mother's, you know. But regrettably, his valet disdains to travel north of Oxford Street."

Delacourt looked at her darkly. "Yes, yes! Perhaps Pringle does deserve a holiday. But I am not at all sure I want another man—particularly not the sort of fellow who decides where he will and will not go."

"I collect that Elliot's man is a very clever fellow in all sorts of—er, *things*," Jonet vaguely insisted. "I shall have him sent to Curzon Street at once. Just temporarily, of course."

His green eyes flashed. "Let be, madam!"

Jonet drew nearer and brushed one hand down his cheek. "David?"

"What?" he snapped.

"Just trust me, my dear."

But any further protest Lord Delacourt might have made was conveniently forestalled. Agnes, the parlor maid, stuck her head inside the book room to tell Jonet that the trunks had been brought down from the attic and that her dresser awaited packing instructions.

Abruptly, Jonet scooted forward to put on her shoes. "Now, listen to me, David!" she began in a warning tone. "I must look to you to keep an eye on the boys whilst we're away. And pay particular attention to Robin!" She slid on the last shoe and looked up at him gravely. "There's been altogether too much dicing at the Lamb and Flag, and I should prefer his stepfather know nothing of it."

Delacourt stood and offered his hand. "Yes, of course."

Awkwardly, Jonet managed to stand. "And Stuart! Stuart is to be kept away from his cousin Edmund at all cost! That worthless scoundrel had the effrontery to leave a card yesterday!"

"Oh, I'll see to Edmund," Delacourt assured her with utter confidence—and not a little relish.

Jonet leaned heavily on her brother's arm as they walked toward the door. "Oh, and David! You will continue with Stuart's fencing lessons, will you not? Charlie will give you a key to the ballroom."

"Yes, of course," said Delacourt for the third time as he gently propelled her out the door and down the hall.

When they reached the stairs, Jonet lightly kissed him. "Now, you must go to Cole. He has a heap of files and correspondence for you."

Abandoning her brother, Jonet leaned on Agnes's arm and made her way up the steps to her sitting room. As soon as the door closed, she turned urgently toward her maidservant. "Agnes, can you carry a message to Lady Delacourt at once?"

"Over tae Curzon Street?" asked Agnes curiously. "Aye, sure."

Jonet flew to her writing table beneath the window and jerked out a piece of foolscap. *"Success is within our grasp,"* she muttered, reading aloud as she scribbled. *"Send your servants on holiday and come to me in Cambridgeshire as soon as you may . . ."*

Throughout his two-hour briefing with Cole, Delacourt's mind kept returning to his sister's strange remarks. Although Lord Delacourt took orders from virtually no one, he was always reluctant to question his sister's commands. Sometimes, he inwardly considered, it was as if Jonet had the gift. Certainly, many in the Cameron line had possessed it; the English had even burnt a couple.

The viscount, however, could not predict the future. Had he been able to, he might have hastened home. But instead, Delacourt dropped by Brooks's to peruse the *Times* and partake of a late luncheon with friends, whose company he found unaccountably tedious and whose conversation seemed oddly trivial. Nonetheless, after this deliberate delay, he returned to his town house in Curzon Street with the bizarre intention of putting Pringle on the next mail coach to Brighton.

But he had strolled no more than halfway toward the blue drawing room to enjoy tea with his mother when he spied Charlotte wheeling her ladyship down the hall toward the stairs. "Mother?" he called sharply, "Charlotte? Are you not having tea?"

Abruptly, Charlotte stopped and spun her ladyship's chair about. "David, my dear!" they chorused. Just then, a footman descended the steps behind Charlotte, a heavy trunk braced high on one shoulder.

"Mother—?" Delacourt stared at the trunk in amazement. "Is that your luggage coming down?"

"No, no, dear," Lady Delacourt murmured, craning her head and lifting her lorgnette. "I daresay that would be Pringle's."

"Pringle's—?" Delacourt stared at her. "Where the deuce does he mean to go?"

Lady Delacourt looked decidedly uncomfortable. "Why, to Brighton, I believe. Lady Kildermore sent a note . . ."

Delacourt darkened his glower. "Did she indeed?"

His mother looked uncharacteristically penitent. "Why, yes. But if you do not wish him to go—oh, but I forget! The other man has come already."

"Other man—?"

"Oh, yes! A lovely, lovely fellow . . . Campbell? Kendall?" His mother managed to look frail and befuddled. Delacourt wasn't fooled. Despite her physical infirmity, the old lady was as keen as a newly stropped razor.

"In any case," Charlotte interjected airily, "he went straight up."

Delacourt felt a stab of alarm. "Up where? To do what?"

Lady Delacourt lifted her narrow shoulders elegantly. "Why, to your dressing room, my dear. To—to *sort things out*, he said."

Just then, with another parade of footmen and luggage trailing him, Pringle came gamboling down the stairs, looking ten years younger. Circling around Lady Delacourt's wheelchair, he paused to press Delacourt's hand between his own. "Oh, thank you, my lord!" the valet said fervently. "I shall see you on the first of June!"

And then he was gone. The next two footmen, trunks carefully balanced, stopped at the foot of the stairs to look inquiringly at his mother.

With another guilty look, Lady Delacourt waved her hand. "Set it down in the foyer, Hanes. My carriage shan't come 'round for another hour."

Delacourt did not bother discussing the matter further. Clearly, Charlotte and his mother were leaving. Off to their Derbyshire seat, he supposed. But at present, there was a far more urgent issue at hand. Someone—*a stranger*—was poking through his wardrobe! It simply would not do!

Mr. George Jacob Kemble was that most feared of personages, an elegant gentleman's gentleman of the new school, with unerringly conservative taste and the good sense to know that it was his mission on God's earth to provide aid and enlightenment to the ignorant. Unfortunately, in Kemble's considered opinion, the ignorant were all too plentiful.

Had he known what sheer force of will awaited him, Lord Delacourt might not have hastened up the stairs with such determined alacrity. But he did not know, and so he paced quietly through his bedchamber and peered into his dressing room with grave suspicion.

Delacourt could have sworn he made not a sound. And yet, the man inside addressed him without so much as lifting his head from his task—which appeared to be a careful accounting of Delacourt's neck cloths. "You rang—?" he sang out melodiously. Then, the fellow lifted a pair of deep topaz eyes to stare at Delacourt. He was a slight, handsome fellow of an indeterminate age and dressed as flawlessly as any member of Brooks's might ever have hoped to be.

"Who the hell are you?" Delacourt demanded.

"I," he proclaimed, flicking out his hand, "am Kemble."

Delacourt was utterly mystified—and, inexplicably, just a little cowed. "Indeed?" he managed.

The fellow paused only briefly, laid aside Delacourt's cravats, and then began to pick through the wardrobe shelves. "I am to have Thursday evenings and every Sunday off," Kemble crisply stated. "Was that explained?"

"Not precisely, no." Suppressing a smile, Delacourt let a knowing eye drift down the man's length. "An active social life, I take it?"

"Quite." Kemble paused in his rummaging just long enough to finger—and frown at—the fabric of Delacourt's favorite riding coat.

"You've taken a dislike to my coat?" asked Delacourt lightly, stepping a little nearer to the door.

Kemble let the coat slide through his fingers, then moved systematically on to a rack of waistcoats. "I suppose it will do, if paired with a neutral waistcoat," he said almost absently. "Have you a problem with that?"

"No, not I," returned Delacourt smoothly. "But I'm

not perfectly sure why you're rummaging through my dressing room."

Kemble flicked him a disdainful look. "I was sent for, my lord. A message came to Strath—my Lord Rannoch's house—telling me I was required here most urgently."

Delacourt felt his eyes widen. "*Urgently?* Why would Lady Kildermore think I needed help urgently when—"

Kemble's horrified gasp cut him short. "*Oh—my— God—!*" cried the valet, jerking back his hand as if bitten.

"What?" asked Delacourt.

The valet's hand seized upon Delacourt's newest waistcoat and ripped it unceremoniously from the others. "Perhaps, sir, it is because of just this sort of— of *manque de goût!*" he announced, shaking the waistcoat accusingly.

But Delacourt, who'd slept through most of Harrow's French lessons, knew only that he'd been insulted. "What do you mean to imply, sir?" he challenged. "That waistcoat is all the rage!"

"Perhaps. If one is a raging lunatic," mumbled Kemble, dangling the crimson silk between thumb and forefinger as if it might be lice-infested.

"But that color is called 'raven's blood!' " Delacourt grumbled. "And I like it! I shan't give it up."

Kemble shoved the offensive garment deep into the row of waistcoats and turned to face his new employer. "Now, let us understand one another, my lord," he firmly began, giving another haughty hand toss. "I have a reputation to uphold. *I* shall agree to work here. But in return, *you* must agree not to go running about town rigged out like some overdressed Bow Street Runner. I simply cannot abide it!"

"*You* cannot?" Delacourt stepped fully into the

dressing room and set one hand at his hip. "Now, see
here, my fine fellow—"

Kemble shot him a withering glance. "No, you must
see," he waspishly returned. "There comes a time in a
man's life when he must stop blowing with the winds
of every new fashion. An age at which he must recognize that more subdued colors become the—"

"An age? An *age?*" Delacourt had never been so
horribly insulted. "By God, sir, I am not old!"

To his acute discomfort, Kemble leaned a little
closer. Clinically, he touched a cool fingertip to the corner of Delacourt's eye, drew the skin toward the temple, then let it snap back into place. "Crow's feet," he
said smugly. "You're three-and-thirty if you're a day."

Delacourt was aghast; not at the valet's words but
by the utter lack of malice in them. Good God, he was
but thirty-two! For a couple more months, anyway.
Still, he hadn't thought it showed . . .

But the doubts crashed in upon him. He had been
awfully tired of late. His zest for life had lessened, and
he was plagued by a restless ennui. Had a life filled
with decadence stricken a few years off his looks?
Was he—heaven forfend—no longer attractive? Was
he well on his way to becoming nothing more than
another aging roué with a bad sense of fashion? And
then what? Chronic gout? A pink frock coat?

"Tobacco?" interjected Kemble.

Delacourt dropped into the chair at his dressing
table. "No, thanks," he muttered. "But a tot of brandy
might hel—"

Kemble hissed through his teeth. "Do you *smoke,*
my lord?"

"Oh." Abjectly, Delacourt looked up. "I have a
fondness for a good cheroot, yes."

"Then you must stop it at once," proclaimed the

valet with another disdainful toss of his hand. "Your sort of complexion cannot take it. It wrinkles the skin and sallows the tone. But not to worry! I'll whip up some of my champagne-and-cucumber mask. Twice a day for a fortnight, and you'll look a new man!"

"But I don't wish to be a new man," insisted Delacourt, struggling to cast off his doubts.

Kemble merely shrugged his thin shoulders. "Then I must echo your original question, my lord," he returned, tossing out his hand again. "Why am I here?"

In frustration, Delacourt lifted his eyebrows and wondered how much strength it would take to fracture Kemble's wrist. "I'm sure I don't know."

"Well, if it's not a fashion crisis, then it must be something worse! Not that there is anything much worse." Suddenly, the valet narrowed his eyes. "Are you being blackmailed, my lord?"

"Good God, no," returned Delacourt. At least the fellow was entertaining.

Kemble crossed his arms over his chest and tapped his toe on the dressing-room floor. "Your mistress—is she unfaithful? Or perhaps you seek revenge on someone who has wronged you?"

Abruptly, Delacourt stood. "By gad, sir, you are a very strange fellow!"

"Perhaps," he lightly admitted. "But I think that you are in some sort of trouble. Perhaps you do not know as yet just what sort—but I daresay we'll soon find out."

5

Scorched by the Lamp of Enlightenment

$\mathcal{M}$onday morning dawned far too early for the faint
of heart. Nonetheless, as he had promised his
brother-in-law, Delacourt bestirred himself at cock
crow, allowed himself to be dressed as befitted a man
of his declining years, then presented himself in
Pennington Street at the god awful hour of half-past
eight, whereupon he was given over to the work-
roughened hands of one Mrs. Mildred Quince.

This steely-eyed matron looked to be a hard price
to pay for just one night of incompetent card playing. But pay he must, and Delacourt did not mean
to whine. Certainly, one did not whine to Mrs.
Mildred Quince, who was a broad-shouldered, battle-
hardened sort of woman. Indeed, she rather resembled his Uncle Nigel when he wore his favorite gray
serge gown. But that was another story altogether . . .

Still, Mrs. Quince seemed devoted enough, and she
gave him a thorough tour of the establishment, com-
mencing with the cellars and ending with the attics. In
between, Delacourt reluctantly observed, lay the vast,
odiferous kitchens; the huge laundry rooms filled

with steaming wooden tubs and nightmarish man-gling machines; and the long, wood-planked sewing rooms. Moreover, for the more deft-handed residents, there was a room given over to leatherworking.

Not once in the whole of his privileged life had Delacourt paused to consider how his gloves were made or his breeches were sewn. Certainly, he'd never given the first thought to how his drawers got laun-dered, and he'd probably just had his last, but never again would he take his staff for granted. The vis-count left the workrooms with a begrudging appreci-ation for manual labor and a deep sense of gratitude that so little of it was required of him.

Each room was filled with young women, their heads diligently bent to one task or another. They seemed civil enough, but their every sidelong glance made plain to him his status as an outsider—and worse, as a member of the Quality. Delacourt felt a mo-ment of profound sympathy. No doubt they were ac-customed to this, the well-meaning upper crust trotting dutifully in to peer at them, as if they were some sort of social experiment. Which, he supposed, they were.

Surprisingly, it pained him to admit as much, even to himself. But as he probed the depths of this foreign emotion—guilt, sympathy, or some complicated fu-sion of both—he received tidings which were even more distressing. Another young woman had gone missing, Mrs. Quince explained.

This time, it was Margaret McNamara, whom he vaguely recalled from Friday's funeral service. "Aye, well, a hard case, that 'un," the matron added gloomily. "There's some you can help, and some as don't really want it. Not when there's an easier living to be made upon their backsides. And you'll learn that quick enough, m'lord."

It was on the tip of Delacourt's tongue to reply that he intended to learn nothing of the sort, that he was stuck in this hellish rabbit warren filled with steaming and clanking and overheated Christian charity because he'd lost a gentlemen's wager. And because no one else was foolish enough to take on the cursed job, which was beginning to assume the characteristics of a stray dog following a fellow home after a late night.

Damn it all, he had no wish to feel guilt or sympathy or pain for these people he did not know. But Mrs. Quince, he quickly realized, would scarce be served by his bitter tongue, and so he'd clamped down on it. Just then, the bell rang for morning Bible study. The matron trundled off, flapping her wings and gathering her chicks, leaving Delacourt to his own devices.

He made his way to the large room which had been given over to office space and pushed open the door. The files and notes Cole had promised him had already been heaped upon the desk farthest from the door. All was bathed in silence, with the morning sun pressing lamely in through windows which were covered in soot.

The room reeked of boiling cabbage, lye soap, and quiet desperation. Slowly, Delacourt strolled across the floor remembering his last visit to this miserable place. Had it only been three days since he had stared across that desk at the woman who looked like an angel and felt like his nemesis?

And then Delacourt remembered helplessly watching her fall, seeing that head of flame-gold curls pitch inexorably backward, listening to the horrible crack as she struck the floor, and knowing with a certainty that had she been badly injured, he could not have borne it.

Delacourt sank into a chair and let his face fall forward into his hands. Thank God Cecilia Markham-Sands had a skull as hard as her flinty little heart.

Lady Walrafen's crested carriage drew up before the mission promptly at eleven. Her footman put down the steps, and she and Etta went in together, just as usual. But strangely, nothing felt as it usually did. On the journey east, the streets had looked far dirtier. Once inside the storefront, the room seemed narrow and more confining than it had the previous week. And she knew that when she went upstairs, things would be worse.

She had really believed that he would not come. Or that if he came, he would straggle in around teatime, looking jaded and lethargic from a night of debauchery, with that arrogant smirk etched upon his too-handsome face. And yet, the moment she crossed the mission's threshold, she knew instinctively that Delacourt was already in her office.

Well, perhaps it was not, strictly speaking, her office. But she cast her eyes heavenward and knew that he was up there. And Cecilia had every idea that the black-hearted devil would be sitting in her favorite chair with his glossy black top boots propped upon her very own desk.

And so she sailed up the steps and through the door, her arms full of ledgers, her head held high.

But to her surprise, Delacourt sat at the desk nearest the wall, which was by far the smallest of the three. His height and shoulders dwarfed it, and in response to her entry, he did not so much as lift his head.

His arrogance was simply too much to bear with any measure of grace. Cecilia dropped her ledgers with a deliberate thud.

Slowly, Delacourt tore his eyes from the letter he

had been studying, and Cecilia was surprised to see comprehension dawning in his eyes. It would appear he truly had not heard her enter. She had thought—dreaded the fact, really—that he would be watching for her. Waiting to torment her.

"Well!" she announced preemptively. "You are here again, I see."

"Where else might I be?" he asked, calmly unfolding himself from the small chair to stand beside the desk. "For unless my sense of time went astray with my morals, this is Monday morning."

Cecilia jerked out her chair with a harsh scrape. "It is eleven o'clock, my lord," she coldly returned. "Your morning, I regret to inform you, is long gone."

"As I'm well aware, ma'am, having spent the better part of it here, as opposed to lounging in my bathwater in Park Crescent." Delacourt gave her a dry smile. "Now, do you wish to continue this childish spat? Or shall we get on with the business of the day? I believe we have some." He held up the letter and gave it an impatient twitch. The Home Office crest was plainly visible.

Cecilia felt a moment of grave uncertainty. He sounded . . . entirely serious. "Really, Lord Delacourt," she managed. "Surely you do not mean to—to stay on?"

Again, he lifted his piercing green gaze to hers. "Most assuredly, ma'am. If that continues to trouble you so deeply, then perhaps you'd best go?" He said the words softly, almost hopefully, she thought. And yet, his eyes were still dark and mocking.

It really was too much for Cecilia. "But I have always enjoyed my work here," she said quietly. "Why do you now wish to torment me when, in the past, you've always avoided me?"

Delacourt's expression was inscrutable. "Avoided you?"

Cecilia tried to harden her glare to no good effect. "Not two months past, you gave me the cut direct and walked out of Ogden's house party."

"What? I—?" Delacourt's face lit with an amusement she could have sworn was feigned. Slowly, he circled from behind his desk. "Cecilia, my dear, perhaps you flatter yourself. Urgent business recalled me to town. Were *you* at Ogden's?"

As usual, Cecilia's cheeks flooded with heat. "Yes— I was—I mean to say, you *did*. Everyone saw it."

Slowly, he crossed the oak floor toward her, his heavy boots echoing through the cavernous room. "Cecilia, you still blush so easily. And so very prettily."

He seemed very close now. Too close. Too tall. Her heart began to race, and then to pound. "I do not believe you," she managed to say.

Carefully watching Cecilia's every move, Delacourt clasped his hands tightly behind his back. "Then what do you believe, my dear? That I left Ogden's because of you?" He dropped his voice seductively. "Or that you do not blush prettily?"

"You deliberately snubbed me." Cecilia tried to lift her chin. "And it was not the first time."

The softening in her gaze disturbed him. He'd rather have her hissing and clawing. But those big blue eyes—oh! They left him awash in awkward emotions; frustration, anger, confusion. Even, devil take it, a measure of temptation. But he'd be damned if he'd show it. Or surrender his pride to it.

He clasped his hands until his fingers felt numb, but his voice was perfectly smooth. "Do you somehow imagine, Cecilia, that I've been suffering from unrequited love these last six years?" He threw back his head and forced himself to laugh. "Unrequited lust, perhaps. But a man does not trouble himself to run from that piteous emotion. Not when it is so easily slaked elsewhere."

Nervously, Cecilia's eyes darted about the room. One small hand fluttered up, then settled uneasily at her waist, as if it stood ready to push him away. Did it? His gaze chased hers. She wished to avoid his eyes. Perversely, he willed her to look at him.

Suddenly, their gazes locked. He stepped nearer, studying her. And then, hidden deeply in her wide blue eyes, he saw it. Anger, yes. And fury. But there was something else, too.

Desire? Yes, the merest hint. But he could sense its keen edge tormenting her, for Delacourt was a master of seduction.

Briefly, his senses reeled. And on the heels of that came relief—and of the worst sort, too: relief of a fear he'd not known he possessed. What the devil was he thinking? Delacourt shut out the questions and slid his finger beneath her chin, tilting up her face. One flame-gold curl brushed the back of his wrist like a trail of silken fire.

And suddenly, something—another confusing emotion—welled up inside him, threatening to choke the very breath from his chest. But he resisted it with his infallible arsenal. Cool flirtation. Biting sarcasm. "Yes, I desire you, Cecilia," he admitted, forcing a blasé tone. "What man with blood in his veins wouldn't?"

"Do not you dare to make a joke of me, sir!" Cecilia jerked her face from his hand.

"A joke?" Delacourt echoed. "Ah, lovely Cecilia! Can you be so naïve, I wonder?" He paused, lifting his eyebrows in deliberate inquiry. "I can easily prove the truth, since the evidence is rather—er, *hard* to conceal."

Cecilia drew back, her eyes flaring wide. Cruelly—for it could only have been cruelty which drove him—Delacourt followed her, backing her up until she bumped into her desk.

"No!" she growled. "Oh, no! You said—"

He knew he should stop, yet Delacourt leaned into her, crowding her. "I said what, my dear?" he murmured, fascinated by the long dark lashes which fringed her eyes.

Cecilia's delicate brows snapped angrily together. "I believe, my lord, that you vowed you'd sooner cut it off!"

"Oh, but what if I lied, Cecilia?" he whispered, snaring her hand in his and dragging it to his mouth. "I may have." He pressed his lips to her skin. "I often do," he murmured, turning her hand over and lightly touching his tongue to her pulse. "And I do it so well."

He studied her from beneath his lashes. Cecilia's breath had sped up to short, desperate pants. She was afraid. And enthralled. Quite deliberately, he drew a tiny bit of her flesh between his teeth and nibbled ever so gently. He watched, spellbound, as her eyes dropped nearly shut and her delicate nostrils flared wide.

Good God, he wanted her.

And she wanted him.

He was not perfectly sure which truth frightened him more.

Both were best put to an end. Slowly, he opened his mouth, pressing two more fervent kisses to her wrist. "Yes, my dear, if one of us is to leave, I think it must be you. As you see, I can but barely control my animal urges. I could be unhinged by my lust for you at any moment."

As if a magical spell had been broken, Cecilia

snatched her wrist away. "You arrogant devil! Must you flirt with every woman whose path you cross? And why in heaven's name do you flirt with me?"

Innocently, he lifted his gaze to hers. "Because you expect it," he softly returned. "Confess it, Cecilia. You want me to flirt with you. To act the rogue. To justify your poor opinion. After all, a true gentleman would not inspire lust in a virtuous woman's heart, would he?"

For a moment, Cecilia was rendered speechless. "You inspire nothing but loathing," she finally managed.

Suddenly, his sarcasm fled, and an emotion far more dangerous seized him. Delacourt leaned nearer, forcing her to bend back. "Really, Cecilia," he whispered, his breath stirring the soft hair at her temple, "I think you lie almost as well as I do." And then— later, he could never quite understand how it happened—he was kissing her, and not entirely without her consent. But Cecilia was by no means unafraid.

It was a novel experience, to kiss a woman who was completely confused, half aroused, and more than a little apprehensive. Delacourt was not perfectly sure how one managed it, since he'd been half drunk the last time he'd done such a witless thing. And so he gentled his embrace and softened his mouth to hers.

It seemed most effective.

Lazily, he let his lips slide over Cecilia's, nibbling, tasting, and very gently probing, while his fingers twisted indolently around another loose curl at the nape of her neck, until her anger receded, then melted away. At last, she relaxed against him, and ever so delicately, he touched his tongue to hers. Asking her, pleading with her, but without the words he was so loath to speak. As if in answer, Cecilia's hand—which had been pressed against his chest—

curled into his lapel in an instinctive, artless caress.

Delacourt tried to tell himself that he was still in control. That he was merely toying with her. Then she moaned softly into his mouth, and he was lost. He slid deeper—metaphorically, literally—plunging inside, covering her mouth with his own, drawing her scent of soap and plain lavender into his lungs. His fingers fisted painfully into her hair while his opposite hand slid to the delicate curve of her spine, dragging her against him until her full breasts were crushed against his chest. He ceased to think of why he did not like her and thought only of how long he had wanted her. Needed to taste and feel and smell her again. He felt a shudder run through him at the admission of the truth.

Suddenly, Cecilia's breath caught, a desperate, urgent sound. And then she hesitated, as if she meant to draw away. Something inside him wanted to cry out. Delacourt tightened his grip, but he could not salvage the sweetness. It lay just beyond his reach. As it had always been.

At once, he felt the stirring of true panic inside her. And this time, he was both old enough and sober enough to know whom he kissed. In short, he had no excuse at all.

Gently, Delacourt lifted his mouth to look down at her and saw something more than fear, worse than anger. It was rejection. And its taste was old and bitter.

She tore her gaze away and stared past his shoulder. "Just leave me alone, David," she asked quietly. "Just take your hands off me, please."

"My hands are by my sides, Cecilia," he said very quietly, feeling the rush of unwanted emotion recede. "Where, pray tell, are yours?"

Her face a dawning mask of horror, she looked down

at the fingers which were still curled into his lapel.

Delicately, he cleared his throat. "I think—but perhaps I am mistaken—that you will find your other one somewhere beneath my coat. At the small of my back, perhaps."

She jerked her hands away as if he'd just burst into flames.

Delacourt forced a jaded tone. "Ah, the consequence of honesty!" he said, stepping back from her. "I am again forsaken."

Her eyes wild and desperate, Cecilia circled around, placing the desk between them. "Get away from me, Delacourt!" she hissed. "Don't—don't force me to—"

"Oh, no, Cecilia," he softly interjected. "You'll not blame me alone. I am not the sort of man who forces women to do anything."

"No?" she challenged. "The others fall willingly at your feet, then?"

Delacourt obliged himself to smile. "Sometimes."

"I shan't!"

To his surprise, Delacourt heard it then—the tormenting uncertainty in her voice. "Cecilia," he said softly, forcing the sarcasm from his tone, "desire is not the simple matter of *right* or *wrong* you wish to imagine it. Forcing one's attention on another is wrong. *Always* wrong. I think you know the level of force I mean—yes?"

Cecilia seemed to grow angrier still. "Well, just tell me this, Delacourt," she challenged. "What sort of woman would wish to be seduced by a man who has assaulted her?"

Suddenly, he understood the emotion which drove her. It was self-loathing—the worst sort of uncertainty. He knew firsthand its malignance. "My dear," he said softly. "Don't you think it's time you forgave me for making you feel sexual desire? And forgave yourself for wanting someone you don't particularly respect?"

Across the desk, all the color drained from Cecilia's face.

Against his better judgment, Delacourt tried again. "Cecilia, the response—the *lust*—which flares spontaneously between two people—that's just fate. Bad luck. Good luck. Call it what you will—but Cecilia, we have it. Heaven help us. But don't blame me. That's not fair."

She made a little sound then. A laugh? Or a sob? He wasn't sure. "It's like an itch, Cecilia," he quietly continued. "It drives you mad. So you scratch. And maybe that's the end of it."

Or maybe not. The words hung in the air, unspoken.

"You're very good at this, aren't you?" she finally whispered.

"Good at what?"

"Seduction."

Mutely, David just shook his head. Why was he even talking to her? What was the point?

Clearly unconvinced, Cecilia let her open palm slam down upon the desk in exasperation. "Oh, why can you not just *go away?*" she pleaded, her voice fraught with torment. "For if you do not, then I must. I shall *have* to."

Suddenly, Delacourt felt a spurt of bitterness. "Oh, fine, Cecilia, leave!" he said softly. "That will be one more thing for me to feel guilty over."

"You have never suffered a moment's guilt in your life."

It was far from true, but Delacourt would not deign to answer it. "You called me a fribble, Cecilia," he said quietly. "A man cannot be expected to bear such an insult without a fuss."

"You impudent dog! You call sticking your tongue halfway down my throat *a fuss?*"

Delacourt had to admire her audacity. And in truth, he had been insane to kiss her. "Very well, Cecilia," he answered with a sigh. "You win. Stay. I swear, I shan't so much as touch you. Then I shall be your captive audience, and you may exact your revenge by doing what you ought to have done years ago."

"What?" she asked grimly. "Shoot you?"

"No." Delacourt smiled weakly. "Reform me."

Cecilia's mouth fell open, and she stood frozen to the floor. Suddenly, a fist rapped energetically against the door. They spun about to face the entrance.

Mrs. Quince sailed in, a veritable clipper ship of Christian indignation, flying her sails of gray serge. "You'd best come with me, my lady," she began, jabbing a finger at the ceiling. "It's that Nan again. Pulling Molly's hair and cursing like a boatswain. And all of it over the boy what delivered the coal this morning!"

Cecilia never returned from lecturing the errant Nan. Delacourt supposed she managed to while away her afternoon in the workrooms, providing the denizens of the Daughters of Nazareth Society with all manner of moral guidance and lady-of-the-manor munificence. Delacourt tried to convince himself that although he missed her presence in the room, it was the sort of *missing* one felt after having a bad tooth drawn; there was a tender, empty hole, yes, but what one really felt was the absence of acute discomfort.

Yet, even dislike could be edged with some perverse sort of attraction. He'd simply been alleviating his boredom as he always did—by flirting with a beautiful woman. But dash it, Cecilia needed to unbend just a tad. She was a lovely, vivacious creature. A widow! She ought to relax and enjoy the freedoms society granted her.

But she wouldn't be enjoying any more of them with him this afternoon, for she did not mean to return. His unerring masculine instinct told him that much. And so he forced his attention to the stack of notes and correspondence which Cole had left him. The letter from the Home Office was the first. Apparently, his bullying down at the High Street Public Office had been effective. The investigation into Mary O'Gavin's death had been permanently given over to the elite River Police, an unusual but impressive step. He felt marginally comforted.

He ripped through the seal of the second letter, which had clearly been hand-delivered to the mission. To his shock, a bank draft from Edmund Rowland drifted down onto the scarred wooden desk. Delacourt picked it up, looked at the neatly etched zeros, and gave a low whistle. Good God! The jesting at Brooks's had been in earnest. Such a sum must have drained the old boy. How the devil had that flame-haired minx done it?

Cecilia again, damn her! Must the woman spring to mind at every turn? Viciously, Delacourt slashed open the next letter with a violent flick of his penknife.

Blankets. David sighed. A parish in the north wished to donate a dozen. That was very good news, he supposed. After that, there were self-important letters from two of the mission's larger benefactors— probably people like Rowland, who gave money to assuage a guilty conscience.

And unlike Cecilia, Cole, or Lady Kirton, none of them was apt to actually *do* anything, other than throw supercilious advice and easy money at the problem. Indeed, it struck him that if one truly wished to make a difference among the East End's crime and poverty,

then one needed to roll up one's sleeves and wade into
the human morass which constituted its population.

And then, it struck him that he was becoming far
too moralizing for his own good.

Gads! He had a reputation to maintain! What the
devil was happening to him? He'd been here but two
days, and already he was thinking like some overzeal-
ous Whig. Next he'd be espousing labor unions.
Brooks's would be compelled to revoke his member-
ship. As a man of honor, he'd have to insist upon it.

After leaving Mrs. Quince with Nan and Molly,
Cecilia could not summon the courage to return to
the office. Her body still trembling with agitation, she
dragged down the darkened corridor feeling like a
prisoner headed for Tyburn Tree. She went so far as
to lay her hand upon the office doorknob, and then,
at the last possible moment, she turned and fled,
darting back down the passageway into Mrs. Quince's
tiny sitting room instead.

Dear heaven, had she lost her wits entirely? She
crossed the room to the walnut sideboard and, bracing
her hands on either side of it, bent her head and drew a
deep, unsteady breath. She had let Delacourt unnerve
her again, drat him. No, she'd let him do much worse
than that. For all his wealth and influence, he was nothing but a rotter and a libertine. So why did he still have
the power to make her feel . . . make her feel so . . .

Damn him! Cecilia jerked upright and slammed
down her fist. Atop the sideboard, a candle bounced
out of its holder and rolled onto the floor. Ignoring it,
Cecilia turned away and began to pace. Heaven help
her, she was to be trapped at the mission with him
three bloody days a week, and every time she looked
across the room at his hungry green eyes, she would

feel *it*. That twisting, snaking sensation deep in the pit of her belly.

She whirled about and crossed to the window. In the street below, traffic lumbered along as usual. A coal cart. A costermonger. Then an elegant coach and four, doubtless conveying some shipping magnate down to the Lower Pool to watch his ship come in. It seemed a perfectly normal day on Pennington Street.

But it wasn't. Slowly, Cecilia turned, letting her gaze slide from the glass. She had to get out, go home. Have a bath. Have a ride. Hell, have a drink. Anything but this.

Just then, the door swung open, and to Cecilia's surprise, Kitty O'Gavin came in carrying a stack of freshly laundered bed linens. Cecilia moved from the window, and Kitty gave a little scream, her head jerking up like a terrified animal.

Cecilia's personal concerns faded. Hastening forward, she took the sheets and set them down in a chair. "Kitty, did I startle you?" she asked softly. "My apologies."

Pressing her lips tightly together, Kitty shook her head. "No, m'lady. I just . . . I just . . ." She was still trembling.

Cecilia laid a hand lightly on her arm and drew the girl toward Mrs. Quince's sofa. "Come sit down, Kitty. I want to speak with you."

Reluctantly, Kitty eased herself down. "I'm fine, m'lady, truly."

Cecilia managed a smile and settled onto the opposite end. Kitty looked tired; dark circles ringed her eyes, and she looked as though she'd dropped a stone, weight she could ill afford to lose. "How are you bearing up, my dear? You look terribly tired."

Kitty refused to hold her gaze. "I'm well enough, m'lady."

Gently, Cecilia reached out to tuck an errant strand of limp blonde hair behind the girl's ear. "Kitty, you are very young to be alone without your sister. Have you any family? Anywhere to go? I can arrange for passage—to Ireland, even to America—if you need it."

Kitty stared into her lap and shook her head. "No, I've no family as I know of."

"Then have you given any thought to your future? Tell me how I can help. Might I look about for a situation for you? A good laundress can always find employment."

Kitty's head came up in alarm. "No! I mean—I like it here. As long as I can stay, I'd like to. I'll work hard, m'lady, I swear it."

Soothingly, Cecilia stroked a hand down her arm. "Oh, my dear, it isn't a matter of working hard . . ."

Cecilia let her words trail away. She'd been about to say that women who came to the mission must learn a skill and move on with their lives. But Kitty seemed too lost to hear that just now. "Of course, you may stay as long as you wish," she reassured her, resolved to change the subject. "Now, tell me, Kitty, have you thought of anything else we might tell the police? Anything which might help them find the person who did this?"

Abruptly, Kitty shook her head.

Gently, Cecilia prodded. "Can you tell me what persuaded the three of you to come to the mission, Kitty? I mean—three friends, all together. It strikes me as odd."

Kitty finally looked at her. "It was Meg's idea," she softly answered. "Her's 'n Mary's. They come upstairs to our room late one night, woke me up, and said they were leaving. So what choice did I have? Stay there by meself? So I came, too. That's all I know." She ended on a strident note, looking as if she were desperate to escape the room.

Again, Cecilia patted her on the arm. "I understand Kitty. Really. Now, run along back to work if you wish. I shan't trouble you any further."

After Kitty left, Cecilia felt marginally calmer, though a great deal more saddened. Her troubles seemed suddenly insignificant in comparison to those of others. On the mantelpiece, the small brass clock chimed the hour. Three o'clock—? Good heavens, it was time to go home. Resolved not to return to the office, she went straight downstairs.

In the shop, there were no customers. Behind the counter, one of the girls was industriously sweeping the floor. Etta, efficient as always, had already gone to call the carriage. Cecilia turned to lift her cloak from its hook behind the door when, suddenly, the girl with the broom spoke.

"Lady Walrafen?" she asked rather nervously. "Mrs. Quince ain't come down in ever so long, and I'm a bit worried about somethin'."

"Worried?" echoed Cecilia, fastening the frog of her cloak. "What's the matter, Betty? Is the till off again?"

Betty put her broom in the corner with a clatter and stepped tentatively from behind the counter. "No, mum, it ain't that," she answered, running her hands down her apron. "It's just that a strange man come in—maybe two hours past. Arstin' questions, 'e was."

De Rohan? His name leapt to Cecilia's mind, but she thought it unlikely that the police inspector would ask questions without permission. "What sort of man, Betty? Was it a policeman?"

Betty looked distinctly uncomfortable. "No, mum. Leastwise . . . I don't think so. But now that I think on it, he did look a bit like a policeman."

Cecilia pulled up her hood and began to tuck her hair in. "Did he ask for me? Or for Lord Delacourt? What, precisely, did he want?"

"He was arstin' questions about that girl—the one what got stabbed." Nervously, Betty twisted her hands in her apron. "He wanted to know if she was 'ere at the mission. So I told him straight out, just like we're supposed to, that I couldn't answer them sort o' questions."

At once, Cecilia's hand stilled. "And then what?"

Betty shrugged. "I tole 'im if he'd wait, I'd fetch someone. But when next I looked around, 'e was gone."

Cecilia felt a wave of relief. Clearly not the murderer, then, since he had not known what had become of Mary. Nor, thank God, had he asked for Kitty. "Perhaps he was a friend? Or a former—er, client?"

At that, Betty's expression brightened. "Now that I think on it, he did sort o' look the type."

"And just what did he look like?" Cecilia pressed. Unfortunately, Betty was not the brightest candle in the mission's chandelier.

Betty shrugged again. "I was awful nervous, mum," she said apologetically. "Tall, 'e was, and dressed nice. But not too nice, if you know what I mean."

Cecilia really didn't know, but she rather doubted much more would be had from Betty. Just then, she saw her carriage draw up in front of the shop. "Listen to me, Betty," she said carefully. "You did precisely the right thing by not answering his questions. And if you should see that man again, I want you to send for Mrs. Quince at once. Can you do that?"

Dipping her chin shyly, Betty bobbed a quick curtsy. "Yes, mum. I will. I promise."

As Delacourt had suspected, Cecilia never returned to the office. After another two hours of letter writing, he flung his pen down in disgust and headed for home. But once he'd relaxed into the depths of his coach, his hard-won concentration slipped, and his mind returned again to Cecilia. He tried to relax against the plush upholstery, but it was of no use, for beneath the layers of his expensive clothing, Delacourt was still chaffed by her rejection. And wounded by her poor opinion.

A sore tooth! What a fatuous analogy. He was just a bloody damned fool, and inside the shadows of his carriage, it was easier to admit. Oh, perhaps Cecilia desired him, but she still did not respect or like him. And why had he commenced a flirtation with *her*, of all people? Was he simply feeling the press of years? Or was he remembering something that had almost been?

Delacourt shut his eyes and let his head fall back. Good God, how he hated that, hated to admit he even possessed such a memory, hated to think of it.

Barely a hope, less than a dream.

With his eyes squeezed shut, he could see it still. A shaft of brilliant sun. And a gentle face, a lithe, vigorous body, turned toward the light, gilded by it. A gasp. And then soft, tentative lips pressing uncertainly against his. A young girl's innocence. A confirmed rake's nightmare.

And yet, it had not been a nightmare. Not precisely. Not until the end.

Delacourt squeezed shut his eyes, but his mind spun as relentlessly as his carriage wheels, while the trees and buildings along the Strand dappled the interior with dying sunlight. Delacourt sat up, stretching out his hands to study them.

His were the hands of a man who was no longer precisely young, it was true. But he had a dreadful suspicion that his flirting with Cecilia had been driven by something worse than a young blade's inexorable slide toward middle age. Delacourt shifted uncomfortably on the seat. The truth was, Cecilia Markham-Sands was not the accomplished flirt he'd expected a society widow to be. In fact, she'd kissed as if she were dreadfully inexperienced. Which ought to make him feel a deep sense of remorse.

It did not. It pierced him with a dangerous sense of exhilaration.

For two years, she'd been another man's wife. Yet Cecilia still seemed oblivious to her own charms. He'd never known such a woman. And Delacourt had known more women than he cared to count. They were all the same, save for the minor details. He was not a vain man—well, not inordinately so—but he knew how to please a woman with flawless expertise. Delacourt could read their every emotion—feigned passion, sincere timidity, false modesty. But in the end, they all succumbed to his attentions.

Never before had he kissed a woman so set upon resisting him. Or resisting herself. And Cecilia's tempestuous emotions—fear, anger, deep desire—all of them had been frighteningly real. Delacourt would have staked his rather sizable fortune on it. It had been cruel of him to torment her. And while Delacourt could honestly be called a great many things, a few of them not so flattering, he had never been deliberately cruel to a woman.

He did not like her, it was true. He felt a deep sense of anger when he thought of all that had passed between them—of how she had made him *feel*, both before and after he had kissed her that very first time. It really was too awful to consider.

What he needed was to think of something else.

Or, more honestly put, what he needed was sex.

Badly, too, for beneath all the guilt and anger, his body still ached with an old, familiar hunger. The need to thrust and burn and spend himself inside a woman as she sighed with breathless anticipation. To feel her legs band about his waist, urging damp flesh against flesh. To smell his scent mingle with hers and swirl about them in a sweet, sensual heat.

How long had it been? Too long. Far too long for him. And it had grown worse with every passing day. For the last three nights, he'd fairly smoldered with lust, tossing in his bed until well past dawn. Yes, he was a hedonist. Some would say a sybarite. But he neither knew nor cared what others thought. His appetites were well known, but he played fairly, he paid well, and he gave as good as he got. If not better.

Delacourt was always in control, but his sensuality was a strong, undeniable part of himself. The heritage of his iniquitous sire, perhaps?

The thought made him want to put a fist through the glass of his window.

No, by God, he was *not* like that. He might be a licentious rakehell, but he was not a rapist. He would never take an unwilling woman. Not when he *understood* she was unwilling, for God's sake. And at base, Cecilia Markham-Sands was still an unwilling woman. She always had been. And he did not need another misunderstanding on that score.

At Charing Cross, Delacourt picked up his gloves and his stick, then rapped violently on the carriage roof. He was tired of being trapped in a dark, confining coach with his rigid cock and newfound conscience. It was a virulent combination. Moreover, another duty called.

He sent his driver on to Curzon Street, then turned north to make his way up St. Martin's Lane and deep into yet another rabbit warren brimming with trouble, the narrow lanes and alleys which formed the fringe of Covent Garden. It was but a short walk to Rose Street, and the Lamb and Flag, an iniquitous public house often called the Bucket of Blood for its history of hosting rather violent fistfights. Usually, the place teemed with rabble, of both the higher and the lower orders. Tonight, however, Delacourt was driven not by boredom or thirst but by an obligation so annoying that he paused on the threshold to consider it.

But it had to be done, damn Cole and Jonet both. And as he stepped inside, Delacourt knew that his journey had not been in vain. Deep in the rear, Lord Robert Rowland sat with one hip hitched upon a worn trestle table, watching dispassionately as two young swells fervently diced.

Pausing at the bar just long enough to snare a pint of something wet, Delacourt pressed through the smell of sour ale and unwashed bodies, making his way to Robin's elbow. In the dimly lit corner, raw tension hung as thick as the tobacco smoke, and Delacourt's worst suspicions were confirmed when he caught a glimpse of the older man's face. *Damn and blast!* No wonder Jonet worried.

Sprawled opposite Robin was Bentham Rutledge, a rogue so notorious his exploits could almost put Delacourt to the blush. He was surprised to see young Hell-Bent back in town. Two years ago, he'd reportedly fled London after a duel had sent his opponent to what was believed to be his deathbed. It was rumored Rutledge had traveled through the Near East and on to India. But clearly, the devil was back. He sat near Robin's elbow, a raven-haired dolly mop draped over his shoulder and a neat stack of banknotes at his elbow.

Opposite Rutledge, the second player had broken into a sweat. Good God, what a lamb amongst the wolves Robin was! As Delacourt considered how best to intervene, the sweating man shoved what looked like a Sèvres snuffbox into the pile of coins and vowels which lay upon the table. Then, in an unsteady voice, he called the throw.

Delacourt leaned toward his nephew's ear. "A sovereign says he rolls another seven," he offered quietly.

Robin jumped as if he'd been shot. "Good God!" he exclaimed, nearly falling off the table. But, like his mother, the lad quickly recovered. "What, ho!" he said jovially, thrusting out a hand. "It's you, Delacourt!"

The players glanced up, greeting him without enthusiasm.

"Well!" proclaimed Robin. "You've met my pal Weyden, eh? And old Hell-Bent, too, I daresay?"

He had not. Nonetheless, Delacourt stiffly inclined his head. "A pleasure, Mr. Weyden. Mr. Rutledge."

Robin gave him a nervous smile, hung his thumbs in the bearer of his trousers, and rocked back on his heels. "What the devil brings you into Rose Street, m'lord?"

Ignoring the question, Delacourt drew back to stare at the lad's waist. "Really, Robin!" he exclaimed, mimicking one of Kemble's stricken looks. "Not the thumbs! You look like one of Nash's bricklayers. Not to mention that it ruins the drape of one's trousers!"

Robin yanked out the offending digits, jerking to attention. "Oh," he said, his beaming bonhomie fading.

Delacourt inclined his head toward the dice game. "This reminds me! I'd promised to avenge my loss at whist by trouncing you in a hand of piquet, had I not?" He smiled dryly. "Why don't you come up to Curzon Street right now? I'll give you supper, too."

Robin's face fell completely. "Now?"

"Why not?" Delacourt lifted one brow and tilted his head toward the table. "Surely you're not fool enough to play in this pernicious rat hole?"

"No, no!" Eyes wide, Robin shook his head. "No, indeed!"

"Oh, you restoreth my faith," replied Delacourt smoothly, throwing an arm about the boy. "Now, what will you have? Cook set a rack of lamb on to roast this morning. Will that suit, do you think?"

As he propelled Robin out the door and into Rose Street, Delacourt kept chatting companionably, forcing the boy to do likewise, until they entered the shadows of Goodwin's Court. Carefully, he slowed his pace, looking for footpads and pickpockets. Delacourt was desperate to get the boy home, but dusk was upon them, and the high, narrow passageway, which was never inviting, felt particularly menacing.

Perhaps he possessed a bit of his sister's intuition, or perhaps it was just extraordinary hearing, but Delacourt sensed trouble before it exploded. Quickly, he pushed Robin behind him just as a door onto the lane hurled outward, flying back against a brick-fronted row house. In an instant, a beefy hand shoved a sobbing woman through the door, sending her reeling backward in a whirlwind of pink satin and red velvet.

She landed ignominiously upon her backside in the filth of the alley, cracking her skull against the opposite wall. The man followed her out, storming across the cobbles to tower over her. He was a big fellow, run to fat, with expensive but garish clothes.

"I said we'll do with yer as we please, yer stupid cow," he rasped, grabbing her by her red cloak in one fist while drawing back the other. "An' none of yer bloody maundering! Now, go an' see if that slut you work for'll have you back now, yer tight-arsed nun."

Even at a distance, Delacourt could see that the woman's nose had been bloodied and one eye was already swelling shut. "Stay put," he ordered Robin as he strolled toward the brawling pair.

The woman—a girl, really—was now quietly sobbing. "I'll give you back yer money, Grimes," she gasped. "Just le' me go."

The man uttered a vile oath, dragged her from the cobblestones, and gave her a threatening shake. Delacourt literally heard her teeth rattle. Lightly, he reached out and tapped his walking stick on the man's shoulder.

His grip slacking marginally, the fellow turned to face Delacourt with a gape-mouthed stare. "Aye, wot?" he growled, his eyes skimming the viscount's length. His voice rasped coldly, like rusted metal.

"My good fellow!" Delacourt smiled quite deliberately. "I really don't believe the young lady fancies your attentions. Perhaps you'd best unhand her."

"Oh?" asked the fellow querulously. "An 'oo the 'ell 'er you?" But he straightened up and released the woman, who darted down the lane to cower in a doorway.

Delacourt deliberately set his elegant walking stick against the tip of the man's toe and leaned intently forward. "Let's just say I'm an admirer of feminine beauty," he said very softly. "And I do not greatly care for what you've done to hers."

The man shifted his weight uneasily, and again, his eyes drifted down Delacourt. Finally, he took one step backward. "You don't know 'oo yer messin' wif, you bleedin' nob," he growled. "Fink you can just up an' trifle in a man's rightful business pursuits, eh?"

"Actually, I'm rather certain that I can."

"Sod off," returned Grimes, spitting vehemently into the street.

"Thank you, no." Again, Delacourt smiled. His left hand curled ruthlessly into a fist, but for Robin's sake, he shoved it against his side. "Now, let us be reasonable. What does the lady owe you?"

"Two quid," he snarled. "Not that the bow-legged bitch is werf it. Reckon you'd 'af to pay the culls to ride 'er."

Delacourt withdrew his purse and dropped a few coins into the man's callused palm. "That squares it, I believe. Now, I strongly suggest you forget your acquaintance with this girl." Very deliberately, he lifted his gaze to hold the man's. "And you'll take that suggestion, I hope? For I should regret above all things having to trouble you with the magistrates. Or someone rather less benevolent. I daresay you know the sort I mean."

"Fuck you," said Grimes, shoving the coins into his pocket.

"Excellent," purred Delacourt. "We have an understanding."

It was well after dark by the time Lord Robert and his uncle arrived at Delacourt House with their unwilling angel of the night. Delacourt had no notion what had possessed him to take the girl, but he was sensible of the fact that one did not drag a Covent Garden prostitute through the front door of one's home. Not if one lived in Curzon Street.

So he made his way toward his back door, taking Robin and the frightened girl with him. Delacourt was not perfectly sure what he ought to do with her. And the girl apparently did not care, for throughout the walk to Mayfair, she had said not a word nor asked the first question. Even when he dragged her into the alley behind his house, she remained stoically silent. He thought it a rather horrifying testament to the utter despair in which she must have lived.

Grimly, Delacourt poked his head inside the servants' entrance. To his chagrin, however, the back hall was already occupied by his new valet, who had apparently come belowstairs with the express intent of setting the under-staff on its collective ear.

"Starch? *Starch?*" Kemble was screeching at the laundry maid as he brandished a fistful of cravats in her face. "Do you dare to call this *starch*, ma'am? Because I call it plaster of Paris! And I'll not have it on good neck cloths, do you hear?"

"Evening, Kemble," the viscount said softly as he entered the door. "Seton, you may return to the laundry."

"Insolent piece," growled the valet, critically watching the maid's withdrawal. Then he turned to Delacourt with a somewhat smoother expression. At once, however, his eyes swept over the young prostitute's filthy velvet cloak and pink satin dress. Then he saw young Robin lingering in the shadows. Kemble's glower returned. "Really, my lord! I disapprove most vehemently!"

"Of what?" returned Delacourt dryly. "My new *ménage à trois?*"

Kemble eyed him nastily. "The boy is rather too young, do not you think?"

Boldly, Robin stepped from the shadows. "No, I'm not," he protested, misunderstanding Kemble's insinuation. Or at least Delacourt hoped it was a misunderstanding.

"Do hush, Robin," he quietly instructed, turning back to his valet with a smile. "Kemble, this is Lady Kildermore's son, Lord Robert Rowland. I'm to keep an eye on the boy whilst she's in the country."

"And pander for him, too?" asked Kemble darkly. "Her ladyship will be singularly impressed!"

Too tired to argue, Delacourt tossed his hat and stick onto a wooden settle by the door. "And you have the audacity to call my laundry maid an insolent piece," he returned. "I'm sorry to disabuse your perverted sensibilities, Kemble, but Robin and I happened upon this woman in some distress as we were returning from Covent Garden."

His anger obviously melting, Kemble stepped a little nearer, studying the girl. "Indeed?"

With quick, efficient jerks, Delacourt stripped off his gloves, tossing them atop the stick. "Yes, there was a regrettable disagreement with a customer who gave her the razor's edge of his tongue."

"And a bit of his fist, too," added Kemble darkly. He made a little *tsk-tsk* in the back of his throat and gently dragged the girl into the light of a nearby wall sconce. Strangely, she did not resist. "What's your name, love?" cooed the valet, tilting her bruised face to the candlelight.

"Dot," she whispered.

Kemble smiled. "Well, Dot! We'll need a bit of beefsteak for that eye, and some of my chamomile ointment for that split lip." He moved as if to propel her toward the kitchen.

Delacourt heaved a sigh of relief. Clearly, he'd been out of his depth, and just as clearly, Kemble was not. Then, a prick of guilt stabbed him. "See here, Kemble," he said uncertainly, "just what do you think we ought to do with her?"

"Do?" Kemble shrugged his elegant shoulders. "I mean to patch her up a bit. Beyond that, I rather doubt there's much one can do."

At once, Delacourt withdrew his purse. "Look

here, old boy, I know a shelter—Amherst's place on
Pennington Street—could you send the bootboy for a
hackney and take Dot there tonight?"

Finally, a flash of alarm lit the girl's face. Delacourt
stepped nearer and laid his hand lightly upon her
shoulder. "It is a safe place, my dear. A religious mission, not a brothel. Mrs. Quince, the matron, will give
you a bath and a place to sleep, all right? And if you
do not wish to stay, then tomorrow we shall see
what's best done with you."

6

Mrs. Quince administers a Dose of reality

On Wednesday morning, Cecilia dragged her feet all the way to Pennington Street, then avoided the office altogether by bolting straight for the schoolroom. She was barely in time to conduct the eleven o'clock Bible study. Moralizing was a duty for which Cecilia had never felt particularly qualified, and it was worse now that Delacourt had come back into her life to remind her so acutely of her own ignoble inclinations. But it was her turn. She would do it.

As she dashed through the door to take her position at the lectern, fifty pairs of eyes turned away from their bench mates, and all chatter ceased. With practiced good cheer, Cecilia flipped open her Bible to the Book of Daniel, rattled off a hasty prayer, then ripped through the story of Shadrach and the fiery furnace. But the women looked singularly bored and unimpressed. No doubt the horror of Shadrach's stroll through the inferno paled just a bit when one had walked the mean streets of Shadwell.

The lesson concluded, Cecilia thumped shut her book and the babble resumed. With a brisk step, Mrs. Quince hastened forward to herd her lambs into the workrooms. Just then, Cecilia's gaze caught on a slender, dark-haired girl in the back. She sat huddled on a bench, her face mottled with shadowy bruises. She had one arm around Kitty O'Gavin, and they were making no move to file out with the others.

"Mrs. Quince?" Cecilia called, still watching the pair.

The matron hastened to her side. "Aye, my lady?"

"Is there still no news of Meg?"

"None, ma'am. I'm sorry."

Cecilia's spirits sank, though it was the answer she'd expected. Just then, the dark-haired girl smoothed a hand gently over Kitty's temple. "And that dark-haired girl with Kitty—is she new?"

"Yes," answered Mrs. Quince, screwing up her face in thought. "Name's Dot King. That nice Lord Delacourt sent her in night before last night."

"D-Delacourt?" Cecilia stuttered.

"Oh, aye! Took 'er off a customer what was roughing 'er up out Long Acre way, so his man said," the matron reported matter-of-factly. "And a good thing it was, too. Poor mite was tore up something dreadful— and in some places his lordship don't know nothing about, I daresay."

Her words were blunt, and Cecilia understood at once. "You mean she was raped, Mrs. Quince?"

The matron nodded. "Aye, and then some. And by more than one, from what I gather."

Violently, Cecilia slapped her Bible onto the lectern. "Then that man—that *devil*—ought to be arrested," she retorted hotly. "I shall ask Lord Delacourt to see to it at once."

Mrs. Quince tossed her a kindly patronizing look. "Now, that just ain't how it works, my lady, and well you know it. Besides, I know Lord Delacourt's type.

You go squawking to him, and it mighn't be an arrest he sees to."

Cecilia looked at her in surprise. "Why, I cannot think what you mean."

Mrs. Quince narrowed her eyes appraisingly. "It's like this, my lady—all them smooth words and lazy looks o' his are naught but table dressing. Underneath, he's a hard man. And that sort won't bother the constables with a gang of sodomites. Not when there's more efficient means of handling 'em."

Cecilia cut a glance toward the two girls who still had not moved. She had thought herself inured to the horror of such cruelty. But she wasn't. And pray God she never would be, for then she would be fit for nothing save for teas, ridottos, and well-meaning rhetoric.

For a long moment, she merely stared into the depths of the room. "Do you think Lord Delacourt a very bad sort of man, Mrs. Quince?" she finally asked.

The matron smiled and shook her head. "Lud, no! Not a bad man a' tall, just a—"

But in that instant, Kitty staggered to her feet, sending a rack of prayer books into the floor. For a moment, she swayed alarmingly, and Cecilia realized she looked paler and thinner than ever, if such a thing were possible. It seemed that only Dot's arms kept her from collapsing onto the floor.

Desperately, Dot looked up. "She's in a bad way, mum," she whispered, trying to help Kitty up the aisle. Alarmed, Cecilia had already started toward them, but just then, Kitty swayed again, her hand flying to her mouth. Her chin jerked up, her eyes wide with alarm.

With amazing speed, the knowledgeable Mrs. Quince bolted for the coal scuttle, but she was a moment too late. Cecilia reached Kitty just as her breakfast came up on an awful retch. Mrs. Quince hastened forward, and between them, Cecilia and the new girl managed to support Kitty until the worst was past. Then, gingerly, they settled her onto the front bench.

Pulling a handkerchief from her apron, Mrs. Quince knelt down to mop Kitty's brow. "There, there, ducks!" she cooed. "Feel a bit better, do you?"

Solemnly, Kitty nodded. Then, with a horrified expression, she caught sight of Cecilia's soiled skirts. "Oh, m'lady!" she gasped. "Look what I done!"

"Never mind that." Cecilia patted her cold hand. "Let's worry about fetching you a doctor."

"Hmm," said Mrs. Quince knowingly. "A midwife, more like." There was no censure in her voice, only certainty.

Abjectly, Kitty turned her gaze to the matron.

"How far gone, dearie?" asked Mrs. Quince softly.

Dejected, Kitty fell back against the bench, shuddering against Dot's shoulder. "I don't know," she whispered miserably, her hand going to her belly. "Four or five months."

Cecilia gasped in horror. "But Mrs. Quince, that cannot be! Look at her! She's frail as a blade of grass."

With a grunt, the matron rose from her stooped position. "Aye, too thin by half. And fretting herself nigh to death, if I don't miss my guess." She tipped up Kitty's chin on one finger. "Look 'ere dearie—are you bleeding? Best to tell me."

Kitty barely nodded.

Mrs. Quince turned to the new girl and sighed. "Help me get the poor child up to her bed, Dot. I daresay 'er ladyship's right. We'll be needin' that doctor after all."

Lord Delacourt's first order of business Wednesday was to drop by the River Thames Police Station at Wapping New Stairs to inquire into the progress of the murder investigation. Now that he'd kindled a fire under them, he supposed he'd best keep it stoked. Unfortunately, the man he needed to see, Chief Inspector de Rohan, was not in.

Bristling with impatience, Delacourt snatched a pen and paper from the wide-eyed officer who stood at the front desk, and jotted out a list of questions. He had worn no seal and saw no need for secrecy, so he passed the paper back with a snap. "See that de Rohan gets this immediately," he demanded.

The officer blinked, then finally reached across the desk, but the paper trembled slightly as he took it. "R-r-right, m'lord!"

Suddenly, Delacourt looked at the man and wondered which of them was more uncomfortable. In all likelihood, the policeman had never seen a member of the nobility in his office before. And as for him, he'd not spoken a word to a policeman in nearly twenty years—not since a doddering old night beadle had dragged him home to his mother following an adolescent romp through the Haymarket.

But unleashing a week's worth of frustration and worry on someone who'd done nothing to deserve it was unjust, he belatedly realized. So he looked at the officer and tried to smile. "Look, I'm sorry. I've had rather a bad week. A young girl was murdered, and I just . . ." Delacourt let his words trail away. "I just need to hear from Mr. de Rohan rather urgently," he continued more gently. "Would you be so obliging as to tell him that?"

It was amazing what a kind word could do. "Right, m'lord," the officer responded, his voice sympathetic.

Delacourt turned to go, then spun about abruptly. "Oh, one more thing for de Rohan." He took back the letter and scratched out a word in the margin, then turned the paper about so that the officer might look at it. "Would you by chance know this fellow?" he asked, tapping his finger thoughtfully on the name. "His storefront in Goodwin's Court says he is an importer of lace and silk, but I have a strange suspicion he's in a less reputable line."

"Oh? O' what sort?"

Delacourt smiled tightly. "I'm not sure. Perhaps just a little procuring for friends, but he's a nasty piece of work."

The man's brow furrowed. "*Grimes* . . . name's mebbe familiar, but we mostly handle thievery and smuggling out o' this office." Suddenly, the furrow vanished and his face brightened. "But Mr. de Rohan used to work out 'er Bow Street and remembers every scalawag over there, 'e does. What, precisely, would you be wantin' to know?"

"Whether there's any way to ensure that the fellow suffers a miserable life," answered Delacourt with a tight smile. "Preferably one fraught with far too much attention from the constables, the bailiffs, the customs officers, the tax man; in short, anyone with a sharp pencil or a heavy tipstaff."

"Oh, ho!" said the officer cheerfully. "Well, if it's legalized harassment you're wantin,' then de Rohan'd be your man. I'll ask him straightaway."

Delacourt smiled broadly. "I should be obliged."

He leapt into his carriage, which had been left waiting by the door, and traveled the short distance to Pennington Street with a strange sense of exhilaration coursing through his blood.

No, he had not forgotten Mr. Grimes. And the more he thought on Dot King's swollen eye, the more he ached for a little rough justice. Not to mention that if a man was sick enough to hit one woman, he'd likely hit another, and prevention was better than a cure for that sort of sickness.

At the mission door, he jumped down again and hurried through the shop and up the stairs. He had yet another moral obligation to discharge on this particular morning. An apology.

But Cecilia was not there. And when she had not appeared in the office by two, Delacourt began to wonder. He knew better than to assume she'd merely given up the mission's cause and left him to his own devices. She was just too bloody stubborn. Which could mean only one thing.

So the impudent wench meant to avoid him, did she?

Delacourt grinned and felt his blood stir again. Though it made no sense at all, he was perversely determined to run her to ground. And so he went wandering through the grim, gray corridors, finding instead her chatterbox lady's maid, who blurted out the whole dreadful story of Kitty O'Gavin and the doctor who'd been brought over from Southwark.

All exhilaration, all eagerness, and everything but sick fear was forgotten as soon as he saw Cecilia, slumped in a rickety chair by the third-floor dormitory entrance. She sat with infinite weariness, her narrow shoulders rolled forward, her elbows braced on her knees, her forehead in one hand. She looked incredibly fragile. And incredibly beautiful.

Fleetingly, Delacourt feared she might be crying, and froze. He'd seen her on the verge of tears once before, and the long-ago memory tormented him still. What in God's name was she doing here, anyway, in this place of bleak desolation? The very thought of it made him bitterly angry.

Reality was not supposed to be inflicted upon

gently bred women. Who the devil was responsible for her? That witless Harry? Her pompous stepson, Giles? Why, a woman like Cecilia should be safely tucked away in some comfortable country house, playing with her children by the fire, sheltered from the world's iniquity by a devoted husband.

But that was none of his business, was it?

He shook off the bitterness and wrestled his anger into submission. "Cecilia?" he called softly, one foot on the landing, his hand resting lightly on the newel post.

She looked up at him, blinking uncertainly, as if she did not recognize him.

Delacourt climbed the last five stairs, and paced anxiously toward her chair. "Cecilia, I'm so sorry about Miss O'Gavin. Is the doctor still with her?"

Mutely, Cecilia nodded as she raked a tangle of hair off her forehead with a heavy hand. She looked so wretchedly weary—and damnably alone—in the cold, murky light of the unlit corridor. Abruptly, he let go his pride and knelt by her chair.

"And what of you?" Gently, he took her small, bloodless hand and lightly chafed it between his own. "Are *you* all right?"

Cecilia never answered his question. Instead, she leaned back in the chair, making no effort to withdraw her hand from his. "Kitty is going to lose her baby, David," she said very quietly. "And she will lose it because she's a fifteen-year-old child who's been too cold and too malnourished, and left alone in a bad world for too bloody long." Deeply, she sighed, her chest shuddering with the intensity of it.

Just then, the door opened, swinging outward on hinges which squalled in protest. A tall, middle-aged man with a leather medical bag ducked under the low lintel and stepped into the hall. He was followed by

Mrs. Quince, who gingerly carried a basin of pink-stained water which she put down on a small hall table. Delacourt winced at the reality of it.

"Sir James, how is she?" Cecilia rose slowly from her chair. "And the babe? Will it live?"

Grimly, the doctor shook his head. "She's weak, Lady Walrafen," he admitted. "Very weak. I hold little hope for the child."

Cecilia made a strange, choking sound and stepped back a pace. Gently, the matron leaned forward to pat her on the shoulder. "Now, now, my lady! Don't take on so! We've been through this before. Sir James has done what he can. The babe's in God's hands."

"Well, God certainly seems to call a prodigious number of them home." Cecilia's voice was tormented and bitter. "And I, for one, have grown weary of it. These girls want their children just as much as any woman."

For a moment, Mrs. Quince looked as though she might argue, but apparently, she had not the heart. "There, there, Lady Walrafen! I know how you take on when a wee one is lost."

Delacourt could bear Cecilia's pain no longer. "Just what would it take?" he interjected, blundering in without an introduction. "I mean, what would Miss O'Gavin require in order to be well again?"

Apparently, no introduction was needed, for the doctor looked at him in mild disdain. "What does she need, my lord?" he echoed incredulously. "Why, she needs good food, clean water, and air free of soot and smoke. She needs a decent job—one which does not require her to walk the streets whilst selling her soul—and a sane, safe world in which to bear and raise her child. Can we simply stitch those up out of whole cloth, do you think?"

Anger spiked in Delacourt's chest. What had he

done to earn this doctor's contempt? Who the hell did he think he was? In blazing arrogance, Delacourt's gaze swept over the doctor, but he saw only a tired, middle-aged man with a drained expression, loosened shirt hems, and bloodstains splashed across what had once been perfectly starched cuffs.

And then comprehension struck like a flash of lightning. On his next breath, Delacourt wished to the devil he'd never had to see the inside of this wretched place. But he had. And now, no matter how he tried to cling to it, his shield of righteous indignation was dissolving, and uncomfortable reality was seeping in, chilling his soul.

Perhaps like so many of his class, Delacourt wanted to think that the world's social ills could be easily righted—indeed, if one must think of them at all. Such an attitude was no doubt an insult, a cold slap in the face of those who daily swam against a tide of poverty and misery.

Surprisingly, it was Cecilia who leapt to his defense. "I'm sure Delacourt does not mean to trivialize the matter, Sir James," she softly insisted. "It's just that he does not yet understand all our obstacles."

The doctor's visage softened very little, but his next words were more conciliatory. "Yes, yes, to be sure," he muttered. "It has been a difficult afternoon for us all."

Cecilia spoke again. "Sir James, what more can we do for Kitty?"

After rummaging in his leather satchel, the doctor withdrew a stout, brown vial and pressed it into Mrs. Quince's hand. "She's to have this every four hours," he answered. "And other than that, there's little one can do. Keep her warm, feed her well—beef tea, custards, any sort of stewed meat—*if* she will eat, which I question. In addition to being with child, Miss

O'Gavin has suffered tremendous grief and emotional
strain. Her sister's death has affected her deeply, and
she seems disturbed in a way which I am at a loss to
understand."

Mrs. Quince nodded vigorously. "Aye, there's something weighing heavy on that child's mind, but she'll
not say a word. Hard and forbearing, the Irish."

Abruptly, Delacourt spoke again. "Can she be
moved, Doctor? If there were, perhaps, a healthier
place for her to stay?"

"Moved?" Sir James looked taken aback. "Perhaps,
if the bleeding and nausea subside, and she begins to
take a little nourishment. But wherever would the
poor child go?"

The doctor did not wait for the answer which he
clearly believed was not forthcoming. Instead, he
shut his leather valise with a businesslike snap, buck-
led it, and headed for the stairs. "I shall be in the
surgery at Saint Thomas's until five," he said over his
shoulder. "Send for me if she worsens."

At once, Mrs. Quince picked up her basin of water
and followed Sir James down, leaving Delacourt
alone with Cecilia in the corridor. Cecilia sank back
into her chair.

With an odd twinge of sadness, Delacourt realized
that for the first time in the whole of their strange relationship, he and Cecilia had passed more than five
minutes together without quarreling. What a pity it
had taken a tragedy to achieve it.

Lightly, almost instinctively, he reached out and
laid his hand on her shoulder. "Cecilia, my dear, I
have something to say to you, but I think that it must
wait. Will you permit me to call your carriage and
send you home?"

Vaguely, she shook her head. "I don't know."

"You can do no more here today. Your dress has been ruined, and you need to rest."

Cecilia stared past him, into the depths of the passageway. "Perhaps you are right," she answered quietly.

"I'm sure of it."

She stood, and his hand slipped from her shoulder. "Then I shall gather my things," she said, moving toward the stairs with a slow, sad grace. Suddenly, she looked back over her shoulder at him, her expression soft but otherwise inscrutable. "Shall I see you tonight, my lord?"

"Tonight?" he echoed, a foolish sort of hope coursing through him.

"The board meeting," she answered hollowly. "It is my turn to host it."

"Oh, the board meeting," he quietly echoed. Then hope surged again. "I'm to call at your house?"

"Number Three, Park Crescent," she answered. "We meet the third Wednesday of each month. Of course, if you've other plans . . ."

For one infinitesimal moment, Delacourt remembered the voluptuous auburn-haired actress he'd espied at the Theatre Royal last month. Tonight her play was closing, and he had previously thought to offer her a new, more stimulating role by way of consolation. But he stepped a little nearer to Cecilia, and the thought was gone, vanishing on a whiff of her sweet, simple scent.

"No, I've no plans," he insisted a little roughly. "Other than to fulfill my agreement with Amherst."

Much later, in the falling February dusk, Henrietta Healy pulled her thick wool cloak a little closer and stared across the grass of Regent's Park as a slender canal boat slipped quietly past. Devoid of cargo, it skimmed high in the water, floating back down to Limehouse for reloading. On the narrow deck, a boatman stood, legs spread wide, coiling a rope about his arm. Lazily, he turned, winking over his shoulder at Etta.

The wind shifted then, teasing at the scarf about her throat, and sending a visible shiver down her spine. "Etta, you are cold," said Cecilia fretfully as they strolled, their cloak hems catching on the stiff winter grass. "How thoughtless I am. Should we go in? I daresay you'll want to be off to your aunt's soon."

"Brr!" said Etta. "It *is* near darkmans, mum. Don't the cold never get ter you?"

Cecilia laughed, but it was a sound devoid of humor. "I've a bit more flesh on my bones than you, Etta," she answered, pausing abruptly on the towpath. "I wish I could give you two stone of mine."

Etta's laugh was rich and knowing. "Oh, no, mum! Got a proper figure, you have. Round and full and in all the right places. That's just the thing to turn a man's eye."

Cecilia cast an appraising eye down Etta's lanky figure. "I doubt that, Etta. But to be sure, you are too thin . . ."

Suddenly, a vision of Kitty caught in her mind, a frail, bloodless girl, trembling with nausea on her cot. For a moment, the image was so strong, Cecilia found herself unable to speak. How could Kitty have failed to comprehend the significance of carrying a child? Perhaps in her world, it was not something to be treasured but, rather, just another problem in a life filled with hardship. Still, had the mission known, Kitty could have been given extra food, more meat and milk. But would it have made any difference if the girl wouldn't eat?

Etta looked at her strangely. "Aye, you'd be thinking of poor old Kitty again," she said knowingly. "But like me Aunt Mercy says, you can't fix all the world's ills, mum. No, not by a long shot."

Slowly, Cecilia resumed walking, turning away from the towpath to cross the wide expanse of grass which lay between the canal and her front door. "Tell me, Etta, how in God's name does it happen?"

Equivocally, Etta shrugged her narrow shoulders. "Wrong time o' the month, and the poor goose forgot her sponges, most likely."

Cecilia looked at her strangely. "Her what?"

Across the grass, two dapper young gentlemen were approaching, their tall beaver hats nearly touching as they bent low in conversation. Ignoring them, Cecilia turned to Etta. She was stunned to see the maid blushing. "Lor, mum!" Etta finally answered. "You bein' a widow an' all, wouldn't *you* know?"

"Know what?" asked Cecilia.

Etta sighed impatiently. "If a fellow won't use a skin, then you just soak a little bit of sponge in vinegar—or brandy, if you got it—and then you . . . well, you put it *in*. Don't they teach proper ladies that?"

"No. No, they don't," answered Cecilia, mystified. "What do you put them in?"

The approaching men were much closer now, but in her discomfiture, Etta apparently did not see them. "Gawd, m'lady!" she squawked. "Sponges! To keep from 'aving a child!"

On the path ahead, one of the young men burst into a giggle, but struggled valiantly to conceal it behind an elegant kidskin glove. It was Cecilia's turn to blush. "Good heavens, Etta!" she hissed. "I didn't mean how did Kitty get with child! My question was rather more abstract than that!"

"*Abst*-what?"

"Oh, never mind," insisted Cecilia. At least Etta could be relied upon to jolt one out of the doldrums. She watched as, one by one, the windows began to light up in the elegant sweep of terraces which edged the park. And suddenly, she wanted to go home; to shut herself inside her ivory walls and shut out all the world's iniquity.

She quickened her pace, and they strolled home-ward in silence until curiosity bested Cecilia. "Just what did you mean, Etta, about the time of the month?"

This time, Etta looked around before speaking. "You count orf the days, mum, to yer mid-cycle. That's when a gal's most apt to conceive. And *that's* when you *got* to use them sponges," she whispered in-sistently. "Didn't yer ma tell you anything?"

"Mama died when I was born," said Cecilia quietly. "I didn't have a sister, just an aunt who lived far away. I suppose I must seem very stupid."

"Well," said Etta in a warning tone. "You might best be learnin' a thing or two, mum, what w' that company you been keepin'.' No insult, mind."

"You mean to tease me about Lord Delacourt, I see," said Cecilia. "But even I am not that stupid. Besides, he isn't really interested in me, he just wishes to torment me."

"Oh, a man like that 'un will torment you, mum, and no mistake," said Etta softly. "But I'm thinking you don't fully appreciate how. Now, step lively, cause I got to get that mess o' hair put up afore I pike off to me Aunt Mercy's for the night."

Obediently, Cecilia picked up her pace, thinking as she did so that Etta could not be more wrong. Cecilia understood exactly how a man like Delacourt could torment a woman. Indeed, she had to admit that he'd been tormenting her in just that way for years, and he had been doing it quite effortlessly. The memory of his very first kiss haunted her still. She had desired him then as she desired him now.

And yet, Cecilia had resisted him, because that sort of man was easily resisted. One had only to remember the difference between right and wrong. Morality and immorality. But the man she'd seen at the mission this afternoon—oh, that was another thing altogether! Resisting a man with anguish in his voice and tenderness in his touch was far more complicated. Resisting a man who gave a damn about those around him was nearly impossible. And while Delacourt might be a scoundrel, it was becoming apparent that he did, surprisingly, give a damn.

7

~

The midnight Guest

$\mathcal{L}$ord Delacourt was somewhat delayed in his journey to Park Crescent that night, for despite Kemble's best efforts, the viscount had again been plagued by a less than perfect neck cloth. In frustration, he'd finally given up and left wearing an ordinary *en cascade* which, only a fortnight prior, would have been wholly unacceptable.

Tonight it mattered very little. Indeed, a great many of his priorities seemed to have shifted, and in ways he could scarce understand.

As his coachman made his way through the traffic rolling up Regent Street, Delacourt rummaged in his pocket for the letter which a messenger had delivered at dusk. Chief Inspector de Rohan had been both succinct and prompt in his response. But the writing was too small and too precise to be reread by the faint light of his carriage lamp. No matter. He knew what it said.

He looked up to stare through the window at the passing carts and carriages which rumbled over the cobbles and through the busy night. The evening was bitterly cold, the darkness heavy with the promise of rain.

In the pools of streetlight beyond his window glass, Delacourt watched the passersby dart from their storefronts and hasten from coffee houses, and he could not but wonder if they had a mission in life. Where did they go with such smart steps and such a strong sense of purpose? And had he ever gone anywhere at all? Or was he forever *Delacourt*—sophisticated, languorous, and so very nearly useless?

Finally, the coach rocked to a halt, and he bounded up the steps to find Cecilia's small drawing room already crowded. Cecilia's butler, a tall, pale fellow with a rasping throat and watery eyes, escorted him in, and at once, Delacourt's gaze caught upon Lady Kirton, the quiet widow who, like Cecilia, served as patroness to the mission.

Delacourt had met her the previous day, and to his surprise, he had liked her very much, and so he moved in that direction, nodding to the other board members as he went. Surprisingly, he knew them all, though none well. And they were not, he inwardly admitted, the silly social butterflies he'd once thought them. Instead, all were active in either politics, reform, or social welfare, and none was considered the highest of *haute ton*.

Giles was there, of course, his welcome cool at best. Quickly, Lady Kirton introduced her friend Colonel Lauderwood, whom he vaguely knew, but almost at once they were called in to dinner. Delacourt found himself seated between Giles and Lord Ridge, where he was meant to act as a buffer, no doubt. Prior to old Walrafen's death, Giles had sat in the Commons, his leanings notoriously pro-reform, whereas Ridge was an inveterate Tory. Delacourt was mildly surprised to see that Sir James Seese, the physician from the mission, completed the board.

As to Delacourt's reception, he was greeted with everything from overt suspicion on the part of

Colonel Lauderwood to a hearty back-pounding from
Lord Ridge. Nonetheless, he obliged himself to be
cordial to everyone, an easy task when he set his
mind to it. And then, he urged himself *not* to gape at
Cecilia, a mission of monumental proportions.

Her smile almost unnaturally brilliant, Cecilia sat at
the head of the table, turning from one person to another, her dangling diamond earrings winking in the
candlelight. Though she usually dressed with unerring
conservatism, tonight she wore a daring dress of dark
green crepe over ivory satin, the very same he'd seen at
Ogden's house party. The gown had since been altered
and was now less formal. But he would have known it
anywhere, for its plunging décolletage had left him
speechless and feeling absurdly angry. Just as it did now.

Surely she realized how blatantly it exposed the
high ivory swell of her breasts? So why the devil had
she chosen such a thing for tonight's dinner?
Admittedly, it was elegant in its simplicity. And there
was no denying Cecilia's ample cleavage was worthy
of display. And yes, green was the perfect foil for her
pile of rich red-gold hair. But had she meant the dress
to impress someone? And if so, whom?

He looked about the gathering, but almost everyone there was either married or approaching their
dotage. And then his eyes fell on Giles. Damn it. Yes,
he was handsome enough. Very handsome. And a
sober-minded, solid citizen who, if he had any wicked
tendencies, saw fit to keep them circumspectly hidden. And now that he thought on it, Cecilia had
seated Giles at her left. Moreover, the fellow had been
periodically leaning near her, touching her proprieto-
rially on the arm, and speaking just a little too softly.
Delacourt found it oddly disconcerting.

He was almost relieved when, over the fish course,

the dinner conversation promptly turned to business, and he was obliged to participate. Surprisingly, he was better prepared than he had expected, for he was able to answer most of their questions and make a few minor suggestions. The most pressing issue was money, for the January coal bill had been onerous.

Another concern was the death of Mary O'Gavin, and the board murmured approvingly when he explained, in carefully veiled terms, what he had learned about the investigation's progress. At the end, Cecilia was perfectly silent. Sir James looked mildly impressed. But despite being very nearly blind, Colonel Lauderwood somehow kept tossing suspicious glances at Delacourt, just as he had done all evening.

Delacourt chose to ignore him, and soon, he became vaguely aware that the talk had shifted to a lively political debate. But his mind kept returning to the trouble at the mission, specifically the murdered girl and her missing friend. Was it somehow all of a piece? Or was he simply making too much of it? And what should be done with the sister? He felt strangely responsible for the whole tragic situation. And in a way, he was.

While dressing for dinner, he'd spoken to Kemble at length about it. The man raised a wealth of theories and questions, all of which Delacourt meant to discuss with de Rohan. It seemed his valet was a student of human nature—the very darkest sort of human nature.

Mentally, he reviewed the salient points of de Rohan's letter. The inspector had confirmed that Mary had indeed had an illegitimate child, now deceased, father unknown. Kitty O'Gavin insisted that her sister had possessed no jewelry, no finery, and no money, thus making her an unlikely target for robbery. A visit to Mary's former brothel netted nothing further.

At the foundling home, Mary had left at eight that

night, just as she'd done weekly for well over a year. The physician's report said that Mary had neither struggled against her attacker, nor had she been raped, although Delacourt had neatly avoided mentioning that before the ladies.

But Cecilia had been too much exposed to the harshness of life. Eventually, she would ask. Oh, yes. She would. At the thought, Delacourt squeezed shut his eyes. He did not think he could find it within himself to answer. If that poignant vision of Cecilia slumped in her chair this morning had taught him nothing else, it had taught him that it was more likely his own callousness he'd been justifying when he thought of her as a cold, heartless bitch. She wasn't. He almost wished she were. Sometimes, it was safer that way.

He looked up again to see that Cecilia was engaged in a heated conversation with Lord Ridge. He found himself watching the sparks of blue fire in her eyes and listening to the lilt and timbre of her voice without really hearing the words. Then, suddenly, Ridge's retort cut through the fog.

"Oh, no, Lady Walrafen!" he cheerfully boomed. "I am not your enemy! Save your scold for Delacourt here, for he's as High Tory as they come!"

For an instant, Cecilia forgot her impassioned debate with Lord Ridge. David's eyes, which mere moments ago had been closed, now held her gaze with a startling intensity. It was as if he'd been abruptly awakened, only to behold something which he could not fully grasp. His thick, sooty lashes were wide open, his lids no longer heavy with that strange, seductive languor which had always seemed such an essential part of what she believed him.

And then, his confusion cleared, and Cecilia saw something deeper. A quiet, almost sorrowful knowledge. And something else. Frustration? A secret carefully hidden?

She was not sure. But she was distinctly uncomfortable under his scrutiny. Indeed, he may as well have had his mouth on hers again, tilting her world out of focus, as he always did.

Sweet heaven, she did not know herself when he touched her, teased her, and told her things that simply were not true. Still, the desire she felt for him was almost overwhelming. At that moment, to her relief, David's mouth tightened, the thick lashes dropped half shut, and, again, he was Delacourt.

Warmth flushed up her neck. How fanciful she had become! Lord Ridge had issued a challenge which wanted answering, and she was dithering.

Awkwardly, Cecilia set down her fork, and hid her unsteady hand in her lap. "Lord Ridge," she said quietly, forcing her voice to calm. "We have all set aside our differences and come together to make this mission a great success. All I ask is why cannot Parliament do the same? Must we resort to sending ladies into the House of Commons, as well as into our charitable organizations?"

Lady Kirton laughed. "Oh, Cecilia! Your late husband would be aghast to hear you speak so."

Cecilia shook her head. "No, I am still a loyal Tory. I merely seek compromise."

"My dear girl," grumbled Lauderwood, shifting uncomfortably in his chair, "with your views, you are too much like old Giles there—naught but a Peel Tory!"

Opposite the colonel, Lord Ridge shook his fruit knife at her. "And it's not a t'all the same thing, m'dear!"

"Perhaps not," Cecilia lightly confessed. "But I think Peel has done a fine job as Home Secretary, and Giles says it's but a matter of time before he reconvenes a new

Parliamentary Committee to push for police reform. Then your Peel Tories will help ensure we no longer have innocent women butchered in the East End."

"Bah—reform!" chided Lord Ridge. "I've come to hate that word. And Giles needs to watch his loyalties, m'dear!"

Giles cleared his throat, lifting one finger pensively. "I fear our optimism about Mr. Peel's priorities is premature, Cecilia. Irish opposition is brewing again, and the emancipation issue may soon occupy much of his time."

"Yes, and that's another thing we oughtn't waste our time on," groused Lord Ridge as the servants began to clear.

Lauderwood roused again and lifted his wine glass at Ridge. "Here, here," he concurred, draining it.

Inwardly, Cecilia chided herself for seating two such crotchety malcontents near one another. "Perhaps we could use a little Catholic emancipation," she asserted boldly. "For my part, I think the Irish take the leavings of our political system. Fully a quarter of our mission inmates are Irish. Just look at what happened to Mary O'Gavin."

"Really, Cecilia," interjected Lady Kirton gently. "I cannot think her being *Irish* was the problem."

"No," snapped Cecilia, setting down her wine glass with a clatter, "her being *poor* and *Irish* and *raised* in a St. Giles ghetto was the problem."

Abruptly, Delacourt shoved back his chair and jerked a heavy gold watch from his waistcoat. "Good God, look at the time!" he exclaimed, barely glancing at it. "Port, gentlemen?"

After coffee had been taken in the drawing room, Delacourt deliberately lingered in the background as

Cecilia's guests departed. With every hat and stick the butler fetched, Delacourt could see her anxiety ratcheting ever so slightly upward. Almost desperately, she watched each carriage roll up, peering out into the night to study the color of the livery, despite the fact that his coachman had not yet been called. Still, Delacourt hung back, knowing that there were words which must be said between them.

He had expected Giles to linger, but surprisingly, he had murmured something about an engagement at his club and promptly departed. Lady Kirton and the colonel were the last to leave. The obviously ill Shaw looked as if he might collapse under the weight of their wraps.

"Goodbye, my dear," Lady Kirton murmured against Cecilia's cheek. "Do try to stay out of trouble."

Cecilia laughed lightly. "But you have invited me to tea on Friday, Isabel! I can hardly run into trouble in so short a time!"

"Oh!" chirped Lady Kirton as the butler helped the colonel with his greatcoat. "That reminds me—I had a very peculiar caller yesterday. Indeed, it nearly escaped me, but it was so very odd . . ."

Cecilia leaned intently forward. "Who was it?"

"Anne Rowland," said her ladyship, her voice soft with amazement. "Edmund's wife. And since I hardly know her, I was just perishing with curiosity as to why *she* would call on *me.*"

Colonel Lauderwood snorted. "No surprise there! Woman's an inveterate social climber. Thinks she can leave a card at any door she chooses. Surely you were not *in?*"

Lady Kirton tossed him a skeptical look. "Don't be silly, Jack," she fondly chastised. "Social climbers would scarce trouble themselves to call upon me.

Whatever good would it possibly do them? I never go anywhere."

"And did you see her, Isabel?" asked Cecilia curiously.

Lady Kirton nodded, the tiny pink feathers of her toque bobbing merrily. "Indeed, and that is the peculiar part. You see, her husband wishes her to volunteer!"

"Volunteer for what?" asked the colonel roughly.

"Why, for the Daughters of Nazareth Society! Indeed, she was most keenly interested."

Cecilia shrugged her shoulders elegantly. "Then she may certainly do so. Another benefit dinner or musicale would scarce go amiss."

"A dinner!" snorted Lauderwood. "I rather doubt they can afford to feed themselves after that magnanimous donation."

But Lady Kirton was still shaking her head. "Oh, no, Cecilia! That's not at all what she had in mind. She wishes to work *in* the mission. With the women. But I must say, she hardly seemed the type. And when I pressed her, it became rather obvious that her husband was pushing her to play the lady bountiful—" Lady Kirton stopped, looking appalled. "Oh, dear, that sounded unkind, did it not?"

Colonel Lauderwood drew Lady Kirton's carriage cloak snug about her arms. "What it sounded, my dear, was accurate," he said, patting her affectionately on the shoulder. "Now, come along with you. This air is making Shaw's cold worse, and it's starting to spit an icy rain."

"I'm ordering Shaw up to bed at once," Cecilia firmly announced, rising onto her toes to kiss Lauderwood's cheek. "And dear Colonel! You must watch your step on those slippery stairs."

"Watch my step! Watch *my* step?" grumbled the

colonel, turning toward the now open door. "Sound advice, young lady! Heed it yourself, and remember— sometimes blind old men see more than you think!"

At last, the door was shut, and before Cecilia could direct Shaw to order his carriage and fetch his coat, Delacourt interrupted her. "May I speak with you before I go, Cecilia?" he asked quietly. Shaw discreetly withdrew, giving a tiny muffled sneeze as he left.

Cecilia looked resigned. "Yes, of course," she returned, gesturing politely toward the drawing room. Delacourt followed her in. Absent the crush of guests, the room looked intimate and inviting.

For a moment, he let his eyes drift across the walls, which were elegantly hung with slate-blue silk. The thick Aubusson carpet was woven in a similar shade and accented with a warm red-brown. The ceiling was high and beautifully plastered in panels of slate blue, with white Grecian plasterwork sumptuously applied into medallions and garlands.

Three windows draped in dark blue velvet gave onto the crescent, and Delacourt imagined that from the floors above, the view was magnificent. In the hearth, Cecilia's fire was fast dying, but the room was still warmed by the light of a dozen candles. The furniture was plush and comfortable rather than stylish. Two upholstered chairs and a matching settee surrounded the hearth, with a delicate writing desk just behind them. On the whole, it was a room which invited you inside and encouraged you to linger.

But Cecilia was not encouraging anyone to linger. Instead, she stood by the open door and did not ask him to be seated. No doubt she wished him to be brief and then get the hell out of her house.

But the words were slow to come. Absently, Delacourt picked up one of the Chinese porcelains from the carved writing desk. Cecilia seemed to have several such *objets d'art,* but this one was eye-catching, a small ewer, delicately fashioned into the shape of a dancing girl and beautifully enameled in green and red. Nervously, he balanced it in his hand. "How lovely this is," he finally said.

"It is Ming dynasty," she explained, crossing from the door to the edge of the settee. "That one is my favorite, a gift from Giles for my twenty-first birthday."

"You have a great many," he said, glancing absently about the room.

Cecilia tilted her head gently to one side. "I collect Ming ornaments," she answered, stepping a little nearer. "My one extravagance, I fear."

"They are all . . . quite lovely," he said again.

At last, Cecilia looked directly at him, her deep blue gaze strong and steady. Perhaps she was not so nervous after all. Perhaps the grief which they had shared this afternoon had somehow altered things between them.

"Have you some fondness for Oriental porcelain, my lord?" He was surprised to hear a light challenge in her voice.

Delacourt looked up at her and set the ewer down. "Not really," he admitted lamely.

A wry smile played at one corner of her mouth. "No, I thought not," she said, motioning toward the two chairs which flanked her hearth. "Come, you may as well sit down. Then tell me what it is you really want."

Tell her what he really wanted? Not in a million years, thought Delacourt. *Not even if I knew.* But what he said aloud was, "I wish us to declare a truce."

"A truce?" echoed Cecilia, settling herself onto the edge of one of the chairs, her spine perfectly straight.

Delacourt took the seat opposite. "And I wish to

apologize," he said quietly. "My behavior two days ago was unconscionable."

Cecilia's strong, steady gaze had fallen to her lap. Now, she picked nervously at the folds of her skirts. "Then, I wonder . . . I wonder if you would tell me why you did it?"

"I do not know," he answered honestly. "I know only that I want peace between us, Cecilia. At least until these dreadful months are behind us. And then, when I am gone from the mission, you may resume hating me with the full force of your personality if you wish."

Her head jerked up at that. "I do not hate you, Delacourt. Perhaps I once thought I did, when I was very young and foolish, and thought I knew what tragedy was. But you, my lord—" Abruptly, she pursed her lips and gave her head a little shake.

"What, Cecilia?" he demanded. "Speak! Let us get past this—this *thing* which makes us jab and scratch at one another like bad-tempered children! Good God, I cannot bear it."

Cecilia sighed deeply and stared into the fire which was now dying in the grate. At last, she spoke, but without really looking at him. "You are angry, my lord. And I believe you cling to that anger like—like a shroud, drawing it all about yourself, cloaking yourself in it while shutting others out."

Her insolence—no, her *sincerity*—took his breath away. "Perhaps you do not hate me, then, Cecilia," he tightly replied. "But I don't think you like me very much."

Her gaze left the fire, caught his eyes, and nailed him to his chair. "I don't think you like yourself very much, Delacourt," she returned. "People think you proud, arrogant, even vindictive. But I have begun to believe that you are just a very unhappy man. And I wonder why."

Delacourt felt his heartbeat slow, almost stop. He felt as if a door had cracked open before him, revealing a dark, unknowable void beyond. He wished very much to slam it shut again. And yet he did not. "You spoke of tragedy, Cecilia," he answered instead. "Can you tell me what your definition of tragedy is? I should very much like to know."

At once, Cecilia rose and went to a small mahogany table laid with decanters and glasses. She made an elegant little movement with her hand, as if to pull the stopper from one of the bottles, then abruptly drew back and simply stood, looking at it. "I suppose," she said quietly, without facing him, "that to some, tragedy is simply not having one's life turn out as one had hoped. We go through life with . . . with certain expectations. Perhaps we even take them for granted. And yet, when they do not come to pass—"

She paused, obviously measuring her words, and when she spoke again, her voice was very quiet. "I'm sorry, my lord, but I find I have not the heart for a philosophical discussion tonight. May I offer you some small refreshment before you go?"

It was her way of suggesting he leave, a civil, even generous hint given the circumstances. And yet, Delacourt found himself unwilling to take it. "I should welcome a little brandy, if you have it. The night is very raw."

In silence, he watched as Cecilia poured out a measure of what looked like very good cognac, along with a glass of sherry. Then she crossed the room and pressed his drink into his hand. For an instant, his fingers slid over hers. Cecilia's touch was warm, gentle, and oddly comforting. And then, it was gone, and he held nothing but a glass of brandy which he did not really want.

Suddenly, Delacourt realized that he was still staring at her. Good God, she must think him an idiot. Her odd remarks had shaken him more then she could know. He had to grab hold of his wits, recoup his famous composure. He searched his mind for some glib, flattering remark.

"You look very lovely tonight, Cecilia," he managed to say, in his usual indolent tone. "That green silk is most striking . . . but I rather fancy you've altered it in some way since last I saw it."

Cecilia stared down at her skirts, sliding one hand across the emerald silk while holding her wine glass with the other. "Yes, it was a quite new evening gown," she said almost brightly, as if welcoming the return of banal chitchat. "Though I've only worn it once since I put off my black. But then Etta scorched a hole in the shawl, so I just cut off all the trim and made it a dinner dress. I'm shocked that you guessed." Suddenly, her hand froze, and her gaze came up to catch his.

Delacourt swallowed hard.

Cecilia stood before him, staring straight down into his eyes. "You didn't *guess*, did you?" she asked very quietly.

Delacourt looked down into his brandy. A long, heavy silence held sway, pressing the breath from his lungs. "Just tell me why," she said very softly. "Why did you lie about cutting me at Ogden's? I'm not . . . insulted. I simply wish to know."

Delacourt began to stutter some pathetic response, but he was snatched from the jaws of fate by the heavy tread of Cecilia's butler. Shaw paused in the open doorway. "A visitor, my lady," he wheezed. "The chief inspector again."

De Rohan! The very man he'd been searching for. A

moment earlier, Delacourt had been desperate to escape, but now, he wouldn't have quit Cecilia's drawing room had the hounds of hell been nipping at his heels.

Cecilia shot him a look which plainly said she wasn't done with him, but immediately, the inspector was shown in. "Thank you, Shaw," she said coolly. "Now, take yourself to bed. That's an order. It's nearly midnight, and you aren't well."

Shaw left looking grateful. At once, Cecilia turned her attention to her guests, promptly introducing them. Mr. de Rohan's black, hawkish brows went up at Delacourt's name. "My lord," he responded coolly, sketching a surprisingly elegant bow. "I trust my responses to your inquiries this afternoon were satisfactory?"

"There is nothing about this situation which is satisfactory," responded Delacourt tightly, taking in de Rohan's dark frockcoat, plain linen, and polished black boots. "But that's hardly your fault."

The policeman studied David for a moment, his expression mildly resentful. "You had also asked, my lord, that we keep a watchful eye on your acquaintance in Goodwin's Court. I hope you will be satisfied to know that the appropriate people have been assigned."

David inclined his head. "I thank you."

Cecilia looked back and forth between them, her expression curious. "Please, won't you both sit down? Mr. de Rohan, may I offer you a brandy? Or a hot rum?"

"Thank you, no," de Rohan responded, sitting stiffly down upon the brocade settee which faced the hearth. "I can stay but a moment."

Delacourt reseated himself and took up his cognac. "It is rather late, Mr. de Rohan," he said, swirling the dregs absently about in the bottom of his glass. "I hope you do not make a habit of such onerous hours?"

De Rohan's expression further darkened, as if he suspected he were being reproached for the lateness of his call. "Lady Walrafen asked that I report to her as soon as I had news of Margaret McNamara. One can rarely choose the timing of a tragedy."

"Oh!" Cecilia gave a small, strangled cry, her hands tightening spasmodically on the chair arms. "Meg is . . . dead?"

De Rohan turned to face her. "Yes, ma'am. I'd hoped to bring you better news, but it was not to be. I am sorry."

"What happened?" asked Cecilia quietly.

"I had been uneasy since the day she went missing," de Rohan confessed. "And so I had put the word about that all the public offices should keep a sharp eye out. Tonight, a watchman came in to say a young woman had been dragged from the river."

Delacourt could not bear the grief on Cecilia's face. "Could there have been some mistake?" he asked, grasping for straws.

De Rohan's mouth twisted bitterly. "I think not, my lord. I went to the morgue myself."

Cecilia shut her eyes for a moment. "She drowned?"

De Rohan's voice was grim. "No, my lady."

"What, then?" asked Delacourt archly.

De Rohan cut a sidelong glance at Cecilia, as if measuring her fortitude. "Her throat was cut," he answered bluntly, returning his gaze to Delacourt. "And then someone tied her body—quite deliberately—to the bollard atop Pelican Stairs, and left her floating there as if she were nothing more than a bloody rowboat."

"My God," whispered Delacourt. "Who found her?"

"A pot boy down at the Prospect of Whitby," said de Rohan. "Poor lad had gone along the alley beside the pub to pitch a tub of kitchen scraps in the river. He saw the mooring."

"Why would anyone do such a thing?" mused Delacourt. "Wouldn't the murderer realize she would be discovered?"

"Oh, I daresay he was sure of it," said de Rohan softly.

Delacourt felt a moment of revulsion. "You think someone was sending a message?"

"A message?" whispered Cecilia. "To whom?"

"You think it was meant for Kitty O'Gavin, don't you?" interjected Delacourt, looking at de Rohan for confirmation.

De Rohan looked surprised. "Yes." His voice was edged with a grudging respect. "Those women have been hiding something all along. Indeed, it may be the reason they sought shelter at the mission."

"You mean . . . to *hide* from someone?" asked Cecilia. "Poor Kitty!"

De Rohan shrugged noncommittally. "She is very nervous, that one. And Miss McNamara was almost hostile. At first, I thought it was just an inherent disdain for the police. But soon, I suspected it was something more serious."

"And apparently it was something serious enough to have her killed," added Delacourt, who had risen from his chair and begun to pace the room. "What now, Inspector?"

De Rohan, too, stood. "For now, I mean to go home and get some sleep," he said, running a hand wearily through his hair. "And in the morning, I'll go back down to the Prospect, speak to the pot boy and the staff, and look for witnesses along the river."

"I shall come with you," interjected Delacourt, turning to retrace his steps back to the fireplace.

For a moment, de Rohan looked resentful, but almost immediately, he gave a resigned sigh. "It might be of help. The lower classes fear the wrath of the nobility far more than the power of the police. After all, we have so little of it."

Delacourt nodded. Sadly, de Rohan was right. Perhaps Cecilia was right, too, in her complaints about the need for police reform. And perhaps *he* should take his seat in the House often enough to know why the devil nothing had been done. "I shall pick you up in Wapping at nine, if that suits," he said swiftly. "But what will you do if we learn nothing?"

"I mean to return to Pennington Street," answered de Rohan firmly, "and have the truth from Kitty O'Gavin."

"I shall be there, too," Delacourt added, his voice grave. "Perhaps it will help."

"You cannot press her!" said Cecilia, jerking from her chair. "Kitty is too ill."

Lightly, de Rohan lifted his brows. "With all due respect, my lady, if someone does not press her, she may end up worse than ill."

"Yet Cecilia makes a valid point," said Delacourt thoughtfully. "Kitty does need some time to rest. And as Sir James said, she needs cleaner air and better food. But she also needs safety. I'll hire a couple of men to keep watch at the mission, and in a day or so, we will speak with her."

Cecilia began to interject, and Delacourt raised a staying hand. "Cecilia, we have no choice. But as soon as Kitty is well enough to travel, I mean to send her to my seat in Derbyshire. Once her health has been recovered, I'm sure my housekeeper can take her on in some capacity."

Cecilia stared at him as if he'd just turned purple. De Rohan, however, looked more pensive. "Yes," he said slowly. "I think that will answer very well. And if you offer her sanctuary, she may be more inclined to talk."

"Then I mean to go along when you speak to her," interjected Cecilia with a firm shake of her flame-gold curls. "I tell you, I shan't have the two of you berating her. Not when she is with child."

Hands clasped behind his back, de Rohan nodded. "Perhaps a woman will soften things a bit."

Delacourt felt a moment of panic. He did not like the idea of Cecilia becoming further involved in what was fast becoming a treacherous situation. It was inappropriate. Damned dangerous. But it appeared he would have little to say in the matter. Carefully, he cleared his throat. "Could you give us some idea of what we are to do when we see Kitty?"

At that, the chief inspector shook his head. "I wish I knew, my lord," he admitted. "At the very least, we must find out who their regular customers were. And was their brothel just that? Or something more perfidious?"

"Could they have been involved with white slavery?" suggested Delacourt, remembering some of Kemble's grimmer theories. "Or perhaps smuggling or receiving?"

For a moment, de Rohan studied him, as if he were beginning to wonder what to make of him. "No, I think not smugglers," the inspector said quietly. "However, thieving and fencing had crossed my mind, though none of them looked the part. In truth, they looked to be what they claimed—poor prostitutes."

"But murderers do not go about killing prostitutes for no reason," insisted Delacourt in frustration. "Not unless they are madmen. And if they are mad, then they are very dangerous indeed."

"Oh, they *are* very dangerous," agreed de Rohan. "I believe we have established that. Now, we have only to establish who *they* are." Neatly, he turned on one heel to bow to Cecilia. "Lady Walrafen, I regret having disturbed your evening. I must be off. I shall call on you in Pennington Street on Friday, if that suits?"

If Delacourt had harbored any hope that Cecilia would change her mind, it was dashed when she nodded with alacrity. The plan thus agreed upon, she escorted de Rohan from the room, leaving Delacourt to simmer in his disquiet.

In utter silence, Cecilia walked with Maximilian de Rohan down the hall. She collected his coat and hat and drew open the door. On the doorstep, Lucifer rose to his feet, and Cecilia bent down to say a few soft words of greeting. The gruff dog's face seemed to break into a lopsided grin.

De Rohan smiled faintly, snapped the mastiff to attention, then stepped out. But on the second stair, he paused, looking heavenward. Above Regent's Park, what had seemed like an impenetrable cloud cover had suddenly split open to reveal a brilliant sliver of moon which was almost magical in its intensity.

De Rohan stared up into the night sky. *"La luna crescente,"* he whispered as if in awe.

"I beg your pardon?"

De Rohan turned to look up at her, his expression one of mild embarrassment. "A crescent moon," he translated with a shrug. "It puts me in mind of an old saying of my grandmother's, that's all."

Cecilia smiled at him. She was beginning to like him very much. "You are Italian, Mr. de Rohan?"

De Rohan shrugged his broad shoulders again. "Among other things," he answered. "But my grandmother, she is from Milan." He regarded her in silence, as if awaiting some gesture of disdain.

But Cecilia had no intention of giving it. "And what is this saying of your grandmother's?" she asked gently. "I'm inordinately fond of old adages."

He looked over his shoulder, as if to see if she were making a joke of him. Clearly, she was not. "A crescent moon," he answered, stepping briskly down onto the pavement. "If you see one on a cloudy winter's night, it means your most secret wish is about to come true." At the foot of the steps, he stopped and turned back, his face a mask of sudden grief. "But it was not so for Meg McNamara, was it?"

Cecilia shook her head.

De Rohan regarded her in silence for a long moment. "Then let us hope that tonight, *bella signora*, it will be so for you," he answered softly, "and so I wish you *buona notte*." Then, abruptly, he spun about and doffed his hat in a sweeping, elegant gesture. And both he and the moon vanished into the mist.

His embarrassment over the green dress all but forgotten, Delacourt lingered in the drawing room, pondering the harrowing specter de Rohan's visit had raised. Delacourt was by no means a fearful or uncertain man—quite the opposite, in fact—and often to his own detriment. But when he considered the deaths of Mary and Meg, a chill of pure evil ran up his spine. He felt thwarted and responsible. Deeply responsible. With Cole away in the country, it fell to him to see the murderer brought to justice. There was no escaping that simple truth. But it also fell to him to keep Cecilia safe. Good God! Which of the two would be the harder?

De Rohan, drat him, seemed perfectly willing to drag Cecilia into the bloody mess. He, of all people, should comprehend the dangers associated with working in the East End, and particularly under these circumstances. What if the killer had infiltrated the mission itself? What if he—they—*whoever*—began to suspect Cecilia knew more than she did? What if, God forbid, she actually learned something from Kitty which *was* dangerous?

It was well enough for de Rohan; solving crime was his damned job. And well enough for him, too, for Delacourt knew how to protect himself. Moreover, in a few weeks, he'd be merrily on his way, headed back to his aimless life of gaming and clubbing and calling upon his tailor. But Cecilia wasn't going anywhere. She would continue just as she always had, toiling three days a week in the docklands like some put-upon shopgirl.

He drained the rest of the cognac and set down the glass with a careless cracking sound. In the street outside, he could hear the watch calling midnight. Vaguely, he listened to Cecilia and de Rohan murmuring on the steps. But his mind was caught in a nightmarish vision of Cecilia being dragged from her carriage into some dark, narrow street.

To busy himself, he took up the scuttle and poker and began to rebuild the fire, to no avail. His imagination kept spinning, and by the time Cecilia returned to the drawing room, Delacourt had managed to lose his focus, his good intentions, and much of his carefully cultivated patience.

"Cecilia," he began, addressing the fire rather than face her. "I really do not like this idea of your going with that police inspector to interview Kitty. In truth, I think we must reconsider the staffing arrangements at the mission."

At once, the tension inside the room ratcheted upward. Cecilia crossed the rug toward the hearth, her silk skirts rustling impatiently. "Precisely what are you saying, Delacourt?" she asked, her voice tight.

"Simply this," he answered, shoving away the scuttle and rising from the hearth. "The dockyards and their environs are dangerous, and we can no longer assume the mission is safe. Two of the women have been murdered, and there's no reason to think they will stop."

"And what has our staffing to do with that?"

Delacourt could hear the edge in her voice, but the danger was too grave to be ignored. "While I have the utmost admiration for your devotion," he sternly explained, "your going there to work with those unfortunate women is no longer worth the risk to your safety."

Her sharp intake of breath sounded through the room. Delacourt looked up to see that Cecilia's eyes flashed with ice-blue anger. He realized at once that his words had been rather imperious.

"Worth the *risk?*" she echoed before he could temper his remarks. "Tell me, my lord, just how do *you* define a person's worth? Do you believe that because I am wealthy and titled, my worth is somehow different from that of Mary or Kitty?"

"That's not what I said, Cecilia," he growled, turning to give the coals one last angry jab.

"No, it is not what you said," she agreed, her voice tremulous with anger. "But I think it is precisely what you meant. Why do I suspect that you think me of some greater worth than those women?"

Because you are, you little fool! he wanted to shout. *You are very important to me, damn you!*

But Delacourt could not get the words out. The awful truth of what he felt for her kept rising up to choke him. Instead, he could only hesitate, as some agonizing emotion he dared not name twisted in his belly.

So he simply stood there, like the overbearing tyrant everyone thought him, staring down into the blazing fire with the poker clutched in his hand, nails digging into his palm. And all the time, Cecilia was pacing inexorably nearer.

"You cannot go to the mission any longer," he said quietly. "I am the director, and that is my decision."

"Why?" she demanded again. "Or are you simply searching for a reason to be rid of me?"

Be rid of her? Good Lord. Delacourt was beginning to fear he'd never *been* rid of her. Not since the very first moment their lips had touched. He rested his empty hand on the mantel, and leaned into it.

"Answer me, Delacourt!"

An answer. She wanted an answer. By God, he would give her one. "You are the daughter and the widow of a nobleman," he snapped, still addressing the fire. "You are gently bred, Cecilia. I am simply telling you how life *is*, and you are just too bloody stubborn to listen."

"I am *gently bred?*" she echoed incredulously. He

turned to see that Cecilia stood by his elbow now, her arms crossed over her chest.

"That is what I said."

"Well, shall I tell you about those women in the mission, my lord?" Inside the elegant silk gown, she trembled with rage. "Shall I tell you of their *breeding?* Yes, some are of lower birth than others, but trust me—they all began life as innocents."

Delacourt had no wish to hear it. "I am in no mood for your moralizing, Cecilia," he said in a warning whisper.

But Cecilia would not be silenced. "I don't give a damn about your mood," she returned. "Many of those girls began as parlor maids, tweenies, shop-girls—and, yes, even the occasional governess—and most of them were ruined by some man, some-one who no doubt professed himself a *gentle-man—*"

Behind his eyes, a horrible vision flashed, like the explosion of gunpowder. "Be quiet, Cecilia!" he de-manded, gripping the iron poker so hard his fingers went numb. "I won't listen to this! I swear it!"

"Yes, a *gentleman,*" she repeated, her voice rising. "One who thought it his right to simply take what he wanted and damn the consequences. Does that sce-nario sound familiar, my lord? Does it?"

Blood pounded in his temples. Her words hit too close—and in a way she could not possibly under-stand. "Don't do this, Cecilia!" he rasped, scarcely aware that he was brandishing a poker. "For once in your life, just do not push me!"

"No! Tell me, Delacourt—" Cecilia whispered, her eyes now flooding with tears. "Tell me! What stands between a woman's good name and outright ruin if she has no one willing or able to speak for her? Who will keep her safe? And who, God forbid, will help her raise her children—*bastard* children, I might add?"

Delacourt was blinded by anger. Fear and rage pressed in upon him. "Damn you, Cecilia!" he shouted as, seemingly of its own volition, the poker swung high and came crashing down upon her desk. The exquisite Chinese ewer shattered into a thousand ugly pieces.

8

~

In which Lord Delacourt marks the Earth with ruin.

In the aftermath, Cecilia could do nothing but gape at the spray of porcelain which covered her desk, her settee, and even the tips of her slippers. For a timeless moment, she stared at what was left of Giles's extravagant gift.

Suddenly, David tossed the poker onto the marble hearth with a clatter, shattering the awful silence. He came toward her, jerking her hard into his arms and against his chest, crushing her. "Damn you, Cecilia."

His was no gentle lover's kiss. David took her without hesitation, forcing his tongue into her mouth and sliding one hand into her hair, fisting his fingers into it until her scalp burned. And still he kissed her, desperately, recklessly, without finesse or tenderness. He raked her mouth with his, abrading her face with the shadow of his beard.

Cecilia let herself rise on the tide of emotion, tasting the rage which coursed through him. And yet, she knew that it was not her whom he raged against. She had tormented him quite intentionally. But this time, she'd unleashed something she did not understand. Still, the molten need welled up against her will, and with it came that old, familiar ache. It drew at her, evocative and tempting, pulling at her breasts and her belly, down into her empty womb, and leaving her trembling with hunger. Just as she'd always felt when David touched her.

But this time, it was different. This time, he wanted her with something more than lust. She could feel his need and his pain. When she came fully, willingly, against him, crushing her breasts against his chest, David moaned, and slid one hand down her spine, dragging her hips hard against his own. In an instant, she ceased to worry that what she felt for him was wrong.

She gave no thought to the past. All the stubborn never-evers and a hundred bitter insults simply melted from her memory. And Cecilia was left drowning in David, knowing only that he hurt. And that she wanted to soothe him. Just plain *wanted* him. And had since that frightening afternoon when he'd urged her back into the hay, thrusting his swollen manhood against her.

Oh, God, she'd been so tempted. It had been madness. *Was* madness. And yet, for the briefest of moments, she now wished that no one had stopped them. She wished she had simply opened herself to him then, surrendered to her own wicked urges, and saved herself six years of torment.

Then he'd been half in his cups. But now, he was not. Clearly, he still wanted her. And it was not too late to allay her own burning desire. So Cecilia kissed him back. She kissed him as he kissed her, urgently, greedily, with her mouth and her tongue, sliding inside his warmth, tasting and touching and learning.

"Oh, Cecilia," he murmured, burying his face in

her hair, sliding his open palms up her shoulder blades. "Why must you possess me so?"

The heat of his anger had died, but the hot scent of him lingered, waiting to be drawn into her lungs. Her mouth open against his throat, Cecilia slid her lips along the edge of his high, starched collar, savoring his exotic sandalwood cologne and his own ethereal male scent. Sweet heaven, she'd never known a man could smell so enticing.

Cecilia let her hands drift over him in wonderment. David was tall, much taller than she, and slender, like a cat, narrow-hipped and broad-shouldered. A tailor's dream. A woman's fantasy. God knew he'd haunted her sleep often enough.

Cecilia let her hands slide beneath his waistcoat and up his back, feeling him shiver under her touch. Raw, sensual energy coursed through him. Into *her*. As if to push her past all reason, David's hand slipped between them and over her breast. Then he paused, gently lifting his face from hers.

"Yes," she whispered, refusing to hold his gaze.

It was enough. With one hand, David jerked the green silk dress off her left shoulder, baring one breast. Cecilia had always thought them rather too ample. But David, apparently, did not. "Oh, God," he whispered reverently. "So perfect." He cupped her breast in his hand, then lightly brushed his thumb over her nipple, watching as it hardened to his touch.

And then, to her shock, he bent his head and took her in his mouth, suckling gently, almost reverently. It was the end of Cecilia's restraint. To hell with *shouldn't*. She wanted him. Wanted to claw off her clothes. Strip off the skin which had bound her for so long to something she wasn't. The right and the wrong could wait. Under the onslaught of David's fingers, her hair was tumbling down. She shrugged the other shoulder out of her dress, fighting the urge to rip the silk from her flesh.

But David had other thoughts. Abruptly, he tore his mouth from her breast and drew her back to him. "Enough, Cecilia," he rasped against her cheek. "Good God, that's enough. We—I—must stop. This is insanity."

Cecilia forced herself to look up at him. The sheer beauty of him nearly wrenched her heart from her chest. "Do you not want me?" she whispered.

In her arms, he trembled, his eyes falling shut. Without looking, he lifted his hand and ran the back of it along the softness of her cheek. "*Wanting* doesn't make this right," he answered softly. Nonetheless, his hand fell away, and slowly, oh so slowly, he dropped his head to hers.

If his first kiss had been like fire, this one was like molten lava. It poured over her, weighing down her muscles, dragging her against him. His mouth molded to hers as his tongue slid sinuously inside, coaxing and probing the depths of her desire. The desperate need to possess him, to take him inside and make him a part of her, was undeniable. Cecilia was only dimly aware that she had begun to drag his shirt hems from his trousers. That she was sliding her hands up the taut smoothness of his bare back.

And then, his deft fingers were unfastening the buttons down the back of her dress.

"Stays," she managed to murmur against the hot flesh of his throat.

"Wild horses couldn't drag me away, sweet," he answered, shoving the green silk down her arms.

"No," she whimpered. "My *stays!*"

But it seemed not to matter. Together, they had collapsed onto the floor. David dragged his body over hers, pressing her down into the softness of the carpet.

"Oh, God, Cecilia," he whispered, barely lifting his mouth from hers. "I have to be inside you. *Now!*"

"Yes," she answered as he fisted his hand in her skirts. David raised himself up on one arm, tugging at the fabric with rough, frantic motions. Suddenly, cool air breezed up her calves, then her thighs, even as the heat rushed up her face.

David sat back on his haunches, pitching her shoes, stockings, and drawers aimlessly aside, as if he were afraid sanity might return. His motions were desperate, clumsy, too unlike the man she thought she knew. And dimly, Cecilia realized she looked more like a common trollop than a lady, with her bodice down about her waist and her skirts shoved up to her thighs.

But need had overcome both modesty and pride. Eagerly, she reached for him. David ripped off his cravat and coat, and the sound of rending fabric split the air. Carelessly, he hurled them into the darkness. Cecilia's hands slid beneath his shirt and up his belly which was lean and hard. In response, he sucked in his breath and began to fumble frantically at the close of his trousers.

And suddenly, Cecilia froze. David's manhood rose up from the crush of linen and wool, larger and more powerful than she was sure it ought to be. She felt panic light her face. But it was too late to quibble. He braced himself over her with one arm, parted her flesh, and probed rather awkwardly at her entrance.

And then, David went perfectly still. He made no move to enter her as she had expected. Instead, he simply stared down, his eyes drifting over her naked breasts, her shoulders, and finally coming to rest on her face.

"David?" she whispered.

In response, he simply lowered his body onto hers,

his mouth open, his breath rasping against her ear. His hand came away from their joining, drifted up her body, and slid aimlessly through her hair, now loose at her temples.

"What is it?" she asked softly.

David heard the agonizing catch in her voice and felt deeply ashamed. And deeply confused.

God help him, but he just . . . well, he couldn't *do* it.

Never in his life had his body failed him. More often than not, it had been a persistent nuisance. But it wasn't persistent now. For when he had torn open his trousers and stared down at her half-naked body— the very one which had haunted his fantasies night after night—the doubt and confusion etched upon Cecilia's face had brought everything vividly back.

Good God, it might as well have been yesterday. Certainly, Cecilia looked as innocent and uncertain. And he—oh, he could even smell the sweet scent of hay and horse in the air! He could feel the stable floor tipping from beneath his feet and Cecilia's firm, youthful body molding to his, even as her palms pressed him away, and he knew all too well his own reckless intent. His intent to take her, to use her body for his own gratification with little thought for hers. And he felt the shame flood over him. The certainty that he was his father all over again.

"Oh, Cecilia," he breathed against her flushed skin. "Oh, my dear, I—I don't think I can . . . I mean, this just doesn't feel . . . right."

But beneath him, Cecilia was already shaking with rage. Or so he assumed. Right up until the moment he felt the warm wetness of her tears streaming down her cheeks and onto his.

Speechless, he rolled onto his side, dragging her with him until they faced one another, his back to the fire. His hand came up to push the curls back from her face, confirming the horrible truth.

"Y-y-you *don't want me!*" she softly wailed, biting into her fist.

Suddenly, he understood. And she *didn't* understand. Christ, what a nightmare. "Oh, Cecilia, darling!" he whispered. "That just isn't true!"

Lamely, she nodded, her rich red-gold curls scrubbing on the carpet. "Oh, y-yes, it is!" she sobbed weakly. "You d-don't want me an-any more than Walrafen did! You've just been tormenting me. N-nobody ever wants me. The only men I attract are men like that horrid Edmund Rowland!" She drew a snuffled breath. "And wh-what does that say about *m-me?*"

If David had felt like a dog before, he certainly felt worse now. Roughly, he curled his arms about Cecilia and drew her body against his. She felt round and sweet, and he could feel her tears dampening his shirtfront. For a long moment, he simply held her as she cried, not knowing what to do or say. Certainly, he was ill prepared to deal with such an emotional outburst. The women he had known did not cry. Because they weren't paid to.

He wondered what that said about himself. Had he been purchasing something which felt fleetingly real but was, in truth, so deeply flawed and superficial, it bore no resemblance to reality?

God, what a question! He would not—could not—think about it. He bent his head and kissed her lightly on the forehead. "Cecilia, my dear, you are beautiful. Any man in his right mind would desire you."

"Don't lie to me, David," she sniffed miserably into his shirt. "You don't. Decent men never do."

David was taken aback by her phrasing. *Decent?* That sounded a damned sight better than his old depiction of a *devil-may-care fribble*. Somehow he'd gotten promoted. Was there hope? Gently, he pushed her a little away and stared into her limpid eyes. "Cecilia," he said with a sardonic laugh, "you have obviously never noticed how men watch you move through a room. For if you had, you would know how wrong you are."

As if she were embarrassed, Cecilia dashed a tear from beneath her eye. "You kissed me that day in the mission," she said almost accusingly. "I thought then that *you* wanted me."

"And I did," he ruefully admitted. "Cecilia, a man's desire is a complicated thing."

"Apparently so," she agreed a little bitterly.

"Oh, Cecilia," he moaned, dragging her a little nearer, his humiliation all but forgotten. "What am I to do with you?"

Suddenly, a strange thought struck him. A thought which explained a good deal. But how the devil did a gentleman ask? Awkwardly, he grappled. "Cecilia, your marriage . . . did Walrafen not want . . . or I should say, *could* he not . . . um—*perform?*"

"Not really." She snuffled moistly. "He said . . . well, he *said* I was pretty. And he tried. Two or three times. But he never *did* anything. I just don't think I was attractive to him. But afterward, he would always pat me on the head and—and tell me what a dutiful wife I was." Her voice rose pitifully, catching on an agonizing sob. "But I wasn't a *wife*. I wasn't *anything* I wanted to be. And I think he believed me too stupid to know the difference."

"Oh, dear."

"Oh, how embarrassing," corrected Cecilia witheringly. "And I cannot believe I am telling you this."

"Cecilia," David said gently, "you were begging me

to make love to you. Trust me, I would have figured it out."

"Oh, it's too awful!" she moaned.

"Darling, it isn't *awful*," he whispered, trying not to delight in Walrafen's conjugal failures. "It happens. Your husband wasn't a young man. I'm sure . . . I'm sure he did his best." But inwardly, David thought Cecilia's breasts alone could resurrect a man from the dead. Indeed, he was beginning to feel a little hopeful himself.

"Then why did he m-marry me?" Cecilia sobbed, obviously unaware of David's rekindling interest.

Probably to spite his son, whom he delighted in tormenting, David inwardly considered. But he bit back the words, for they were the last thing Cecilia needed to hear. "He married you because you were beautiful and desirable," he softly answered. "And I am sure he loved you very much."

"But you do not even have to *like* someone to want to bed them," she said quietly. "Even I know that much." Gracelessly, Cecilia struggled into a seated position on the rug and began to tug at the sleeves of her gown, discreetly covering herself. Strangely, her quiet, resigned motions made David want to cry, too. It seemed so sad, so wrong somehow.

He struggled onto his knees before her, hitching his trousers over his hipbones. He *did* want her. He had always wanted her, had he not? Indeed, he very much feared that what he felt for her was something worse—and infinitely more confusing—than desire.

But all Cecilia wanted was to be found desirable. And somewhere along the way, she'd obviously misunderstood what that word meant. No doubt he had had a hand in that little bit of cruelty, for six years ago, she had been far too young and inexperienced for a man of his ilk. In response, she'd married someone who, in comparison to him, no doubt looked sane and trustworthy.

And yet, David had very nearly succeeded in seducing her—an eighteen-year-old virgin. And what if he had? Could life have turned out any more miserable— for either of them? Abruptly, he sat up, speaking rapidly before he could change his mind. "I'll tell you what the trouble is, Cecilia," he said awkwardly. "It is this room. I mean, this floor. The rug. Why, for pity's sake, this isn't *romantic*. This isn't the way a gentleman ought to treat a woman as precious as you."

Nervously, she blinked. "I don't understand."

David leaned forward to cradle her face in his hands. Gently, he kissed her. "Look, Cecilia—if you want me," he said softly, "if you are unerringly certain that this is what you want, if you can say it honestly, when your mind is not clouded by lust, then let me take you upstairs to your bed. Let me do a proper job of loving you. In the way that you deserve. And I promise, I will not fail you."

For a heartbeat, Cecilia was silent, then gradually, she reached out her hand for his. "I know," she said softly.

Cecilia had no recollection of how they made their way up the two flights of stairs in the dark. Dimly, she was aware of pushing open her bedchamber door and of being led across the room to her small four-poster bed. And then, David sat down on the edge of the mattress and drew her between his legs. He looked up at her as she stood there, his eyes dark and glittering by the light of the lamp Etta had left burning.

Outside, the freezing rain had turned to sleet, lashing at the windows in sheets. Within, the room was a sanctuary, bathed in warmth and soft firelight. The

flames from the hearth cast shifting light and shadow
over David's face, emphasized the aristocratic elegance of his bones, the dark intensity of his expression. Silently, he reached up and began to pull the
pins from her hair.

When at last her hair was down about her shoulders, David turned his attention to the sagging bodice
of her gown. "Cecilia, you are sure?" he rasped. His
hand trembled almost imperceptibly as he urged the
other sleeve down her shoulder, baring her flesh inch
by inch.

Cecilia stared down at his long, elegant fingers as
they drew the silk down her arm. "Yes," she whispered,
closing her eyes. "Just show me how to please you."

"Cecilia," he answered tenderly, "you do please me.
I have only to look upon you, and I am *pleased* to the
point of madness."

And then, as if he'd said something which made
him uncomfortable, David jerked to his feet and
turned her around. His fingers moved down her back,
swiftly freeing the row of tiny buttons as his lips
brushed first her neck, then her collarbone. "I—I'm
wearing stays," she whispered nervously.

"I shall manage."

"Oh." Cecilia felt her face flush with heat. Of
course he could *manage*. "I daresay you've undressed
a great many women," she added a little miserably.

"Yes, but I mean to undress only one tonight," said
David, bending his head to suckle at her ear. Then his
tone became more compassionate. "Cecilia, love, I'm
no innocent. God knows I'm not good enough for
you, but you've always known that. Still, I can give
you pleasure. And show you how desirable you are."

Gently, David slid the dress to her waist, then let his
arms come about her. Cecilia's breasts spilled from

her stays, molding to his hands. From behind, he caressed her, while his lips brushed over her hair. *He did want her.* She could feel the heat of his eyes, staring over her shoulder, watching her breasts harden and tremble as he touched them. The pleasure was too exquisite to be borne. Almost against her will, Cecilia whimpered as her head tipped back against him, exposing herself to his view.

"Good God, Cecilia," he whispered, lightly pinching her nipples between his thumbs and forefingers. "You are more beautiful now than when I first—"

Cecilia spun about in his arms and kissed him, her mouth opening to his. Even now, held fast in the spell of his seduction, she had no wish to be reminded of the past.

Outside, the driving sleet grew faster, hammering against the glass in rhythm with her pulse. David's eyes fell shut, his thick lashes fanning across his cheeks as he deepened the kiss to a burning intensity.

Suddenly, he broke away, and swiftly undressed her, expertly unfastening what was left of her clothing. It took him but a moment, and then he slid the chemise over her head and buried his face in her hair as his hands ran over her bare shoulders and down her back, cradling her buttocks.

With a low, masculine growl of impatience, he pushed her onto the bed, stripped off his shirt, and shucked out of his remaining clothes. Cecilia found him only marginally less alarming in his half-aroused state. She realized he was still staring at her breasts.

"They are . . . ample, are they not?"

David looked at her and smiled almost wistfully. "They are just as I have always dreamed of them— perfect, ripened peaches," he whispered, following her onto the bed. "I haven't tasted one in years without thinking of you. Such untainted beauty. Such art-less simplicity."

The honesty of his words made her blush. Cecilia had never lain naked with a man. Not even her husband, in his fumbling and futile efforts, had fully undressed her. In the hearth, the coals sheared off, heightening the glow across her skin. Shyly, she moved to draw back the shielding bedcovers.

At once, David's hand came down to cover hers. "Don't, Cecilia," he whispered. With his body, he pressed her down against the linen counterpane, the fabric soft and cool against her back. Bracketing himself over her, he bent his head to kiss her breast, his tongue seeking the tip, drawing it into his mouth until she arched and cried out at the spike of pleasure. As his dark, heavy hair fell forward to sweep over her feverish skin, his teeth gently nipped at her, suckling until that strange liquid warmth ran through her belly and between her legs.

Good Lord. She had not known . . . had never dreamed of such a thing. Nor of such exquisite torment. Oh, she'd known that David was sought-after for just such skills. A relentless libertine, she'd thought him. But suddenly, she did not care. And he did not relent.

Still hanging over her, one forearm braced above her shoulder, David turned his attention to the other breast, nursing and nuzzling as his other hand slid down and smoothed over the swell of her belly. "Perfect," he whispered. "So beautiful, so womanly you are, my sweet." He opened his hand and caressed her lower still, until one finger slid into the silken cleft between her legs. She was wet. Embarrassingly slick. His fingers slid through her flesh like an erotic breeze, the dampness trailing through her curls.

His fingers traced through her again, a whisper of pleasure, and then his thumb touched what felt like the very core of her soul. It was too much. Too powerful. Cecilia gave a faint, breathless gasp and tried to jerk away. Against her breast, David growled, a sound of intense pleasure deep in his throat. With one hand, he stilled her, while his thumb brushed the wonderful place again, making Cecilia want to writhe and sob with pleasure.

"Oh, oh . . ." she breathed into the darkness. "Stop, David . . . oh!" Cecilia felt on fire with shame and pleasure. But she pressed her heels into the mattress, arching hard against his hand. Searching. Eager.

David trailed the heat of his tongue over her nipple. "*Sweet Peaches* . . ." he whispered hoarsely. "A taste of you could drive a man insane." Along her thigh, she felt his rod stir and grow hard again. She pressed herself against him, and David let his full weight come down on her, urging her down into the firmness of her bed.

With womanly instinct, Cecilia lifted one leg and curled it tight about his waist, dragging his hips into hers, and letting her tongue trace a salty path down his throat. She wanted. Oh, how she wanted . . . something.

Gently, David pushed her leg down again. "Slow," he rasped. "Go slowly, Cecilia . . . don't rush . . ." His skin was burning now, too, his back taut and powerful as she skimmed her hands down to the tightly bunched muscles of his buttocks.

He raised himself up slightly, bracing his weight on both arms as he studied her, his once indolent eyes burning with raw emotion. "Oh, Jesus, Cecilia . . ."

Suddenly, he slid down her length, burying his face in the thatch of gold curls between her thighs. Strong and heavy, his hands slid inside her thighs, pressing them apart. With wild abandon, he thrust his tongue into her wetness, probing until he found the place his fingers had teased to hardness. Cecilia stifled a scream. Her hips arched off the bed, but David's powerful arms forced her down again. Sweetly, deliberately, he tormented her, sliding first his tongue, then his fingers, inside her.

David found himself grappling for control. She was beautiful. Too beautiful for him. Greedily, he suckled her, drawing in the scent of her passion, sliding his fingers through her warm velvet flesh, and then beyond, into the forbidden tightness. Gently, he probed her, wondering what it was going to feel like when he tore through such exquisite innocence. Could he bear her pain? His own pleasure? Yet he burned to take her, make her his. God knew he had no right. Never had. Still, he'd been given a second chance, though it might be madness to seize it.

But he meant to, because this time nothing—*nothing*—would stop him. Certainly Cecilia wouldn't. She was writhing against the bed now, murmuring incoherently, her hands fisting in the coverlet, her hair spread over the pillow in a glorious tangle of flame-gold. In the firelight, her skin glowed, her beautiful breasts and rounded belly were flushed with pink.

With a hushed whimper, David closed his eyes and tasted deeply of her, remembering six long years of carnal fantasies—obsessive, heated dreams—not one of which could compare to this reality. Suddenly, Cecilia bucked hard beneath him, her breath fast and rasping.

David had broken into a sweat. Still, he resisted the urge to take her, touching her again with his tongue, stroking and teasing. He'd promised her pleasure, and she'd damned well get it, even if he exploded from restraint.

But it was Cecilia who exploded. Her release came upon her quickly, leaving her shuddering and trembling, her body rigid against him. *"Ah, ah . . . aaah, David,"* she moaned, her hands flowing over her body, touching her throat, breasts, her belly, and finally coming to rest over his own fingers.

In response, he slid up her length and held her as the trembling subsided. "Come inside," she finally whispered, her voice hoarse and foreign. "I want you inside me now. *Please.* I know it's wicked, but I want you."

Against the back of her head, David felt his hand spasm as he pressed her cheek against his chest and held her. "Oh, my sweet Cecilia," he murmured into her hair. "You must understand—there is nothing *wicked* about this—not if it is what we both want."

"Do you want . . . it?" she asked uncertainly. "Do you want me?"

David gave a sardonic laugh. "So much it hurts, you little fool." He covered her with his body and kissed her again. She was round and pretty and delicate all over. Too delicate. His cock was hard and pulsing as he ran one hand down its length, considering what he was about to do to her. To both of them, perhaps.

Mesmerized, Cecilia watched him touch himself. "What will it feel like?"

Such an innocent question. A less selfish man would have stopped. But David leaned forward, spread her with his hand, and slid inside her snug warmth just an inch. "Like that," he whispered, holding himself in check.

Cecilia shivered at the newness of the sensation, of David's heavy, heated flesh searing and stretching hers. It felt good. Perfect. As if she'd waited a lifetime. Instinctively, she urged against him. David's hardness slid deeper, rubbing high over the sweet place his mouth had found, and at once, Cecilia understood. She reached out for him, trying to pull him nearer.

David resisted. Slowly, he withdrew, and Cecilia cried out, stung by the emptiness. With his hand still holding the weight of his manhood, he shoved himself in again, sliding deeper this time. And again, and again, flesh into flesh, a little at a time. Strange. And wonderful.

Still, she wanted something more. His head bent, his eyes focused on their joining, David began to shudder, his muscles taut. "Please," she sighed, reaching out for him again.

"Not yet," David whispered, his voice straining.

"Yes," she begged. "Now. All."

"No!" he growled.

Then, suddenly, he moaned deep in his chest, a low cry of agony, and moved his hand. On a sudden thrust, he slid deep inside, stretching her, seemingly beyond her tolerance. There was a moment of sharp pain, a sense of intense invasion, and finally acceptance, as Cecilia's body took him fully inside.

"Oh, my God," David whispered, his voice rich with awe.

His head went back. His eyes were squeezed tight, the tendons of his neck corded and slick with sweat. "You are . . . unhurt?" he rasped, his voice weak, his body trembling with what felt like superhuman effort.

"I—I'm fine," she managed, feeling him throb and pulse against the entrance to her womb. Her pain gone, she craved only the return of sensation, of David's heated hardness sliding into her. Again, he shuddered, a bone-deep tremble. Greedily, Cecilia rocked her hips against him, instinct drawing her hands to his buttocks.

His eyes flew open in alarm. "No!" he shouted, shoving her hips harshly back down against the bed. "Oh,

Christ almighty! Don't . . . don't pull," he whispered
hoarsely. "And don't push. Oh! Cecilia! Just *don't* move."

Outside, the sheeting ice had lessened to a soft
rain, swathing the room in perfect silence, save for the
harsh breaths that sawed in and out of David's chest.

"It isn't good?" she asked softly, reaching up to
push the heavy curtain of hair back from his face.

"Too good, Peaches," he muttered. "Too bloody
good . . . I think I'm going to die."

She tried. Oh, heaven help her, she tried to do as he
asked and lie still beneath him. But her leg began to
slide sinuously back and forth along his, and of their
own will, her hips rose against him, hungrily seeking.
He stroked once, high against her, sweet and true. A
blinding sensation slid nearer. In the darkness, David
cried out, a soft sound of torment, a man pushed beyond restraint. And yet, Cecilia pressed against him,
yearning for something she did not understand.

"Please . . ." she whimpered. "Please don't stop."

David stared at her, his eyes wide and dark with
warning. "I won't," he rasped, "but just . . . let me do it."

Mutely, she nodded, and he shoved himself inside
her again. It was too much. Too sweet. She reached
out for him, clawing impotently against the tight
muscles of his shoulders. In truth, she clung to him,
dragging herself high against him, urging him to
move against her, to give her what he'd given before.

"Oh, give me strength," he whispered, bowing his
head and drawing himself out with a warm, silken
glide through her flesh. Again, he drove himself into
her, this time spreading her wide with one hand, forcing his stroke against her core of fire and pleasure.

Oh, that was it. Yes. So perfect. So deep. Cecilia
moaned and rose up again, writhing beneath his
thrust. Again, and again, he pounded into her, his

breath heaving in and out, his head back, his hips pumping feverishly. What had once been pain became torment, and then . . . something more. Blindly, Cecilia reached out again.

This time, David fell full on top of her, forcing her shoulders into the mattress, roughly shoving himself in and out until Cecilia could do nothing but whisper his name. Until, at last, she exploded inside, surging around him, drawing him deep, into her heart and her soul.

"Oh—Cecilia!" he cried. "Oh—my God!" His voice was hoarse and desperate. His teeth caught in her hair as he bit into her neck. His hips bucked against her twice more, pounding the headboard against the wall. He clutched her tighter, dragging her against him, shuddering, shoving, pulsing inside her until he was spent.

For a long moment, he held her, clutching at her awkwardly, as a drowning man might clutch a log in the ocean. His hard, unyielding jaw, the very one she'd once thought so haughty, fell against her forehead, damp with sweat. At last, a sigh—a whimper, really—escaped him, and finally, his body collapsed, his shoulders shuddering one last time.

Slowly, he rolled to one side, taking her with him as he went. And Cecilia fell into a deep and dreamless sleep.

9

In which Delacourt Awakens to an Epiphany

*R*eality returned to David through a dense fog, as if
he were walking toward a place he did not know.
Drowsy and uncertain, he lifted his head from the pillow of Cecilia's breast and looked about. In her
hearth, the fire was dying. In the shadows sat a pair
of armchairs, a Louis Quinze dressing table, an armoire, all very normal things. Indeed, it was a very
normal lady's boudoir, done up in frilly fabrics of
green and gold. Surely, he'd seen countless like it?

And yet, when he looked back at Cecilia, a sensation which felt far from normal squeezed the breath
from his chest. He forced himself to inhale. Something—a bedsheet—was tangled about his ankle. He
threw it off with a harsh thrashing motion. In her
sleep, Cecilia sighed and turned onto her side to snug-
gle deeply into the pillows. Entranced, David studied
the lush curve of her hip, the mass of burnished hair
which fell over one shoulder, and a feeling of intense
possessiveness—the need to wrap himself about her,
to feel the instinctive tightening of her body against
his—almost overwhelmed him.

Sweet Jesus, what was he thinking? Roughly, he

lifted himself away from her and went to the window, parting the draperies to peer out into the night. The air, it seemed, had warmed. A thick, murky fog had enveloped Marylebone, swaddling the glossy cobbles in silence. In a corridor above, he could dimly hear a clock striking. Four? Or five?

He turned to look over his shoulder at Cecilia once more, and realized that he had to get out of her house before he did something unspeakably foolish. Like waking her up, falling at her feet, and babbling incoherently about having loved her since the first day he'd laid eyes on her.

Damn! He couldn't afford to even consider such a thing. His hands trembling, David drew the cover around her nakedness, jerked on his clothes, and went slinking down the stairs like a thief—which, in a way, he was, since in a moment of supreme idiocy, he'd seized something which had not been his to take.

Once inside the drawing room, he shrugged hastily into his coat and threw his cravat about his neck. But Cecilia's clothing was still scattered over the floor. David had never before faced such a point of etiquette. Surely, it would be ungentlemanly to leave a lady's unmentionables to be discovered by the first person down tomorrow? And he rather doubted that it would be Cecilia, a woman who obviously slept the sleep of the innocent.

Quickly, he gathered up her things and crept back to her room, piling everything on a chair just inside her door. Then, unable to resist, he turned back for one last look at her, snuggled into the covers like a sleepy kitten. It was almost his undoing. Impulsively, he snared one of her silk stockings and stuffed it into his pocket. Then he hastened down the stairs to snatch his coat and dash out into the damp February morning.

Soon, he was alone in a dark, cold carriage, rumbling toward Portland Place. David tried to tell himself that his leaving so quietly was an act of consideration. Cecilia was not the sort of lady who would wish her servants to catch sight of her lover skulking out at dawn. But the truth was, he was driven by cowardice. Delacourt simply did not know what to say after last night.

Last night. Oh, God.

Was it the beginning of something wonderful? Or simply a fitting end to an enduring obsession? In the darkness, he bowed his head. Pray God, anything but that. Perhaps he did not know precisely what he wanted. Or, more accurately, did not know if he deserved what he was beginning to *think* he wanted. But he knew he needed Cecilia in his life.

So . . . what now? Did he fling himself at her feet? Beg her to—*to marry him?* Damn. He'd done that before. And the little cat had all but spit in his face. Surely she wouldn't now? But why not? What had changed? All her high talk about *decent* men aside, would she think him somehow nobler, more honorable, now that he'd finally managed to take her virginity? David snorted aloud.

No, Cecilia would not blame him. But it was entirely possible—quite likely, in fact—that she would wake up with grave regrets. And certainly, those regrets would not be eased by learning the truth of who—and what—he really was. And this time, he would have to tell her. This time, he could not assuage his guilt by telling himself he was trying to marry her for her own good, and because she had no better option. This time, Cecilia had many choices. She could marry where she chose—and *if* she chose.

Suddenly, Delacourt looked back to see the elegant

entrance to Park Crescent disappearing in the distance, and he knew that at a bare minimum, he had to make love to her again. But would she be willing? God knew he'd given a pitiful performance. How ironic! At the time when it had mattered most, the celebrated and notoriously profligate Lord Delacourt had first succumbed to an attack of the scruples and, in the end, had been unable to muster any measure of restraint.

And when she awoke, would she think him a cad? Or a gentleman? Certainly exploding into a rage and crushing her precious Chinese dancing girl had been beyond the pale, even if that stiff stick Giles had given it to her. And now, he was slinking off like a dog with its tail between its legs. He must go back and face her. Apologize.

Yes, but was not that the very thing which had gotten him into this whole bloody mess? Still, it was important he not press her. In the first place, Cecilia did not press particularly well. He'd learned that lesson years ago. And in the second place, her trust had been taken advantage of by the men in her life—himself included—altogether too often.

Perhaps he ought simply to ask her what she wanted of him? It was a novel concept—but yes, by Jove, it seemed fair. Give her the choice. Let her take her time. But it was a deuced risky game, that.

For what if she didn't choose him?

Humming a rousing little tavern tune under her breath, Henrietta Healy lifted her ladyship's best petticoat from its puddle on the chair and eyed it critically. Stubbornly, she snapped it, as if expecting the wrinkles might be intimidated into fleeing of their own accord.

Reluctantly, Cecilia cracked another eye. Etta came fully into focus. "Ungh," Cecilia murmured, fisting her hands above her head and stretching languidly under the sheets.

"Mornin' to you, too, mum," announced Etta cheerfully, picking up Cecilia's chemise. "Slept snug, did ye? Lor, I didn't! The chimney down at Snead's coffee house caught fire. Oh, you can't think what a racket that was! Then the sleet. And after that, them grandbabies o' Aunt Mercy's cried the whole live-long night. And a funny thing, too," she continued, draping Cecilia's clothing over one arm. "One o' them stockings is gone missing."

Cecilia gave another lazy stretch. "Your Aunt Mercy lost her stocking?" She yawned, struggling mightily to wake up and follow the conversation.

"No," fumed Etta, a deep frown puckering her brow. "Them pale ivory ones what Madam Germaine ordered made up special for that green dress."

Suddenly, Cecilia focused on the pile of clothing. Memory stirred. "Oh, my God!" She sat bolt upright in bed, frantically patting the covers all around her.

"Well, it's just a stocking, mum," said Etta flippantly. "And it ain't like ter be in yer bed."

"Oh, my God!" Cecilia repeated. Her head jerked up, and, stark naked, she bolted from the bed, shoving her arms through her wrapper as she went. "What is the time? Where is Shaw? Has anyone swept out the drawing room?"

"The drawing room?" asked Etta, puzzled. "Couldn't say, mum." But Etta answered in vain, for her mistress was already heading for the door.

"Well!" said Etta with a sudden, knowing wink. "I reckon you've finally gone 'n dipped a toe in the water!"

By seven in the morning, David found himself propped back in his favorite reading chair and staring at his bedroom ceiling. At least, he wanted to stare at it. However, when he opened his eyes, all he saw was a pale green mist.

"I feel like a bloody garden snake trying to shed its skin but finding it caught on my ears," he fumed.

At his elbow, he could hear Kemble, and the rhythmic *thwack*, *thwack* of a razor being stropped. "Snakes," the valet said airily, "have no ears."

"Well, how much longer, blister it?" David tried to sound cross, but it was awkward, given all the plaster Kemble had troweled onto his face.

A dark shadow bent over him, and he felt the valet's cool fingertip poke about beneath his eye. "I can take off the cucumber slices now," he said saucily. "But the mask must stay another quarter-hour."

"Another quarter-hour? Good God, man, I have to be in Wapping by nine."

"Do you wish to be prompt or presentable?" retorted Kemble.

"Prompt, damn you. I'm going riff-raff hunting with a bloody police inspector! Who cares what I look like?"

"Well, you needn't snap at *moi!*" said Kemble archly. "A man of your age simply cannot keep such hours. Home at five, and your bed not even rumpled! My dear boy, that's what I call a sleepless night."

"I slept through part of it," groused David

"Indeed?" tittered the valet. "Not the important part, I hope."

"Has anyone ever told you you're damned insolent?" muttered David struggling in the chair. "Now, get this bloody mess off my face. I have to sit up. We must talk."

"Oooh! This sounds rich," purred Kemble, snapping out a towel and tying it about David's throat. "Was she married? Were you caught? Must I go and bribe her footmen?"

"Not yet, no, and not yet," grumbled David.

"*Oh, really—?*"

Suddenly, David realized what he'd said. "Blast it, I mean—*no, no,* and not yet!"

"Was that a telling slip of the tongue, my lord?" asked Kemble on a choke of laughter.

David tried to change the subject. "Damn it, never mind. Now, listen here—I need you to do something for me. Tomorrow afternoon, I want you to go down to Bow Street and hire a couple of runners. Big ones. Then take my traveling chaise over to the mission. Pick up that girl—Kitty, the one whose sister was murdered—and have the runners escort her quietly to my estate in Derbyshire."

"My lord, it is done," returned Kemble, his voice suddenly more serious. "I take it you are worried for her safety? Two down and one to go, so to speak?"

"Just so," answered David as Kemble plucked the cucumber slices from his eyes and tossed them into the rubbish bin. "And so far, we can get very little information out of this younger sister."

"Hmm," said Kemble, laying a razor to David's face and stroking off a swath of the cucumber concoction. "Perhaps I could be of help?"

David crooked his head to peer up at Kemble. In a perverse way, he was beginning to like him, undoubtedly another sign of his disordered mind. The man's presence was something like an icy rain, not precisely comfortable but infinitely refreshing. Sometimes he found himself wondering if the Marquis of Rannoch might part with the fellow. Probably not.

Nonetheless, Kemble's suggestion had merit. The old boy had a way about him, there was no denying it. Perhaps de Rohan and Cecilia would not need to speak with Kitty at all.

"People of the lower orders—well, they do not greatly trust the gentry, do they?" mused David. "It's unfortunate."

"Unfortunate?" Kemble laughed dryly, shaving off another swath of cucumber. "If you think that's unfortunate, my lord, observe how they behave in the presence of a Bow Street Runner or a policeman." He spoke with a certain knowledge.

"What do you know about life in the East End, Kemble?" David asked curiously.

For once, Kemble was reticent. "Enough to survive, my lord," he said quietly as he worked. "What would you have me do?"

"This girl," said David returning to his topic. "She knows something which I fear is very dangerous. Do you think you could get her to share it?"

With two neat flicks of his wrist, Kemble was done. "Your wish is my command, oh my Pasha!" he answered with an elegant, fluid salaam.

"Jesus, watch that razor!" David drew back in horror.

But Kemble's smugness—as well as the rest of him—was still intact. Sharply, David exhaled. "As to Kitty, yes. Probe. But gently! She's been through a vast ordeal."

"Just trust me, my lord," he responded, drawing clean his blade against the edge of a copper basin. "With a knife. Or with anything else."

And he could trust him, David realized. Kemble was very charming when he wished to be, and for all his fussing and scolding, he had that air about him—an air of competence, yes, but also one of kindness. Women would respond to it instinctively, he thought.

Kemble unfurled the towel from his neck, and for the next few minutes, Delacourt permitted the valet to dress him in relative silence. He did not look forward to spending a morning traveling through Wapping and Shadwell. But he dreaded even more what he knew he must do in the afternoon.

Just as David began to tie his cravat, he saw a way out—or at least a mitigation—of his dilemma. "Oh, and Kemble?"

"Yes?" The valet poked his head out from David's dressing closet.

"Do you know anything about antique Chinese porcelain?" he asked casually, drawing the last end up and around into the loop.

The valet's fine brows went up as he snapped open David's coat. "As in Ming vases and such?"

"Why, yes, that very thing!" answered David, drawing back from the mirror to critique his knot.

"Sorry, my lord," Kemble said mournfully. "I'm a Ch'ing dynasty man myself."

"Oh." David's face fell as he shrugged into his coat. "But isn't it all very like? I mean, you're quite resourceful. Could you not dig up some of the other kind?"

"Well, of course." Proudly, Kemble drew himself up. "I know a few fences in St. Giles. And a couple of legitimate artifact dealers in the Strand. What did you have in mind?"

"Oh, I don't know . . . maybe half a dozen? And get a couple of greenish-looking ones."

"Half a dozen?" asked Kemble archly. David thought he caught a flash of humor in the valet's eyes, but it was quickly veiled. "But, of course, my lord. You need only tell your man of affairs that I shall require the cash with which to purchase them."

"Oh, you tell him," muttered David, tugging on his gloves. "Just be quick about it. I'm in a devil of a fix."

"Yes, of course," answered Kemble smoothly. And

when Delacourt next looked up from his toilette, his valet had disappeared.

By a quarter past nine, London's fog had not dissipated. Indeed, near the river, it hung thicker still, cloying, cool, and metallic in David's nostrils. Standing beside de Rohan along a curving stretch of roadway, he stared past the Prospect of Whitby and down the adjacent alley as a man in a damp leather waistcoat rolled a hogshead toward Pelican Stairs. David could barely make out a second man who stood at the end of the alley, clutching a rope. Their boat no doubt floated in the river at the foot of the stairs.

"She was found there?" asked David.

De Rohan nodded, his expression grim.

The men with the hogshead carried their burden down the stairs and disappeared below. De Rohan then stepped briskly into the street, snapping his fingers to the huge black dog which seemed to follow him everywhere. In the morning fog, with his long, black greatcoat swirling about his boots, the inspector looked like a dark, avenging angel.

David followed him into the alley—it was more of a narrow passageway, really—and single-file, they walked the few yards to the river. The alley widened at the end, opening out into a space behind the Prospect and the adjacent building. After pacing about and staring at the ground for a moment, de Rohan stepped up onto the ledge and stared down into the water just as the two men rowed away.

The wash of their small boat slurped forlornly against the stairs as they melted into the mist. "High tide in half an hour," muttered de Rohan. "There's nothing left to see anyway. Let's visit the Prospect."

"What will we do once we go inside?" David asked

as they reached the door. Automatically, the mastiff flopped down beside the entrance, grunted, then dropped his head to his forepaws.

"Speak to the lad first, if he hasn't already vanished," said the inspector with a shrug. "After that, we'll drift about, see who we might know."

"I rather doubt I know anyone who might frequent such a place," David murmured, eyeing the door with grave suspicion.

But he was wrong. They had no sooner entered the door, their eyes slowly adjusting to the gloom, than who should come clattering down the narrow stairway but Hell-Bent Rutledge, whistling a hornpipe jig as he buttoned his waistcoat beneath a hastily tied cravat. In the crook of his arm, he carried a limp blue coat.

Across the room, a thin, narrow-faced man stood at the bar, carving a hunk of Stilton cheese. A platter of quartered onions sat at his elbow. He lifted his gaze to Rutledge, an expression of recognition on his face. But before he could speak, David stepped smoothly away from the door. "Good morning, Mr. Rutledge," he said quietly. "Fancy meeting you here."

Rutledge's head jerked up and around as he peered blearily into the weak shaft of daylight. "What! That you again, Delacourt?" he cheerfully returned. "These low taverns do have a certain charm, don't they?" With a sardonic wink, the young man crossed to the bar, leaned across, and snared a crumbling chunk of cheese, stuffing it into his mouth with a shameless grin.

"Morning, Rutledge," sighed the tapster, setting aside his knife. "You'll be wanting a bit o' something for the road, eh?"

Still chewing, Rutledge shrugged into his coat, a sad affair which looked as if he'd slept in it—or perhaps *on it* was a better guess. But with whom and doing what,

David couldn't bear to consider. "Coffee'll do me, Pratt," Rutledge answered on a swallow. "And set the cheese down on my shot, right?" Then he sauntered across the room and flung himself onto a bench by the bank of sooty windows which gave out onto the river.

It had become obvious that the man at the bar hoped to ignore his two visitors. With a slow, steady gait, de Rohan approached, leaning over the counter on one elbow. "I've come to see the boy who found the body out back yesterday, Mr. Pratt."

The tapster cut him a nasty look. "The boy didn't 'ave aught to do with it, de Rohan. 'Ave you fellows down at Wapping New Stairs run out o' mudlarks and lumpers to hound?"

De Rohan drummed his fingers on the scarred oak surface. "Just fetch him, Pratt," he said with infinite weariness. "I've had three hours' sleep, my boots are wet, and I've got better things to do than roust every fat-pocketed lighterman who sets foot through your door from now 'til Michaelmas. So save me the chore, won't you?" Without another word, de Rohan pulled away from the bar and crossed the room, passing by Rutledge's table to take a seat around the corner near the kitchens.

Delacourt followed him, cutting a glance toward Rutledge as a thin, sleepy-eyed serving girl leaned over his table to set down a crockery mug and a tattered newspaper. Absently gazing into the fog, Rutledge ran a hand up her leg to settle on her rump. Then, with a jerk, he looked up, as if she was not who he'd expected. The girl gave him a half-hearted slap and went about her business.

"You know him?" asked de Rohan as they settled into chairs in the corner.

"Very little," he answered. "His name is Bentham

Rutledge, a bit of a blue-blooded ne'er-do-well." Which was probably just one step removed from being a *devil-may-care fribble*, David wryly considered.

He found himself looking over his shoulder at Rutledge, studying the carefully crafted façade of affability which undoubtedly masked a deep, youthful anger. An anger which was destined to boil down to a middle-aged rage, hardening his heart as well as his too-handsome face.

At the thought, a bitter smile pulled at his mouth. Funny how easily one recognized the telltale signs from a distance. Was that what he had looked like at Rutledge's age? And just how hardened had he become?

David remembered when he'd been but a few years younger than Rutledge and newly come to town after a blissful tenure at Harrow and Oxford. Rich, titled, and not unattractive, he had fancied himself very much the man about town, and society was to be his oyster. Then had come the letter from his father—no, *from the man who had abused his mother.* And life as he had known it, or life as he had expected it to be, had come crashing down about him.

So David was left to wonder . . . what was Rutledge's secret? For, most assuredly, the young man had one. Inwardly, David shrugged. It was none of his concern. Just then, the kitchen door swung open, and a tall, slender lad of about sixteen came out, wiping his hands on a dingy apron. "I'm Thomas," he said, hesitating at the edge of their table.

De Rohan's mouth turned up, but the smile did not reach his eyes. "This gentleman and I should like to hear about the girl you found in the river."

Thomas dropped the apron. "Don't know much," he said with a shrug.

Idly, David drew a couple of coins from his pocket.

De Rohan made a disapproving noise in the back of his throat as David slid a crown across the deeply scarred table. "Well, let's hear what you *do* know," he suggested very softly, snapping the coin against the wood with a neat *click*. "And then let's hear what you *might* know." Neatly, he plunked down a sovereign next to it.

The boy's eyes widened. "What d'ye mean? *Might* know?" he asked suspiciously.

David shrugged. "I daresay there's a vast deal of gossip in a place like this."

The boy crooked an eyebrow and let his eyes drift over David's clothing. Apparently, he was persuaded. "I went out right at dusk," he began, "to pitch the potato peelings 'n such, and there was this mooring, knotted up at the bollard. But there weren't no boat. So I peered over the edge, and that's when I seen 'er, just a-floating. Facedown, 'er arms spread out like an angel."

De Rohan looked disappointed. "You didn't get a good look at her?"

"Oh, I hung about whilst the watchmen pulled 'er out," answered Thomas ghoulishly. "Swole up something ter'ble, she was. But it looked like old Meg, right enough."

"You knew her?" interjected David, leaning across the table.

"Mostly I recognized 'er workin' dress," he admitted. "Dark red satin, it were. She wore it all the time."

"She was known here?" asked de Rohan urgently.

"I've worked at the Prospect well nigh four years, and she's a reg'lar," said the boy proudly. "We get sailors, stevedores, 'n lightermen a-comin' in here night 'n day. Even the odd gent or two. A good place for things you want done on the quiet."

De Rohan glanced at Rutledge again. "You've rooms upstairs, I take it?" His meaning was plain.

Thomas shook his head. "Meg didn't use 'em. She 'ad a place—a 'ouse she worked out of."

"But she also came here to pick up flats?"

The lad nodded.

"Who were her regular customers?"

"No one particular as I ever saw." He leaned a little nearer to David and jerked his head in Rutledge's direction. "But you might arst him. I'm thinkin' he knew some of 'er friends. He's been arstin' a lot o' strange questions."

David cocked an eyebrow at that, but de Rohan just stared out across the river toward the foggy quagmire of barges and merchantmen which crowded the lee of the Lower Pool. "Tell me, Thomas," he said musingly, "how was she tied?"

Thomas looked at him as if he were daft. "She 'ad a bleedin' rope around 'er neck."

"But how was the rope made fast?" insisted de Rohan. "What sort of knot?"

Suddenly, understanding lit the lad's eyes. "A clove hitch," he said swiftly. "A proper 'un, too. Neat and tight. And it was a brand-new rope."

"Good lad," answered de Rohan. "And how long before that since you'd seen Meg in here? Would anyone remember?"

"Why, t'weren't more'n three days ago," said the boy calmly.

"Three?" interjected David skeptically. "Are you sure?"

Earnestly, the boy screwed up his face. "Monday, it was. She come in early, near eleven. Pratt 'ad taken the trap to the Garden to fetch vegetables, so it was just me 'n Nell 'ere."

"Was she alone?" demanded de Rohan. "How was she dressed?"

For a moment, the lad looked confused. "In 'er dark red dress, like usual. By 'erself. But she was looking for someone."

"For a customer?" pressed de Rohan.

"Can't say," answered Thomas. "All she said was, 'Tommy, keep a sharp eye out for a man who might come in asking for me.' Then she winked and slipped me a bob. But no one came. At least, no one she paid any mind. At noon, I come out again, and she was gone."

De Rohan paused, tapping his long fingers on the tabletop. Like his face, his hands were long and olive-colored. Not for the first time, David wondered at his ancestry. "So she had a little of the ready in her pocket," the inspector mused. "Was it her habit to slip you something?"

"No, never," admitted the pot boy with a snort. "Caught my notice, it did. That, 'n her just a-sitting there like the cat wot got in the cream. But maybe not, eh?"

"No," returned de Rohan softly. "Maybe not."

Their conversation with Thomas was at an end. Clearly, Meg had come in to some money, and even David could guess she'd been blackmailing somebody. He looked about the room to see that Bentham Rutledge had slipped unnoticed out the door.

David was not overly worried. Men of his ilk were easy to find—just look for the nearest cockfight or the hottest gaming hell. David knew just where to search, and if he did not, undoubtedly his not-so-innocent nephew would.

In Park Crescent, Cecilia was almost at her wit's end by ten o'clock. Her morning had been one wretched calamity after another. Despite her frantic search, the mysteriously missing stocking had not been found. Weakly, she'd slunk back up to her bedchamber and taken the rare step of having her breakfast sent up, unable to endure the humiliation of going down to face servants who might be snickering behind her back. So, while Etta prepared her bath, Cecilia had tried to eat her toast, literally choking on it. Then she'd knocked over her tea while coughing bread crumbs all over her sheets.

Etta bolted from the bathroom to pound her between the shoulder blades, her expression sly and knowing. Weakly, Cecilia had waved her off with the tray and headed for the tub in hope of drowning herself—or at least soothing her wounds with a long, hot soak.

To her acute dismay, she found that she was terribly sore, and as she settled into the water, she found that one of her wounds was as physical as it was mental. The merest trace of blood stained her left thigh— almost nothing, really. After a life lived in the saddle, it was a wonder she'd bled at all. Still, it was irrefutable evidence. Her virginity was well and truly gone.

With a deep, agonizing groan, Cecilia let herself slide beneath the surface. When her lungs felt as though they might burst, Cecilia slowly surfaced, marginally resigned to her fate. It wasn't as if she hadn't expected a little blood, or even regretted the loss of what it represented. But good Lord! To lose it to Delacourt, of all people. Dragging the wet hair back off her face, Cecilia tilted her head against the rim and stared up at the high, wainscoted walls of her bathroom.

It was almost laughable, really. All these years, she'd gone to such lengths to avoid Delacourt, just as he had done with her. And now fate—helped along just a tad by Mr. Amherst—had conspired to fling her into bed with the man!

But that really wasn't true, was it? She hadn't been flung anywhere by fate. It had been her own undeniable lust which had done the job. Yes, she'd taken David by the hand and dragged him willingly up the stairs to her bedchamber. When he had discouraged her, she had pushed. When he had offered to stop, she had begged.

It was just as she had always expected. She had an abnormal and indecent attraction to handsome, green-eyed scoundrels. At least, she wasn't alone in her failings. David's smoldering gaze could make a woman rip off her clothes and hurl herself at him. Indeed, if rumor could be believed, more than a few had. The thought stung. Was she nothing more than another ninny-brained conquest in a long string of David's sexual triumphs?

But it hadn't felt quite like that, had it? Indeed, it had felt like something quite, quite different. Cecilia was beginning to suspect she did not know him as well as she had once believed. Certainly, he was far more complex. His anger last night had been palpable, yes. But it had been driven by a pain so obvious and so deep, it had torn at her heartstrings. And when he had dragged her into his arms and kissed her, it had felt as if he were fighting off demons.

She had once thought him simply vain, profligate, and decadent. But last night, what she had felt was decency, honesty, and . . . yes, *insecurity*. Strangely, the memory stirred in her breast, warming her with hope. But hope for what? Had she become some sort of besotted fool?

Suddenly, Cecilia began to giggle, and then to laugh out loud. She felt as David must have done that day in her carriage—a Bedlamite, she'd thought him. Mad. Insane. And perhaps she was, for the truth had finally dawned on her.

She was in *love* with him. With *Delacourt*!

Oh, yes. She'd fallen deeply, hopelessly, head-over-heels for the most inveterate rake in all of England. The one man she'd sworn to avoid. The man who'd sworn to avoid *her*. Cecilia beat at the water with her fist, unable to restrain the great whoops of laughter.

Suddenly, Etta was pounding at the door with the heel of her hand. "M'lady!" she called through the heavy wood. "M'lady, are yer all right?"

Slowly, Cecilia regained herself. "No, Etta," she gasped, pressing the back of her hand to her brow. "I'm not. I'm afraid I'll never be all right again."

For once, Etta was nearly speechless. "No?"

"No," returned Cecilia, standing up in a cascade of water and grabbing a towel. "But I'm afraid there's no help for it. Just lay out my brown merino habit and send Jed around to saddle up Zephyr. I feel the need for a thundering ride. Maybe I'll fall off and break my neck."

Cecilia reached Hyde Park at an hour which was, by Town standards, appropriate only to costermongers and street sweepers. Still, she always preferred to ride early so that she might move at something rather more exhilarating than a canter. The alternative was the pokey afternoon promenade of the *bon ton* and their hangers-on, which she assiduously avoided.

At the top of Park Lane, Cecilia nudged her mount through the gate and toward the main path. At the bluff, she paused to watch the fog rising off the Serpentine below. The park was indeed empty, save for a couple of gentlemen strolling along the water's edge, where a swath of purple crocuses were bravely heralding spring's return. Satisfied, she drew in a deep, cold draught of air, gave Jed the signal, and cut Zephyr loose.

For almost an hour, they circled the park, slowing as they reached the footpaths, and thundering along the bridal lanes where possible. All the while, Jed stayed on her heels, watching out for her, yet urging her forward in their enduring competition to see who was the more bruising rider—not that they could kick up their heels much in Town.

Finally, she slowed her horse to a walk and let Zephyr pick his way back along Rotten Row. The ride had had its hoped-for effect. Her head was clear, her hands steady. Last night was becoming a real and rational problem, rather than the dream it had seemed last night, or the nightmare it had become this morning.

She was still apprehensive, yes. But by the light of day, she realized there was little she could do to resolve matters. The next move would have to be David's, heaven help her. Mostly because she had no notion what to do, no understanding of how to go on. No idea as to what she wanted out of this strange, new relationship.

She knew only that she wanted *him*—the man he'd been last night. Not the haughty, preening aristocrat he showed the public.

Yet she had made David a pariah in her own mind for so long that now to be jerked from one mindset and thrust into another left her reeling. And David was as confused as she, Cecilia suspected. Still, the passion which had blazed between them had been like nothing she'd ever known, nothing she'd ever dreamed of.

But any blaze could burn itself out, and rather quickly, too. She was well aware that David had taken many lovers, and had stayed with none of them above a few weeks. So what hope did she, with her inexperience, have against such odds? Deeply, Cecilia sighed. It was time to go home. Time to set aside this obsession with David for the nonce, since it could not be resolved.

And so Cecilia forced her attention to the mission—specifically, the mysterious deaths of Mary and Meg. Clearly, Chief Inspector de Rohan felt she could be of help in his investigation, even if David disagreed. And so she had decided that this afternoon she would take a carriage ride along Black Horse Lane. She very much wished to see the house known as Mother Derbin's. Sometimes a woman's eye noticed things which a man's did not.

She gave Jed the signal to head homeward and reined uphill. But at that moment, she saw the two gentlemen, still standing by the edge of the Serpentine. Cecilia could not see the first man's face, but the second man was elderly, his long face pinched and pale. Abruptly, he turned away and set off slowly toward the Knightsbridge Road. Attired in a long gray coat and a very elegant hat, the man walked with an uneven gait, as if he favored one leg. Suddenly, he turned onto a graveled path, revealing a glimpse of his walking stick which reflected a dull silver in the daylight.

A faint memory stirred. Cecilia cut her gaze back to the man by the water. But Edmund Rowland had already spied her. "Good morning, Lady Walrafen," he called out, lifting his hand as he approached her.

Cecilia had no choice but to stop and acknowledge him. "Good morning, Mr. Rowland."

"What a charming sight you make on such a dreary day," he said, moving as if to snare Zephyr's bridle.

But the feisty gelding took exception to Edmund, jerking his head away with a hearty equine snort. The result was damp and disastrous. Shaking off his hand, Edmund reached delicately with the other, withdrawing a linen handkerchief from his pocket.

"My deepest apologies, Mr. Rowland," exclaimed Cecilia, trying to maintain a straight face as Edmund wiped his cuff. "I'm afraid the cold makes Zephyr's nose run. And unfortunately, he's a bit skittish of strangers."

Rowland smiled up at her tightly and shoved the handkerchief back into his pocket. "Then it seems I must befriend both horse and mistress," he smoothly returned. "Come, my dear, will you not dismount and take a stroll along the water?"

Cecilia was left in an awkward position. Rowland was now a very generous benefactor of the mission, thanks to her conniving. It seemed churlish to refuse him, and so she allowed him to help her dismount and gave her reins over to Jed.

Lightly, Edmund curled his hand beneath her elbow. "I have often heard it said that the beautiful Lady Walrafen sits a horse better than any other woman in London," he proclaimed as they strolled toward the water. "But I had scarcely credited it until I saw you with my own eyes. And that horse! Why, I am persuaded that few men could handle such a big, magnificent beast."

A warm glow swept up Cecilia's face, and her dislike of Edmund was fleetingly forgotten. "Why, thank you, Mr. Rowland," she said, knowing full well that her horsemanship was her only vanity. "I must confess, I love riding above all things."

Edmund's brows rose elegantly, and it seemed he tightened his grip on her elbow. "Above all things?" he said softly. "Why, I'm almost sorry to hear it. How dreadfully . . . confining it sounds."

Cecilia suspected at once what he was about, subtle though he was. "I live a rather confining life, Mr. Rowland," she returned a little sharply. "And I very much prefer it that way."

Edmund looked stunned. "My dear child!" he said gently. "I perceive I have insulted you! That was far from my intent. Indeed, I wish merely to be your friend."

"My friend?" returned Cecilia, trying to suppress the suspicion in her voice.

"Simply that," insisted Edmund as they drew alongside a bench. Reluctantly, she sat, and to her relief, he situated himself at a proper distance. "And as both your admiring friend," he continued, "as well as my cousin Cole's nearest relation, I'm grateful for this opportunity to speak with you privately—" He stopped abruptly, looking suddenly uncertain.

"Yes—?" urged Cecilia.

Edmund gave a bemused smile and shook his head. "No, no, my dear." He cast his gaze heavenward. "I should be horsewhipped for airing such contemptible speculation. Let us speak of more mundane things. Tell me, do you go to Lady Kirton's tea on Friday? I believe that Anne and I have had the honor to be invited. And to the ball as well. No doubt she is grateful for our donation to your worthy institution."

The remark about invitations passed almost unheard. "What sort of speculation?" Cecilia asked very softly.

Edmund tossed his hand in a disdainful gesture. "Lady Walrafen, a virtuous woman should never heed innuendo. Nor pay any mind to even the merest *expectation* of gossip."

"Mr. Rowland," she said tightly. "I believe I must insist."

Edmund looked deeply aggrieved. "Oh, very well,"

he whispered, cutting a glance toward Jed, who stood some distance away. "I am sure that Cole, in his airy, impulsive way, gave no thought to the *appearance* of the thing—" He stopped again and looked away.

"The appearance of what?" she insisted, growing increasingly ill at ease.

Edmund's gaze returned to hers, holding it unsteadily. "Of your working so closely with that scoundrel Delacourt," he blurted out. "I mean—*really*—what *was* my cousin thinking? Everyone knows you jilted that man, and with good reason. After all, you were so very innocent, and he was already . . . well, already *what he is*. Moreover, Delacourt is the vengeful sort. But now, to have it written down! Really, it is too awful!"

Cecilia felt as if she might be sick. "Written . . . down?"

Edmund looked truly miserable now. "The, er, the betting books at Brooks's. I fear the odds are very much against you, my dear. And the speculation— well, it is not a pretty one."

Edmund's meaning was plain, and given such news six years ago, Cecilia Markham-Sands would have promptly bent over and cast up her accounts in the grass. But the Countess of Walrafen would sooner die. Well—that, and the fact that the countess had had no breakfast to speak of.

So, instead, Cecilia threw back her shoulders and drew herself up, stiffening her spine as if she were a queen. "Mr. Rowland, I'm sure you mean well," she said gravely. "But Lord Delacourt and I have no differences. Indeed, I believe I can safely say that we are . . . yes, that we are friends now. If people choose to speculate that our relationship is anything more, then I fear they shall find themselves rather lighter in the pocket for it."

Edmund leaned over and patted her gently on the shoulder. "My dear, I confess, you have greatly relieved my mind. For some reason which escapes me—account it a devotion to family duty, if you will—I fear that my dear cousin will hold me responsible should any ill come to you whilst he's away."

Cecilia managed a weak smile. She wouldn't have guessed Cole and Edmund were particularly close. In truth, it took her aback. Had she misjudged Edmund? She thought not.

"Then rest assured your family duty is done," she answered. Then, deliberately, she changed the subject. "Now, you must tell me—who was that very tall gentleman I saw you speaking with? He looked quite familiar."

Edmund furrowed his brow. "I rather doubt he is anyone with whom you might be acquainted."

Suddenly, Cecilia recalled the walking stick. "Oh, I know! He was a guest at your soiree."

"No, my dear, you're mistaken."

"Oh, no, I'm very sure I saw him there."

Lightly, Edmund laughed. "You may well have seen him. In the corridor, perhaps? But he was not a guest, just my broker—Leadenhall Street, don't you know," he said, wrinkling his nose. "And a Jew. So, certainly not anyone whom one would invite to one's parties."

Cecilia thought his attitude rather cruel. "Oh? How dreadful to be disturbed in the middle of an entertainment," she responded rather coolly.

"Quite," returned Edmund, perfectly oblivious. "But there were some papers which most urgently required my signature. By the way, I trust that Walrafen left your affairs in good order? I do not mean to pry, my dear, but I have quite a head for business. Should you ever have any concerns, you have only to call upon me."

"Thank you," she said firmly. "But Giles is forever offering the very same sort of guidance, and no doubt wishes I'd heed it more often." Cecilia had no inclination to discuss business, particularly not with Edmund Rowland. Nor with Giles, for that matter. She managed her own affairs, as far as the law permitted, and she was perfectly adept at doing so.

Just then, the sound of the clock at St. James's Palace carried on the breeze. "Good heavens!" she exclaimed, seizing the opportunity to jerk to her feet. "Is it one already? How time does fly. Mr. Rowland, I fear I must abandon you, or Cook shall never forgive me!"

Smoothly, Edmund stood, but Jed hastened forward to help her remount. As they rode back along the edge of Park Lane, Cecilia turned around in her saddle. Edmund was strolling toward a barouche which had just rolled down Park Lane.

Along the Thames, Lord Delacourt and Chief Inspector de Rohan spent another futile hour interviewing Mr. Pratt and the girl named Nell. Following that, de Rohan, David, and the dog—Lucifer, the wicked-looking beast was aptly called—went prowling up and down the streets, knocking on the door of every shop and tavern within five hundred yards of the Prospect. Universally cagey-eyed and reticent, the denizens of the East End would admit to knowing little more than the time of day.

Unfortunately, David got the feeling that they were telling the truth. Certainly, no one piped up to say they'd seen a dead woman in a red dress being dragged out of a clearly numbered hackney coach by two easily identifiable thugs—which was what David had naïvely hoped to hear.

But as de Rohan pointed out, the murderer could

more easily have brought the corpse up by boat through the Limehouse Reach, or even down by the Upper Pool. In short, from anywhere. Moreover, he could have been anyone—anyone who knew how to tie a seaman's knot. Which was most everyone south of Whitechapel Road. Deeply, Delacourt sighed, his admiration for de Rohan's perseverance growing with every passing minute.

At noon, de Rohan tightly informed him that he had other business to attend. Two Portuguese smugglers had been taken up the day before, and his presence was required before the magistrate at a two o'clock hearing. David was almost relieved. Briskly, he informed de Rohan of his plans for Kitty, dropped him and his dog off near Wapping New Stairs, and then ordered his coachman home. Chilled to the bone and dull-witted from lack of sleep, he found himself unable to make sense out of anything they'd heard.

In Curzon Street, Kemble was nowhere to be found, so David stripped off his clothes, washed and redressed, then went downstairs, automatically sliding into his usual chair for his usual luncheon. So lost in thought and sleeplessness was he, David did not immediately notice that his usual beefsteak had not been promptly placed before him.

Quietly, a footman by the doorway cleared his throat, and Delacourt became aware of a strange sort of tension in the room. He focused his bleary gaze upon the table and, in mute amazement, stared at the horrific visage which looked back at him, its bright black eyes glinting ominously.

The little fellow sat squarely upon his table, right where Delacourt's grilled beefsteak ought to have been. His cheeks were puffed out and painted a bright shade of grassy green, and he wore nothing but a little yellow towel hitched about his nether regions like some sort of nappy. Slowly, Delacourt's eyes caught on the row of similar—albeit far less appalling—porcelain ornaments which lined the top of his dining-room sideboard.

Suspicion bloomed.

"Kemble!" he bellowed.

At once, a brace of footmen leapt from the shadows, and it took but a moment for the valet to be hauled into the dining room. "What the devil is this?" Delacourt demanded, pointing at his afternoon intruder.

Out came the wrist. "Maaarvelous, isn't he?" the valet simpered. "I just knew you'd be thrilled."

"Scared witless, more like," muttered Delacourt. Impatiently, he motioned for his coffee and his steak, shoving back the porcelain figurine with his other hand. "Honestly, Kemble, that's the ugliest damn thing I ever laid eyes on. I sincerely hope you did not pay good money for a squat, green, half-naked—"

With a great huff, Kemble leaned forward and snatched the thing off the tablecloth. "Don't blame me!" he hotly began. "You'll recall I prefer Ch'ing. But nooo! You wanted *Ming,* and you wanted *green.*" He settled the figurine's strangely carved base gently atop his forearm and thrust it at him. "So here is your green Ming!"

"Good God, you're going to *ming* and *ching* me straight to Bedlam!" said David, rubbing his temples with his fingertips. "What the hell is it, anyway?"

"It's a roof tile."

"A roof tile?" sputtered Delacourt, shoving back his plate distastefully. "I send you off to buy porcelain—little Chinese dancing girls, vases and bowls, that sort of thing—and you bring me back a bloody *roof tile?* With a—a damned oriental leprechaun standing on it?"

"I have some vases," insisted Kemble indignantly. He jerked his head toward the sideboard. "And two bowls. But you said not one word about a Chinese dancing girl! Besides, these roof tiles are all the rage—"

"Oh, yes!" exclaimed Delacourt melodramatically, throwing his arms open wide. "All the rage! Just like those damned dreary waistcoats you've been forcing me to wear."

Lovingly, Kemble stroked the green man's shiny pate. "These are quite rare," he huffed. "One mounts them over one's door to ward off evil spirits."

"Yes, and it would bloody well work, too," muttered Delacourt, sipping at his coffee. "I wouldn't go near the damned thing in a drunken stupor."

"Upon my word, you're an ungrateful wretch!" Hugging the porcelain to his chest, Kemble looked truly offended. "And after I ventured into St. Giles in the fog this morning! Have you any notion how dangerous that is? I risked life and limb—perhaps even *worse*—merely because you want to impress your way into some woman's bed—and do not try to deny that that is precisely what you're about here. And now *you* want to play the discerning connoisseur? As if you could tell Ming from Meissen!"

"Oh, hell!" interrupted Delacourt, setting down his coffee cup with an awful clatter. "Box up the lot of 'em, and call my carriage."

10

In which Lady Walrafen receives a Trojan Horse

To anyone who knew Lady Walrafen well, and this certainly included her staff, her ladyship's restless unease and monosyllabic conversation that afternoon would have been construed as a sign of a troubled mind. Under normal circumstances, there was nothing very arcane about their mistress. Lady Walrafen said what she meant, meant what she said, and, for the most part, did it with a breezy, blithe attitude.

But today, she was neither breezy nor blithe. In fact, for the better part of the afternoon, she had been pacing up and down the length of her drawing room, chewing first on her left thumbnail, then on her right, and muttering to herself. Eventually, however, Cecilia paused long enough to give the vague instruction that her carriage and her lady's maid were to be made ready to leave within the hour.

Thus, when Lord Delacourt dropped the knocker at Number Three Park Crescent, he was received by Shaw with a degree of hesitation. The still-wheezing servant stared past his shoulder to the beribboned wooden crate two footmen were unstrapping from David's carriage.

"Perhaps I ought to see if she is at home first?" the butler suggested delicately.

"Be so good as to inquire," said David, standing firm. "But if she is not, I shall simply leave this for her."

Inwardly, he almost hoped she wasn't at home. It seemed suddenly more prudent to abandon his peace offering on the steps and flee, since he still didn't know what the devil to say.

But she was at home. And she did receive him, albeit with a measure of restraint. Or was it uncertainty? Delacourt had little experience with females who were either. His footmen set down the crate in front of her brocade settee and withdrew, drawing the door shut behind them.

"A gift," David muttered, waving awkwardly toward it. "By way of an apology."

Cecilia's delicate brows flew aloft at that. "An apology?" she said, her voice bemused. "I did not realize that an apology was in order under such circumstances." She managed what looked like a weak grin.

Delacourt forced himself to smile back. *Oh, God.* She was so beautiful, more so today than the day before, and he had the uneasy suspicion that with Cecilia, it would always be so. This afternoon, she wore a day dress of heavy teal-blue silk. The neckline fell just below her collarbone, the sleeves and the waist cut snugly in the latest fashion, emphasizing the sweet flare of her hips.

Cecilia stared down at the crate, resting her hand along one of the armchairs. In the privacy of her home, she wore no gloves, and the dark cuff fell slightly below her wrist, trailing a ruffle of ivory lace across the back of her hand. Her fingers were slender and capable, and he wondered what it would be like to stretch out across her bed in the afternoon light and watch Cecilia make love to him with them. How he would love to feel her palms go skimming down his chest, and further still, until her fingers tangled in the curls at the base of his manhood.

Atop the armchair, she let her hand slide restlessly over the curving back, and in his mind, he saw her fingers wrapped around his rigid cock, caressing him, then guiding him toward—

"David?" He realized Cecilia was looking at him very curiously. "You wished to apologize for—?"

David felt heat flood his face. Good Lord. He couldn't remember ever having blushed in the whole of his life. Uneasily, he stepped a little further behind the chair, very much afraid that a little discretion was in order. It would not do for her to glance down and think him some sort of rutting boar—even if he were.

He made another uncertain gesture with his hand. "The gift is in recompense for my having broken your Chinese girl," he explained awkwardly. Then he dropped his voice to a hoarse whisper. "Really, Cecilia . . . I cannot think what came over me last night."

Cecilia studied him for a moment. "You have regrets?"

At that, he laughed bitterly. "Darling, my regrets are legion. But the only thing I regret about last night is losing my temper. In truth, it shook me."

Cecilia let her eyes drift over his face, her gaze catching on his mouth. "I confess to having been a little shaken myself."

Unable to restrain himself, he came away from the chair and strode toward her. He wanted so much to draw her into his arms, to share with her not just the ugliness inside him but the beauty which she had brought into his heart. And yet, he could not find the words. And even if he could, it was entirely possible she would not wish to hear them.

So, instead, he merely lifted his hand and stroked the back of it across her cheek. "Cecilia, my dear, I think we have much to talk about. Last night was . . . like a dream to me."

As if she could read his mind, Cecilia slid her arms about his waist. "We seem to have gotten over our dislike of one another rather thoroughly."

"Oh, Cecilia," he said softly. "It is certainly not dislike which I feel for you."

"What do you feel, David?" she quietly responded, tearing her gaze from his and pressing her cheek against the lapel of his coat. "I should like you to be honest with me. Please."

Uncertainly, David stared down at her. What did she wish to hear? He felt as if he were perched upon an icy mountainside and that a deep, unfathomable chasm lay at the bottom. He remembered his resolution not to push her; not to press for anything she wasn't ready to give.

"I respect you," he finally answered. "Too much to do or say anything which might cause you a moment's unease."

"Respect?" Cecilia pushed away and let her eyes drop half shut. "How very . . . *reassuring.*"

Suddenly, David braced his hands on her shoulders, his fingers digging into her flesh. "Then tell me," he demanded, his voice hoarse. "Just say it, Cecilia. What is it that you expect of me? What would you have me do? You have only to name it."

Cecilia realized at once what he was asking: Did she mean to insist on marriage? Well, she'd not done so the first time, and she certainly would not do so now. Whatever he offered, it must be freely given, as she had given herself to him last night. And even if he should offer her marriage, such an invitation would require careful consideration.

She was in love with him, yes. But she was not a fool. Any intimate relationship with David would still lack the one most essential element of true intimacy. His unwillingness to share of himself all but ensured it. David was too brooding, too quiet. And because of that, she would never be able to feel the closeness—that oneness of both body *and* soul—which she now understood she needed.

Moreover, his even hinting that she might hold out some sort of expectation stung just a little. "I think you mistake me," she said, drawing a little away from him. "I expect nothing."

David lessened his grip on her shoulders, his fingers trembling ever so slightly. "Forgive me, my dear," he said, gently lowering his forehead to touch hers. "My choice of words was poor. Perhaps I implied . . . I mean, what I ought to say is—"

Suddenly, David seemed to lose his legendary nerve. "Oh, dash it, Cecilia! I'm no good at this. I just think you're splendid. Now, look here—why don't you just open my gift?"

Despite her frustration, Cecilia felt a flash of wry humor light her eyes. Oh, let him keep his secrets and offer her his bribes, if that was all he had to offer now. She loved him, and she would be patient. For a while.

"Very well," she relented, "but this had better not be a trained monkey with bells around its neck!"

"A *trained monkey?*" David's voice was arch. "Who the devil would give a woman such a ludicrous gift? Come, will you not have a look inside?"

Carefully, David studied Cecilia's face, still afraid she might refuse. He was taking the easy way out, and she knew it. He was plying her with gifts, because they were easier to give than words, just as he'd done with countless women before her—but for entirely different reasons. On this particular occasion, he was buying time, not affection. God help him, he was terrified. Terrified of losing her. And yet, he could not press her; indeed, he hardly knew what he could fairly offer her.

At last, Cecilia surrendered and allowed herself to be led toward the settee. In a few moments, David had sliced off the ribbons, opened the crate, and persuaded Cecilia to begin unwrapping the vases and bowls.

She seemed outwardly pleased, *oohing* and *aahing* as she gingerly lifted each to the light. He sat beside her, watching suspiciously. Was that a smile playing at the corner of her mouth? Or was she peeved? Most assuredly, she had every right to be. His behavior last night had been abominable, even for him. And today, when he so desperately needed his smooth words and persuasive ways, he was bumbling about like the veriest clod. Still, it seemed to David that Cecilia was softening ever so slightly. And then she reached into the bottom of the crate.

Damn! Anxiously, David's hand came out to stay hers. Leaning awkwardly over the crate as they both were, he realized that their faces were so near his breath was stirring the soft hair at her temple. Abruptly, he jerked away.

"That last one," he hastily insisted, "it is nothing, I assure you. A mere trifle. I rather doubt you will even want it."

"Oh, I'm quite sure that I shall," averred Cecilia politely. "After all, your taste in Oriental porcelain is amazingly flawless—not to mention almost frighteningly extravagant." Very carefully, she unwrapped the paper. And then, she sat perfectly silent for what seemed an eternity.

"Oh," she finally said, her voice breathless with amazement. "Oh, my!"

Delacourt panicked. "I told you it was a trifle. And an ugly one at that."

"Oh, David!" Without looking at him, Cecilia lifted the figurine to cradle it in her lap, and slowly, almost lovingly, she ran the tip of her finger across the green man's yellow towel. "I think he's the most horrific thing I've ever seen!"

His disappointment acute, Delacourt exhaled sharply. At once, Cecilia's head jerked up, and her gaze locked with his. He was shocked to see that her eyes looked damp and gentle. "I first suspected you were just trying to placate me," she whispered. "Yet you gave this a great deal of thought, did you not? But how on earth did you find one so quickly?"

Confused, David spread his hands open wide. "I begin to fear that I don't *know* anything. Not about porcelain, certainly. And probably not about women."

Suddenly, Cecilia grinned and leapt to her feet. "Let's take him upstairs and see how he fits."

Before David could grasp her meaning, he was being dragged through the hall and up the stairs toward her bedchamber. In the first-floor corridor, Shaw glared at David disapprovingly, and on the next landing, a housemaid paused in her sweeping, gape-mouthed.

But resolutely clasping his hand in her right and clutching the statue to her bosom with her left arm, Cecilia made her way to the back of the second floor, into the shadows just beyond her bedchamber. There, in a deep, shell-shaped alcove lined with shelves, sat almost a dozen of the peculiar little figurines mounted on strange, arching bases—roof tiles,

Kemble called them. Last night, blinded by lust and stumbling through the dimly lit corridor, David had failed to notice the collection. Well, truth be told, he never noticed such things. But he suddenly understood why Cecilia had believed him so thoughtful. And since God so rarely favored him, David was not about to look askance at his good fortune.

But more important, it was hard not to take pleasure in her joy. Most women would have behaved a little coyly, but Cecilia was not most women. Lovingly, she put the green man down next to a red one, gave another sigh of delight, and began deftly rearranging the entire collection, muttering to herself as she went. Her eyes were bright, her cheeks deliciously pink, and David decided right then and there to have Kemble fetch another dozen of the ugly little devils, and damn the cost.

Delicately, Delacourt cleared his throat. "My dear, I'm given to understand that these fellows are meant to keep wickedness from your door," he said softly. "So perhaps you ought to mount him there."

"Oh, no," insisted Cecilia, turning the green man a little toward the light. "I am sure some passerby would climb up and steal him."

Impulsively, David wrapped one arm high about her waist, drawing her back against his chest. "I meant—" he whispered, crooking his head until his mouth could nibble at her neck. "Over *there.*"

Blushing brightly, Cecilia glanced up to see that he was pointing at the lintel over her bedchamber door. Hesitatingly, she licked her lips. "Ah, perhaps . . ." Suddenly, Cecilia's face broke into a teasing grin. "But you know, now you have me wondering. Do you think it would have the same effect if I just set him on my bed table?"

Quite deliberately, Delacourt leaned closer, curving

his body about hers. "Oh, I really do doubt it," he said, just before he ran the tip of his tongue down her ear. "I feel a terrible spate of wickedness coming on. But I suppose we could go in and give it a try."

Suddenly, heavy footsteps could be heard ascending the staircase. Like guilty young lovers, they sprang apart just as Shaw appeared at the top of the steps. "Your pardon, my lady." The butler cut a glance toward David. "Do you still wish your carriage brought 'round?"

David shifted his gaze from Shaw to Cecilia. "Ah! I collect you are on your way out," he said, trying to conceal his acute disappointment. "Forgive me. I did not mean to keep you."

Cecilia looked uncertain, and not a little guilty. "Well, yes. I had a mind to go down to Black Horse Lane and take a look around."

At once, all David's amorous thoughts drained from his loins as his heart thudded to a stop. Somehow, he managed a tight smile. "Shaw, please be so obliging as to excuse us a moment."

The butler looked taken aback but withdrew. David turned to Cecilia, struggling to measure his words. "Please tell me," he softly began. "No—*please swear to me* that you do not mean to go haring off to that Mrs. Derbin's brothel."

Cecilia tried to feign an innocent expression, but David was not fooled. "I mean only to have a look around," she said defensively. "And Etta will go with me."

David was nonplussed. Just what was he supposed to do? If he ordered her not to go—which was his wish but not his right—she'd simply hop into her landau and vanish the minute his own dust settled.

Suddenly, another horrific fate loomed up before

him, and he felt as if he were once again staring down at Cole's black queen. The prophetess. And once again, there was nothing else to be done. She meant to go, and so he would have to take her, rot it. It was the only way to ensure that she was safe. Two women had been murdered, and they did not yet know why or by whom. Perhaps there was a connection to Mother Derbin's. And perhaps not. But the risk was too grave to be ignored.

"You shan't go anywhere with Etta," he said in exasperation. "She's no sort of protection at all, you goose! If you must insist upon such rash behavior, then you'll go with me."

"With you?" Cecilia's brows went up.

"Yes," he hissed, "and in my carriage. With the blasted crests covered." He glared at her tangle of flame-gold hair, her kittenish face and big blue eyes. Surely, there wasn't another woman in all of London who resembled her. "And for pity's sake, Cecilia, cover yourself with a veil. A heavy black one. Make it two. Otherwise, you'll be seen the moment you crack the curtains—which I know perfectly well you mean to do."

By the time they reached their destination, it was nearing twilight, the evening emerging unusually clear. Already, the waxing moon was dimly visible, shimmering silvery-white against a dusk-blue sky. The alleys and side streets along Black Horse Lane were cloaked in shadows, but no lamps had yet been lit.

Given its location between Wapping and the West India docks, the environs surrounding Black Horse Lane were quite busy despite the hour. The street was filled cheek-by-jowl with pawnbrokers, wine merchants, import-export dealers, and chophouses, and

all of them catering to seamen, tradesmen, and busi-
nessmen.

Throughout the journey, David had sat rigidly opposite her, his muscles tight, his thighs flexed. Even
as she turned away to peek through the window,
Cecilia could feel the tension which thrummed
through him. For the most part, he had avoided looking at her, choosing instead to stare blindly into the
depths of the carriage. He was angry, she thought.
And perhaps a little worried. But not for himself.

In the heavy silence, Cecilia found herself wondering at the impetus behind his unexpected call this afternoon. Had he, as he claimed, merely come to apologize? If not, what else had he meant to say? Clearly,
something more compelling than guilt had driven
him to her door, and despite his denial, Cecilia very
much feared it was regret. Would he laugh, she wondered, if he knew how deeply the thought of losing
their fragile bond terrified her?

No, he would not. Despite what was said of him,
Cecilia was beginning to understand that it was not
within David's nature to be deliberately cruel without
provocation. Moreover, a man did not bring precious
gifts and gentle words to a woman he meant to forswear. Were she of a suspicious nature, Cecilia might
have feared David had cleverly orchestrated her seduction out of pure revenge. Just as she might have chosen to believe that he had been a party to those dreadful wagers at Brooks's. But Cecilia believed neither.

It was strange, really, how sure she was of his
honor, when mere days ago, she had been all too
eager to impugn it. How dreadfully wrong she had
been. David *was* honorable. Deeply honorable. How
had she ever believed otherwise?

She remembered the complex melange of emotions

she'd felt during her come-out, when, at long last, David had ceased in his efforts at flirtation. Yes, she had been relieved. But now, she was ashamed to admit that there had been another, darker emotion. Disappointment.

Yes, it was true. And what a foolish child she had been! On a deeply intuitive level, she had been a woman playing with fire, and when that fire had burnt down into nothing more than the cold ashes of loathing, she had felt both hurt and angry.

Now she understood. Lord Delacourt was not the sort of man one toyed with—not deeply, not intuitively, not in any way at all. Never had he publicly pursued a woman, yet twice he had tried to court her. Would he ever do so again? Cecilia prayed to God it was not too late for them. Unable to resist, she glanced up at him beneath lowered lashes. How grave he looked. How sternly his jaw was set.

No, David was not a man easily manipulated. Perhaps she would pay a dear price for her treatment of him these many years. Oh, he still desired her, and he might take her as his lover for a time. But perhaps his pride would not permit him to court her publicly? Certainly, he was unlikely to—well, to pursue anything more than a discreet *affaire d'amour.* Yet Cecilia wanted so much more. Was she a fool to have hope?

Suddenly, Cecilia sensed the carriage slowing. David gestured toward a nearby building. The establishment known as Mother Derbin's, a double-fronted town house with heavily draped windows, was strategically placed near a corner, tucked in between a well-lit coffee house and a tobacconist's shop. Strangely, the place did not look as nightmarish as Cecilia had envisioned. Indeed, to the uninformed observer, it simply appeared to be a private home, albeit in a relatively undesirable location.

Abruptly, David lifted his walking stick and rapped three times on the ceiling. At last, he spoke, his voice dark. "Well, there you have it, Cecilia. And as you see, one can observe nothing from its exterior."

Slowly, his coachman pulled up along the pavement just opposite the alley. A very elegant barouche was approaching from the other direction, rumbling slowly to a halt beside the tobacconist's. Cecilia thought the carriage vaguely familiar, but on a second glance, she could not place it.

Suddenly, the door of the coffee house was thrown open, spilling a shaft of lamplight into the street. A well-dressed man wearing a hat and cloak hastened forward, pulled open the carriage door, and without putting down the steps, helped a slender, elegantly dressed woman alight. As her feet touched the cobblestones, she tipped back her head and laughed, letting her hands slide lingeringly down the man's chest. This woman, too, was heavily veiled.

The man waved the barouche away, and then, to Cecilia's shock, he escorted the laughing lady into Mother Derbin's. Cecilia recognized at once that the woman was no prostitute. But perhaps an expensive courtesan? Though why a man—a man who looked suspiciously like a gentleman—would bring his high-flyer to such a place escaped Cecilia.

On the bench beside her, David made a faintly disdainful gesture. Cecilia turned to stare at him. "Why do they go into such a place together?"

David looked as if he'd anticipated her curiosity. "A liaison, no doubt," he explained with an awkward shrug. "The lady is probably married. There are many amongst the *ton* who enjoy illicit pleasures, and God only knows what else. They find it wickedly titillating to indulge themselves in such a neighborhood, particularly where there is little fear of recognition."

Cecilia found herself both intrigued and horrified by his explanation. She had begun to imagine herself well informed, almost sophisticated, but Etta's tutelage had never extended to this. Clearly, however, David knew what he was talking about. No doubt he had visited just such places himself, and left many a lady *illicitly pleasured*. The thought made her acutely uncomfortable.

Just then, another carriage rolled up, this time a hired hackney. A man stepped out, tossed the driver a coin, and strolled lazily toward Mother Derbin's. He moved with the grace of youth and pushed open the door with an easy familiarity. On the seat beside her, she heard David's sharp intake of breath. To her surprise, he quickly withdrew a slender notebook from his coat pocket and jotted down the hackney's plate number.

It was time to spring into action. She hoped David could be persuaded. Urgently, Cecilia leaned forward to draw the curtains wide. David's free hand lashed out, snaring hers and jerking it away from the window. "Damn it, Cecilia, do you wish to be seen?"

Cecilia avoided the question. "That man—did you know him?"

David sighed and snapped the notebook shut. "For a moment, I thought so. But . . . no. I fancy I was mistaken." He regarded her sardonically. "A product of my overactive imagination, no doubt. I have been much troubled by it of late."

Cecilia avoided that remark as well. "David," she whispered persuasively. "I think we should go *in.*"

"Oh, God." David let his head fall forward into one hand. "Now I'm clairvoyant."

Plaintively, she leaned nearer, whispering into his

hair. "But David, you have been inside such places before, have you not? How bad can it be?"

David merely lifted his head to stare at her. A quirking smile teased at one corner of his mouth.

Eagerly, Cecilia continued. "Look, I am heavily veiled. No one shall see me. Can we not simply go in and pretend to—well, to do whatever it is that people do in such places?"

At that, David burst into soft laughter, lifting his brows lecherously. "Oh, be still my heart!" he whispered, leaning forward and abruptly yanking her into his arms. "It seems my fantasies are about to come true! Let us proceed apace to Curzon Street."

In mock severity, Cecilia socked him over the head with her reticule, but David did not stop laughing. "Oh, be serious!" she hissed, sliding back onto her seat. "I merely wish to go inside just long enough to look around. Perhaps we shall even meet someone who will know about the murdered girls."

"Good Lord, Cecilia!" he exclaimed, collapsing back against the squabs. "They aren't having a bloody tea party in there! One does not simply wander about, nibbling on cucumber sandwiches and chatting. Indeed, I really think you have no notion of what such places are all about—which is precisely as it should be."

"But I cannot help it!" she wheedled, crushing her reticule dejectedly into her lap. "I am perishing of curiosity."

"Ah!" he softly exclaimed, stroking a finger beneath her chin. "I begin to comprehend! Then let me take you back to the privacy of my home, my sweet. If it's your curiosity you want slaked, I promise to leave you well satisfied. But there, darling. Not here."

His soft, wicked words flowed over her, sending a tremor of sensual awareness down her spine. *He still wanted her!* Why—and as what—she did not know, but just now, it scarcely mattered.

Slowly, she lifted her eyes to his, watching as the flickering light of the carriage lamp caressed his sinfully perfect features. For a moment, she let her gaze feast upon his dark, unfathomable eyes and then his full, almost feminine mouth. Good heavens, but she was sorely tempted.

Still, there had been the faintest hint of surrender in his tone, and Cecilia wanted desperately to get inside Mother Derbin's house. "I think it would be wicked fun to go inside," she insisted, looking up at him from beneath lashes which were, she hoped, seductively lowered. "And of course, I should feel ever so much safer going with you than with Etta."

That got his attention. All semblance of tenderness fled as David seized her by both shoulders and jerked her toward him with such fervor her bonnet slithered over one eye. "By God, Cecilia, if you so much as dare to poke a toe over that threshold—!"

Abruptly, he let his hands drop away. "But you won't listen, will you?" he said bitterly. "Not even if I get down on my knees and beg. And if I do not take you, I do not doubt for one moment that you will come back with that ramshackle maid of yours."

Then, with slow, resigned motions, David leaned forward, withdrew a heavy pistol from its carriage holder, and dropped it into a deep pocket inside his greatcoat. Cecilia felt excitement coursing through her.

As if he sensed it, his head jerked about. "You'll pull that veil all the way down, and keep it down," he harshly demanded. "And don't speak one blasted word, do you hear me? This must be your lucky day, and I must be insane. But I'd best have a look at that

man who just went in, and if I leave you here, you'll
dog my every step."

After ordering his coachman and footmen to keep
watch, David took Cecilia by the hand and dragged her
across Black Horse Lane and into the street beyond.
Together, they pushed through the front door, finding
themselves in a narrow, dimly lit vestibule. A short,
broad-shouldered man stepped forward, but in the
poor light, Cecilia could not make out his face very well.

David asked to see Mrs. Derbin, and with a grunt
of acquiescence, the man motioned them through the
vestibule and into a large drawing room. Inside, comfortable chairs and curving chaises were clustered
about tea tables, and each sitting area was sheltered
by an artful arrangement of potted palms—fake, by
the look of them. But clearly, the room's clever com-
position was meant to ensure an element of privacy.

The room was almost empty. To Cecilia's left, a
buxom woman in a yellow satin dress was speaking
plaintively to a man who stood cloaked in the shadows. In the rear, two men lounged, wine glasses in
hand, as they watched a slender blonde drape her as-
sets over the curving back of a red satin settee.

Apparently coming to some agreement, the two
men rose, one of them throwing an arm about the
blonde. Together, the trio left through a heavily
draped door in the back of the room. Cecilia was
aghast at the implication. Heat rose to her cheeks,
and she was deeply grateful for the privacy of her veil.

At once, the woman in yellow turned around and
came toward them, her hands outstretched in greeting. She paused, eyeing David's length. "My lord," she
said, her voice dark and husky. "I am indeed honored."

David did not recognize the woman who approached him. Unfortunately, it was clear that she

knew him. And Cecilia realized it, too, for her hand tightened spasmodically about his arm.

Oh, hell. But what had he—and what had *she*—expected? As Cecilia had so boldly said, he'd been in such places before. Indeed, he had paved his own road to hell by strolling in and out of them. Reluctantly, he strolled in a little further.

"Good afternoon," he said, sounding far more calm than he felt. "My lady has expressed an interest in discovering what you can provide in the way of . . . *entertainment.*"

Mrs. Derbin smiled wolfishly. "Well, my lord, we are not so elaborate as the establishments you are doubtless accustomed to," she whispered. "But I daresay we can provide ample accommodation for the lady's whims. I assume you've come for a partner? I have many young girls—"

"No girls," interjected David firmly. "And no other women."

Fleetingly, Mrs. Derbin looked confused. But quickly, she recovered, flicking an appraising glance at Cecilia. Clearly, she was eager to please her well-born customers. Then a knowing gleam lit her eyes.

"Perhaps you'd be better pleased with a strapping young man?" she suggested, glancing over her shoulder at the fellow she'd left in the shadows. "Normally, that is not our stock in trade, but perhaps this gentleman will deign to join you? The particular entertainment he seeks is, alas, no longer available." She inclined her head suggestively.

Apparently sensing that he was under discussion, the man stepped forward, catching a flash of muted candlelight across his face. David reeled with shock, then shame, finishing with a searing curiosity.

It really was him! *Bentham Rutledge.* Again.

But this time, he did not look so carelessly amiable. Indeed, words could not possibly have described the twisted look upon his face. Before David could refuse and drag Cecilia away, Rutledge's mouth curled mockingly.

Stiffly, he bowed to Cecilia, letting his dark eyes drift hotly over her. "Your taste in women is known to be exquisite, my lord," he said, his voice lethally soft. "But I think not tonight. I await your pleasure, Mrs. Derbin, for our business is not yet concluded to my satisfaction." He turned, inclining his head toward David. "And as to you, my lord, it would seem I can anticipate seeing you again quite soon." And with that, Rutledge returned to the shadows.

Mrs. Derbin looked distinctly uncomfortable. Whatever was going on here, David now had little doubt that Rutledge was in it up to his neck.

Suddenly, Cecilia spoke. "Do you know, darling, I've changed my mind," she said, her voice deep, throaty, and cleverly disguised. Then she turned to Mrs. Derbin. "Do send us that extra girl. But please, let us have a more private place at once."

"But of course," said the hostess smoothly. Immediately, she left the room and entered the vestibule to speak to the man who'd let them in. As soon as she was out of earshot, David wheeled on Cecilia, incredulous. "What the hell do you think you're doing?" he whispered.

Cecilia's eyes flashed impatiently. "But we have learned nothing yet! Nothing at all which helps us!"

David barely resisted the urge to shake her until her teeth rattled. "You, madam, may have learned nothing. But I have learned that you are daft. Moreover, I've seen what I came to see, and I'm ready to get out."

Unfortunately, he could say nothing further, for

Mrs. Derbin was returning. In her hand, she held a key. "Angeline will not disappoint, my lord," she whispered, sliding the key through her fingers with a slow, suggestive motion. "You may go up to room number seven at your leisure, and she will join you there."

She pressed her fingers into his hand, and reluctantly, David took the key, closing his fist about it, letting it dig deep into his flesh. By God, Cecilia was going to pay for this one. He had half a mind to haul her upstairs and spank her soundly, or tie her to the bedposts and tease her till she begged, or otherwise avail himself of whatever perversion room number seven afforded. Surely, there would be many, and a rude education was precisely what Cecilia deserved for disobeying an order which had been solely designed to protect her.

Ruthlessly, he dragged her upstairs. The room was the last on their right. Along the way, Cecilia stared up and down the dimly lit corridors. The air was filled with a cloying scent and the muted sounds of masculine laughter.

Along the passageway, vulgar paintings adorned the walls, and explicit plaster statues were tucked into niches throughout. Beneath a flickering wall sconce, a recumbent statue of some pseudo-Grecian god was being enthusiastically fellated by a water nymph on her knees. As he dragged her past it, Cecilia craned her head halfway around to stare.

Then it got worse. In an alcove by the door of number seven, a hoofed-and-horned statue of Pan had managed to bend a scantily clad shepherdess rather artfully over a rock and was impaling her crudely from the rear.

Cecilia jerked to a halt. "Good heavens, is that—" She bent a little closer, peering at the woman's white plaster buttocks. "Is that s-sodomy?" she finally managed.

David wanted to sink through the floor in mortifi-
cation. "Not quite," he hissed, dragging her away by
the arm. "Sodomy is something rather different—and
don't *even* ask!"

By the time he unlocked the door, the room had already begun to feel like a sanctuary. Roughly, he
shoved open the door and dragged Cecilia inside. In
the hearth, a pile of coal blazed hotly, clearly kindled
in anticipation of a customer. Unfortunately, the heat
only managed to heighten the stale smell of sex and
the sweet, cloying scent which had pervaded the corridors. At once, David lifted Cecilia's cloak from her
shoulders and slid out of his greatcoat. As there were
no chairs, he draped them across the footboard.

By West End standards, the room was abominably
tasteless. In the center sat a sagging four-poster bed
with the obligatory leather strappings tied to the bedposts. Covering it was a red velvet spread slashed
with black. A selection of black leather whips was
mounted on one wall, but for the more faint of heart,
red silk ropes were twined about their handles. In the
corner stood a crooked wicker screen, and behind it
sat a close-stool and a washstand. David felt a shudder run through him. Yes, a man would definitely
want a wash upon leaving a place like this.

Cecilia was already staring around the room, her
mouth agape. David could only pray that she did not
begin rifling through the armoire. God only knew
what Mother Derbin kept hidden there, and he was
not in the mood to answer any more of Cecilia's probing questions. Good Lord, the woman was going to
try his fortitude in the worst sort of way.

Just then, a light knock sounded at the door, and a
voluptuous girl with dark hair entered. "Well, good
evenin', ducks," she announced the moment her eyes

lit upon David. Then she saw Cecilia, and her expression faded a bit. "Wot's yer pleasure?"

David strolled slowly forward. "That's an impressive accent you've got there," he said dryly, "for a girl named Angeline."

Angeline screwed up her mouth and narrowed one eye. "Mother Derbin says it's good for business," she retorted. "Now, wot's your pleasure? You want ter watch me awhile with her?" she asked softly, inclining her head toward Cecilia. "Or would you be man enough ter do us both?"

David smiled tightly. "I daresay I could manage, though I don't make a habit of it," he answered lightly.

Beneath the black veil, Cecilia gasped in outrage. Before he could say anything further, she darted forward and produced a banknote from her reticule. "All we want," she hastily interjected, "is to ask you some questions."

Angeline drew back in alarm, but her eyes never left the banknote. "Yeah? And o' wot sort?" she asked.

"We're searching for information about three girls who used to work here," Cecilia explained.

"Three—!" Angeline eyed David up and down again. "G'orn!"

Impatiently, Cecilia shook her head while David tried not to laugh. "Not like that," Cecilia insisted. "Two sisters, Mary and Kathleen O'Gavin, and a friend of theirs, Meg McNamara. Did you know them?"

Uncertainly, Angeline licked her lips. "No—" She stopped, then eyed the banknote once again. "Might 'ave 'eard a little something about 'em, though. But they don't work 'ere n'more."

David stepped forward, crossing his arms over his chest. "What we'd really like to know," he said softly, "is why they left. Was there some sort of unpleasantness? Are you women being abused? Made to do something you don't wish to do?"

Angeline seemed to take umbrage at his implication. "Now, look 'ere, mate—I likes me job just fine. And as to whatever we get, why, we get paid well enough ter take it, I'd say."

David smiled crookedly. "I see," he said quietly. "I'm glad you find satisfaction in your chosen career, but pardon me if I assume that the other three ladies did not. They fled this place in the middle of the night, and I should like very much to know why."

"Well, they weren't roughed up by no customer, if that's wot yer sayin'," Angeline warned. "Like as not, they'd all still be here, if it weren't for Meg and Mary a-pokin' their nose where it had no business."

"What do you mean?" asked Cecilia. Stubbornly, Angeline dropped her eyes to the floor.

In response, Cecilia boldly rattled the banknote. No withering violet, his Cecilia. "Madam," she continued quite ruthlessly, "this is more than you'll earn in a month. And all we want for it is information. You tell us what you know, and we'll go happily back downstairs and tell Mother Derbin what a stellar performance you've given us."

Angeline looked up, shifting her gaze from Cecilia to David and back again. "It all happened afore I got here," she reluctantly began. "But I heard as how they went sneakin' down in'ter the cellars to give away a little tickle-tail to a couple o' Frog sailors they'd got a soft spot for. Everybody knows you don't do *that* around here."

Cecilia frowned. "You mean—do it with a *Frenchman?*"

Angeline let out a loud snort. "Ol' Derbin don't care if yer does it with a lamppost, long as somebody's payin'. But them cellars, now—we particular ain't ter go down there."

Abruptly, David stepped forward. "Why not?" he demanded.

The prostitute shot him a withering glance. "Have yerself a guess. We're sittin' pretty amongst 'alf the dockyards in London. But me—" Angeline paused to shake her head violently. "I don't need ter know nuffin' about it."

"Does Mrs. Derbin know what goes on in the cellars?" asked David pointedly. "Or is there someone else involved?"

Again, she shrugged. "There's a Mr. Smith what comes weekly to collect the rent. She's afraid o' him. And he's got a key to the cellars. That's all I know."

Mr. Smith? David rolled his eyes. "This Mr. Smith, is he a young coxcomb of a fellow with black hair and brown eyes?"

Angeline laughed, a harsh, brittle sound. "Not hardly. I've given 'im a tumble or two, and he's a big buck of a man. A nasty piece of work, too. Likes it rough, yer knows wot I mean? But young he ain't."

It was clear they had learned all that the prostitute was willing to tell. Cecilia passed her the money. "Angeline," she said, her voice suddenly softening. "If ever there comes a time when you are no longer happy in this work, I hope you know that there are places you can go."

Sarcastically, Angeline snorted. "Yeah, like a bleedin' workhouse? Or one of them Methody-missions?" Slowly, she shook her head. "Not in this lifetime, ducks. I'll take me chances with the Mr. Smiths o' this world."

Clearly, Angeline knew her own mind. Deep in thought, David slid his fingers through his hair. "Look here, Angeline," he said slowly. "This is what I want you to do. Go back to your room, or to someplace you can hide for a while. When you hear the bells at St. George's toll six, return to this room and make it appear as if it has been used."

"Sure," the prostitute agreed, turning to go.

Suddenly, David held up a staying hand. Good God, what an idiot he'd been! "One more thing—have we any peepholes in this room?"

"Peepholes!" Cecilia said, horrified.

Angeline tossed her a scornful glance, then jerked her head toward the armoire. "On the left side of that clothes cupboard, but there ain't nobody wot's paid to watch ternight." And then the prostitute shoved Cecilia's banknote into her bosom, gave it a little shake, and strolled out the door.

At once, David moved to the wall, easily locating the peep. Drawing out his handkerchief, he wadded up the corner and stuffed it inside the hole.

"David?" asked Cecilia uncertainly. "Wh-why are there holes in the walls?"

Another question. Damned if she wasn't full of them. Reluctantly, he turned away from the armoire. "Because there are a great many perverted people in this world, my dear," he said roughly. "And places like this cater to them. Do you understand now why I did not want you here?"

At that, Cecilia lost a little of her color, and, unable to restrain himself, David went to her, gathering her into his arms. Cecilia did not resist, and only then did he truly appreciate the toll which her bold act with Angeline had taken. Cecilia could be daring, but it was not, precisely, her nature to be so. In this case, no doubt she'd done what she thought necessary. But now, in his arms, she trembled.

Just then, Cecilia drew a long, shuddering breath

against his shirtfront and let her hands—those perfect, sweet hands—slide up his back. The fact that she wore gloves, and that his bare skin was covered by three layers of Bond Street tailoring, in no way mitigated the pleasure which coursed through him. And her next words were not helpful.

"David," she said quietly, "while we wait, will you make love to me?"

"No." He said the word firmly and swiftly, his eyes taking in the tawdry room, the wall hung with whips and ropes.

Cecilia realized at once what David was thinking. He thought her too pure, too innocent. He still saw her as Lord Walrafen's virginal wife, not as she was: a woman with needs and desires. A woman who was willing—no, eager—to learn how to give and receive physical pleasure. And since David's sexual appetites were perhaps too sophisticated to be pleased by anyone's virginal wife, Cecilia would have to become the sort of woman who could hold his interest long-term. And she could do it.

Steadily, she held his gaze, willing herself to stop shaking. "Don't treat me as if I were a child, David," she said quietly. "If last night was enough for you, then say so. But if not, don't make me play the innocent. I'm not. Not in any way that matters."

David gave a soft, exasperated hiss from between his teeth. "I don't know what you're talking about," he insisted.

"I wish us to be lovers," she clarified. "There. I have said it. Now, you may accept my offer, or you may laugh in my face as you choose. All I ask is that if you accept, you give me the courtesy of your fidelity until you tire of me."

"Oh?" David's expression darkened, and his mouth

turned up into a sneer. "And where shall we conduct this illicit liaison?" he demanded, dropping his hands and turning away from her. "Am I to come to your home and strut about as if I had paid for it? As if I had paid for *you?*

Despite his bitter tone, it was at base a reasonable question. Cecilia had never considered the how and where of her offer. Yes, she was a widow, and entitled to some moral latitude. Still, the thought of entertaining him in her home gave her pause. And David . . . well, David lived with his mother and sister. That was worse.

At least her servants were loyal and discreet. But suddenly, she realized that if David could not be persuaded to wed her, she would likely never marry again. Therefore, she did not have a pristine reputation to maintain. "Yes," she said abruptly.

He spun about on one heel and looked at her.

"Yes, you will come to my home," Cecilia firmly clarified. "I would be in no way ashamed to have my association with you known."

In the blink of an eye, he had closed the distance between them. "Perhaps you should be, you fool," he growled, taking her by the shoulders and giving her a good, swift shake. It was a response which was becoming increasingly familiar.

"I've asked you to be my lover. There's no shame in that."

"Is that what we are, Cecilia?" he whispered. "Are we lovers? And if so, for how long?"

"I think I'm waiting for you tell me," Cecilia softly replied.

At once, David seemed to collapse inwardly, his shoulders sagging and his eyes closing. To her shock, he drew her into his arms and onto the tawdry bed. Together, they tumbled onto it. David rolled to her side, opened his eyes, and levered himself up on to one elbow.

But other than sliding one hand about her waist, he made no effort to touch her. For long moments, he merely held her, studying her face, her hair, his arm where it encircled the turn of her waist.

"Do you not wish for something more out of life than a lover, Cecilia?" he finally asked, his voice infinitely weary. "And why a rogue like me? You should have children. Beautiful blond babies." Gently, he skimmed the palm of his hand down her belly and around her hip. "If ever a body was made to bear children, my dear, it is yours. You should marry again."

Cecilia knew that he spoke of another man, not himself. Clearly, the thought of anything serious between them had not crossed his mind. Or perhaps he had rejected such a notion. Perhaps the idea of being faithful to one woman was loathsome to him, no matter who the woman was. Men often were terrified by the very thought of love and commitment. Was that the source of the unease which she sensed behind David's façade?

But instinctively, she knew that if David should ever commit himself to a marriage, he would be committed for life. And by heaven, she meant to convince him. Seduce him. Tempt him. Beyond restraint, until she melted his reason and splintered his resistance. Somehow, she would become the one woman with whom fidelity would seem worth the sacrifice. The one woman with whom he could share himself—and his darkness.

But with David, a woman would be wise to move slowly. Still, there was no time like the present to get started. Tentatively, she reached up and slid her fingers through the heavy curtain of hair which had fallen forward to shadow his face. Then, unable to resist, she slid the ball of her thumb across his full lower lip. At once, his eyes fell shut and he softly kissed her finger.

"Kiss *me*, David," she whispered. "Kiss my mouth, as you did last night."

"Not here," he rasped, nuzzling his lips against the palm of her hand.

"Yes, here," she insisted, rising up to take his mouth.

At first, David indulged her, dipping his head and allowing hers to fall back against the bed. Lightly, his lips pushed against hers, molding warmly over her mouth. But when Cecilia tried to deepen the kiss, opening beneath him and sliding her tongue across his lower lip, David drew away.

"Do not push me, Cecilia," he said, opening his eyes. "And don't try that trick of accusing me of not wanting you. I do, and you know it. But this place . . . it disgusts me. Besides, you are merely trying to avoid a serious conversation."

"And what conversation would that be?"

David rolled to her side and dragged one arm across his eyes. "I believe we were speaking of your unborn children," he said quietly. "And in my heart, I was praying to God one isn't already in the making."

Cecilia shifted onto one elbow and stared down at him. She had not missed the solemnity in his voice. She thought again of Etta's advice—advice she didn't want. In an attempt to forestall the blue devils, Cecilia let her hands trail playfully down his chest. "Oh, perhaps someday I will marry again," she admitted lightly. "If the perfect man ever asks. Because yes, I would very much like to have children. Lots of them."

On the bed beside her, it sounded as if David laughed, but the sound was muffled by the coat sleeve drawn over his face. "Lots of them? You sound very brave, Cecilia. How many would you like?"

"Oh, I don't know," Cecilia confessed, toying with the folds of his cravat. "Four or five? Does that sound a great many? I collect you have some experience with children. Your friend Lady Kildermore has five, does she not?"

David seemed to ignore her question, but at least he dragged his arm off his face. "And this man—this father of your children—he would have to be a pattern of rectitude, would he not?" he lightly responded. "A man of flawless breeding, with indisputable bloodlines."

"Why, of course," she said laughingly. "And let us add handsome, wealthy, and possessed of impeccable taste. Moreover, he would have to bow to my every whim, and shower me with expensive gifts. If you have an applicant for such a demanding position, I do hope that you will pass it along?"

On the bed beside her, David seemed to stiffen. "I don't," he said, his voice suddenly rough. "Make no mistake, Cecilia—I can suggest no one who will meet your needs."

At once, he rolled toward her until he looked her straight in the eyes. "I'll gratefully accept your offer to be your lover," he continued. "However, you must understand that when you are ready for your perfect man—when you are truly serious about it—then I think you will need to move on, my dear."

"I understand," she said quietly. "Perhaps—well, perhaps I understand more than you think."

"This is not a complicated situation, Cecilia," he interjected dryly. "And I am not a complicated man."

"Are you not?" she asked briskly. "How glad I am to hear it. Now—what must we do until six, David, if we cannot make love?"

Wryly, he grinned and draped one arm around her. "We will do what lovers really do much of the time, my dear," he responded, neatly jerking her hips into his. "We will sleep. I, for one, am a few hours short—and you know why."

"Oh—!" Cecilia's fingers flew to her mouth.

"What?" asked David suspiciously.

"My stocking!"

"Ah," moaned David, flopping onto his back. "You wish to have it back?"

Cecilia's eyes grew round and hopeful. "You have it?"

"An accident," he said swiftly. "It got . . . tangled in some of my clothes—my coat—in the drawing room."

Cecilia exhaled a low sigh of relief. "No, just throw it in the dustbin. But oh, David! You cannot imagine the dreadful morning I had. I imagined one of my staff had found it, and I was simply beside myself. And then! Oh! Jed and I went out for a ride, and who should I stumble across but Edmund Rowland."

"Edmund Rowland?" said David disgustedly. "I hope you were able to avoid that fatuous ass."

"No, not entirely," said Cecilia. "I had to stroll about with him for a few moments . . . and he did say something—something which I hope will not overly distress you."

David shifted his head to look at her. "Yes—?"

As usual, Cecilia felt herself blushing. "But you belong to Brooks's, do you not? Yes, of course, I know that you do. But perhaps you did not know that there was a wager? A very unpleasant one, I'm given to understand."

David gave a deep groan. "Oh, hell."

"You knew?"

"Yes, and Edmund Rowland was in the middle of that mischief, too, I daresay," insisted David grimly.

"He encouraged a couple of drunken louts to write it down in the betting book. Cecilia, I'm very sorry that you had to learn of it."

"David?" Her voice was very tentative. "What, precisely, does it say? Of course, I could not give Edmund the satisfaction of my asking for particulars."

Fleetingly, David felt relieved. "So you do not know."

But Cecilia's impatience was growing. "I said I did not. Do you mean to tell me? Or must I ask someone else?"

David felt like a trapped animal. With everything else he'd had on his mind, he'd somehow managed to forget Sir Lester's vile wager. Good God. He wished very desperately to get his hands on Edmund Rowland. At this moment, it would have taken very little effort to ring his skinny neck. But Cecilia was still waiting for her answer.

"As usual, you give me no choice, Cecilia," he complained. "Very well. It seems that Sir Lester Blake and Mr. Reed found it humorous that I had been entrapped into managing the mission. It may surprise you to know that there are some people who still delight in the fact that you once jilted me, and apparently, it is common knowledge that you worked with Cole. But I can assure you that I did not know it. Not, at least, until that night."

Cecilia was surprised. "Did you not?"

David shook his head. "No, but my so-called friends wasted no time in telling me. And even less in making bets on how long it would take me to bed you."

"Oh!" said Cecilia softly. "And . . . precisely how long did they give you?"

David cleared his throat uncomfortably. "I believe it was until May Day. Thereabouts."

"Well, they possess a remarkable underappreciation for your skills, do they not?" she mused. "And the amount of the wager was—?"

"Er—fifty guineas."

"And quite a lot of money, too!" Abruptly, Cecilia spun to a seated position. "I'm glad I didn't come cheaply. And now that you've had your wicked way with me, there's nothing else for it, is there? You'd best pay up."

David stared up at her in amazement. "Cecilia, that's not how it works. If two drunken idiots choose to make a wager on something which is none of their business—"

"Oh, gentlemen make a habit of that," Cecilia interjected with surprising good cheer.

"—then I'm under no obligation to help them settle it," he finished. "What would you have me do, confess over a game of loo in the card room?"

Cecilia grinned. "You, sir, may do as you wish. But perhaps I meant *pay up* in a different context altogether?"

David was saved from further interrogation by the low, mournful tones of St. George's bell tower. It was six o'clock. Abruptly, he sat up and grabbed Cecilia by the hand. He certainly had no wish to be there when Angeline returned to muss up the room.

11

In which Delacourt leaps out of the Frying Pan

*I*t took David but a few moments to effect a smooth escape from Mother Derbin's. On his way out the door, he slipped the buxom bawd an ungodly sum of money, whispered how pleased he'd been with Angeline's performance, and assured her—quite truthfully—that he would be back. Then he shoved Cecilia out of the house and into the street.

Outside, dusk was swiftly falling. The side lane was now swathed in darkness. Ahead, at the intersection of Black Horse Lane, David watched carefully as a brewer's dray went rumbling past. Another hackney approached from the opposite direction. The hackney driver tapped his hat brim with his whip, and both carriages clattered on into the night. The coast was clear.

Still clutching Cecilia by the arm, David stepped into the main thoroughfare. Most of the shops had long since closed, but a public house a few yards along the lane was doing a brisk business, and through the narrow windows of the coffee house, David could see that it, too, was crowded. To his relief, his coachman and footmen were waiting at the corner as instructed.

Efficiently, he bundled Cecilia into the carriage and motioned for his footman. "Hand me a lamp, Strickham," he said quietly. "And then keep an eye on the lady while I have a little stroll."

At once, Cecilia stuck her head out the door. "David?" she said sharply. "What do you mean to do?"

David quirked one brow and looked up at her. "Perhaps answer the call of nature—?"

Cecilia looked skeptical. "Then go behind that stack of barrels further down the pavement," she hissed, wrinkling her nose. "Half of Black Horse Lane already has."

David feigned embarrassment. "My dear, you shock me. I'm very shy."

"And so you want a lamp for the job, do you?" she returned. "And I daresay you mean to take it down that alley behind Derbin's brothel. A very private place indeed."

Caught out, David grinned. "Yes, I want to see if there is a rear entrance into the cellars," he agreed as Strickham passed him the lamp. "Or perhaps in back of the tobacconist next door. These places are built like rabbit warrens, half of them connected." He moved as if to shut the door.

Swiftly, Cecilia's gloved hand thrust forward to stay it. "But you cannot go alone," she whispered, her asperity slipping. "It mightn't be safe."

"I hope, my dear, that you do not mean to guard me," David murmured, hefting the lantern to adjust the flame. "My masculinity is already a tenuous thing. I shudder to think what impairment your lack of faith could engender."

Cecilia flopped back onto the carriage seat, stubbornly throwing her arms over her chest. "Well, someone should guard you, Your Royal Insolence," she complained bitterly. "Will you take Strickham if I promise to stay here?"

In an effort to soothe her concern, David took on a teasing tone. "My dear, do you value my safety so greatly that you would forgo an opportunity to fling yourself into the jaws of danger? I'm truly touched."

"Oh, go ahead and make a jest of me," she retorted, her words finally catching on a sincere sob. "I hope that bawd's henchman knocks you over the sconce and pitches you onto the next freighter to Calcutta!"

She was more than concerned. She was truly frightened. David *was* touched. Feeling like a cur once again, he passed the lantern back to his footman and crawled halfway into the carriage. With a brush of his arm, he lifted her veil and swiftly kissed her. "I'm sorry, minx. You're right, of course. Strickham will come along."

And then, he was gone, setting back off in the direction from which they had just come, with his footman on his heels. Cecilia waited impatiently in the lamplit carriage. It seemed an eternity before she spotted the faint hint of lamplight trickling back out of the alleyway. Mere seconds later, both men appeared in the street.

Apparently unseen, they strolled toward the carriage as if they really had done nothing more interesting than water the alley. David passed the lamp to his footman and climbed inside.

Throwing up her veil, Cecilia leaned forward. "Well?"

"It's there," David responded. "And there's a well-worn path leading to the steps. That—and the fact that the door has three locks on it—could make a fellow suspicious."

Clearly relieved, Cecilia exhaled and collapsed

against the velvet squabs. "What do we do now?" she asked, screwing one fist sleepily into her left eye.

David shook his head. "Nothing, Cecilia. *We* do nothing. I shall tell de Rohan—though how the devil I'm to explain our little exploit tonight is beyond me." His voice was resigned. "I daresay he'll be left with a very poor impression of my sexual preferences."

At that remark, Cecilia fell silent, and he was reminded yet again that their little escapade had probably left her more shaken than she wished to admit. In a few moments, they passed from Black Horse Lane and onto the Ratcliffe Highway. As if she were exhausted, Cecilia let her head tilt back and her eyes drop shut.

Entranced, David studied her. She was beautiful, his drowsy kitten. Beneath her left eye, there was the tiniest mole, a dark brown speck against her flawless skin. It had always intrigued him, that tiny dot, and now that he could study it at his leisure, it seemed to David the greatest of luxuries.

Traffic thinned, the carriage sped up, and still Cecilia did not wake. After the turbulence of his afternoon, David was glad to settle back and feast his eyes upon her. The frothy black netting of her veil lent a beautiful contrast to Cecilia's porcelain skin, not to mention the flame-gold curls which peeped from beneath her bonnet. And her mouth. He loved it, for it was sweet, full, and bow-shaped, like a cupid's. And he loved her nose, with its little tip-tilted end.

Cecilia's lashes were long, surprisingly dark, while her cheeks were always lit with a shade of peach or pink, or oftentimes bright, burning red. Cecilia's every emotion showed in her face, and he loved that, too. It was, he thought, a form of honesty. Most women of his acquaintance were experts at deception, but a beautiful blush could not be feigned. It made Cecilia perfect.

And so what the devil was he to do with her?

He deeply disapproved of this idea of hers, this understanding that they would conduct an affair—and apparently not a particularly discreet one—continuing it indefinitely. Well, perhaps he did not disapprove stridently enough to refuse her. Good God, could any mortal be man enough for that task? Assuredly, he was not.

And yet, she had not denied her intent to remarry. She wanted children. Four or five, she had said. And of course, she wished them to have impeccable bloodlines. Oh, he had not missed the teasing tone in which she'd responded to his questions, but that did not alter the essential truth—and wisdom—of her answers.

David had not thought a great deal about children until Henry, Jonet's first husband, had died suddenly, leaving her a young widow with two little boys. Stuart and Robin had charmed him, yes. But when Jonet's little girls had come along, he'd been a lost man. There was something about baby girls—the way they smelled, the way they cooed, the way they would clutch at his finger with their little fists and look at him as if he'd hung the moon—oh, yes—*something* about them appealed to his deepest male instincts. It engendered in him an overwhelming desire to touch, cosset, and cuddle. An almost bone-deep need to protect.

And it had hurt.

Across the length of the carriage, he studied Cecilia, pale and serene by the light of the lamp. Yes, she would make an admirable mother. Like Jonet, she would be as a tigress to her children, watchfully guarding, patiently teaching. He wanted. Oh, God, how he wanted.

Was it possible? Certainly, the thought had been in his mind, buried deep beneath a heap of guilt and a mountain of pride, since the moment he'd first seen

Cecilia Markham-Sands. Still, David did not believe
in love at first sight. He was not, by his nature, a romantic man. But he did believe that kindred souls
knew one another. And that with the right person, a
perfect sense of oneness could be achieved. He believed it, for he had seen it happen to his sister. And
he had seen it change her life.

Could he have that with Cecilia? Perhaps. Damn it,
he needed to think! What choice did he have? This affair was not going to work, no matter how much he
loved her. Indeed, it would not work *because* he loved
her. He had not the heart to sully her name by her association with him. It did not matter that she had
more or less granted permission to do precisely that.
Even a marriage would not alter the fact that he was
generally thought a roué and a blackguard and an all-
around vengeful, heartless bastard.

Because it was true. All of it. Or had been—until he
had landed in the middle of the Daughters of
Nazareth Society. And within a matter of days, his
rage and his guilt and his burning belief that he had
somehow been wronged by fate had faded in comparison to what he'd seen there.

Then there had been Cecilia. And the constant, chaf-
ing emotions he felt for her. He couldn't even tell her
the truth about why he'd stolen her bloody stocking—
and yet, he was supposed to tell her the truth about his
life? That he was not, after all, the Viscount Delacourt?

But with Cecilia, that would not be the hard part.
She was too honest, too egalitarian. He understood
that now. Unlike most women, he could trust her. Even
if she should refuse him, even if she should be horrified
by it all, she would not run up and down Piccadilly
whispering the news in every passerby's ear, until someone who mattered—one of his enemies—got wind of it.

No, the hard part would be reliving his honorable mother's shame. And letting down—*completely* down—the defenses he'd built about his heart. And asking for the privilege of siring those four or five children she wanted, while implying by that very question that he thought himself good enough to do so. And admitting, after all these long and lonely years, that it had been *his* naïveté, not hers, which had been so violently stripped away at Newmarket on that long-ago summer's day.

It was too much. Too fast. He had not the strength.

"David?" Cecilia's drowsy voice cut through the fog of his introspection. "Where are we going?"

Suddenly, it occurred to him that he did not know. He had merely ordered his coachman to drive on, with no thought to where they were headed. Straight toward a catastrophic collision, he feared. But Cecilia's question was more literal than that.

"To my house," he said, with far more decisiveness than he felt. "We're going to Curzon Street for dinner . . . and for whatever follows."

For the first time that evening, Cecilia looked mildly distressed. "But surely you don't take your mistresses there? I mean, your mother . . . ?"

His emotions already on edge, David felt his temper spike. "You are *not* my mistress," he said harshly. "And it would be perfectly permissible for my mother to entertain you in her home. Indeed, she would account it a great honor."

Cecilia managed a weak smile. "But—?"

She had heard the uncertainty in his voice. She knew him too well. David let the scowl slip from his face. "But as it happens, I am a man unencumbered by female relations at present," he said more softly. "Mother has gone to attend Lady Kildermore's confinement. She has taken Charlotte and sent most of the servants on holiday."

"Oh," said Cecilia, her voice a little mystified. "They are friends?"

"The very best of friends," he clarified.

Again, Cecilia shifted uncomfortably on the carriage seat. "David," she tentatively began. "May I ask a question that is none of my business?"

David tried to sound lighthearted. "By all means, my dear. I should be afraid to stop you."

Refusing to hold his gaze, Cecilia began to twine the cords of her reticule nervously in her fingers. "Was your mother dreadfully disappointed when you did not marry Lady Kildermore?" she asked uncertainly. "After all, despite your being younger, she is rich, and accounted a great beauty."

Well. How to answer that one?

"No," he said slowly. "We are friends, all of us, but there was never any question of our marrying. Indeed, I wouldn't have her. Nor she me, I do not doubt. We are exactly alike in both character and temperament—"

Abruptly, he broke off, all too aware that he had almost revealed too much of himself. He drew a deep breath. "Cecilia, I do not want to talk about Jonet," he said on a sigh. "What I want is to make love to you. Badly. Will you put down your veils, come home with me, and let me take you to bed?" Across the narrow carriage, he held out his hand.

Slipping her fingers into his, she smiled. "I do not need these veils."

David frowned. "I think I must insist, Cecilia," he said slowly. "I am not perfectly ready to commit us to this life of scandal you so heedlessly wish to rush into."

Cecilia looked at him, confused. "Widows take lovers. Indeed, it is often done."

"Not by you," he said succinctly.

"As you wish, my lord." With a fluid, elegant gesture, Cecilia lifted both her hands and drew down the froth of black netting about her face. "Kindly observe that in order to get what I want, I can occasionally be obedient."

Cecilia recognized at once that David's home in Curzon Street was the epitome of restrained elegance. And it was also, just as he had claimed, terribly short of staff. After a long wait, the second footman let them in, and as casually as if he did it every day, David ordered a light supper sent up to his bedchamber.

The footman did not so much as blink when he took Cecilia's cloak. David offered his arm and escorted her through his home. Cecilia was deeply intrigued. The first floor was made up of the dining room, the breakfast room, a blue and gold drawing room, and a beautiful, airy parlor with French windows which gave onto a tiny garden.

"My mother's morning room," he said softly, and then, he led her up the stairs. Two flights of them, to be precise. As if sensing her confusion, he explained. "My mother has retained the master's suite here. She is an invalid, and so it is easier for the servants, and for Charlotte. I have taken a room on the floor above. It suits me well enough, and as you see, the house is quite large."

Soon, he pushed open a heavy mahogany door, and Cecilia found herself inside a startlingly austere room. David's bedchamber was well but sparsely furnished in shades of brown and ivory. In the center of the room sat a massive bed without hangings or canopies of any sort. To the right, in front of the hearth, was a small sitting area with a table, a brown leather sofa, and a pair of sturdy armchairs. To the left of the bed sat a huge walnut armoire, a very masculine writing desk, and a doorway which obviously gave onto a dressing room.

In the hearth, a cheery fire burned, and on a small side table sat a decanter of what might have been port, along with several glasses. It was not a large room, but it was warm, unpretentious, and, best of all, it smelled of him.

Determined to behave as confidently as he had done, Cecilia folded back her veils and lifted off her bonnet, tossing it onto the bed. Then, suddenly, an uncomfortable thought struck her. "Your valet?"

David shrugged out of his coat and threw it across the settee. "Kemble insists upon having Thursday evenings off," he returned, his voice quiet and a little uncertain. And then, as if he'd made up his mind about something, he whipped decisively around, caught her hand, and pulled her against him in a motion so swift and fluid it made her breath catch.

His mouth came down on hers in a kiss which was rich with possibilities. Lazily, his lips met hers, molded to them, and slid languidly back and forth, as if he meant to take all night. At once, Cecilia decided she didn't mind if he did. Her heart began to hammer, and a fierce, primal need rose up inside her as she melted her body against his.

David's lips were perfect, warm and faintly sweet. He slid his mouth over hers again, lightly nibbling, gently sucking, and raking her skin with the dark shadow of his beard. Cecilia's nostrils flared, drawing in his warm, musky scent. He was tall, and Cecilia was very short, and so she rose up onto the toes of her slippers to meet him, realizing as she did that it should feel awkward to kiss a man in the privacy of his bedchamber. Certainly, Cecilia had never done so before.

But as if they'd done it just this way a thousand times, David kissed her thoroughly, opening his mouth over hers, teasing at her lower lip, then sliding his tongue sinuously inside, probing, tasting, and touching her very soul, it seemed.

And yet, it was not enough. Cecilia let her hands slide from his shoulders to his waist, and then to the buttons of his waistcoat. She felt David shudder under her touch as she slipped the first one free, and at once, he pulled incrementally away, without really lifting his lips from hers.

"*Dinner* . . ." he murmured against her mouth. "The servants will be bringing dinner."

As if he had commanded it, a sharp knock sounded. Tearing himself away from her, David went to the door, took one tray from the servant, and ordered the rest of it set down in the corridor. With a wink to Cecilia, he crossed the room and put down the tray on top of the table. A bottle of white wine and a bowl of fruit followed.

Cecilia raised her brows. "A well-trained staff," she remarked.

David's grin merely deepened. "Perhaps just an optimistic one," he muttered.

Cecilia wanted to ask what he meant, but at that moment, David picked up the wine bottle and poured it into glasses. He closed the distance between them, pressing a glass into her hand.

"To tonight, then," he said, softly holding her gaze.

Cecilia stared over the rim of her glass. "To tonight," she repeated.

David drained his glass, then stared at her. "I would dash this against the hearth, my dear," he said jokingly, "but it's Venetian. I hope you don't mind."

Laughing, Cecilia lowered her eyes to the bowl of

her glass. "You sound rather like my old Scottish auntie, my lord. So infinitely pragmatic."

To her surprise, he made no response, and it seemed to Cecilia that the silence grew deafening. What on earth had she said? Embarrassed, she drained her wine, which was perhaps unwise.

"If you have no valet," she said, setting her glass aside, "may I offer my services?"

At that, David finally laughed. "My lady, I can think of no greater luxury," he answered, sounding almost himself. "Will you accompany me to my dressing room?"

Following him, Cecilia passed by the foot of his bed, across the rather ordinary brown and gold carpet, and into the dressing room. If his bedchamber had been simply appointed, this room was quite the opposite. Cecilia found the difference telling indeed. While the simplicity of the inner man was hinted at by the stark bedroom, the public persona of Lord Delacourt was quite obviously crafted, layer upon layer, within the confines of his dressing room. It was almost as if the two chambers belonged to different men altogether.

In addition to several built-in wardrobes and two oak chests-on-chests, the dressing room contained a long brass hip-bath, a dressing table, bandboxes topped with a tower of hatboxes, a wooden frame filled with walking sticks, a tall jewel chest, and a walnut rack piled high with freshly laundered cravats. A large mahogany cheval glass provided the crowning touch of elegance to the quintessential gentleman's dressing room.

"I fear the stench of Mrs. Derbin's yet clings to me," David murmured, tilting the glass to better untie his cravat. "You'll forgive me, my dear, if I put on a dressing gown?"

Cecilia stepped boldly forward. "Permit me, sir," she said, lowering her eyes to his throat. And then,

with fingers that were surprisingly steady, Cecilia unfastened the intricate knot, unwrapped it from
around his collar, and let it slither onto the carpet at
David's feet.

On tiptoes, she rose up to kiss him lightly. "And
now," she mused, dropping her gaze, "the waistcoat, I
think." Swiftly, she unfastened the remaining buttons, pushed it off his shoulders, and let it fall.

David lifted one eyebrow. "This shall certainly
teach my man not to take Thursdays off," he remarked, eyeing the growing pile of clothing on the
floor. "Please, madam, have your way with me."

Emboldened, Cecilia knelt and pulled off his
shoes, hurling them into one corner. Then, she stood
and began to tug free his shirttails. Impassively,
David lifted his arms, his mouth quirking into a side-
ways grin. "You're impatient," he remarked.

But Cecilia was scarcely listening. His shirttails
now free of his trousers, she slid her hands beneath
the fine, starched cambric, skimming her palms
around his waist and then up his body, spearing her
fingers through the fine thatch of hair which covered
his chest. Cecilia could feel the male heat and
strength surge inside him, and it made her ache with
a strange new longing.

She knew David felt it, too. Under her touch, all
humor suddenly vanished, and he made a deep noise
in the back of his throat, a low, sweet sound of agony.
Empowered, Cecilia found his nipples, hard and erect
beneath her fingertips. For a moment, she let her fingers tease and play uncertainly, and then boldly, she
withdrew her hands to shove the cambric up his
chest. With another guttural sound, David stripped
the shirt over his head.

At once, Cecilia's mouth found his nipples. As he

had done with hers, Cecilia took one into her mouth, wondering if it would please him.

It did. "Ah, Cecilia!" he choked.

Lightly, she brushed her tongue across his flesh, and David's fingers seized her shoulders, digging into her skin. Again, he moaned hungrily, but Cecilia did not intend to rush. She wished to torment him. As he had tormented her.

Yes, this was her fantasy, and she meant to revel in it. Moreover, she would have been worse than a fool had she not sensed David's doubt about their relationship. It was remotely possible that this might be her only chance to savor, to learn. And Cecilia meant to do both.

As if drawn by an irresistible force, her fingers found the close of his gray wool trousers. Awkwardly, she fumbled, and to her relief, David's hands came down to slip loose the fastenings and shove the fabric free. His erection rose up between his hands, jutting from the white linen of his drawers, straight and strong and throbbing.

Strangely, the next step seemed perfectly natural, and it had nothing to do with the wicked paintings and statues she'd seen that afternoon. Unhesitatingly, Cecilia went to her knees in a crushing puddle of silk and petticoats. Greedily, her hands found him.

"Oh, God," David whispered, one hand sliding down the back of her hair, gently cradling her head. "Oh, my God. Cecilia. You can't. *I* can't . . ."

But he made no move to stop her.

Deeply, Cecilia drew him into the warmth of her mouth. To steady herself, she slid one hand around him to cradle his taut buttocks. It seemed perfectly natural. She felt powerful. Feminine.

Her mouth moved on him inexpertly at first, and then more confidently, as the stroking rhythm built. Still cradling the back of her head, David let his other

hand clutch at her shoulder, his fingers flexing spasmodically against her skin. "Oh . . . love, have mercy,"
he whispered, choking out the words. David's buttocks
had drawn tight, his pelvis had thrust urgently forward.

Suddenly, the fingers which had so gently cradled
her head fisted into her scalp, pulling the pins from her
hair. "Stop!" he hoarsely rasped. "Oh, God, stop . . . !"

Cecilia lifted her eyes to see that David's head was
thrown back, his mouth open in a silent, strangling
cry. In one swift, demanding motion, he hauled her up
and against his chest. Awkwardly, the heel of her shoe
caught in her skirts. Cecilia stumbled and fell against
him. The sound of rending silk tore through the room.

And then, Cecilia could never remember quite how,
David dragged her down and onto the floor. His elbow
struck the walnut rack, sending a pile of white cambric cascading, unnoticed, onto the carpet. Urgently,
wordlessly he shoved up her skirts, fumbling for the
slit in her drawers. David's need was primal and ruthless, his impatience palpable. With a primitive male
grunt, his fingers speared into her. At his touch, she
shuddered, opening for him. Wildly, his eyes flared.

Instinctively, Cecilia threw one leg about his waist
and pulled him down. Her slipper slid off and tumbled down his back. David entered her on one hard
stroke, roughly shoving himself inside, bracing himself over her with one hand. The tendons of his arm
and neck went taut as he thrust himself inside her
like a man possessed.

And then, his eyes squeezed shut. His head went
back, jerking repeatedly. "Ah, Cecilia . . . oh, *Jesus* . . ."
he rasped, furiously pumping himself inside her, driving her backward. Cecilia felt the top of her head
bump against something hard. Behind them, the rack
of walking sticks rocked wildly, then clattered against

the hip-bath and onto the floor. A hatbox tumbled, fell open, and rolled across the carpet. David shoved himself home one last time, then collapsed limply, trembling against her.

Cecilia pressed her lips to the damp skin of his throat. Convulsively, he swallowed. "Oh, love," he rasped. "I am so sorry. So sorry."

Soothingly, Cecilia stroked the palm of her hand down his back. "Why?" she whispered.

David buried his face in her hair, now tumbled into wild disarray. "I have never—" he panted. "Oh, God—*never* lost myself so dishonorably."

Cecilia brushed her lips across the base of his throat. "I think I'm flattered."

Clumsily, David lifted himself up, staring down into her face for a long moment. "I don't know what's wrong with me, Cecilia," he finally confessed, his breathing still ragged. "I apparently cannot touch you without losing control. Perhaps . . . well, perhaps it really is old age. I was once accounted quite skilled at this."

Cecilia grinned. "Oh, David, you're still *quite skilled.*"

With a grunt of resignation, he shifted his weight slightly to one side, as if to make her comfortable. "It's not supposed to be like this, Cecilia," he gently explained.

Cecilia let her fingers skim down the wall of muscle which formed his chest. "But what if—" She paused for a heartbeat. "What if it *is* supposed to be like this?"

David closed his eyes and shook his head. "Good sex is like music or ballet," he softly insisted. "It should have grace and rhythm. But most important, it should be equitable."

"And what if you are wrong?" she asked, stroking back the heavy, dark hair which shadowed his face. "What if it is supposed to be raw and untamed? What if it isn't always equal? Or graceful? Of course, I realize I'm merely a novice," she softly added, "but did someone write rules I know nothing of?"

David stared down into Cecilia's wide, innocent blue eyes and felt his heart lurch. Slowly, he lowered himself, resting his forehead on hers. "Cecilia," he whispered. "I'm scared."

She looked at him in astonishment. "Of what, pray tell?"

"*You*. Us. All of this."

Cecilia returned his gaze unflinchingly. "David, just make love to me," she said, her voice soft and certain. "Undress me slowly as you did last night, and take me to your bed and love me—"

"Cecilia—" But there, words failed him. Just as his body had done. What in God's name was he going to do? His world was turning upside down. "Cecilia, darling, I can, but . . . it will take some time. That's how it is. For a man. That's what I'm trying to tell you."

Gently, Cecilia urged him off her. "And we have all night," she reminded him. "Or most of it. And I would have you show me ways in which we may pleasure one another."

David levered himself onto one elbow, then stood to help her from the floor. He drew her up into his arms, gathering her against his chest. "You know too much already, Cecilia," he reassured her, speaking softly against her ear. "That trick that you pulled on me just now—I know perfectly well where you learnt it. I know perfectly well what has made you so curious, and it is not necessary for you to do or even to know of such things."

Cecilia pushed herself away from him and stared straight into his eyes. "I want to know," she persisted. "Don't treat me as if I am some fragile bit of Chinese porcelain which you might smash to pieces were your emotions to overcome you. Don't treat me as if I am less than a flesh-and-blood woman. That is hardly fair to me."

They still stood in the middle of his dressing room. David released her, viciously jerking up the close of his trousers. "Cecilia, I'm trying to treat you like a lady," he said, sliding his free hand anxiously through his hair. "Not a whore."

At once, she returned to him, brushing her hands over his chest and tilting her chin to look up at him. "I have been alone for a long time, David," she said, her voice soft and throaty as she lowered her lashes. "I am tired of living without passion. Teach me—and I promise I will satisfy you as you have never been satisfied before."

God help me, David thought, *but she already does* . . .

He bit back the words before they were spoken, but he was beginning to fear that that was the very problem. He had no notion what he would do if she learned anything new, for he was already lost. And yet, he knew that he was being unreasonable, even harsh. Perhaps the truth was that he feared what she might become. To someone else, if he could not win her heart.

Yes, and the truth hurt, did it not? Gently, he took her by the hand and led her from the dressing room to the bed. As he had done last night—dear Lord, had it only been last night?—David pulled the remaining pins from her hair. Slowly, David began to undress her.

As he gently eased the teal silk down her shoulders and over her hips, he remembered his dark, erotic fantasies of the afternoon. How desperately he had wanted to see her hands on him, how seductive he had found the ivory lace which draped across her fingers. But it had been a fantasy. Nothing he had ever expected to happen. Not with a woman as artless as

Cecilia, for it seemed he had already stripped away far too much of her innocence.

And yet, he could never have imagined how her touch would feel—or how he would react to it. Like an untried boy with his first woman. It had been all he could do not to spill himself in her mouth, or across her beautiful dress. All he could do to restrain his lust long enough to thrust himself inside her.

And now she wished *him* to teach *her* about passion? It would have been laughable, had her question not been so earnestly asked. With his trousers still draped loosely about his hips, he stood behind her, unfastening bits of lace, ties, and stays, until Cecilia was naked in his arms. He held her an arm's length away and let his hungry gaze drift over her.

"You are so beautiful, Peaches," he murmured. "So ripe. So womanly."

And she was. She was all woman, from her fine, full breasts, to the elegant turn of her waist, right down to the generous swell of her hips. Her mouth was already love-bruised and swollen, her pink nipples hard, her hair down about her shoulders in a cascade of fiery golden curls. David sucked in his breath, long and slow.

She had won. He would do anything she asked.

Anything, right or wrong.

He sat down on the bed and stared up at her, his expression as open and encouraging as he could make it. "What do you wish to know?"

12

~

Semper Veritas

"*H*ow a man and a woman best please each other," she swiftly answered, lifting her hand to brush the hair from his eyes. "I wish . . . I wish to know where to touch you. Where you like to touch me. And the positions in which—" She jerked to a halt, blushing all the way down to her breasts. "The positions in which a man and a woman can have sexual inter—"

"Make love, Cecilia," David interjected. Swiftly, he snared her about the waist, angling his head to kiss the swell of her belly. "*We* make love, you and I. We don't have *intercourse*. We don't *copulate*." He punctuated his words with kisses across her abdomen. "Nor do we *do* any of those other impersonal euphemisms. Do you understand the difference?"

"Do you?" she softly challenged, cradling his head against her stomach. "Or are those pretty words meant to make me feel better?"

David lifted his head to stare up at her, feeling her fingers entwined behind his head. "Oh, Cecilia," he said softly. "I can assure you that I know the difference. I know all too well."

Silently, he stood to strip off his remaining clothing, and then he drew back the covers, motioning her into bed. Already, he could feel the stirrings of desire. It would not be long. He let his eyes slide down her naked body as she lay stretched across his bed.

Her breasts were heavy, swollen with passion, her head tipped back into the softness of his pillow. No, not long at all. Cecilia made him feel as if he were again one-and-twenty, and possessed of all the vigor of his youth.

David slid into bed beside her, the mattress creaking under his weight. Propping himself up on one elbow, he let his fingertips brush over her breasts. He loved the contrast, his dark hands skimming over her luminescent flesh. "Cecilia," he said softly. "I've a better idea. Why don't you tell me where to touch you?"

"Umm . . ." Cecilia's head tipped back, and she swallowed hard. "Yes."

David continued, barely touching her. "Do you like this?" he whispered, lightly grazing the swell of her belly, feeling her tremble beneath his touch.

Urgently, Cecilia moaned, squeezing her eyes shut. "Yes, please . . ."

"Let's go slowly," he murmured, dipping his head so that his lips could skim the curve of her ear. Lightly, he ran his tongue around the inner edge. "What about this, hmm?"

"Oh!" was her breathless response.

David circled the shell of her ear, then plunged inside. He was barely touching her. And yet Cecilia felt desire surge through her like nothing she had ever known. He withdrew, sucked the lobe between his teeth, and gently nipped.

The quick, sharp pain was wildly arousing. Instinctively, Cecilia's hips bucked against the mattress, the surge of desire growing, heating, flooding her stomach, her womb, and then drawing at her, hot and hungry between her legs. Cecilia thought she might die of the pleasure.

His finger skimmed through her cleft, and she gasped. "Yes, Cecilia," he whispered. "Just a little bit at a time, I'll discover all your sweet, secret places. But slowly, love. So slowly."

Cecilia felt her hands fist into the bedsheets. She opened her mouth to plead with him but could make no sound. And then, he touched her more surely, drawing two fingers between her thighs, sliding them up through the wetness, delicately tormenting her. Sharply, she drew in her breath, a whisper in the darkness.

Again, David stroked. Over and over, sweet and perfect. She lost herself to the pleasure. It was frightening. Exhilarating. Until at last, his touch tore at her like a rip tide, snatching her from the moorings of sanity and hurtling her through the stars, casting her far away, into the warm waves of rapture.

Tenderly, David curled himself about Cecilia as her trembling slowly subsided. *Good Lord.* He'd never seen a woman come so easily. He found it both gratifying and frightening. Not to mention erotic beyond belief. Already, he was half hard, pressing greedily against her thigh.

At last, Cecilia's eyes flew open. "Oh," she said simply. "Oh, my."

David slid down her length, gently urging her legs apart with his body. "No," she whimpered. "I can't . . . I can't *bear* it!"

"Shush, love," he whispered, his mouth pressed against the swell of her belly. "Just let me taste you."

David spread his hand over her upper thighs, opening her wide. Gently, he soothed her with his tongue, nibbling first at the tender flesh of her mound, savoring her sweetness. He wanted to bring her pleasure again. To make her feel as if she had been made love to. *By someone who loved her.*

And he did.

All about them, the room was quiet, save for the soft ticking of the mantel clock and the quiet hiss of the coal in the grate. When he sensed that Cecilia was ready—when he knew that his touch would not overwhelm her—David lightly traced his tongue to the folds of her flesh. But at the scent of her, it was his own need which spiked, suddenly pooling hot and heavy in his groin.

He felt his cock begin to throb, hot and insistent. Ruthlessly, David dragged in a breath and forced his attention back to her, stroking across the sweet, hard nub until he heard a sound—a soft cry of surrender—catch in the back of Cecilia's throat.

As he sensed her breath begin to quicken, he lifted his head. "I want my fingers inside you now," he said, his voice surprisingly thick. "I need to feel you come again. The contractions—I want to share your pleasure."

"Yes—" Cecilia felt the word tear from her on a sob. She felt the trembling begin again, deep in the pit of her belly. She was afraid. Afraid of drowning in the pleasure. Of never finding herself again. She now understood just what he was capable of. Why women flocked to him. And the temptation was beyond her.

His fingers slipped inside, and at once, her hand lashed out to grab a fistful of bedsheet. "Oh, God!" she cried, her eyes flying open. His gaze locked with hers, his eyes dark with desire. She called out his name—or tried to—pleading for release as she moved urgently against his hand. And all the while, David gazed at her through eyes which were sultry yet brilliant. "Ah—ah—*David*—!"

He felt the first surge of her climax hard against his fingers. Cecilia's body went rigid, her lush hips coming fully off the mattress, her mouth opening in a silent cry. Unable to resist, he dragged himself up her length and mounted her roughly. "Inside, Cecilia," he growled, spreading her flesh as he took his cock in hand. "Please," he whispered, plunging himself into her in one smooth stroke.

Cecilia rose up to meet him, dragging herself against him, pulling David into her. Her gentle eagerness left him wild, primal. She gave him herself, in a way no other woman ever had. And he wanted her; his body cried out for her, with a longing he'd never before felt.

How he loved her. Always before, though, he'd held something back. But this time, the torment tore through him, ripping out his soul, and spilling it into her. All of him. He pumped himself into her in hard, hot bursts of lust and love and need.

No, he could not win this struggle.

Not against Cecilia.

At last, David collapsed against her, waiting for body and spirit to reunite. And wondering if they ever would. It felt as if some essential part of him had flown to her now, to be forever united in a bond which could not be undone.

Cecilia awoke to the muted sounds of the watch calling three o'clock in the street below David's bedchamber. Awkwardly, she levered up onto her elbows and looked about the room. The fire was burning low, and one of the lamps had already gone out, but the sweet scent of wine and passion still lingered in the air.

Cecilia looked down at the sleeping man beside her and knew a sharp and sudden yearning that defied all logic. Not a yearning for physical release but something far deeper, less tangible. The need to touch, to smell, to embrace. The need to *stay*.

She put up a hand and dragged the tumble of hair back off her face. Good Lord. It was time to go home. Past time, in truth. Afraid to return to sleep, she slid away from David's warm, lanky length and forced herself out of his bed. Her feet hit the floor, but, unable to resist, Cecilia looked back. David was even more handsome than when awake, for in sleep, he appeared relaxed. Almost innocent. Well, save for the dark shadow of beard which made him look a little bit like a pirate. She cocked her head. Or perhaps it was a highwayman.

Still, he was a charmer of the worst sort. Sleepily, she stretched, touched her toes, and considered what he might have looked like as a child. Beautiful, no doubt. She wondered fleetingly if his mother had spoiled him. Certainly, Cecilia would have done.

Trying hard not to wake him, she drifted through the room, her bare feet padding silently across the wool carpet. Near the hearth, she paused to stare at the portrait which hung above it. In an elegant Queen Anne chair, a white-haired lady sat ramrod stiff, her hands resting along the curving arms. But for all the imperiousness in her grip and posture, one could see that a certain amount of frailty already showed in the lines about her mouth. Still, her expression was implacable, her eyes wide-set and nearly black.

David's mother. There was no doubt, for though their coloring was vastly different, the likeness in the bones of the face was there. They shared that same arrogant tilt of the chin and that steely look of pur-

pose in their gaze. And Lady Delacourt certainly did
not look like the sort of woman who had ever spoiled
anyone.

Cecilia left the hearth and crossed the room. On the
opposite wall hung a beautiful oil painting of a huge
country house set in a landscaped park. His Derbyshire
seat, perhaps? Or one of his lesser properties? Either
way, it was an impressive display of wealth.

Cecilia turned from the painting and yawned, once
again tempted to return to the warmth of the bed. But
if she did, she mightn't wake again before dawn. In an
effort to occupy herself, she moved on to David's
desk, pausing to toy with his old-fashioned pounce
box, his mechanical pen, and then a palm-sized
miniature of a delicate, dark-eyed girl.

Curious, she flipped it over. *"Miss Branthwaite,
1794"* was boldly inscribed on the reverse. His sister
Charlotte! Cecilia smiled. David was far more sentimental than he let on. She set down the miniature,
and suddenly, her gaze caught on a tiny porcelain
dish—more of a covered jar, really—which sat next
to it.

With a collector's eye, Cecilia bent down. Even in the
sparse light, the jar appeared to be beautifully painted.
Wishing to examine the seating of the lid, Cecilia
picked it up. She was surprised to see that the dish was
lined with velvet. Curious, she poked her finger into it.

A ring—a very heavy, masculine ring, by the feel of
it—was nestled inside.

Unable to resist, she drew it out and crossed back
to the hearth to examine it. The metal felt incredibly
cold to the touch. She knelt down and held it to the
light. Certainly, it was nothing she'd ever seen David
wear. It nearly filled her palm, an ancient, crested
piece, heavily carved on both the top and the band.

Old-fashioned cabochon rubies were set deep into the gold on either side of the crest.

Tilting it a little nearer to the fire, Cecilia could see its design: an outstretched falcon's claw clutching a Scottish thistle. The inscription was in Latin. *Semper veritas.*

Always truth. How oddly familiar . . .

Abruptly, Cecilia stood, dropping the ring onto the floor. It bounced once on the carpet, then landed on the hearth with a *clunk!* Cecilia sucked in her breath, her gaze flying to the bed. But David still snored softly. Cecilia knelt down, seized the ring, and returned it to the dish. This piece of jewelry was not meant for prying eyes. She was certain, because it bore the crest of the earldom of Kildermore. Cecilia had seen it a dozen times, emblazoned on the doors of the elegant black coach which occasionally delivered the Reverend Mr. Amherst to the mission.

The ring must have been a gift from the Countess of Kildermore. But when? And why? Obviously, the ring meant something to David, or he would not have kept it in such a place of honor. Indeed, it was a deeply personal gift, the sort of thing Jonet Amherst might have given a lover or the man she hoped to marry.

But her husband did not have it. David did. Had there been some truth to the old rumors about them after all? Perhaps that explained David's deep-seated anger, his mild antagonism toward Amherst. The thought made Cecilia poignantly sad, but there was no point in pretending that she was the first woman in David's life. Slowly, she crept back to bed and curled herself about David, tucking her pelvis against his bare buttocks and sliding one arm over to hold herself against him.

Still, he did not stir. She almost wished he would.

She wanted to ask him about the ring. But that would be deeply intrusive. And how would one explain having snooped through another person's belongings? Unfortunately, her discovery of the ring in no way affected her feelings for David. Whatever people thought him—rake, rogue, arrogant aristocrat— Cecilia loved him, because at last she had seen the man behind the myth and rumor. She had even seen things which he had not, perhaps, wished anyone else to see. And what she felt for him now was a woman's love, one which transcended all her confused, youthful emotions.

She was certainly not the first woman to share his bed, but on some level, she was beginning to believe that David loved her. Still, he was *scared,* he had said. But of what, precisely? Of commitment? No, she no longer believed it was that. Something deeper, then. Something he was struggling to come to terms with. And he would. Of that much, Cecilia was confident. She was also very patient. She would wait for him. She owed him that, at the very least.

Gently, she bent her head to kiss his cheek. It was time to go. She must wake him and ask that he see her safely home, lest her servants realize she'd stayed out all night. As it was, she could expect to endure a harsh ribbing from Etta, especially after her asinine behavior over the lost stocking. The girl was no fool. She would put two and two together and get a ribald laugh out of it.

But despite her kisses, David did not stir. Very tenderly, she sucked his earlobe between her teeth and nibbled ever so gently. At that, his eyes fluttered open, and beneath the sheet, he rolled into her embrace. Blinking, he stared up at her. Then, almost immediately, his face broke into a beautiful, drowsy smile.

"You are so beautiful, Peaches," he whispered, his voice still thick with sleep.

Playfully, she jabbed him lightly in the ribs with one finger. "You are such a flatterer," she complained as he jerked away.

"Oh, no," he said, suddenly serious. "I may be a great many wicked things, Cecilia, but not that. I will never lie to you."

Oh, yes. *Semper veritas,* she thought dryly—almost wishing he would lie to her. Wishing he would say, *I love you, Cecilia, as I have never loved anyone.* But that might not be precisely true, she feared.

Just then, an uncomfortable expression clouded his face. "And since I've promised you total honesty, my dear, there is just this one little thing," he said rather awkwardly, lifting his eyes to hers. "Something I think I must tell you. About the porcelain box."

Cecilia assumed at once he'd seen her examine the ring. "No," she swiftly interjected. "I really wish you wouldn't. Don't . . . please just don't spoil this, David."

He grabbed her wrist and pulled her nearer. "But I must be completely truthful with you," he urgently persisted. "It is only right that I should explain precisely how I came by them—especially the roof tile."

The roof tile? Cecilia felt her body sag with relief. "Oh. Of course."

David paused, looking as uncertain as a young boy. "It's just that I didn't pick it out. My . . . er, my valet did. Picked them all out, truth be told. But I believe he has rather good taste in such things."

Cecilia wanted to laugh, but she didn't. "So . . . the roof tile was just dumb luck?"

Ruefully, David nodded. "I fear so."

"Oh, well!" With an impish smile, Cecilia shrugged. "There goes the romance of the thing!"

"Romance?" he growled, dragging her deep into the bedcovers and crawling atop her with the full force of his weight. "By God, I'll show you romance, you lusty little wench. Real romance. And it doesn't come in a crate tied up with bows and ribbons."

13

~

In which Lord Robin sweetly sings

David found himself unable to drift back to sleep upon his return from Park Crescent. Oh, he was tired—bone-weary, in fact—and dawn was some time distant. But Cecilia's scent on his tousled sheets made it impossible to consider crawling back into the warmth of the covers alone. So, instead, he lay on top, staring up at his ceiling while absently pondering just how vast his bed was in relation to the modestly sized room.

Really, had he any need for a bed half so large, particularly when he always slept alone? Despite his audacity in bringing Cecilia here last night, it had been the first time he'd ever entertained a woman in Curzon Street. But then, never before had his desire drawn him to his own hearth and home. Why was that, he wondered? His mother and Charlotte were often away. Still, it always seemed less complicated, somehow less personal, simply to pay for the privilege of venting his lust elsewhere.

David crawled from bed again, silently resolving to get rid of it and replace it with something smaller if . . . well, if he could not convince Cecilia to fall in love with him. And that was what he wanted, was it not? He wanted her not just in *lust*, as she was now, but in *love*. It seemed a serious challenge. Last night at her house, he had been driven to the edge of declaring his undying devotion to her, and loving her tonight had damned near pushed him over and into that black, unknowable void below.

It was odd, really. For so long, he had feared the exposure of who he was—or, better put, who he was *not*—and the loss and embarrassment such exposure might cause his mother. For years, Jonet had kept his secret, remaining silent even when her own situation with Cole had made it imperative that she explain the truth of their relationship. And yet, she had stoically kept her sworn oath to David, because she knew he had disliked and distrusted Cole.

At the time, he had been deeply touched, for in a world fraught with dishonor and deceit, his sister's word had been her bond, though the cost to her could have been dear. But now, strangely, he would have given up all that Jonet had held so sacred on his behalf simply to know what was in Cecilia's heart. It was a sensation which was dreadful in its uncertainty, since never before had he feared rejection.

Well, perhaps once.

In an effort to push back the memories which threatened, David went to his desk and abruptly withdrew a sheet of writing paper from the center drawer. He had a missive to send to de Rohan. There was urgent work to be done this day. But even as he trimmed and relit the wick of his lamp, the uncertainty would not be shut out. Even as he stared down at the paper, white against the mahogany of his desk, he could see another letter written on paper just as blindingly white.

It had been just a little over five years ago when he had finally understood that his brief and extraordi-

nary betrothal to Cecilia Markham-Sands was over. It
had been early August, and the letter from her Uncle
Reginald had arrived in Curzon Street by private
courier. *"I regret to inform you that my niece cannot be
persuaded to your suit,"* he had written in a hand as
heavy and dark as his words. *"Sadly, I must ask that
you sever all contact, and cease any attempt to convince her . . ."*

Until that point, God help him, David had thought
it all a game. And yet, he had wanted her so badly, he
had played it. Not six weeks earlier, he had gone
down to the *Times* to deliver the announcement of
their engagement, thinking as he did so that it should
have felt frightening to take such a step with one's
life. And yet, it had not. It should have felt as if he
were sacrificing his personal happiness to set right a
grievous error. But it had not felt like that, either.

Moreover, the absence of those emotions had had
nothing to do with the belief that the betrothal was a
sham. Because he had *not* believed it. In some pathetic,
inexplicable way, he had imagined he could make it so;
that his grim implacability would impel Cecilia to the
altar if his wealth and position did not. Worse still, he
had convinced himself that the fact that he was being
forced to marry her relieved him of any obligation to
tell her the truth about his origins. What kind of
twisted logic was that? And what did it say about the
level of respect he had shown her?

Afterward, as he had read her uncle's letter over and
over, it had left him incensed, reassured, and relieved.
Incensed that she had rejected him. Reassured that she
had had the wisdom to do so. And relieved that she had
not meant to trap him after all. He had understood,
once and for all, that she was not acting the coy young
miss in order to play upon his sympathies, or to gain a

more generous marriage settlement. She simply did not want him. He had frightened her. And that was that.

Suddenly, a light knock sounded upon his door, jolting him from his reverie. David's head jerked around, and he stared at the mantel clock. Damn! His bathwater, judging from how the time had flown. He called out permission to enter, and a servant came in bearing two brass cans.

Behind him, Kemble floated in, called out a cheery good morning, and sailed into the dressing room to help situate the tub. David bent his head to the task of writing de Rohan, but at once, a shrill shriek of displeasure assailed him.

"Oh, my *God!* Oh, *my God!*" Kemble wailed. He marched out of the dressing room, hands balled into fists at his sides. "Just *what* in heaven's name caused that desecration in the dressing room—?"

David winced as memory stirred. "Is it dreadful?" he asked sheepishly.

Kemble crossed his arms, tapped his toe furiously, and jerked his chin toward the dressing room. "Well, your best top hat is ruined," he said, as if that explained it all. "Crushed! Crushed beyond repair! It is a sacrilege! A travesty! Your shelves and bandboxes tipped over! Shirts and cravats wrinkled! Indeed, I should not have come here had it been explained to me that you—that you—"

He broke off, apparently too enraged to finish. But David, perhaps in some misplaced wish to be punished, egged him on. "That I *what?*"

"*Drank!*" proclaimed Kemble with a haughty flourish of his hand. "*Drank to excess,* I should have said. For there is no other explanation which might justify the brutality which has been perpetrated in your dressing room. And when a man imbibes to the point that his wardrobe must needlessly suffer, then that is indeed excessive."

David bowed his head so that Kemble would not see his expression. "I shall endeavor to sober myself up," he said as humbly as he could manage. "Would you be so obliging as to ring for coffee? I fancy that would be of help."

Against the backdrop of his valet's ongoing histrionics, David managed to down his coffee, scratch out de Rohan's letter, post it by way of his groom, then plunge into the tub. Quickly, he bathed while Kemble, still seething with indignation, laid out his morning clothes. When he stood up in a cascade of warm, soapy water, Kemble came forward with a bath towel.

His eyes lit on the scratches down David's left shoulder. At once, a curious little smile quirked up one corner of his mouth. "Hmm . . ." he softly mused, draping the towel over David. "Now that I think on it, I've never seen a brandy bottle make marks quite like that."

As best he could, David ignored Kemble's suspicious looks and dressed hastily, on the off chance his pretty kitten had left some other scratches of which he was unaware.

"I mean to be out for most of the day," he announced as Kemble slid a sober gray superfine coat up his arms.

"As shall I," responded Kemble, giving the shoulders a mollifying pat. "I'm to hire your runners, you'll recall. Then I'll see what can be had from Kitty O'Gavin before I pack the lot of them off to Derbyshire."

"Right!" said David. "I hope that she is well enough to travel."

"She is," said Kemble, drawing back to squint at David's silk neck cloth.

"You've checked?"

"I sent a note 'round to that steely-eyed matron of

yours last night," murmured Kemble, giving the silk a little fluff. "Yes, the small diamond, I think."

"Well, you're very efficient," answered David appreciatively.

"Oh, I always say that gray wool calls for the simplicity of the diamond," agreed Kemble as he situated the pin into the folds. "Does she have ballocks under those dark serge skirts, do you think?"

At that, David managed to laugh. "Until tonight, then," he said, seizing his hat. "I shall likely have need of you, for I have a vast deal planned this evening."

Kemble trilled with laughter. "Anything which will require bandaging?"

"Let us pray not," said David grimly as he went out the door.

In short order, he was in his carriage and rolling along to Brook Street. At such an early hour, Mayfair was free of traffic, and the journey took but a few minutes. Since Charlie Donaldson and most of the footmen had accompanied Jonet to Cambridgeshire, he was admitted by a housemaid whom he scarcely recognized.

The girl looked a little alarmed when he announced his intention of calling upon Lord Robert Rowland. "I'm sorry, m-my lord," she managed to stammer. "But I'm not all sure that I ought—or what I mean to say is, that it's entirely possible he mightn't be at—"

"At home to ill-mannered, early-morning callers?" Delacourt finished helpfully, tossing down his hat on the hall table. "Worry not, for you needn't disturb him. I claim that honor for myself." At once, he slid out of his greatcoat and handed it to her, then leaving her openmouthed in the hall, went swiftly up the stairs.

Outside Robin's door, he paused to knock. There was no response. David stripped off one glove and, with all his strength, knocked again, hammering out a thunderous tattoo on the mahogany. Still, there was no answer. Abruptly, David drew back his foot and kicked, rattling the door in its frame.

Across the hall, David heard Stuart's door crack open. "Good God, leave off!" muttered a tormented voice behind him. "Just go on in! Drag his arse out— murder him in his bed—anything! Only stop that infernal banging!"

David turned around. "Sorry," he whispered.

At that, the young Marquis of Mercer poked his head fully out, puffing away at the tip of the nightcap which threatened to tickle his nose. "Oh, just you, eh?" he mumbled, squinting out into the passageway at David. "Well, go in. You'll never wake him from out here. Indeed, he mayn't even be in yet. God only knows."

David flashed him a teasing grin. "Are you not, then, your brother's keeper?"

Finally, Stuart opened both eyes, lifting his eyebrows in lordly disdain. "Rather fancied that was to be your job this trip," he said, shutting the door with a thump.

Well. Not a morning person.

Inwardly, David shrugged and twisted Robin's doorknob. It was, as he expected, unlocked. He crossed the room and jerked back the bed curtains, much to his regret. The stench which roiled up to assail his discerning olfaction would have been enough to fell a less experienced man.

Apparently, his nephew had been steeped in cheap gin, then doused with an even cheaper perfume. Robin was stretched diagonally across the mattress, bare-bummed and on his belly, with one big foot dangling crookedly off the edge.

"Wake up!" David ordered, smacking Robin hard on his lily-white buttocks.

Robin jerked spasmodically, then rolled over onto

one elbow, a shock of chestnut hair falling forward to cover one eye. "Damn," he mumbled, dragging the hair back off his face. For a moment, he stared in bewilderment as David neatly drew his glove back on.

Reality finally dawned. "Oh, David..." Robin managed. "Awful bloody early, ain't it?"

David grinned and clapped his hand over his heart. "Yes, but happily I think on thee, like the lark at break of day arising," he quoted. "Now! Awake, sweet Robin, and sing to me at heaven's gate."

"What the hell!" muttered his nephew irritably as he sat up in bed. "Is that any way to wake a fellow up? With a butchered sonnet and a flock of damned birds?"

"Ah, perhaps not," agreed David, dragging Robin by one arm from the bed. "But sing you shall, my boy!"

Robin staggered along behind until they reached the chair, then he tripped and tumbled into it, sitting down with the gracelessness of the near terminally inebriated. He leaned forward, catching his face in his hands. "Bugger me, then," he muttered into the carpet. "What the devil am I to sing about?"

David jerked hard on the bellpull, hoping that some merciful servant would have the foresight to bring coffee, then joined his nephew in sitting down by the hearth. The floor all about their feet was littered with the clothing Robin had apparently worn last night.

"What you will sing about, my dear boy," he answered, "is the Honorable Bentham Rutledge."

At that, Robin's head jerked up. Never had David seen a man so seemingly near death become so swiftly sober. "Why, I don't know a thing about old Bentley," insisted Robin hotly. "What the devil would I know? If anyone told you I knew anything at all, they were much mistaken. I see him about town, no more, no less."

A blatant lie. Heaped with partial prevarications

and passionate denials. Not a good sign. A shudder of unease ran through David. "You mistake me, I think," he said softly. "I merely wish to know where you met Rutledge. And where he lives. Where he spends his evenings. I understand he has a fondness for gaming hells, and I should like to know which one he favors. I somehow fancied you might know these things."

Robin blinked in stupefaction. "Why . . . I met him at the Lamb and Flag, I seem to remember."

Which meant he probably *didn't* remember. Another bad sign. "And how long ago would you say that was?" David prodded. "I understand he had recently been in India, and I have a very keen interest in discovering which ship he came in on, and when it disembarked."

Just then, a chambermaid came in to set down a tray laden with a coffee service. Almost as an afterthought, she cut a casual glance toward Robin, then abruptly, a quick, earsplitting scream tore through the room. In the silence which followed, a teaspoon clattered off the tray and onto the floor.

Swiftly, Robin crossed his legs and arms, but the girl's black skirts were already disappearing through the door. David lifted a wrinkled shirt from the floor, gingerly pinching it between his thumb and forefinger, then tossing it at Robin.

"Mr. Rutledge's itinerary?" he again inquired.

After dragging the shirt over his head, Robin resumed blinking. "Why, I don't think he's been in town above a month or two. And I believe he came from India. But you needn't look up which boat," he added more cheerfully, "for I do know that much."

"Do you indeed?" asked David, amazed.

His eyes narrow, Robin nodded. "The *Queen of Kashmir*," he said swiftly. "Nina—that's old Hell-Bent's dolly-mop—she was in her cups one night and carved it into the table with a penknife. Said it was her lucky ship come in, since he'd been on it."

Well. That was a bit of luck for David, too. He wondered if the *Queen of Kashmir* was still in port. It was possible, given the time it took to offload and refit. De Rohan would know about such things. David made a mental note to ask him. If Rutledge were part of a smuggling operation, his ship could have easily hauled ill-gotten gains. There were probably any number of things which could be profitably brought in from India, provided they could be got past the Customs House. But how many of them were worth killing over?

Thoughtfully, he rose and crossed the room to the coffee service, pouring out two cups. He pressed one into Robin's hand and sat back down. "What can you tell me of Rutledge's family? Or where he lives?"

Robin seemed to hesitate. "I believe he hails from Gloucestershire," the boy said slowly. "But he doesn't go there often. His elder brother is Lord Treyhern, but Rutledge lives in Hampstead, in his sister-in-law's childhood home."

Quietly, David took it all in. "I have heard it said," he suggested, "that Rutledge plays deep. Would you know?"

Robin looked as if he might choke on his coffee. "I know nothing of his habits to speak of," he waffled, setting the cup back down with a clatter. "But I daresay it may be true."

David sipped at his coffee pensively. "Well, know this," he said softly. "If you play with him, you are a fool, and you will lose. And a debt of honor is a debt of honor, whether or not the man to whom you lose is a scoundrel, and whether or not you have reached your majority. You understand that, do you not?"

Robin nodded with alacrity. "Indeed, yes. But you need have no concern on that score."

"I'm exceedingly glad to hear it," returned David. "You should also know, my boy, that while Rutledge may be young—perhaps five-and-twenty at most—he is accounted a very dangerous character."

"Oh, I think you go too far, David," Robin averred. "I find him a perfectly pleasant fellow."

David simply nodded. "Yes, well, your perfectly pleasant fellow murdered his first man before his eighteenth birthday. And since then, he has sent a couple more on to an early reward. And so I hope you will have a care, Robin. I should deeply regret to hear that you have ended up on the wrong end of either a gaming table or a brace of pistols with one such as he. I hope I make myself plain?"

Apparently, he had. What little color Robin's skin had possessed was gone.

David crooked one eyebrow and put down his coffee. "And now, the name of that gaming hell?"

"Lufton's," said Robin swiftly. "In Jermyn Street."

His business with Robin concluded, albeit rather uneasily, David ordered his coachman to drive on to Pennington Street. He was eager to see Cecilia, desperate to reassure himself that the passion of last night had lingered. He wondered if he would ever escape the fear that this tenuous, fragile relationship would somehow vanish. Indeed, Cecilia had seemed a little subdued on the journey back to Park Crescent in the wee hours of this morning, but that could easily be attributed to a nearly sleepless night. He hoped that was all it was.

As his coach spun along the Strand and into Fleet Street, he tried to turn his attention to his conversation with Robin. Some of it, particularly Robin's guilty expression, worried him just a bit. Nonetheless, if Robin had gotten himself into serious trouble, David would surely have heard of it by now. He always kept one ear to the ground, and little escaped him. No, he thought it was not that.

Not yet, at any rate. But clearly, Robin was running with a fast crowd, far too fast for his age. He certainly wanted watching, just as his mother had said. And as for Bentley Rutledge, David was a little confused. It seemed out of character for a man of his sort to live in a bucolic village like Hampstead. And in his sister-in-law's house, no less. One must therefore assume he was not wholly estranged from his family. It also explained his occasionally racking up in town—but not his choice of hostelries, a smuggler's den along Wapping Wall.

It was all very confusing. Particularly Rutledge's visits to Lufton's. It was a notorious gaming hell, true. But the clientele was a decent one, and unpleasantness a rarity. David had played there himself, though he found it a little tedious for his taste. Still, some of the finest families in town had been ruined within Lufton's portals, and as with all such establishments, the house skimmed liberally.

Yet it did not seem the sort of place which would entertain a man like Rutledge. The play was deep, yes. But the vicious edge was missing. And so perhaps Rutledge went there for some other purpose? But what? To fleece foolish young rams like Robin? Or for something more dastardly? It was time, he supposed, to pay another visit to Lufton's, but to what end, he did not yet know. As he tried to puzzle it all out, he realized that he had reached the mission's front door.

Swiftly, he went through the storefront. The three women working there greeted him cheerfully, and coming down the stairs, a laundry worker with a teetering stack of linen wished him good morning. Oddly enough, it all made him feel as if he belonged. And the thought did not make him particularly uncomfortable.

Though it was only ten o'clock, he cracked the office door to find that Cecilia had already arrived. Even better, she was alone. He felt relief wash through him. At once, her head jerked up from her work, and she stood. David closed the distance between them, opened his arms, and tried to draw her to him.

Sensing her reluctance, he kissed her swiftly and let her go. "Good morning, my dear," he said as his lips left hers.

Cecilia's lashes fell nearly shut, a surprisingly maidenly gesture given her uninhibited demands of the previous night. "Good morning, David," she returned, her voice warm but just a little distant, as if there were something weighing on her mind.

David felt a wave of disappointment. He supposed that he had wanted to hear fervor in her voice, had wanted her lips to open beneath his, and her hands to cling to him, as it had been last night. He squashed the feeling. He was being unrealistic. This was a place of business, and, more important, it fell to them to set a good example. The very thought of his attempting to set a good example for anyone should have made David laugh, but it didn't. Yes, Cecilia was right to maintain a degree of distance.

So why did he dislike it so greatly? Why did he fear her mood was driven by something altogether different? "You've come early," he remarked, hoping that it meant she had missed him. "And you look particularly lovely. That gown—it is far more elegant than the dresses you usually wear to the mission."

"Oh, Giles and I are going directly to Lady Kirton's tea this afternoon," she explained casually as she

shuffled through the papers on the corner of her desk.
"Her daughter is to be wed in a fortnight's time, and
there are many entertainments planned."

David felt something inside him collapse just a little. He had hoped that her daffodil-yellow gown with
its rows of lace and flounces had been meant for him.
"I missed you, Cecilia," he said softly, brushing the
back of his hand across her cheek. "My bed was so
empty this morning. You left a void, my dear. A hole
in my heart, perhaps."

Cecilia looked faintly amused. "Why, I have heard
it said that you do not have one, my lord," she teased.

With a flourish, David snared her hand and lifted it
to his lips. "I have not, my love," he answered dramatically, staring over her knuckles and into her eyes.
"For I have given it into your safekeeping."

Cecilia drew back her hand, holding it at her
breastbone and staring down, as if searching for some
physical evidence of his touch. "Do not make a joke of
me, David," she said softly. "For I am easily wounded."

David wanted to reach out and hold her, but her
voice made him fear she would not permit it. "My
dear, I assure you, I am all seriousness. Why the
solemn face and quiet voice?" he prodded. "Where is
my hissing little kitten this morning?"

Cecilia's expression brightened marginally. "Forgive me, David," she swiftly answered, throwing out
her hand, palm first, as if she feared he might attempt
to console her. "I am fine, honestly. It was wrong of
me to tease you, for I know very well that you are a
good and generous man, no matter how you may
wish to pretend otherwise."

Unable to resist, he again stroked her cheek with
his hand. "Oh, how you flatter me!" he teased.
"Indeed, I do not think I can bear to go home alone

tonight, Cecilia. I can only pray that the chambermaid has changed my bed linen today, or your scent will still linger, and I'll find myself burning, sleepless with lust."

Cecilia smiled. "Oh, David, are you never serious?" Absently, she picked up a pencil from her desk and began to toy with it.

Impulsively, he grabbed both her hands in his, causing her to drop it. "But what, pray, am I to do about this delightful sensation which I feel when you are near? Or this equally miserable one I feel when you are far away?"

Steadily, she lifted her gaze to his. "Well, what do you suggest?" she asked. The challenge in her words struck fear into his heart.

David paused for just a heartbeat. "Well, I daresay we could get leg-shackled," he lightly suggested, almost afraid she might implode on the spot. "*If* that is what you wish," he hastily added.

At that, Cecilia merely stared at him, her mouth opening and closing soundlessly. "No, thank you," she said very coolly, jerking her hands from his and turning to face the bank of sooty windows. "I have already had one husband marry me for the wrong reason, and I do not care to have another."

"What do you mean?"

But Cecilia did not turn around. "If ever I marry again," she said quietly, "it will be to a man who is sure he cannot live without me. It will be for love, not convenience. It will be a partnership, with all that the word implies. Complete trust. Total honesty. Commitment. And it will be entered into reverently and seriously, not impulsively and frivolously."

Unsure of what she was asking—or if she was asking anything at all—he stepped close behind her, lightly placing his palms on her shoulders. But her shoulders were still rigid, and in his heart, he feared that the worst was happening all over again.

Good God, what had possessed him to speak of such a thing now? This was hardly the way—or the time or place—in which a man ought to propose to a woman. Particularly one he full well expected to refuse him. Moreover, there was much he needed to sort through in his own mind before speaking of such a thing. And following that, a great deal that needed saying before he could ask so much of her. Was he going to have to slice open a vein and bleed the truth? And then, what if she wouldn't have him? He wasn't ready to hear that yet.

"Cecilia," he said, his voice choking a little as his lips brushed her hair. "You mean to stay with me, do you not? As my lover, I mean? You have not changed your mind?"

"No, I have not," she responded, finally turning around to look up at him. Her wide blue eyes searched his face. "Is that what you fear?"

David managed to laugh. He couldn't bear this seriousness which hung over them. The lighthearted banter they usually maintained was so much easier. Was there no way he could cajole or tease her back into good humor? It seemed so much safer.

"Yes, darling," he lightly responded. "My greatest fear is that you will see the error of your ways and—"

But just then, a swift knock sounded. David and Cecilia sprang apart just as the door burst inward. Mrs. Quince stood on the threshold, her face the bright red of a potential apoplexy victim. "Well, if it isn't one thing, it's another!" she announced in the voice of doom.

"*What?*" asked David and Cecilia at once.

The matron drew herself up to her full five feet. "That horrid pinchbeck necklace of Maddie's went missing," she announced, jabbing one stubby finger at the ceiling. "Nan stole it—and more's the pity she didn't just pitch it out the window instead of hiding it beneath her pillow for all the caterwauling going on upstairs."

"How dreadful," murmured Cecilia, nervously smoothing her palms down her skirts. "I shall speak to her at once."

Succinctly, Mrs. Quince nodded. "You do that, ma'am, for that Nan's in need of some proper moral guidance, and I daresay another ten commandments lecture wouldn't go amiss."

"Yes, a—a lecture, to be sure," echoed Cecilia, starting toward the door.

Suddenly, Delacourt held up a staying finger. Cecilia froze in her tracks, giving him an odd, side-long look. Mrs. Quince turned to stare at him. "You've a question, m'lord?" the matron asked.

"As a matter of fact, I do." Delacourt struck a thoughtful pose. "About those commandments—forgive me, Mrs. Quince, but it's been a while. And you are clearly an expert."

"On the commandments?" answered Mrs. Quince tightly.

Delacourt did not miss a beat. "Indeed, yes. Or maybe I'm thinking of the seven deadly sins? Anyway, does not one of them admonish us not to covet our neighbor's wife?"

Color flushed down the back of Cecilia's neck. Mrs. Quince looked at him as if he were witless. "Why, the commandments do, to be sure!"

"But what exactly does that mean, ma'am? I mean, *coveting.* That's rather more wicked than just—oh, say, *wishing* or *admiring,* isn't it? It's more like—like *lust,* is it not?"

Looking deeply confused, Mrs. Quince managed another nod. "Yes, and a terrible sin it is, too."

Delacourt deliberately drew his brows together. "But what if he were dead?"

"Who?" asked Mrs. Quince fretfully.

"My neighbor. The one whose wife I covet. Metaphorically." Delacourt smiled warmly, and opened his hands in an innocent, expansive gesture. "I mean—just how stringently are these commandments and rules and things applied? That, you see, is what I've never understood. Indeed, Mrs. Quince, I am persuaded that a lack of specificity has led many an otherwise well-intentioned fellow right down the wrong path."

The matron set her ample fists on her ample hips. "Well, no disrespect intended, m'lord, but there's no lack of specificity when the fires of hell are licking at your bum, now, is there?"

Delacourt scratched his jaw thoughtfully. "No, ma'am," he said gravely. "I confess, you have me there."

Mrs. Quince looked somewhat mollified. "Still and all," she demurred. "If the poor devil's dead—why, then he really don't have a wife, does he? I daresay it wouldn't apply, would it?"

Pensively, Delacourt lifted a finger. "See, now, Mrs. Quince—that's just what I think. But you have to think these things through pretty carefully, do you not? Otherwise, a fellow could make an egregious misjudgment. But it would probably be safest just to make an honest woman of her, would it not?"

The matron's expression of misgiving began to return. "M'lord, I'm not perfectly sure I take your meaning."

Cecilia snapped back into motion, hastening toward the door in a rustle of yellow silk. "Humor him, Mrs. Quince," she sweetly whispered, brushing past her out the door. "I think his valet hitched his cravat just a notch too tight this morning."

After a curious parting glance, Mrs. Quince followed Cecilia from the room, but her gray serge had scarce swished out of sight when Maximilian de Rohan appeared on the threshold, filling and darkening the door with his grim, unrelieved black. Beside him stood Lucifer, his glossy black head reaching almost to the inspector's hip bone.

14

~

The corruption of Inspector de Rohan

"*I* got your letter," said the police officer by way of introduction. He was, David had noticed, a man of amazingly few words.

"Good." With a wave of his hand, David motioned the inspector toward the worktable. "Sit down, de Rohan, if you will?"

"I've brought in the dog," he said, his words barely apologetic. "There were children playing in the street below, and if they should taunt him—"

"To be sure," David interjected, understanding perfectly. "Now! I think we have much to discuss."

If de Rohan resented David's ongoing involvement in the case, he was far too clever to show it. With a harsh scrape, the inspector drew a chair from beneath the table, tossed down a leather folio, and took a seat on David's right. "I somehow sense that there is going to be an interesting story behind this request," he said with a bemused smile as Lucifer flopped down at his feet.

David lifted one brow sardonically. "Regrettably so," he admitted. "But it will keep. Were you able to make inquiries into the ownership of Mother Derbin's brothel?"

De Rohan's smile shifted. "I was," he said hesitantly. "But daresay it will do us little good. It appears to be held by a company—a business partnership, on its surface. These things can be very difficult to unravel, particularly if deception is the owner's goal."

Thoughtfully, David tapped his silver pen on the desk. "Did you get an address?"

"A counting house in Leadenhall Street, but there was a sign on the door which said the office was closed due to influenza." De Rohan smiled faintly. "It may even be the truth, for there's a great deal of it going around."

"Bloody hell!" David swore, letting his fist crash down onto the table. "Is there nothing we can do? Can we not force the door? Drag someone from their bed?"

Cynically, de Rohan laughed. "Spoken like a true aristocrat, my lord. Certainly, *you* may break down the door, and quite probably with impunity. But the police have no authority to do anything at all. Indeed, at this point, I don't even have the evidence to compel them to speak with me, nor have I the right to search for it," he snapped. "Not even if I should find the front door blown off its hinges and all of their records spilt upon the floor."

David pushed himself away from the desk. "Look here, de Rohan, I'm sorry," he admitted. "I know you are doing your job. And you are right. We don't have any evidence. But perhaps we could get some?"

De Rohan looked askance. "I don't care for the sound of this."

"Perhaps you ought not listen, then," suggested David with a dry smile.

De Rohan frowned, deepening the lines about his mouth. "Perhaps *you* ought to tell me just how you came to find yourself inside Mother Derbin's," he countered darkly.

Reluctantly, David sighed and leaned back a little in his chair. "I rather feared it might come to that," he admitted. "May I just say I went in under false pretenses, and leave it at that? There is a matter of gentlemanly discretion involved."

Succinctly, de Rohan nodded. "Go on."

Just then, Cecilia swept back through the door, her yellow silk skirts instantly brightening the room. At once, de Rohan and David jerked from their chairs. To David's surprise, the police inspector made Cecilia a very elegant bow.

"Lady Walrafen," he said warmly. "Good morning."

"Good morning, Inspector," she responded pleasantly, her gaze catching on Lucifer. "And you've brought your lovely dog!"

Curled on the floor at de Rohan's feet, the big dog gazed at her with a look of utter devotion. Then, like the gentlest of puppies, he rolled onto his spine, letting his legs splay open and his tongue loll out—which was pretty much what David was inclined to do whenever he saw Cecilia. He suppressed a grin as Cecilia knelt to scratch Lucifer's ears.

"De Rohan has come to report on some information I requested," he explained, watching her small fingers stroke the dog's glossy fur. "Really, Cecilia, you need not concern yourself with it."

Cecilia merely stood and laid her hand on the back of the chair opposite David's. "Nonsense," she said lightly, seating herself. "I'm keenly interested."

De Rohan looked perfectly comfortable in having her join them. Indeed, the man seemed to have some singular notions as to what well-bred ladies should be exposed to. Perhaps his middle-class upbringing had not made such things plain to him. Inwardly, David sighed. Or perhaps de Rohan's notions were not altogether wrong. David was no longer perfectly sure, particularly where Cecilia was concerned. He just prayed she kept her mouth shut about last night.

"You were saying, Lord Delacourt?" de Rohan interjected, returning to their topic.

"Er—yes," David resumed, toying with his pen once more. "Let us simply say that I gave Mother Derbin the impression I was seeking companionship for the evening," he began. "And while in her drawing room, I caught sight of Bentham Rutledge. You may remember him from the Prospect of Whitby?"

De Rohan looked concerned. "The blue-blooded ne'er-do-well?"

"The very same. A remarkable coincidence, is it not?"

"In my line of work," said de Rohan slowly, "there is rarely such a thing as coincidence, remarkable or otherwise. Where does he live?"

"In Hampstead, or so I am given to understand."

"Not the sort of place a bold young blade normally resides," de Rohan quietly commented.

"No," murmured Delacourt. "That fact had not escaped me."

Cocking one eyebrow, de Rohan flipped open a leather folio and scratched out a few notes. "What else do you know of him?"

David shrugged. "Very little, in truth," he answered. And then, as succinctly as possible, he explained what he had learned about Rutledge's background and proclivities, including the fact that he had fled to India after a duel gone wrong. "A bad seed," he concluded, lifting his gaze to meet de Rohan's. "But . . ."

"But what?" pressed de Rohan.

David cut a swift glance toward Cecilia. She was staring at him intently. "But perhaps not a vast deal worse than I was at his age," he softly admitted. Then sharply, he cleared his throat. "Nonetheless, I can tell you that Rutledge was not at all pleased to see me. Indeed, he looked distinctly uncomfortable—seething with suppressed violence, I should have described him."

"And you would know?" de Rohan softly returned, looking at him from beneath his black, angular brows.

David felt the skin about his mouth tightened. "Yes, I think that I would know."

"The man Mr. Rutledge shot in the duel," interjected Cecilia suddenly. "Did he die?"

"No," said David quietly. "But he was expected to. And since he was the rather pampered son of a duke, the outcome would likely have been very bad for Rutledge had he remained in England."

Cecilia looked pensive. De Rohan leaned back into his chair. "And as for your female companionship," he continued. "Did you find any?"

Swiftly, David nodded. "I bribed a prostitute named Angeline to tell me what little she knew." He lied with alacrity to keep Cecilia from admitting her involvement. "Apparently, the two murdered girls had gone down into the cellar—a place which is strictly off-limits for the women who work there."

Lifting one finger from the table, Cecilia looked as if she might speak. Rapidly, David continued. "It seems they had a rendezvous there with two French sailors, and one can only assume they saw something they oughtn't, for that very night they packed their things and fled with the younger sister in tow."

As a precaution, David slipped his foot from his

shoe just in case he should be required to kick Cecilia
in the shin.

De Rohan seemed not to notice anything amiss.
"And did your songbird have an opinion about what
they had seen?"

Cecilia opened her mouth as if to answer. Swiftly,
David moved to intercede. Unfortunately, at the last
second, he decided to aim for her ankle, and when his
toes brushed beneath her skirts and his flesh
skimmed up her calf, the sudden jolt of desire caused
his heart to drop into his stomach. He was compelled
to fight for control of his tongue.

"She—ah, she implied that the cellar was being
used for smuggling," he managed.

"Smuggling?" asked de Rohan archly.

But to David's shock, Cecilia had mistaken his gesture and had slipped off her own shoe. Seductively,
she slid her stockinged foot along his arch, and up his
ankle, leaving a trail of heat along his skin.

It should have felt silly, almost adolescent. But what
it felt was erotic. Deeply so. A mixture of lust and relief
coursed through him as Cecilia let her toes play up his
shin. At least she no longer seemed indifferent toward
him. He struggled to remember de Rohan's question.

De Rohan made a soft hiss of impatience. "My lord,
did she say there'd been smuggling, or did she not?"

David tried to focus. "Er—*not*. Not exactly. She
merely suggested it, but whether she knew that for a
fact or merely surmised it was not clear to us. Er—
to *me*."

"Anything else?" asked de Rohan, apparently oblivious to David's heated emotions.

Abruptly, David swallowed hard. To his acute discomfiture, Cecilia was still stroking his leg like a cat,
her head tipped slightly back, her lips slightly parted,

and her long dark eyelashes almost shut. His insides felt as if they'd been turned to mush, but a part of him was feeling quite the opposite.

Ruthlessly, David snagged his lip and bit down hard. "Ah—yes," he managed to answer after the pain cut through his lust. "Yes, indeed. She also claimed that there was a man, a Mr. Smith, who called on Mother Derbin every Monday morning to collect the rent."

"And is that all?" asked de Rohan, more impatient now.

David felt his face flush with warmth. "I believe so."

Suddenly, de Rohan looked at him curiously. "My lord, are you well? I hope you have not succumbed to the influenza yourself, for your color has taken a bad turn."

At that, Cecilia's eyes snapped open and her foot fell away.

Relief coursed through him. David tried to feign surprise at de Rohan's question. "Why, I am perfectly well," he announced with a degree of hauteur. "Now, as I was saying, it was her opinion that Mother Derbin was very frightened of this Mr. Smith. Moreover, Mr. Smith possessed a key to the cellars. Unfortunately, Mr. Smith does not answer Rutledge's description by any stretch of the imagination."

De Rohan laughed bitterly. "Mr. Smith is probably just a lackey," he answered. "A man with Rutledge's family connections mightn't wish to sully his hands with the goods."

"A good point," responded David. "And as for my songbird, whatever she knows—or doesn't know— she's not apt to speak with the police or give evidence of any sort."

Slowly, de Rohan nodded. "And so you mean to break into this cellar, do you not?"

"Well," David coolly responded, "you know what we aristocrats are like when we get bored."

De Rohan's eyes narrowed. "I really don't think I wish to hear any more about this."

Faintly, David smiled. "I thought not."

De Rohan's black expression relaxed just a bit. "Good," he said. "I'm glad you see reason."

David waved one hand airily. "Oh, do not mistake me, de Rohan. I'm going. And I rather doubt you'll attempt to stop me. But I understand completely if you choose not to be involved."

At that, the police inspector shoved his leather folio across the table with disdain. His eyes flashed, black and vicious. "You put me in an untenable position, my lord."

"There's nothing untenable about it," answered David. "I mean to go."

Obviously no longer able to restrain herself, Cecilia burst in. "My God, David! Do you mean to get yourself shot—or worse?"

De Rohan smiled grimly. "She is right, you know."

"I mean to go," David slowly repeated, fixing his stare on de Rohan. "And yes, I agree that you'd best be out of it."

"You know I cannot do that," the policeman bit out. "You're apt to get yourself killed. And I can assure you that a dead peer in the East End will draw a vast deal more attention than any sort of smuggling you care to name."

"Regrettably, I've done far more stupid things than break into the cellar of a whorehouse," said David with a tight smile. "So, touching though it is, I wish you would not overly concern yourself with my welfare."

"What I wish," said de Rohan, his glower darkening, "is that the Home Office had sent this bloody case to Bow Street where it belongs."

Lightly, David lifted his brows. "Then shall we say tonight?"

Angrily, de Rohan flipped open his folio and took up his pencil. "Blister it! What time?"

"Well," said David softly. "That all depends on whether or not you wish to accompany me first to St. James's. There is a gaming hell in Jermyn Street which Mr. Rutledge frequents."

Finally, Cecilia shoved herself a little away from the table. "Really, David! You go too far. You are like to get yourself hurt if you insist on poking about in this matter."

De Rohan tilted his head toward Cecilia. "She is right, of course."

David turned his gaze on Cecilia. "*I* am apt to get hurt?" he asked archly. "And who, madam, was the one who insisted upon going inside—" He let his words break away, then began again, more conciliatory. "Look here, we none of us want someone else harmed. But what if it is Kitty next time? We cannot hide her forever."

Cecilia blinked a little too rapidly and looked away. "Yes," she said quietly. "Yes, I take your point."

De Rohan shifted uncomfortably in his chair. Belatedly, David realized that their argument had taken on the tone of a lovers' spat. "I cannot attend a club in St. James's," the policeman said firmly. "I have neither the clothing nor the credentials for admission."

"It's a hell, not a club, so the only credential is to look like a well-heeled wastrel," said David with a casual shrug. "So if you're in my company, you'll be admitted without question. Come to Curzon Street at nine o'clock tonight, and my man will fit you out.

Really, you want only a different coat, perhaps a silk neck cloth. Kemble will see to it."

De Rohan's discomfort appeared to increase. Abruptly, Cecilia butted in. "I mean to go as well," she said firmly. "I shall be at your house by nine."

"Absolutely not. It is not appropriate for a lady."

Cecilia rolled her eyes. "Oh, David, that is ridiculous, and you know it! Besides, which hell do you mean to visit?"

"Lufton's," he snappishly admitted.

Cecilia spread her arms wide, lifting her shoulders expressively. "Well, there you have it! It is a hell, yes, but not an especially grim one. Some married women and widows go there. As for you, Inspector de Rohan, you will blend in perfectly well. Moreover, I daresay it will look far less suspicious if the three of us go together."

"She is right, you know," de Rohan said for what seemed like the fifteenth time.

David looked at him darkly. "Why must you keep saying that? Do you agree with every harebrained woman whose path you cross? I vow, you must be a married man. Your defenses seem to have been worn down by them."

"*Them?*" Cecilia's brows went up. "Who, pray tell, is *them?*"

David found himself at a loss for words. But clearly, de Rohan had had enough of their arguing. He shoved back his chair and jerked to his feet, snaring his folio from the table. "Tonight at nine o'clock, then," he said gruffly. "I bloody well don't like it, but I will go."

15

~

In which her ladyship receives some Prudent Advice

Cecilia found afternoon tea at Lady Kirton's a trying affair indeed. Giles had arrived at the mission in one of his haughtier moods, a state which had not been improved by David's insistence on escorting her down to his waiting carriage. The two men seemed to dislike one another on sight.

She and Giles had arrived to find that Lady Kirton's drawing room was hot and overcrowded, the company abysmally dull. People drifted from one part of the room to another, speaking to those they knew and showering congratulations on the affianced couple. Cecilia was happy to add her good wishes, but she should have preferred to do it without Edmund Rowland breathing down her neck.

Was it impossible to offend the man, she wondered? Or should she simply attempt to extort another five thousand pounds from him as punishment for inflicting his company upon her? Terribly tempted, Cecilia stood with her teacup in hand, watching Giles and the other guests mill about the happy couple. Beside her, Edmund yammered on about his bootmaker, his new cabriolet, and his plan to redecorate his home in Mount Street.

Good God. The man was an insufferable bore.

Suddenly, a low, feminine voice resonated at her elbow. "Darling," Anne Rowland purred to her husband. "Do share Lady Walrafen with the rest of us."

Cecilia watched Edmund's face drain of color, like a schoolboy caught out in some bit of wickedness. "But of course, my dear," he returned, stepping away from Cecilia at once.

But if Anne Rowland's request had been motivated by jealousy, Cecilia certainly could not discern it from her expression. Mrs. Rowland was possessed of a dark, brittle beauty, but just now, her countenance was as open and friendly as Cecilia had ever seen it.

"My dear Lady Walrafen," she said brightly, offering Cecilia her elbow. "I believe we never had that turn about the room which I promised you at my soiree. How lovely you look. And how handsome your stepson is."

Cecilia had little choice but to accept the proffered arm. Over her shoulder, she watched as Edmund turned his attentions toward Lady Kirton.

Mrs. Rowland inclined her head a little closer to Cecilia's. "I apologize, my dear," she said softly. "My husband does tend to drone on rather dreadfully, does he not?"

"Not at all, Mrs. Rowland," Cecilia lied. "I find him most diverting."

At that, Anne Rowland tilted back her head and laughed richly, a hauntingly familiar sound. "My dear girl," she replied, her voice brimming with humor. "Such tact must have stood you in good stead during your marriage to Walrafen."

"I'm sorry," Cecilia managed to reply. "I'm not sure I take your meaning."

"Well, it is just that some husbands can be a bit tedious, can they not?" answered Anne Rowland in a confessional tone.

They had made the turn to walk back down the length of the room. "I never found Walrafen boring," answered Cecilia softly, "if that's what you mean. In truth, I scarcely saw him. He was very busy with his political career."

Mrs. Rowland simply nodded. "But now, my dear, you're a widow. You are free to do as you please, and many women would envy your freedom. But then, I daresay a clever woman can always find a way around a man's dictates."

Cecilia looked at her uncertainly. "I wouldn't know," she said simply. "I don't think Walrafen ever dictated to me." In truth, he'd paid very little attention to her one way or another, but Cecilia was not about to admit that to Anne Rowland.

But it seemed that Mrs. Rowland ascribed another meaning to her remark. "No, perhaps he did not, at that," she mused. "Perhaps he did not dare."

Cecilia felt distinctly uncomfortable. It must have shown in her face, for suddenly, Anne Rowland lost a little of her color. "Oh, my! I hope you do not think I am implying that dear Edmund bullies me? We have the most congenial of marriages."

"I am relieved," said Cecilia a little breathlessly. But inwardly, she wondered if Anne were afraid of her husband.

Anne simply smiled, patting Cecilia on the hand, and changed the subject. "Now, my dear, tell me about this mission of yours. I own, Edmund speaks of it incessantly."

"But of course," said Cecilia smoothly. "Nothing should please me more, given that you and Mr. Rowland are such generous benefactors."

Anne's face brightened. "As I told Lady Kirton," she said fervently, "Edmund is very keen upon paying you a visit. And he wishes me to find a way to be of help to your organization."

Cecilia could see no way out of it. "We should be honored."

"In fact, I have already thought of a small way in which I can assist." Mrs. Rowland smiled, a look of genuine warmth. "I need, you know, a new lady's maid. You do let your girls be taken into service, do you not? I heard you had obtained yours in just such a way, and your hair—well, it is always so cleverly done."

Nervously, Cecilia put up one hand to pat the back of her hair, finding only the usual untidy mass of tumbling curls. Had Etta unknowingly set some sort of trend? Cecilia wanted to laugh. "Well, we do not precisely *let* our women be taken into service," she demurred.

Mrs. Rowland looked surprised. "No?"

Cecilia shook her head. "They choose a job which interests them, and we try to facilitate the training. Etta was simply bold enough to choose highly, and I thought she ought to have the opportunity. That's all."

"Oh," said Mrs. Rowland, looking vaguely confused. "I daresay Edmund will wish me to think of something else, then."

But at that moment, Giles came sweeping across the room toward them, bearing an ancient, doddering dowager on his arm. It was Lady Kirton's elderly aunt from Shropshire, to whom she had been promised an introduction. But apparently, ancient dowagers held no interest for Mrs. Rowland. Gently, she patted Cecilia on the hand again. "I must go," she said softly. "But a bit of parting advice, if I may be bold?"

Mystified, Cecilia nodded. "Of course."

"Your handsome stepson, my dear," Mrs. Rowland whispered. "You really should be seen less often in his company. A snarling guard dog tends to put off suitors." And then she drifted away and into the crowd.

By a quarter past nine, the tension inside Lord Delacourt's dressing room could have been cut with a knife. And Max de Rohan looked as if he wished to brandish his own—and use it on his lordship's valet.

With his chin pinched thoughtfully between his thumb and forefingers, Kemble circled the police officer, first this way, then that, like a spinning top which hadn't quite found its center. Periodically, he made odd little clicking noises in the back of his throat.

Seton, the laundry maid who had been brought in on the off chance that some emergency stitchery might be required, stood in quiet awe to one side. Across one arm she held a black superfine coat, and across the other, six luminescent silk neck cloths. Clearly, Kemble had whipped her into shape, for her eyes were round as saucers.

At last, Kemble ceased his pacing and let his hand fall away from his chin. "Extraordinary," he announced, glancing at David. "Simply extraordinary. The calves are of an excellent length, and the shoulders! Almost perfect!"

David let his gaze run down de Rohan's length. "He's taller, and rather heavier, don't you think?" he said, looking at Kemble uncertainly.

De Rohan's black eyes flashed. "I'm not one of your

bloody overbred horses being sold off at Tattersall's,
Delacourt."

David's gaze drifted back up again. "Forgive me,
sir," he smoothly responded. "I perceive that we have
offended you. Don't take it personally. For good or ill,
gentlemen of fashion talk of such things all day long."

"No wonder you wish for a second career as a
cracksman," sneered de Rohan. "You must be bloody
bored to tears."

"Do you know," mused David, quite unoffended, "I
rather think that I was."

Suddenly, Kemble's wrist flicked out and he
snapped his fingers twice. Seton hastened forward,
and after his hand hovered over her outstretched arm
for a moment, Kemble lifted one of the cravats and
delicately draped it around de Rohan's neck.

Again, he stepped back, running an appraising eye
down de Rohan's length. "He has a few inches on you,
my lord," said the valet as if they'd never strayed from
their topic. "But the trousers are of a good material,
and so they will do. The coat is . . . not irredeemable.
But the waistcoat—no, no, no!"

As de Rohan rolled his eyes, Kemble fashioned the
cravat into the flawless folds of a mail coach. Then he
stepped back, frowned, and rewrapped it even more
simply. "Stock!" he cried out, and Seton darted forth
with the stiff black fabric. Expertly, Kemble fastened
it, then nodded. "Excellent! Severe, yes. But with his
black hair and good neck, he wears it well."

"Well indeed," said David appreciatively. "What
about the waistcoat?"

Kemble snapped his fingers again and motioned
toward the rack of waistcoats. "The crimson one,
Seton," he ordered. "Fetch it here, if you please."

David gasped in outrage. "But—but—but that's my

raven's blood! You said it had to go! You said only a raging lunatic would wear it!"

"Well, that's that," muttered de Rohan. "The bloody thing was surely meant for me."

Ignoring de Rohan's aside, Kemble lifted his brows in disdain. "You dare to question *moi?*" he asked David archly. "His coloring is different! His skin is swarthy! It looks good on him, whereas on you, it looks like a gunshot wound."

"But—but—" David tried to protest.

Kemble turned to de Rohan and patted him neatly on the chest. "I hope you'll feel free to keep it, Inspector," he said quietly. "And now, the coat, Seton. Then you may go."

David could see that the battle for the crimson waistcoat was lost. He sighed and moved on to less divisive issues. "You have sent Kitty on her way to Derbyshire?" he asked Kemble as de Rohan was eased into his coat.

Kemble gave a neat jerk on the coat cuffs, then nodded in satisfaction. "Yes, she and the two runners started off around mid-afternoon," he explained, cutting a quick glance toward David. "And yes, I did speak with the girl at some length. You have the right of it, I collect—what little you have. She knows almost nothing, save for the fact that her sister went into the cellar with two men whom Miss McNamara knew well. French sailors, she says. And recently arrived from India on a merchantman—"

At that, David jerked to attention. "A merchantman? Do you know the name?"

The scowl slipped from de Rohan's face to be replaced by a look of acute interest. He stepped incrementally closer.

Kemble's glance shifted back and forth between

the two of them. "She did not know, but it seems that Miss McNamara's friendship with these men was of long standing, and she knew when they were expected in port."

David turned to de Rohan. "It seems Mr. Rutledge came in from India on the *Queen of Kashmir* several weeks ago. There, perhaps, is another of your coincidences which does not exist."

"Perhaps." De Rohan paused pensively. "It will be a simple matter to check the ownership and registration of the *Queen of Kashmir*. And depending on her schedule, we might be able to roust some of the crew if it comes to that."

David sighed and picked up his black evening cloak. "Well," he said wearily, "let's get on with this, de Rohan. The night lies before us, and we have much to do if we are to go from St. James's to Black Horse Lane. For my part, though, I wish we had a few hours to catch some sleep."

De Rohan barked with laughter. "What you'd best wish for, Delacourt, is someone who can pick locks— quickly and in the dark, too."

In the process of selecting a pin for de Rohan's cravat, Kemble's hand froze over the jewelry box. Slowly, his head turned toward David. "You wish to have a lock picked?"

"Er—yes," admitted David. Suddenly, he felt a shaft of hope. Inquiringly, he lifted his brows. "But surely you cannot . . . ?"

Slightly alarmed, Kemble's gaze flew to the police officer and then back to David. Then he lifted his shoulders in a casual shrug. "Oh, why not?" he returned, selecting a small oval ruby and poking it into de Rohan's cravat. "When and where?"

*   *   *

It would have been too much to hope, David inwardly considered, that perhaps Cecilia had failed to show up for their appointed mission. It was. She sat upon the long brocade sofa just inside his mother's morning room, her gloved hands demurely folded. As soon as she saw them descend the stairs, she rose and swiftly crossed the distance between them.

Her face flushed with anticipation, Cecilia wore a daring dress of dark rose with a gossamer shawl to match. The color should have clashed with her hair, but instead, it brought out the golden blonde highlights and deepened the blue of her eyes.

"Inspector de Rohan!" she exclaimed, taking him by the hands and lifting them as if she might dance him about the room. "How handsome you look! And that stunning waistcoat! Pigeon's blood, is it not?"

"*Raven's* blood," muttered David.

"Yes, that's it!" agreed Cecilia. "I've never seen anything half so elegant."

De Rohan looked acutely uncomfortable. "Thank you, my lady," he said, drawing his hands away.

"Oh, dear," said Cecilia with a frown. "We'd best call you *Mr.* de Rohan tonight, oughtn't we? And David," she added, smiling at him as if he were an afterthought, "you are looking very well, too."

The carriage awaited in the street. David offered his arm and escorted Cecilia out and down the steps. "Where is Lucifer tonight, Mr. de Rohan?" asked Cecilia, looking disappointedly over her shoulder.

"He does not care for formal affairs, my lady," the officer solemnly returned. "He begs to be excused."

Cecilia laughed, and soon they were off and traveling the short distance to St. James's. But they had not yet reached Half Moon Street when Cecilia attempted a *coup d'état.* "I've decided we need to alter our plan," she said, lifting one finger delicately.

"Have you indeed?" David archly replied.

"Yes," she said with a succinct nod. "After reconsidering, I fancy we will arouse less suspicion if we go in separately. I shall go first, and take Mr. de Rohan with me. I shall introduce him as my cousin come down from Upper Brayfield to see the sights and sins of town."

"Why, my dear," said David, staring at her across the darkened carriage. "I did not know your mother was so . . . continental."

"Lady Walrafen," said de Rohan gently. "We really do look nothing alike."

Cecilia was undeterred. "My mother's *distant cousin*—she was a nobody, the daughter of the local squire—so no one will know the difference. Then, David, you will wait five minutes and come in behind us."

David crossed his arms over his chest. "I cannot see why this is necessary," he grumbled.

Cecilia lifted her chin. "I shall tell you why, my lord. If you and I go in together, it will set half the room on its ear, and you know why. Any hope of discretion will be lost to us."

"Oh, very well," complained David. "But perhaps you ought to have thought of that before you insisted upon joining in."

Inwardly, however, he knew that Cecilia was right. David very much wished to slip unnoticed through the crowd, ascertaining who the regular gamesters were, asking a few pointed questions of Lufton's staff. Indeed, bribing them if necessary. And he would just as soon do that away from de Rohan's disapproving eye. His only purpose in bringing the police inspector

along was the hope that de Rohan might get a good
look at Bentham Rutledge, on the off chance that he
might recognize the fellow. And of course, they might
have the opportunity to see him again elsewhere.

Left with little recourse, David turned to de Rohan,
who sat beside him on the seat. "You will look after
her, then," he ordered gruffly. "Now, do either of you
know enough about play to bumble through this?"

Cecilia laughed. "Oh, I can play, my lord. I am a vicious whist player, and not bad at the loo table, if they
have one. And Jed and Harry taught me to play hazard."

David made a sound of exasperation. "You will *not*
play hazard," he warned her darkly.

"You may watch me play, my lady," said de Rohan
kindly. "I am not a bad hand at it. Or, if you wish, we
may play at maccao."

The plan thusly agreed to, Cecilia and de Rohan
alit at the door. The porters recognized neither of
them, but it took only a glance at Cecilia's elegant
coach and de Rohan's ruby stickpin to win them ad-
mittance. Inside, the place was filled with a surge of
people. A few moved from room to room socializing
and seeking play, but many more were already bent
frantically over card games or hazard tables. The few
ladies present played strictly at cards, and along the
fringes of the room, Cecilia caught sight of one or two
of London's more exclusive *demimondaines*, clinging
to the arms of their benefactors.

Together, she and de Rohan strolled through the
rooms, Cecilia staring first to her left and then to her
right. The walls were ostentatiously hung with a tabaret
of gold silk, and matching carpets of gold and red
adorned the floors. Each room was lit by huge chande-
liers with wall sconces strategically placed along the
walls above the card tables. It took but a few moments

before heads began to turn and lips began to whisper as the players caught sight of Cecilia on the arm of an arresting olive-skinned man no one recognized.

Stiffening her spine, Cecilia merely smiled and nodded at those who similarly greeted her. Suddenly, she caught sight of Sir Clifton Ward playing at a nearby hazard table. The young baronet was a particular friend of Giles's. And he was coming their way. Drat it, Giles would ring a peel over her head for sure now. There was no hope of escape.

At once, Cecilia tilted her head toward de Rohan's. "Mr. de Rohan, I fear I have forgotten—what is your Christian name?"

"Maximilian." The word was a whisper. "Or just Max."

Sir Clifton came boldly toward them and bowed. "Lady Walrafen," he said, lifting her hand as he raised one brow in barely suppressed disapproval. "What a pleasant surprise. Does Giles know that you are here?"

"Giles?" Cecilia felt her knees give. "Surely he is not playing?"

The baronet shook his head. "Not at present, no."

At once, Cecilia recovered her manners and introduced the two men. "Max de Rohan?" mused Sir Clifton, flicking a curious gaze down the inspector's length. "From Upper Brayfield, no less! Welcome to London. You must let me know if there is anything I can do to facilitate your enjoyment of town."

Just then, one of the players shrugged his shoulders in resignation. Cecilia could not see his face, but he stepped away into the shadows, as if he now meant merely to observe. Cecilia seized the opportunity. "My cousin wishes to play at hazard," she interjected breathlessly. "And I should very much like to watch, if that is permitted? Would you mind terribly?"

"Not at all." Sir Clifton waved an expansive arm toward the table.

In short order, de Rohan had taken his place, and play had recommenced. Cecilia stood behind Sir Clifton and Max de Rohan, one eye on the table, the other scanning the room for David. Surely, more than five minutes had passed. Where was he? She was beginning to suspect he'd been right in telling her she had no business coming here. The heated desperation of the crowd made her acutely ill at ease, and the women in attendance looked as wan and feverish as the men.

Suddenly, Cecilia felt an intense warmth radiating along her arm. Instinctively, she sensed that the man who had abandoned his place at the table had stepped from the shadows to watch more closely.

"Fair cyprian?" inquired the soft, suggestive voice near her ear. "Or jaded wife?"

Shocked, Cecilia jerked away. "Sir," she said haughtily, snapping her head to eye him over her shoulder. "I believe we've not been properly intro—" At once, her words failed, for she was staring straight into the face of the handsome young man she'd seen at Mother Derbin's.

Almost bashfully, Bentham Rutledge lowered his gaze, brushing a knuckle across his upper lip as if missing a newly shaved mustache. "Oh, dear," he said quietly, looking up at her from beneath a pair of dark, heavy eyebrows. "I've rendered you speechless. I often have just such an effect on women. I never know whether to be pleased or wounded."

"In this case, sir, you may settle upon *wounded*," snapped Cecilia, coming suddenly to her senses. "And *widow*, to answer your first question. Now, do go away."

Rutledge looked deeply contrite, and to her surprise, he backed away with a subservient bow. "I beg

your pardon, ma'am," he said, his voice suddenly
grave. "I have insulted you, when I meant only to flirt."

To her shock, Cecilia realized he really did mean to
withdraw. In fact, he looked genuinely distressed.
What the devil was she thinking? This was an un-
hoped-for opportunity. At once, she pressed her fingertips to her temple. "Forgive me, Mr.—?"

A faint look of hope crossed Rutledge's face, and he
stepped forward a pace. "Rutledge," he returned,
clasping his hands before him like a choirboy. "The
Dishonorable Bentham Rutledge, at your service.
However, you may call me Hell-Bent if you wish," he
added, a beatific smile spreading across his face. "All
the very best people do."

Cecilia fought the grin which threatened at one
corner of her mouth. "Well, Mr. Rutledge," she responded a little more civilly. "You must forgive me,
for I fear I am suffering from the headache. I daresay it makes me snappish. I am Cecilia, Lady
Walrafen."

Rutledge's expressive eyes widened at that. "So . . .
definitely *not* a fair cyprian," he said in a disappointed voice. "I confess, I had hoped to steal you
away from whoever had been fool enough to bring
you here, and offer you my protection."

"*Protection* hardly appears to be what you would
offer any woman, sir," she said smoothly.

At that, Rutledge threw back his head and laughed,
his dark eyes crinkling handsomely at the corners.
"God help me," he said, "but I do tend to fall in love
with witty, sharp-tongued women." He lowered his
head and looked at her intently. "Whatever do you
think will become of me, my lady?"

"It is quite likely," said Cecilia warningly, "that one
of those witty women will eventually hoist you by

your own petard, Mr. Rutledge, and flay you with the edge of her sharp tongue for the rest of your life."

"Good God!" Rutledge feigned an expression of agony. "My petard shrivels at the thought."

Cecilia felt her face turned three shades of red. Even Rutledge looked suddenly aghast. "Oh, dear," he said miserably. "I've done it again, have I not?"

"Done what?"

Rutledge looked penitent. "Insulted another rich and beautiful woman. And now you'll never agree to run away with me and support me in the style to which I wish to become accustomed."

Again, Cecilia found herself struggling against laughter. "A refusal is precisely what you deserve," she chided. "Indeed, Mr. Rutledge, what a man like you wants is a serious-minded wife and a half-dozen children to keep you out of mischief."

Was it her imagination, or did Rutledge looked suddenly stricken? For a long moment, he studied her with a gravity she would not have guessed he possessed. "Do you know," he finally said, "I have recently begun to wonder if you mightn't be right. But alas, I can think of no one who would have me."

Cecilia was shocked by the strange undertone of despondency in his voice. She stared up at him, now only dimly aware of the rattle of the dice box. In the distance, she heard de Rohan call an eight. Laughter and hearty backslapping followed. And still Rutledge held her gaze, his eyes oddly shimmering. Logically, she knew that such a man was dangerous, that he could probably enthrall a woman like a snake charmer. But emotionally, she could not help but react. His emotions were *not* feigned. Surely she would know.

"Persevere, Mr. Rutledge," advised Cecilia gently.

"Use that obvious charisma of yours, and decent women will fall at your feet."

Rutledge smiled weakly, and Cecilia was left with the impression that she had struck a nerve, though how, and in what way, she did not quite understand. Again, he fell silent, merely staring at her. "Have *you* ever wished for children, Lady Walrafen?" he finally asked.

Fleetingly, Cecilia thought she'd misunderstood. "I beg your pardon?"

"Children," he repeated awkwardly. "You see, I'm given to understand that most women do want them—indeed, that they want them very desperately."

Now Rutledge had struck a nerve. A deep one. Strangely, Cecilia found herself wanting to slap him for his impertinence.

But he had not meant to be impertinent, had he? The hint of grief yet lingered in his face. He did not know her, could not begin to understand—or care about—her secret pain. What a strange young man he was. And how peculiar it felt to be here, in this place, engaged in what had begun as a silly flirtation but had somehow become an intensely personal conversation. And yet, Cecilia was left with the oddest impression that they were both dancing around dark edges which neither knew existed. And that they were both perfectly sincere.

"Yes," she said quietly, willing her voice not to choke. "I should very much like children. And what of yourself, Mr. Rutledge? Would you?"

At that, Rutledge laughed, but it was a sharp, almost brittle sound. "My dear Lady Walrafen," he said archly. "I daresay I already have a few. That's the way of us incorrigibles, don't you know."

Cecilia should not have been surprised, particularly with a man like Rutledge. But strangely, she was.

And she was shocked, too, at the sudden chill in his voice. "And just how old are you, Mr. Rutledge, if I may make so bold?"

Such a personal question was a mistake. The faint edge of grief had already slipped away. Abruptly, the irreverent light flared anew in his eyes. Until that moment, Cecilia had not realized how close Rutledge stood, but now, she could feel his body heat.

"I am just turned three-and-twenty," Rutledge softly answered, lowering his lashes and bending his head as if he fully intended to brush her lips with his. "Come, my lady—will you not kiss a young rogue happy birthday?"

Suddenly, Cecilia felt a proprietary, iron-hard grip clamp down on her bare shoulder. "Cecilia, my darling," growled David, jerking her back against the wall of his chest. "Collect your cousin. *Now.* It is time we went home."

A dark sneer had spread across Rutledge's face. "Why, we meet again, my Lord Delacourt," he said very formally. "I'm shocked."

"For my part," snapped David, "we seem to meet altogether too often."

Rutledge looked suddenly bored. "I confess, my lord," he said very quietly, casting his gaze about the room as he withdrew a silver cigar case from his coat pocket. "I grow excessively weary of this game we seem to be playing. Are you not man enough to put an end to it?"

"If it is an end you seek, Rutledge," David snapped, "then I am man enough to put a period to your existence at Chalk Farm tomorrow morning."

Cecilia gasped at the blatant threat, her knees almost buckling beneath her weight. The hand clutching her shoulder went immediately to her waist, anchoring her to David's side. At least half a dozen people were staring at them now, and they could not possibly mistake the possessiveness of his gesture or the anger in his tone.

Rutledge cut a swift glance at Cecilia. "Perhaps we should defer this discussion to another time, my lord," he said, inclining his head in Cecilia's direction. "But soon, I think. Very soon."

Cecilia turned about, forcing David either to loosen his grip or to clutch at her like a madman. She was relieved to see that Max de Rohan was watching them out of the corner of one eye, and counting out his winnings in preparation to leave. Thank God.

She looked back to see that Rutledge had vanished into the crowd. But David remained, his expression dark as a growing storm. There would be hell to pay, she knew, as soon as he saw her alone. But that wouldn't be tonight, would it? For he was going back to Black Horse Lane with de Rohan. And if he lived through that, Bentham Rutledge would try to do him in.

Cecilia did not know which she feared more. There was little she could do about tonight, other than to pray to God they would be safe. But as for Rutledge, she simply had to think of *something*. And quickly, too. For it was just a matter of time before one of them blew the other's brains out—and for no good purpose, she was beginning to think.

16

~

In which Lady Walrafen concocts a Plan

During the short, silent journey back to Curzon
Street, David refrained from giving Cecilia the scolding she had earned for permitting a scoundrel like
Rutledge to flirt with her so outrageously. Instead, he
bit his lip and stared into the darkness somewhere
beyond her shoulder, for he knew it would not do for
de Rohan to overhear another lovers' spat.

But what the devil had she been thinking? Had
she not listened to his conversation with de Rohan
this morning? Yes, she had. But as Cecilia was wont
to do, she had simply sailed into dangerous waters
on her own. But then again, many would have said
Cecilia's greatest risk had been in taking him to her
bed, since he was viewed as far more hardened than
Rutledge.

Though masculine jealousy bit at him just a little,
David inwardly admitted that she had probably been
well intentioned. Cecilia was not, by her nature, a
flirt. No doubt she had hoped to lure Rutledge into revealing himself. While it was possible Rutledge was
not involved in the murders, he was still a treacherous man. Perhaps Cecilia had failed to understand

that. Perhaps he had best call on her tomorrow and explain it in terms which could not possibly be misunderstood.

And sooner or later, he meant to catch Rutledge away from the prying eyes of society and finish what they had started. But Rutledge had been right, damn him. Under no circumstance should Cecilia be a witness to such a sordid discussion.

At last, Cecilia spoke, breaking the fragile silence. "You mean to go on with this foolishness in Black Horse Lane, do you?" she asked, her voice more tremulous than challenging.

"I do."

Almost nervously, she smoothed her hands down the black velvet of her evening cloak. "Then you will return, if you please, past Park Crescent," she said firmly. "And you will throw a stone at my bedchamber window so that I may know that you have returned safely. If you have not done so by four o'clock, then I very much fear I shall have to come looking for you."

David wanted first to laugh, and then to rail at her. Still, underneath it all, he was touched. And of course, he had not the heart to tell her that she'd just publicly proclaimed that he knew the location of her bedchamber. On the seat beside him, the police officer coughed discreetly and stared out the carriage window.

"I'll be there by four," David reassured her.

"But what if—"

"I *will* be there," he said more certainly.

After a long pause, Cecilia nodded. "Very well."

"Lor, mum!" exclaimed Etta as soon as Cecilia strode through the door of her bedchamber. "A quick trip, that was. Can't think why you got all rigged out for so little."

Wearily, Cecilia stripped off her gloves as Etta lifted the evening cloak from her shoulders. "Oh, I fear I made Lord Delacourt very angry," she grumbled, tossing the gloves on to her bed. "He insisted we leave early."

Etta's brows went up at that. "What now? I vow, I wonder if you don't torture that man deliberately."

Cecilia felt her cheeks grow warm. "I'm afraid I let Bentham Rutledge flirt with me just a bit."

"Rutledge?" said Etta archly as she folded the cloak over her arm. "That fellow you spied at Mother Derbin's? The one his lordship thinks is up ter no good?"

Biting her lip, Cecilia nodded. Had she been wrong to tell Etta so much of what had gone on these last few days? "Really, Etta, Mr. Rutledge was ever so nice," she insisted. "Almost sad, I thought. And he cannot possibly be mixed up in these murders. I only wish I could convince Delacourt of that before one of them kills the other."

Etta pulled a skeptical face. "No disrespect, mum," she said warningly, "but 'ow would you know what's what? I mean—you ain't exactly experienced in them sort o' things. Best let Lord Delacourt handle it as he sees fit."

Crossing to her dressing table, Cecilia sank down in the chair, crushing her fists into the folds of her silk gown. "Oh, Etta! Spare me your lecture, for I know perfectly well that Delacourt will give me one at the first opportunity," she moaned. "I just *know* Mr. Rutledge is innocent, that's all."

"Oh, ho!" exclaimed Etta as she began to pull the pins from Cecilia's hair. "*Innocent*, now, is he?"

Vigorously, Cecilia shook her head. "Well, perhaps not precisely innocent—"

"Stop yer twitchin', mum," ordered Etta around a mouthful of hairpins, "afore I poke out an eye."

Cecilia tried to sit still. "All I'm trying to say," she explained as her long, unruly hair tumbled about her shoulders, "is that Rutledge is an incorrigible flirt, to be sure. And quick-tempered, too. But underneath it all, there is something else I cannot quite make out. And I greatly begin to fear that someone will get hurt! Indeed, I begin to suspect Delacourt is on the wrong trail altogether, and I shall never forgive myself if something terrible happens to him because of it."

At that, Etta slapped a handful of hairpins onto the dressing table and barked with laughter. "Worrit about Delacourt, are you? Oh, mum, that's a rich 'un, that is. He knows what he's doing, count on it."

Cutting a glance up at Etta's reflection in the mirror, Cecilia pursed her lips. "Oh, you think so, do you? Then let me tell you that at this very instant he is with Chief Inspector de Rohan, breaking into Mother Derbin's cellar!"

Pensively stroking a brush through Cecilia's hair, Etta grew silent for a moment. "Well," she reluctantly admitted, "that does sound a bit dicey."

Cecilia frowned into the mirror. "Indeed, the whole of his behavior has been nothing but dicey these last few days. And if he lives through tonight's foolishness, he next means to schedule a dawn appointment with Rutledge. I begin to believe I must take steps to put a stop to it."

"Oh?" Etta's stroking hand slowed. "An' just what do you mean ter do?"

For a long moment, Cecilia considered it. "I believe I must speak with Mr. Rutledge alone. He and David obviously despise one another, but I daresay I can persuade Rutledge to tell me what he knows."

At once, Etta's hand froze. "Oh, m'lady . . . I don't like the sound o' that one bit."

After sending Cecilia home, David and de Rohan swiftly changed into boots and dark breeches, then sent 'round for his carriage. Together with Kemble, the trio made their way east toward Black Horse Lane. To David's surprise, the neighborhood which had been relatively quiet during his visit with Cecilia now thronged with boisterous people, mostly of the lower classes, and more than a few of them looking a trifle castaway.

De Rohan apparently sensed his disquiet. "The workers have all come to the public houses tonight to be paid," he said by way of explanation.

In the darkness of the carriage, David looked at him pointedly. "To be paid?" he echoed. "In the tap rooms?"

"A common practice, my lord," interjected Kemble.

De Rohan snorted. "Allegedly for the convenience of the employer."

At that, Kemble laughed bitterly. "Convenient for the tapsters, more likely. And not at all convenient for the women and children who are apt to see next week's rent drunk up before daylight."

Again, David found himself stunned into silence. Soon, his coachman was pulling over as instructed, some distance beyond Black Horse Lane. Quietly, the three of them got out, David taking down an unlit lantern from his footman as they left.

"Follow me," ordered de Rohan, jerking his head toward a dark alley. "This route runs parallel to the main thoroughfare and approaches the brothel from the rear."

They set off, the clamor of the street quickly fading into oblivion. With de Rohan in the lead and Kemble closing the rear, they proceeded through the moonlit, twisting lanes at a good clip, the silence broken only by the howl of a distant dog and a faint but rhythmic *clink, clinking* sound.

"What the devil is that racket?" David finally hissed over his shoulder.

"Tools," whispered Kemble.

"Aye," interjected de Rohan bitterly. "Cracksman's gear, by the sound of it."

"You mean there are tools for such a thing?" asked David, incredulous. "I somehow imagined one used a hatpin or a hammer."

De Rohan gave a grunt of astonishment. "For a man with such diversely skilled servants, my lord, you are remarkably ill informed."

Again, David made no answer, for he did not know what to say. Kemble *was* deuced odd. Where on earth had Rannoch found the fellow? David was willing to lay a goodly wager that the man had not spent the whole of his life as a valet.

It took but five minutes of walking before David recognized that they had come out in the opposite end of the alley which ran behind Mother Derbin's and the tobacconist. In a shaft of moonlight, de Rohan paused and pointed into the shadows. "The stairwell is beneath that window," he whispered. "I'll stand watch."

"Now, let us see what we have here," said Kemble with a measure of relish. Without misstep, the valet made his way down into the black pit of the stairwell. In the darkness, David could hear his gloved hands sliding expertly back and forth across the wood.

"Afraid of wandering through St. Giles to buy my porcelain, were you?" whispered David dryly.

Intent upon his work, Kemble ignored the sarcasm. "Three locks," he confirmed, sounding very unlike the persnickety, effete gentleman's gentleman David had thought him. "And all of them remarkably alike. Exceedingly considerate, I should say." With another *clink-clank*, the valet put his tools down.

To David's surprise, Kemble had eschewed his normally dapper dress for trousers and an old frieze surtout, all in solid black. Now, but a few feet below, he could barely be seen. With de Rohan standing above, David listened as the valet knelt to rummage through his small black bag. Gingerly, he withdrew two or three silvery objects, and then struck a tinderbox to light a small stub of candle. After passing it up and down the door, he blew it out again, then set to work.

Almost at once, David heard the little *snick* of the first lever tumbler as it eased into place. The locks were obviously well used, and the next two followed shortly. It was just that easy.

In a matter of seconds, David had descended into the cloud of stale urine and damp mold which hung about the stairwell. Cracking open the door, he pushed it inward just an inch. Inside, no light shone, but the musty odor of an unused cellar was remarkably absent.

Carefully, David slipped past Kemble to step inside, pausing to listen. Above, he could hear the faint tinkle of an ill-tuned pianoforte and the rumbling tread of people moving about Mother Derbin's drawing room. But below, all was bathed in silence.

Quietly, he knelt to light the lantern. If someone were to be caught, he wished it to be only himself, since this bit of foolishness had been his idea. The wick sputtered, then flared to life, bathing the low-ceilinged room in yellow light. Lifting the lantern, David passed it about, chasing shadows from the corners as he moved. The windowless room was all but empty.

He exhaled a sigh of relief, unaware until that moment that he had been holding his breath. Over his shoulder, he motioned to Kemble and de Rohan. "You two needn't come in if you don't wish to risk it," he said, even as they both slipped inside.

De Rohan pushed shut the door and began to prowl through the room, as a panther might prowl in search of his next meal. His boots were silent on the earthen floor which was smooth and free of debris. Along the rearmost wall, two wooden trestle tables flanked a tall cupboard. The inspector's eyes lit upon it, and swiftly, he yanked open the doors, which swung free on well-oiled hinges. Empty.

In silent warning, David gestured to their right, toward the narrow wooden stairs which descended from the main floor. Opposite them, the center wall was set with a small, crudely fashioned door made of planks and bolted shut with a rough-hewn wooden bar.

For a moment, de Rohan studied it. "Another room," he said quietly. "Let's have a look."

One by one, they squatted down and crawled through the door. Inside, the floor beneath them dropped down another two feet, but there was a great deal more to see. Here, the ceiling was even lower, and the floor neatly laid with flagstone. Against one wall sat four crude wooden bunks with what looked like straw mattresses. On a low table, a candle stub sat in a clay dish which overflowed with melted tallow. A broken teacup lay in pieces beneath it. Other than that, this room, too, appeared empty.

"I think we're beneath the tobacco shop," whispered de Rohan as David moved through the room, lifting his lamp and passing it all about. He looked back at the plank door, noting the bolt affixed to the inside. A room designed for privacy, then.

Suddenly, something crunched beneath David's

boot heel. He stepped back and squatted down to pick it up. It was a small wooden slat with a bit of brass hinge fashioned into it. "Look here, de Rohan," he whispered in the darkness. "What do you make of it?"

De Rohan and Kemble drew near, facing each other across the piece of wood. Kemble stroked his index finger over the brass hinge, then lifted his eyes to the police officer, his expression knowing. "The metalwork is elaborate—Asian or Indian, I should guess," he said.

His face grim, de Rohan took the slat and roughly drew his thumbnail over the wood. For a moment, he regarded it in silence. "Mangowood," he finally said. "And you've a good eye for metalwork."

Just then, David's eye lit on a small footlocker shoved beneath one of the bunks. "Look there," he whispered, jerking his head toward it. "A seaman's chest, do you think?"

De Rohan knelt to drag the chest from beneath the bed. Inside lay a bundle of rags, a brass bowl, a few tallow candles and a small, four-bladed knife, curled like long, wicked fingernails.

Gingerly, the police officer picked up the strange tool. "A *nashtar*," he whispered hollowly.

"What the hell is that?" asked David, holding the lantern over the open chest. "It looks like some tool of the devil."

"In a manner of speaking, it's precisely that," answered de Rohan darkly. "This is a lancet used to harvest poppy juice. Someone must have kept it as a souvenir."

"Opium smuggling," said Kemble succinctly.

David looked back and forth between them. "But opium is perfectly legal," he said tightly. "So someone is bringing in opium for unlawful purposes, I take it?"

Grimly, de Rohan nodded. "For the very worst sort

of purposes, I should say. And bypassing the Customs House to do it."

"It sounds as if we need to pay a visit to the *Queen of Kashmir,* does it not?" said David.

In the dim light, de Rohan shook his head as he stared down at the elaborate lancet. "I do not know," he mused. "Certainly, this looks Indian. But opium is usually imported from Turkey, perhaps Egypt."

"Legally taxed opium, you mean," interjected Kemble. "But if a person had regular access to an India-bound merchantman . . . ?"

Absently, David knelt and plucked the brass bowl from the contents of the sea chest. "What does its origin matter?" he mused, studying the intricate design. "I cannot imagine one would store anything legally imported in the cellar of a brothel."

With a grunt of agreement, de Rohan shoved the wooden slat into the pocket of his greatcoat. "You are right about that," he answered, as David touched the bottom of the brass bowl, which was covered with dark resin. "What have you there, Delacourt?"

Still holding the bowl in one palm, David reached out a hand to Kemble. "Look here, old boy, give me one of those silvery tools of yours."

At once, Kemble drew two from his bag, his brows drawing into a puzzled frown.

David took one, then scraped a little of the resin onto the tip and knelt to hold it over the flame of the lamp. Kemble and de Rohan squatted down to watch as David tilted the tool this way and that over the heat. Quickly, the lump turned pale, softening like a glob of candle wax. Soon, it began to swell, and then bubble and hiss.

Immediately, David carried it to his nose, gingerly

inhaling just a whiff. "Ugh!" he exclaimed, jerking away from the smell. "Definitely opium."

Kemble's expression darkened. "You've visited opium dens, then, my lord?"

With two quick swipes, David raked off the residue onto the toe of his boot. "Once or twice," he quietly admitted, addressing the cobblestones. "The unfortunate consequence of a dissolute life, you are no doubt thinking."

"I should certainly be pleased to hear otherwise," de Rohan growled.

David laughed a little bitterly as he rose from the floor. "Let's just say I've had occasion to go searching for lost souls," he confessed. "Regrettably, friends can disappear into such places, and one never knows if or when they will emerge."

Abruptly, de Rohan stood. "Foolish friends you have, my lord."

"Neither opium eaters nor fools are rarity amongst the *beau monde*," admitted David.

"And it is in part your frivolous *beau monde* which creates a black market for this vile merchandise," de Rohan bit out.

David passed the tool back to Kemble. "I know that," he said quietly. "And I'm not proud of it."

"Well, I just wish to God they would use their wealth to bribe the legal substance from some greedy physician," de Rohan snapped. "Then they might stay in the West End and die in their own beds, rather than bring their filthy habits into my neighborhood."

Kemble assumed a bored posture. "While you fellows stage your little passion play, I'm going back in the other room," he interjected, heading for the door. "I seem to have dropped a pick." But he had no sooner dragged his last boot through the opening than the squeal of hinges could be heard overhead.

"Blister it!" hissed de Rohan. "Someone is coming down. Get out, Kemble!"

At once, Kemble disappeared into the shadows. De Rohan swung shut the wooden door, shooting the small metal bolt.

In a trice, David had put out the lamp and pressed himself against the wall beside the door. On the other side of the entrance, he could hear de Rohan's soft breathing. There was no place else to hide. They could only pray that Kemble had escaped into the alley, and that whoever was descending had no interest in this room.

Over the pounding rhythm of his own heart, David could hear the clatter of footsteps trammeling down the wooden stairs—more than one person, by the sound of it. Suddenly, a clear, feminine voice could be heard through the door planks.

"Ugh! I 'ate this bleedin' cellar," said Mother Derbin, her voice now edged with strident Cockney. "And it ain't Monday, so I've not got the rent money. Besides, I can't think why we 'ave ter come down 'ere to talk."

"For this, you ignorant bitch," a deep, rasping voice growled. Simultaneously, the crack of someone's palm striking flesh split the darkness, and David heard what sounded like a skull thud back against the makeshift door.

"And that ain't all yer like ter get if you can't keep your whores out'er this place," the voice continued. "Now I've got ter contend wi' that son of a bitch de Rohan and his hell-hound sniffing up and down Wapping Wall, arstin' questions, God rot you."

Mother Derbin gave no ground. "Look 'ere, now," she said coldly. "I can't stand watch over these girls all the live-long day! I got me a business ter run, and I told you that from the first." Through the door, it sounded as if she dragged herself up from the floor and leaned back against the planks. They creaked inward, but de Rohan had rammed the bolt safely home.

"Then keep that pox-riddled bunch o' sluts upstairs," the rasping man demanded. "Or move yer business elsewhere. The boss 'as need of this cellar, and that's 'ow it's ter be. Now, you listen, and you listen good—there's a ship laid anchor in the Blackwall Reach, just come in from Constantinople."

David racked his brain. Where had he heard that strange, cold voice before?

"I've got no ship on my schedule," she hotly protested.

"Schedule be damned," growled the man. "The shipment was ter come in by dray through Covent Garden, but seems I got me a problem. Someone's set the Bow Street constables ter watchin' me shop—that bastard de Rohan belike—so if the coast ain't clear, the shipment's coming upriver ter you. And you'll not be whining about it if yer knows what's smart."

Mother Derbin was displeased. "Well, this time make bleedin' sure the seamen you bribe 'ave got a teaspoon of brains between 'em," she demanded, her voice rich with sarcasm.

The man gave a low, wicked laugh. "Aye, I've hired us some Chinamen this time—not them witless Frogs what 'er always thinkin' with their cocks. Chinamen might 'appen ter smoke a bit o' the merchandise, but they won't drag a couple o' wide-eyed whores down 'ere ter keep 'em company while they do it."

For a moment, Mother Derbin said nothing. "All right," she finally snapped. "When do they offload?"

"If 'n when you needs ter know, I'll send word," he

said coldly. "You probably won't, cause the boss means ter handle this one personally."

"The boss?" she echoed incredulously. "Why?"

"Because o' the bleedin' constables 'oo'er watching us," he spat. "Not that it's any o' yer business. But someone plainly tipped 'em off. That's wot I'm trying ter tell yer. We got ter be careful 'oo we trust. Now, swish yer wide arse back upstairs and fetch me that skinny little black-haired whore I'm partial to. I'm in the mood, and you ain't my type."

The planked door gave a little groan as Mother Derbin apparently pulled herself away from it. Suddenly, the man inhaled sharply. "Well, God damn you for a fool," he bit out. "Look 'ere, you stupid cow—someone's gone and left the bleedin' storage room unbolted."

Stupid cow.

The cruel phrase finally struck a cord. *Covent Garden. Bow Street.* By God, he could place that cold voice unmistakably now. It was Grimes. The man who'd beaten—and probably raped—Dot King in Goodwin's Court.

And Grimes was going to shove open the door any second. In the pitch black, David felt for his pistol. The butt of the weapon felt cool to his touch, and he suddenly found himself eager to blow Grimes's brains to kingdom come. Yet it was an easier death than a woman-beater deserved.

But the door did not fly inward. Instead, Grimes merely struck Mother Derbin again, then drove the wooden bar home with a harsh scrape. Now they were locked in with no way to escape, unless Kemble was either brave enough or foolish enough to return to the cellar. Through the planks, David could hear footsteps going back up the stairs.

"Christ Jesus!" breathed de Rohan in the darkness. "You just shaved a decade off my life, Delacourt."

David withdrew his hand from his pocket and felt for the metal bolt, sliding it backward. Not that it would do any good when the door was now braced from the opposite side. "Kemble will think of something," David said, with more confidence than he felt.

Just then, as if David had willed it, the wooden bar could be heard scraping back from its slot. On silent hinges, the planked door swung inward. "Move!" whispered Kemble urgently. "Get the hell out before they return."

David felt the valet's arm thrust through the door to give them a hand up. "How the devil did you get back in?" he asked, pushing de Rohan toward the door.

"I never left," said Kemble as he helped the police officer crawl through. "I hid in the cupboard. A most enlightening little *tête-à-tête*, was it not?"

With de Rohan through, David handed Kemble the lantern and scrabbled up next. It took but a few moments to make their exit, with Kemble neatly relocking the door as they departed. With any luck at all, Mother Derbin would never know they had been inside.

As they made their way swiftly through the dark and twisting alleys, David explained just who he believed the raspy-voiced man had been, and de Rohan did not question his judgment. "So Mr. Grimes *is* right about being scrutinized by the police," the inspector chuckled. "But not for the reason he thinks!"

"No," agreed David grimly. "I asked that he be watched because of what he did to Miss King. One look at the fellow told me he was up to no good."

By the time they reached the carriage, David's blood-lust had calmed somewhat, and reason was slowly returning. De Rohan, however, was one step ahead of him. "We must *prove* that Grimes is the mysterious Mr. Smith," he said pensively. "I do not doubt you, Delacourt, but it mightn't be enough for a magistrate. We could board the ship he mentioned—there won't be many lying at anchor answering that description. Still, Grimes is working for someone on shore, and I should sooner reel in a big fish than a small one."

In the dim light, David studied de Rohan. "Then it seems we must pay a visit on Mother Derbin," he agreed. "Why do I not meet you in Black Horse Lane after a few hours' sleep? Say, ten o'clock at the coffee house? From that vantage point, we can observe all who come and go from the brothel. And then we can question her."

He could sense de Rohan's hesitation. "And so it is still *we,* my lord?" he asked sharply. "You mean to continue with this fool's errand?"

"Oh, yes," said David softly.

17

~

Hell-Bent to Hampstead

Cecilia was possessed of many fine virtues, but to the frequent frustration of those around her, patience and prudence were rarely among them. And so it was that by noon of the following day, she had ridden halfway to Hampstead Heath, leaving Jed trailing reluctantly behind and Etta's dire admonitions floating on the wind somewhere over Marylebone.

As the miles passed, and greater London vanished in her wake, Cecilia was increasingly confident of her mission. Thank God David had done as she'd asked and awakened her in the early hours of the morning. She had looked out into the street below to see him standing on the pavement in a pool of lamplight, his expression grim. He had found something. She could sense the ruthless determination which radiated through the darkness.

And now, like a bloodhound on the scent, he would step up his efforts to flush out a murderer, poking about in dark, treacherous places, in the belief that Bentham Rutledge was behind it. And in so doing, Cecilia was beginning to fear he might be blindsided by a threat which could come from an altogether different quarter.

And it would be all her fault. Yes, from the moment he had set foot in the Daughters of Nazareth Society, she had maligned his integrity and laughed at his sincerity. How wrong she had been! And now she feared he felt compelled to prove just how wrong—and in a most dangerous way.

She had to do *something*. Throughout her sleepless night, Cecilia had gone over and over her strange conversation with Rutledge. His words, his face, his carefully hidden emotions—they still nagged at her. There were other things, too. Small things, yes. But taken as a whole, they solidified her conviction that he was not the man they sought. And yet, the enmity between Rutledge and David was palpable. Why she could not say, but David's remark to de Rohan in which he had compared himself to Rutledge had not gone unnoticed by Cecilia. Perhaps David's hostility was more personal?

Still, if she could confirm her suspicions about Rutledge, perhaps both of them might relent? Or at least be spared a dangerous dawn appointment? Moreover, Cecilia was increasingly certain that Rutledge possessed information which they needed, were they ever to find Meg and Mary's killer.

From Regent's Park, the ride to the picturesque village of Hampstead was not long, and even in winter, the scenery was pleasant. Still, Cecilia's mind was not on the stunning vista which greeted her as she approached Downshire Hill. In front of the church, she pulled Zephyr up, pausing to study the neat arrangement of houses and cottages which stretched out along the heath's edge.

"What now, my lady?" Jed asked. "We can't just knock on every door 'til we find the blighter."

Cecilia nudged her horse forward. "We will continue on to High Street until we see a place of business," she said confidently. "Something Rutledge might frequent, such as a greengrocer or a vintner."

But it wasn't that simple. Not one shopkeeper had ever heard of a Mr. Bentham Rutledge. How odd it seemed that a notorious rake would live a life of such quiet rustication. Had the young man been as dissolute as David believed, one would have imagined the villagers would have kept their wives and daughters locked up. But instead, the pretty little lanes of Hampstead were filled with them, and not a one of them knew Rutledge.

In Black Horse Lane, the morning's din inside the coffee house had waned until it was now nothing more than the quiet murmur of voices punctuated by the occasional clatter of a teaspoon against porcelain. The aroma of strong coffee and toasting bread lingered as, one by one, the assorted shopkeepers, clerks, and seamen made their way out the door and back into the street to commence the day's business in earnest.

A man in a brown coat brushed past David's table, a worn newspaper protruding from his pocket, but David scarcely noticed. Through the sooty glass, he stared blindly out at the short flight of steps which rose up to Mother Derbin's front door.

"You are thinking of her, are you not?" asked de Rohan softly. Though he sat just across the narrow table, his voice penetrated David's thoughts as if he spoke from a distance.

Slowly, David tore his gaze from the window and turned to look at the police officer. "Of Mother Derbin?" he asked, vaguely amused.

Almost imperceptibly, de Rohan shook his head. "Ah . . . no," he answered, looking very much as if he wished he'd kept his thoughts to himself. "I meant Lady Walrafen."

Against his better judgment, David smiled wryly. "Yes," he said softly, dropping his gaze to his empty coffee cup. "Yes, I daresay I am."

De Rohan cleared his throat delicately. "I understand," he replied, his voice touched with neither lust nor envy. "She is quite a woman."

Abruptly, David shoved back his chair with a grating sound. "Let's overlook my ill-fated love life for the nonce, shall we?" he replied quietly, dropping two coins onto the table. "I, for one, can probably expect better luck dealing with Mother Derbin, so let us go. There is obviously nothing to be seen from here."

But there was little more to be seen inside Mother Derbin's. It had taken but two minutes for de Rohan to push his way through the busy street, past Mother Derbin's burly porter, and into her private office. She recognized them both at once. The look she gave de Rohan was fearful and derisive. But the cutting glance she shot David was still more telling.

De Rohan she knew, in that age-old way by which the unscrupulous innately sense their enemy. But her lordly customer from the West End clearly unsettled her. His rules of engagement were not known to her. Mother Derbin went immediately on guard, eyeing him up and down with something which surpassed suspicion.

Oh, yes! thought David with an inward satisfaction. *Better the devil you know, eh, Mrs. Derbin?*

Today, the madam wore a tawdry day dress of lavender chintz, her ample arms and breasts lushly oozing from it. David eyed her across a tea table which was marred by water rings and pitted with black scars from at least a dozen forgotten cheroots.

"I've said I know nothing at all which might be of help to you, Inspector," she repeated for the third time, her enunciation far more cultivated than last night. But it was unmistakably the same voice, and David could sense that de Rohan, too, recognized it.

In the back of his throat, the officer made a faint growling noise, sounding very much like the black mastiff he'd left on the pavement outside.

In response, Mother Derbin smiled and lightly lifted her shoulders. "As I've said, I merely rent these premises—three floors, at any rate. I know nothing whatsoever about the cellars or the garrets. If you're looking for Mr. Smith, I fear I have no notion where one might find him."

"Oh, find him I shall, Mrs. Derbin," said de Rohan very softly. "You may be sure of that. And I won't stop there."

A slightly haunted expression sketched across her face but just as quickly vanished. "To be sure," she admitted easily. "For if you wish to watch my front door, I can hardly stop you. Sooner or later, I do not doubt that he will show up."

At once, she stood. Clearly, as far as the madam was concerned, their meeting was at an end. She had deftly evaded all of their questions, sensing that they could prove nothing. David could feel the heat of de Rohan's frustration. Regrettably, they had little legal recourse, save placing the brothel under constant surveillance. And even that might net no immediate result, particularly if the so-called shipment went instead to Covent Garden. Despite Grimes's grumbling, there were scarcely enough officers to watch one place, let alone two, and the Garden was far from the River Police's usual jurisdiction.

So if they had no *legal* recourse . . .

Abruptly, David pushed to his feet and picked up his hat. "Understand me, madam," he said coldly. "Smuggling is one thing, but your business associates made a grievous error when they murdered Mary O'Gavin. Now this has become a very personal matter, so far as I am concerned. If the police cannot resolve this by . . . shall we say, *routine methods*, then there are other ways. I daresay you know what I mean."

In response, much of the color drained from Mother Derbin's face, leaving only the bright red circles of her rouge standing out starkly against her skin. "Why—you—you cannot threaten me!" she hissed, jerking from her sofa.

Lightly, David lifted his brows and tugged a card from the pocket of his coat. "I have not yet threatened anyone," he said, tossing the card onto her table with a disdainful flick of his wrist. "But when I do, the threat is generally clear and unmistakable. Now, should you think better of your reticence after we've gone, you may send word to Mr. de Rohan's office, or to me at that address."

"I rather doubt that I shall," purred the bawd.

De Rohan shook his head. "Let me just ask, Mrs. Derbin, if you've ever seen the inside of Bridewell?" he asked very softly. "Or if you have any notion what happens to your sort inside those cold, miserable walls?"

Mother Derbin paused for a heartbeat, and then, as if she'd made up her mind about something, crossed quickly to a small walnut secretary which stood against one wall. Dropping down the desk, she drew a sheet of paper from one of the pigeonholes, scratched out an address, then thrust it at de Rohan. "I leased this place from a counting house in

Leadenhall Street," she said tightly. "Perhaps you will find the man you seek there. Now, please leave."

It was over—for now. They went out into the surprisingly bright sunshine, de Rohan angrily crumpling the bit of paper into his fist. "The same?" asked David succinctly as they stepped onto the pavement.

"Yes," answered de Rohan. "And now that I think on it, I believe I shall make another visit to Leadenhall Street. Do you wish to come?"

David shook his head as they made their way out of the side street and across Black Horse Lane to his waiting carriage. "I cannot," he said quietly. "I have a little matter to settle with her ladyship yet this morning. Be good enough to let me know what you learn."

Almost two long hours after her arrival in Hampstead, Cecilia found herself near a blacksmith's shop at the end of the village. Bentham Rutledge had proved a most elusive quarry, and Cecilia was beginning to feel desperate. Perhaps he had good reason not to be found? Or perhaps he was using an assumed name?

At that thought, recollection suddenly dawned. *He lived in his sister-in-law's house!* He was not hiding from anyone. Cecilia searched her memory for the name she'd heard David give de Rohan. *Treyhern.*

Jed entered the smithy and returned quickly. "At the end of Heath Street," he announced. "We're to turn at North End Way, pass by the Castle Tavern, and it's the third cottage on the left."

"Thank you, Jed," she said with a sigh of relief.

Soon they had reached the tavern, and then the wooded lane beyond. The third house was small, but rather more than a cottage. Made of vine-covered red brick, the old house was two-storied, with a sharply pitched slate roof and twin chimneys at each end. It was situated very near the street, with what appeared to be fine gardens neatly fenced with wrought iron.

Cecilia dismounted beneath the branches of a bare oak opposite the house, handing her reins to Jed. "I shall be but a few moments," she insisted, more bravely than she felt. But just as she reached the gate, a stooped, elderly woman came toddling out the front door. She was dressed all in black and wearing an old-fashioned white cap with lappets. On her arm, she carried an empty market basket.

Cecilia met her at the gate, heart hammering in her chest. "Good afternoon, ma'am," she said politely. "Is Mr. Rutledge at home?"

Nodding, the old woman lifted the latch and held open the gate, her expression one of polite disinterest. "Aye, if it's young Mr. Bentley you'd be wanting," she agreed, waving her hand toward the rear of the house. "He'd be right around back, puttering about in the garden. Just go 'round and announce yourself."

Cecilia was a little taken aback. She had not thought it would be so simple. Moreover, the woman who stood before her looked nothing like the sort of servant she would have expected Mr. Rutledge to have. "Thank you, I shall," she managed, stepping onto the graveled path the old woman pointed toward.

Behind her, Cecilia heard the woman call out a cheery good afternoon to Jed, and then the iron gate clattered shut. Gravel crunching softly beneath her riding boots, Cecilia made her way past a sweep of well-pruned boxwoods which edged the street. The side gardens were filled with flower beds, now freshly turned and lying dormant as they awaited spring. Soon, the serpentine path wound past a swath of lilac bushes flanking the house, then entered a trellised passageway which was covered with old climbing roses. As she passed through it, Cecilia could only imagine how lovely it must be in the summertime.

Suddenly, the passageway ended, and Cecilia found herself standing in a beautiful rear garden with a stone fountain in the center. Along the wrought-iron fence stood rose bushes, three and four deep in many places, their beds artfully edged with a low rock wall. In the rearmost corner, a man holding a rake was bent down on one knee, fixedly studying the earth around one of the bushes.

At once, he seized the bush by its gnarled base and gave it a violent shake. "Bloody frigging ants," she heard him growl. "It's scarce March, rot you." So frustrated was his invective, so intent was his study, Rutledge did not hear Cecilia approach.

He bent lower, still scowling. Cecilia found herself compelled to suppress a giggle. "Mr. Rutledge?" At once, Rutledge's head jerked up, his eyes squinting against the afternoon sky.

Suddenly, comprehension dawned, and he stood, casually tossing the rake against the fence. "Well, you do surprise me, Lady Walrafen," he said softly, swinging one long leg out of the bed and onto the lawn. "I confess, this is not at all what I expected to happen next."

Cecilia thought it an odd remark. "I'm sorry to disturb you, Mr. Rutledge," she said. "But your servant told me I should come directly back. I believe she was on her way to market."

"Ah—that would be just like Nanny," he acknowledged, still staring at Cecilia with a burning intensity. "Of course, we stand on little ceremony here at Roselands Cottage."

Nanny? Just how dissolute could a man be if he

lived with his nanny in a cottage called Roselands? The thought almost gave Cecilia confidence, but it was a grave mistake. Rutledge was still walking toward her with a slow, predatory grace. His cocksure humor of last night had vanished, to be replaced by something far less benevolent. He looked angry. No, he looked . . . *affronted*.

When he spoke, Rutledge's voice was quiet, almost seductive, as he closed the distance between them. "You are still clutching your crop, my lady," he said, letting his gaze slide over her. "Do you fear you may have need of it?"

"No, indeed!" said Cecilia, nervously dropping it into the grass. "I simply—forgot."

At once, Rutledge bent down to snare it. Cecilia noticed that he wore no work gloves, and that his hands looked capable and callused. "You seem very ill at ease, Lady Walrafen," he said, sliding her crop through his long fingers, his eyes glittering wickedly. "You needn't be, you know. I daresay I already know what you've come for."

Cecilia drew back just an inch. "I'm certain, Mr. Rutledge, that you have no clue," she said, her voice surprisingly calm. "All I seek is information."

"Oh, *information?*" Rutledge said lightly. "Are you perfectly sure, my lady, that there is not something a little more specific which you wanted from me?"

"You mistake me, Mr. Rutledge," she retorted.

"Do I?" he whispered, stepping just a little nearer. "Do you wish me to believe, Lady Walrafen, that your friend Delacourt didn't deliberately send you here?" Almost absently, he lifted his hand to capture the ringlet of hair which brushed her collar.

"I can assure you he did not," she coolly insisted,

slapping away Rutledge's hand. But Cecilia was suddenly uneasy.

"Then I think, my lady," Rutledge continued very softly, "that you'd best convince me your interest is more self-serving."

"You'll not intimidate me with your bold pretensions, Mr. Rutledge," Cecilia insisted. "It won't wash. I've already seen you for what you are, a rather nice young man undernea—"

Cecilia never completed her sentence. Like a strong, sinewy carriage whip, his arm lashed around Cecilia's waist, dragging her against him. As her hand came out to stay him, Rutledge's mouth captured hers, almost gently at first, then harder as she struggled against him. Panic shot through her. His mouth was nothing like David's. Rutledge's touch felt cold and calculating, his grip implacable.

Jed! She had to scream for Jed! Impotently, she struggled against him until she freed one hand, drawing it back to slap him. But just then, Rutledge was somehow torn from her and hurled backward onto the ground, his skull cracking ominously against the base of the stone fountain.

Her hands flying to her mouth, Cecilia stared at the man who towered over Rutledge. It was not Jed.

Oh, dear . . .

"You worthless son of a bitch," David growled down at the man who lay sprawled upon the grass. "I've a mind to splinter your ribs for that."

He moved as if he might draw back his boot, but Rutledge swiftly recovered, rolling away and springing to his feet like a cat. "If it's a brawl you want, Delacourt, I'd be glad to oblige," he challenged, making a fist with one hand while motioning David forward with the other. "Come on, my pretty fellow! It's been deuced dull around here."

"There is a lady present, you swine," growled David. "And you will apologize to her at once."

Rutledge let his fighting stance go, rocking back onto his heels. "Will I?" he asked, his voice lethally soft. "I cannot see why, when the lady has sought me out in the privacy of my home. In my experience, that generally means she either wants something besides information, or she's a woman who's been sent to do a man's job—but with soft words and trickery."

At once, David grabbed him by the coat collar, jerking him forward. "You will apologize for that as well."

"I don't think so," Rutledge sneered, shoving David violently backward.

David stepped back a pace. "Mr. Rutledge," he said, his voice ruthlessly calm, "I am afraid we must meet."

Cecilia rushed forward. "David, you must be out of your mind! He tried to kiss me, nothing more."

David's head jerked around, his eyes blazing almost cruelly. "Cecilia, you *will* be quiet." Immediately, his gaze went back to Rutledge's. "Your second, sir?"

"Lord Robert Rowland?" Rutledge snidely suggested, dusting the grass from his coat sleeves.

"Name another," demanded David. "Or I swear to God I'll kill you now with my bare hands."

At that, Rutledge gave a dry chuckle. "Very well," he said almost amiably. "I suppose it would not do to make a fellow choose between his friends. I shall send Mr. Weyden to wait upon you tomorrow."

From one corner of his eye, David watched Cecilia start forward as if to come between them. Immediately, he threw out a staying arm. "David," she said sternly, "this is foolishness!"

David ignored her. He felt blood-lust thrumming

through him, but with it came the cool certainty that he must have—no, burned for—satisfaction. For some reason, a reason which went beyond even Rutledge's insult to Cecilia, David wanted desperately to teach the younger man a lesson. "Your choice of weapons, sir?" he demanded.

Rutledge was a notoriously sharp shot, and there was little question what his choice would be. And yet, Rutledge seemed to ponder the matter, holding his chin between his thumb and forefinger as he lightly brushed the stubble of his beard. Abruptly, the hand dropped away. "Swords," he said with a bemused smile.

Good God! He would not have made Rutledge for such a fool. David was a good marksman, yes. But with a blade, he was known to be lethal. "Swords, then," he concurred.

Abruptly, Rutledge's face split into a wide grin. "And do you wish to kill me, my lord? Or merely to mar my handsome face?"

David was beginning to believe that Rutledge had some sort of death wish. "That, sir, is up to you."

Rutledge paused for just a heartbeat. "Well, for my part," he said with a smooth bow, "I think I shall aim to slice away at least one of your perfect ears."

"You may well try."

Briskly, Rutledge scrubbed his hands together as if anticipating a treat. "Very well, then," he said almost cheerfully. "And now that I think on it, why wait? I've a lovely set of Florentine blades just inside the house. I've not yet used them myself, for, as I said, it's been dashed boring here."

Mere seconds later, Cecilia found herself being propelled unceremoniously back through the rose pergola, out the garden gate, and into the lane.

"David, are you daft?" she insisted, twisting her

head to look over her shoulder. "This is precisely what I've been trying to avoid! What if you kill him? What if you're hurt? What can you possibly be thinking?"

But it was as if David could not hear her. His grip on her arm was ruthless, the expression on his face dark and hard. Without hesitation, he propelled her across the lane where Jed still watched their loosely tied horses, but now her groom held the heads of four handsome black geldings frothed with sweat.

The beautiful blacks were drawing an equally beautiful black phaeton. An expensive, high-slung vehicle, it was made for speed and elegance. With four horses, it could be handled by none but the most experienced whipsman. No wonder he had arrived on her heels—and Cecilia had no doubt that Etta was the loose-tongued culprit who'd sent him.

Without another word, David dragged her toward the carriage and shoved her rather gracelessly into it. Then he turned to Jed. "You were a fool to bring her here," he snapped, drawing a pistol from his coat and passing it to him. "Now, watch her. And by God, if I'm not back in a quarter-hour, see her safely home."

Stubbornly, Cecilia jumped back down from the high seat, very nearly turning her ankle as she stumbled after him. "David!" she persisted. "You cannot mean to do this! One of you could be killed!"

His expression murderous, David's head snapped around, his angry gaze taking in both her and Jed. "Perhaps, madam, you should both of you hope that I am."

Cecilia felt her anger flash. "David, this is hardly Jed's fault. I gave him no choice. And in case it had not occurred to you, he is in my employ."

David turned to stare at her incredulously. "And in case it had not occurred to *you*, madam," he said, stabbing at her with his finger, "he may shortly be in mine! With all the gossip your coming here will likely cause, I shall probably have to marry you."

"You shan't *have to* do any such thing," she insisted, biting out the words. "I believe we discussed this some years ago."

"Cecilia, I think discussions are over." David's expression was implacable. "I begin to conclude that you require a husband, and rather desperately, too. No sensible woman would come rushing out here to beard a scoundrel like Rutledge in his own den—"

"Rose garden!" Cecilia bitterly interjected. "The man you have pegged as the Antichrist was raking out his rose garden!"

As if he'd forgotten his duel altogether, David spun about in the middle of the lane. "Cecilia, aren't you in the least bit curious about what we found in the cellar this morning? Because I am bloody well eager to tell you."

Cecilia felt marginally contrite. "What?"

David's temper did not lessen. "Evidence of opium smuggling," he answered harshly. "Moreover, Rutledge has killed at least three men that I know of, and ruined more women than I should care to count. And now, I'm going to meet him. Given both my reputation and his, do you really think that there is one person in all of Mayfair who won't hear of this debacle by teatime if I don't run a sword through his heart?"

Cecilia balled her hands into fists. "I cannot think why you called him out," she retorted. "It was just a kiss. And now, you might kill him! Or injure yourself!" Her voice took on a hysterical edge. "Yes, yes, you stubborn, arrogant pig! You could!"

David's eyes narrowed ominously. "Your honor is

at stake, Cecilia," he growled, pacing back toward the gate. "It falls to me to see to it."

"Does it indeed?" Cecilia challenged, lifting her chin. "I cannot think why. I rather fancied it the duty of my brother, Harry. Or even Giles, come to that."

His hand already on the latch, David spun about, the hems of his greatcoat whirling about his high, polished boots. His horses tossed and snorted in disapproval. David ignored them. "I'll show you what duty is, you red-haired witch," he rasped, coming back across the lane. "Just as soon as I finish with Rutledge."

And before she knew what he was about, David had jerked her against the wall of his chest. His touch was swift, almost clumsy with desperation. Ravenously, his mouth took hers in a kiss which was searing. Primal. Proprietary. Nothing like Rutledge's calculated embrace. David bent her back over one arm, stilling her face with one hand, his fingers driving through the hair at her temple. With her hat nearly tumbling off backward—and in front of God, Jed, and anyone who cared to come strolling down the street—David shoved his tongue into her mouth, greedily taking, giving her no opportunity to respond.

And then, as swiftly as it had begun, it ended.

David let his hands fall to her shoulders, all but shoving her away. Lifting one hand to steady her bonnet, Cecilia barely managed to keep her weak knees from collapsing altogether. But David had disappeared through the gate, leaving it to swing wildly in the breeze.

By the time David strode back through the rose arbor, Rutledge was waiting for him, a long leather case laid open beneath the spreading branches of an elm tree. "You may have your pick, my lord," he said with an expansive gesture of his arm. "And if they do not suit, we may certainly defer this meeting to another time and place."

"They will suit," confirmed David, shucking off his coats and pitching them into the dead grass beneath the tree. His top boots and waistcoat soon followed, until he stood in the cold winter air in nothing but his shirtsleeves, breeches, and stockings.

"Ah!" said Rutledge softly. "A serious-minded swordsman."

David made no answer. Instead, he moved to drag a small garden bench away from the space between the fountain and the elm. To his credit, Rutledge took the other end, helping him lift it. That done, Rutledge tossed his own coat and boots almost lazily to the ground.

Jerking his head toward the leather case, he offered David his choice of swords. At once, David seized one, curling his thumb and index finger about the strange Italian grip. It was not, most assuredly, the blade of his choosing. Still, he accounted himself lucky not to be facing Rutledge down a pistol barrel. As it was, he had little doubt of prevailing. Surely, despite the disparity in their ages, Rutledge must know that?

Neither of them mentioned formalities—the rules of conduct, the absence of seconds, not even the point to which they would fight. It was as if Rutledge did not care. Certainly, David did not.

Gracefully, Rutledge bent down and took up the remaining sword, balancing it confidently in the palm of his hand. "They are remarkably fine, are they not, my lord?" he observed dispassionately. "I had them from an Italian nobleman who, shall we say, had fallen on hard times. So let us hope that neither of us meets a similar fate today."

Disinclined to chitchat, David raised his sword in the opening salute. *"En garde,* Mr. Rutledge."

Like the strike of a snake, Rutledge saluted, then lunged. Their blades met low, scraping against one another like the opening cord of an appallingly dissonant melody.

God help him, David's body thrilled to it. He had done this more times than he cared to count, and still, the clash of metal never ceased to electrify him. Everything—Cecilia, the murders, de Rohan, his troubled mind—melted, and he saw nothing but Rutledge's blade glinting wickedly in the afternoon sun.

At once, David responded, lunging forward on his right foot, his blade low, the muscles of his arm taut and eager. Rutledge's eyes lit up as he danced back just a step. David followed him, driving him hard toward the elm tree. But Rutledge was not without experience.

There was a quick scuffle of blades, and soon both men were panting. For a time, David let Rutledge press him as he studied the younger man's moves, taking careful note of his shortcomings. But it seemed Rutledge mistook his patience for reluctance, a common error of the inexperienced. Suddenly, Rutledge delivered a rapid but awkward thrust. He attacked high and left, his movement obviously aimed to slash David's right shoulder.

With an artful guard, David deflected the blow, reveling in the confidence which surged through him. Again and again, Rutledge attempted the attack, but each time, David met him with a swift parry, neatly catching his blade and turning it aside.

Still, Rutledge was a worthy adversary. For one fleeting moment, David let his attention flag. With an elegant motion, Rutledge executed a near flawless *redoublement.* David was ready. He lunged again, this time to the left. Then he followed with a sharp, low thrust which nearly pinked Rutledge in the thigh.

Again, the younger man came at him, propelling him backward, his thrusts made more dangerous by their swiftness. David felt his brow begin to sweat. What Rutledge lacked in finesse he more than made up for in speed. The young man's feet flew across the cold winter's ground, his stockings catching lightly in the stiff grass.

Again, David lunged, pushing Rutledge back with a swift clash of blades, feinting, thrusting, and driving him toward the tree. Fleetingly, he saw fear flash across Rutledge's face. In the air, their blades met again, glided, then clashed low, the metal scraping downward until David's tip caught in the grass.

Rutledge was quick. Too quick. His blade broke free, and Rutledge jumped. David deflected, but Rutledge recovered, performing an awkward but powerful *coupé*, slicing David across the right forearm.

At once, Rutledge dropped his point and stepped back. Fleetingly, all eyes darted toward the slashed shirtsleeve.

No blood.

"En garde, Mr. Rutledge," David repeated, lifting his weapon once more.

And they were at it again. The cold, damp earth was almost invigorating beneath his feet. David felt the muscles of his sword arm bunch, give, and thrust smoothly with his every instinct. Time and again, Rutledge came at him with his glittering eyes and mocking smile. Time and again, David drove him back, turning his blade aside, parrying high, then low, the slice of metal ringing through the cold air.

Once or twice, David suspected he could thrust past Rutledge's swift defenses, but with a calculated deliberation, he pushed the younger man on. Rutledge was good, but he was flagging, his skill more dependent on the physical than the mental.

Again, Rutledge desperately attempted to break through David's guard, to no avail. David caught his blade and, in a swift parry, hurled it aside, catching the folds of Rutledge's neck cloth.

The fabric flapped free in the breeze, a dangerous distraction. At once, David backed away. "Have it off," he demanded, dropping his point. "I wish to draw your blood fairly."

Rutledge was breathing heavily now. Awkwardly, he reached up with one hand to rip away what was left of his cravat, hurling it to the ground. "*En garde,* my lord."

David fairly flew at him, driving back until Rutledge's movements slowed. His body was tiring, but his expression was still vicious, and twice David let pass a clear opportunity to draw his blood.

"Damn you," panted the younger man.

Well! At least Rutledge knew mercy when he saw it. David smiled bitterly, parrying again, their swords ringing. It was clear the younger man had little fight left in him. It was time to have some answers.

Again, David pressed, driving Rutledge almost against the tree. "I wish to know," he ruthlessly demanded, "what business you have in Black Horse Lane."

At that, Rutledge truly faltered. "You wish to know *what?*" he asked, stumbling backward.

"Black Horse Lane!" repeated David. "Tell me! What is your business there?"

Again, their blades met high. "I was—looking—looking for someone," Rutledge insisted, feinting awkwardly.

David drove his point home, drawing back just be-

fore he took Rutledge in the chest. "I shan't stop," he
warned, "until you tell me who and why."

"None of your damned business, Delacourt,"
Rutledge hissed. His jaw was set grimly, but his blows
had lost their rhythm. He was beaten, vulnerable, and
he knew it.

He fought back with a flurry of strikes, but still
David drove him, taunted him. "And what were you
doing in the Prospect of Whitby?"

For the second time, fear and confusion lit
Rutledge's face. Awkwardly, he dropped his point, and
almost unintentionally, David's blade glanced across
Rutledge's right shoulder. The white cambric split in a
long gash of red. The young man jumped backward,
tripped on a tuft of grass, and fell into a graceless
sprawl upon the lawn, his weapon flying backward
into the rose garden.

Ruthlessly, David bent over him, placing his point
neatly above the center of Rutledge's collarbone.

"For God's sake, don't!" shrieked Cecilia, as if from
a distance.

Until that moment, David had not known she had
disobeyed him and returned to the gardens. Now,
with her voice, reality intruded. The soughing wind,
the cry of a bird wheeling overhead, all of it was new
to him. Undeterred, David shook it off, pinking
Rutledge ever so slightly in the throat. With one last
motion of surrender, Rutledge let his head fall back
into the grass.

"Now!" said David, gritting out the word. "You will
first beg the lady's pardon for wrongly impugning her
honor."

"Your—pardon—Lady Walrafen," Rutledge managed weakly. "It seems I . . . was mistaken."

"David, he is bleeding." Cecilia's voice was weak.

David barely heard her. Deliberately, he narrowed his eyes. "And now, sir, we have business to discuss."

"You are a confusing bastard, Delacourt," said Rutledge, the breath heaving in and out of his chest as he stared at David's sword point. "Go on, damn you! Have done if you mean to!"

"Oh, no," insisted David quietly. "First, I want something more. And you know what it is. Now, Mr. Rutledge, you may die slowly. Or you may die quickly. Choose!"

"David!" cried Cecilia more stridently. "I'm trying to tell you! I think we've made a mistake!"

But Rutledge thrust out his left arm, scrabbling through the grass beneath the elm tree. "My coat, then," he rasped. "Give me my damned coat."

Grabbing it in one fist, Cecilia rushed forward, her face drained of all color. "Mr. Rutledge, you are hurt!"

" 'Tis a scratch," he said gruffly. "Give me my coat, my lady."

At once, Cecilia dropped it by Rutledge's hand. He clutched at the fabric, digging desperately through one pocket until he withdrew a fistful of paper, hurling it almost disdainfully at David's face. Not one, but half a dozen bits of paper, scattered across the wintry grass.

"There is what you came for," he spit. "Now, take it, and begone! Or take it, and kill me. I hardly think I care."

Without removing his blade, David knelt and picked one up. With two fingers, he gingerly flipped it open. The words which danced before his eyes squeezed the breath from his chest: *I owe to the bearer, payable upon demand, the sum of £1,150.—Lord Robert Rowland.*

David blinked his eyes, inadvertently letting the point slip from Rutledge's throat. "Well, damn me for a fool," he whispered. *A bloody gaming debt?* Surely, he had not well nigh killed a man for this?

But Rutledge was still breathing heavily. "The other five are there as well," he insisted. "Take them and be damned. I never meant to collect. I wished only to teach the whelp a lesson."

"I don't understand," David muttered. Almost blindly, he stooped and picked up another IOU. *£2,200!* And signed by Robin. Suddenly, it all began to make a frightening amount of sense.

But Rutledge was still speaking. "Good God, Delacourt, what manner of man do you think me?" he continued. "He's little more than a child. If you truly wish to protect him, tell his doting mama to keep him home where he belongs. God knows I wish someone had done that much for me." The last was said bitterly, Rutledge's voice catching at the end.

Against his will, David's fingers unbent, letting his sword drop into the grass. "Let me understand you, Mr. Rutledge. You think I've been following you? And for . . . for *these?*"

Scrabbling awkwardly to his feet, Rutledge looked suspicious. "Well, haven't you?" he demanded. "And I own, I ought not have been surprised, for half of society believes you his father."

It was an old rumor, one which David had hoped had been laid to rest by Jonet's marriage. But Rutledge had been away for two years. Perhaps he did not know. Or perhaps old rumors died a slow death.

Quietly, Cecilia stepped forward, offering Rutledge a handkerchief for his bleeding wound. If Delacourt felt confused, Cecilia looked quite the opposite. "But you did come in on the *Queen of Kashmir,*" she insisted. "From India."

Beside the elm tree, Rutledge slid down, bracing

his back against the tree trunk and pressing the linen against his shoulder. "Yes, amongst other places," he agreed, looking up at her from beneath a shock of black hair. "But what has that to do with any of this?"

Cecilia's pale brow furrowed. "And you have been gambling with Lady Kildermore's son?"

Despite his near-death experience, Rutledge threw back his head and laughed. "I do beg your pardon," he said dryly, waving his arm at the garden, "but was that not the very point of this?"

Roughly, David gathered up the rest of Robin's vowels and shoved them back into Rutledge's coat pocket. "Rest assured, Mr. Rutledge, I had no idea my friend— *my friend!*—was in debt to you. Had I known, I should have insisted that he make good his losses. Indeed, I may yet do. Believe me, a night in the sponging house with the threat of The Fleet hanging over one's head is the best cure for his sort of intemperance."

As if to clear his vision, Rutledge shook his head. "Well, if you didn't want the boy's vowels, why the deuce have you been following me?"

"I've followed you nowhere, Rutledge," David quietly admitted. "But I own, I'm deeply suspicious of your involvement with Mother Derbin. Not to mention your hanging about the Prospect of Whitby and asking suspicious questions."

At once, Cecilia stepped forward, her hands set on her hips. "And you've been asking questions at the mission, too, I think?" she gently challenged. "Perhaps you did not know that we work there. It was you who came to the shop that day in search of Mary O'Gavin, was it not?"

At last, Rutledge nodded, tearing his gaze from theirs as he lifted the handkerchief from his wound.

Thank God the bleeding had stopped. Despite his rage, David had no wish to kill him.

Now, as if drawing some carefully thought-out conclusion, Cecilia nodded. "Yes, after last night, I had almost puzzled it all out. And that is what brought me here."

Immediately, David's hand came down upon her shoulder. "Cecilia, my dear, explain this."

But Cecilia did not look at him. Perplexingly, she stared directly at Bentham Rutledge. "You were the father of Mary's baby, weren't you?" she softly said. "And I daresay you merely wished to find her."

At that, what little façade of strength Rutledge possessed seemed to crumple. He let his head fall back against the tree, the bloody handkerchief clenched in his fist. "I cannot understand," he said, squeezing shut his eyes. "I simply *cannot* understand. How can a woman give up her child—*my child*—and leave it in a foundling home to die? How—?" he cried. "Why did she not simply tell me?"

"You really had no idea?" whispered Cecilia.

Blindly, Rutledge shook his head. "Of course not! Not until it was too late."

Slowly, David was beginning to understand—and yet, it left him feeling all the more confused.

Rutledge's attention was focused on Cecilia now, his eyes searching hers as if he sought some measure of understanding. Or forgiveness. "I got myself into a foolish scrape," he confessed in a tortured voice. "But I sent Mary money by a trusted messenger— enough, I thought, to keep her for a good long while. And then I made for Ostend on the first vessel out. Mary hadn't said a word about a child. Had she done—why, good God! I would have taken her! Or sent her to my family. *Something!*"

David looked at them both incredulously. "And so all this time—" He broke off, shaking his head. "All this time, you've just been searching for Mary O'Gavin?"

"At first," Rutledge admitted. "But eventually, I found out about her murder, and about the babe having died . . ."

David swallowed hard. "And then you went to Black Horse Lane to ask Mother Derbin what happened," he stated flatly.

"I went to Mother Derbin to choke life's breath from her body," Rutledge corrected, rising unsteadily to his feet. "I know damned well she had something to do with Mary's death."

"And what did she say?" asked Cecilia softly.

Solemnly, Rutledge shook his head. "She insisted she knew nothing. She said that when Mary returned to the brothel from the rooms I'd set her up in, she was not pregnant, and hadn't a ha'penny to her name. She claimed she'd done the girl a favor by taking her back in."

David felt deeply confused. "But why did you let me think—" He hesitated, his mind still churning with thought. "I mean, why did you not simply tell me you held Robin's vowels?"

"Oh, gentleman's honor—?" suggested Rutledge sarcastically. "Or if you no longer subscribe to that, perhaps you'll believe I was curious to see what kind of man you thought me."

He had a point, David inwardly admitted. Age, self-discipline, even the limitations of the law aside, a gentleman's debts of honor were his own affair. "My apologies, then, Mr. Rutledge," he said, carefully measuring his words. "You have acted with remarkable restraint and respect toward my

young friend. Lord Robert will be making good his
vowels."

"I don't want his damned money."

David inclined his head. "Then you may donate it
to the Middlesex Foundling Home," he said softly.
"And if it is of any consolation to you, I don't think
Mary O'Gavin knew she was carrying your child
when you left England. As for the money, God only
knows. Any number of things—robbery, misfortune—
anything could have happened."

But Rutledge appeared not to be listening. His eyes
squeezed nearly shut, he still stood in his stocking
feet, leaning back against the elm tree with his arms
crossed protectively over his chest. His suddenly boyish face had drained of all color. It was an appalling
contrast to the brilliant blood which stained his shirtfront from collar to mid-chest.

The afternoon had grown late, and a chilly breeze
had picked up, tossing his disheveled black hair in the
wind. Wearily, David bent down to gather up the swords,
tossing them into the case with a careless clanking
sound. He did not feel good about the emotion—or lack
of it—on Rutledge's face. Nor did he feel proud of what
had just occurred here. And yet, he did not perfectly understand what he could have done differently. Perhaps
he was lacking in some moral compass or intuition
which others possessed. He hoped not. He prayed not.

He did understand one thing, though. He understood why a skilled marksman might choose swords
over pistols: to avoid the temptation of killing a man
who had sorely tempted him to do precisely that. And
perhaps because he cared more about what people
thought of him than he wished to admit. Bitterly,
Delacourt wanted to laugh. It was odd how clearly he
saw such things now.

But his bitterness vanished when he stood up to see Cecilia holding out one hand to him and the other to Rutledge.

"Come," she said softly to the wounded young man—for wounded he surely was, and the cut went deeper than the bite of David's sword.

Slowly, Rutledge lifted his eyes to hers. "Come," Cecilia repeated. "We must go inside and dress that wound."

18

~

In which Lady Walrafen must pay the Piper

"*W*here are we going?" Cecilia finally asked some time later, one hand clamped firmly down upon her bonnet.

His once neat neck cloth now flapping unheeded in the wind, David made her no answer. Upon leaving Roselands Cottage, he had curtly ordered Jed to take Cecilia's horse to Park Crescent, then whipped up his cattle, leaving Jed standing in the dust of Hampstead.

The phaeton had been hurtling madly through the countryside ever since, David's mouth drawn taut and white, his brows knitted into a frown so deep that Cecilia had been afraid to disturb his concentration.

Well, that was rather a lie, wasn't it? She admitted it, just as the carriage hit a deep rut making the turn onto the Marylebone Road. Awkwardly, Cecilia straightened herself on the seat. The truth was, she feared what he might say once the fragile silence was shattered. It was not that Cecilia was afraid to stand her ground. No, not usually. But in the case at hand, her ground was perilously shaky.

David had been right. What she had done had been exceedingly foolish, and she'd known it the moment

Rutledge jerked her against him. In truth, she still believed him a gentleman. But had he been otherwise, Cecilia would have been alone in a very precarious position. And the fact that her rash behavior could have gotten Rutledge—or, heaven forfend, David—killed did nothing to ease her mind.

Still, curiosity ate at her, for they had missed both the turns which would have taken them into Regent's Park. "Where are we going?" she asked again, more breathlessly this time, for it was apparent he did not mean to take her home.

At last, he turned to look at her, his face tight and pale in the early dusk. "To Curzon Street," he said curtly, as if he were surprised she found it necessary to ask.

He whirled the carriage expertly to the right as they hit Oxford Street, pitching her against him again. With an impatient noise, he thrust the ribbons into one hand and lashed the opposite arm possessively about her shoulders, as if he were oblivious to the late-day shoppers who lined the streets.

In response, Cecilia simply tightened her grip on her bonnet. *Good,* she thought. They were going to have it out once and for all. A proper row, she hoped, for there was much which wanted saying between them.

She had not forgotten David's threat of marriage, made in the heat of a coming battle. He had apparently considered being shackled to him something she should wish to avoid, but she did not. It was what she wanted. *Desperately* wanted. She was certain of it now, bizarre though the thought would have seemed just a few short weeks ago. And yet, David resisted opening up to her, going so far as to cloak his proposals as either half-hearted jokes or, in this case, in the guise of a threat.

Cecilia suppressed the impulse to laugh. And then the fleeting temptation was gone, shoved ruthlessly aside by an overriding sense of wretchedness. She'd always assumed that David wasn't the marrying kind, but now she was not so sure. Still, something dreadful and nameless lay between them, like a massive stone dropped immutably into the middle of a marriage bed.

In a few short minutes, they had reached his front door. Passing the ribbons to an expressionless servant, David hastened through the empty house and up the steps to his bedchamber, clutching Cecilia hard by the hand. Obviously, he seethed with emotion.

Swiftly, he pushed shut the door behind them, snapped the key in the lock, and leaned hard against the wood panel as if he expected someone might burst through unbidden. His gaze flicked down her length. "By God, Cecilia," he said softly, "you are going to pay for this."

Cecilia stepped away from the door. "P-pay for what?"

For a moment, he hesitated, his face angry and tormented. And then, strangely, his expression seemed to soften, then collapse. "Good God, I don't know," he whispered, squeezing shut his eyes. "For whatever it is you have done to me."

Cecilia shook her head. "David, I didn't mean to—"

Vehemently, he cut her off with a sharp motion of his hand. "Christ almighty, Cecilia!" he rasped. "You're killing me. I cannot bear this—this *thing* you provoke inside my heart. It's . . . *fear.* And desire. And rage, perhaps? I don't know! I know only that it has begun to feel as if I might explode."

She looked at him through the murky light, and in an instant, his face shifted yet again, into something which looked like an almost agonizing confusion.

The intensity of it frightened her. His were emotions she could not begin to understand. It was as if he wanted her, and yet he fought against the wanting. Was this simply the way of men, she wondered?

Left with nothing but feminine instinct, she lifted an unsteady hand to his face. Sliding her fingertips across the turn of his cheek, she caressed David with the palm of her hand, brushing the pad of her thumb across the corner of his mouth.

Eyes still closed, his nostrils flared at her touch. And then, like a compass seeking north, David turned his head into her hand, pressing his lips into her palm, his breath coming rough and hard against her skin.

David felt the light, warm fingers skim over the hard planes of his face. Cecilia's touch was gentle, sweet, and yet wildly erotic. His nerve endings were on fire. He felt hot and cold. Grief and terror. Anger and lust. *Good God,* he thought. *If emotions had colors, my brain would be a damned kaleidoscope.*

He had to slow down his thoughts. Greedily, his lips sought her touch, and David forced his mind back to the afternoon he'd given her the crate filled with porcelains—how urgently he'd studied her face, searching for any indication of what she wanted to hear. So he would know what to say. How carefully he'd measured his words, in some desperate attempt to give only as much as she demanded, holding back a part of himself. And wounding them both in the process.

But Cecilia would not demand. He understood that now. She was no cloying, grasping female. She would not demean herself by asking of him that which he was unprepared to give of his own free will. Certainly, she had not done so all those years ago when he'd let his pride and his shame keep him from speaking his heart. And she wouldn't do so now. Perhaps it was time he stopped judging and measuring, and gave in to the torrent of emotions which flooded forth whenever Cecilia was near.

His silence frightened Cecilia. "David, I'm sorry," she said softly, hardly knowing what she apologized for.

At that, he opened his eyes, and she saw the desire which burned there, intense and urgent. "I need you," he whispered hoarsely. "Oh, God, Cecilia, I need you. And I need you *safe*. Can you not understand? And I need you . . . *here*. In my arms. In my bed. For you are already in my heart. You fill it. So much so, I sometimes fear I'll choke from the need."

Cecilia lifted both hands this time, reaching up to cradle his face between them. "David," she said softly, "I'm sorry I frightened you. I love you." She stared hard into the unfathomable pools of his deep green gaze. "Don't you know that? I love you."

"I love you, too, Cecilia," he admitted quietly. "It seems I always have."

Shakily, she laughed. "Oh, surely not *always?*"

"Always," he insisted roughly. "Forever. And heaven only knows what I've done to deserve your kind of love, spiteful, mean-spirited wastrel that I am."

She rose onto her tiptoes to kiss away the ugly words, but to her shock, he jerked his mouth from hers, turning his face to stare past her shoulder.

Puzzled, she drew away, and in answer, David jerked her back. "Oh, I want you, Cecilia," he responded, his voice choking. "I want you beneath me. I want to ride you like a wild animal. I want to spend myself inside you so badly I can scarce draw breath."

"Then have me," she answered simply.

He closed his eyes and swallowed, the lump of his throat sliding up and down. David's face was gaunt, his eyes shadowed from lack of sleep, his cheeks bristled with a day's worth of dark beard. It was as if his cool, elegant beauty had finally shattered, to be replaced by an infinite weariness. And yet, Cecilia thought him more handsome than ever.

It was almost dark inside the room now. Quietly, Cecilia turned away. She could not speak, for she did not know what to say. And so she answered his pain in the only way she could, dropping the skirt of her brown wool habit into a puddle on his floor.

David still stood against the door, quietly watching as she fumbled with the buttons of her coat. The rest of her clothing soon followed, until at last she was unfastening her shift.

He stood, simply watching her. "I think . . ." he began, stopping abruptly as the cotton slithered onto the floor. "I think, Cecilia, that you are the most beautiful thing I have ever seen." He spoke with great difficulty, as if restraining some powerful force within himself.

In response, Cecilia returned to him, sliding her fingers into the knot of his cravat and carelessly loosening it. When that was done, she let it slide onto the floor, then lowered her hands to push both coat and waistcoat off his shoulders. His body was still rigid against the door.

"Come to bed, David," she whispered, gently tugging free his shirt. "Come to bed, and show me how lovely you think me. There will be time later for sorting this out."

As if manacles of steel had fallen from his wrists, David jerked violently away from the door and gathered her up into his arms, sliding one arm beneath her knees and lifting her as if she were weightless. Swiftly, he crossed to the bed and settled her onto the edge.

He knelt then, his brilliant green gaze desperately searching hers. He lifted his hand. It trembled. As if to brace it, he spread his palm across her knee, his fingers digging into her flesh. "Cecilia, I cannot promise you—" he rasped, choking off. "I cannot promise you tenderness tonight."

His eyes were mesmerizing; the heat of his hand seared her skin. In acknowledgment, she nodded once. Rising over her, David drew off his shirt, the ruthlessly slashed fabric of his sleeve a testament to the horror which could have been. With an uncharacteristic awkwardness, he began to fumble at the close of his breeches. Then, urgently, he pushed her back into the downy depths of his bed.

Still standing, his head bowed, and one heavy lock of hair falling forward to shadow his face, David slid his hands beneath her hips. Roughly, he dragged her to the very edge of the mattress. With his knee, he shoved her thighs apart, and one hand went to his jutting erection.

"Ah—Cecilia!" he whispered as he entered her, swift and hard. "I'm sorry."

Cecilia gasped at the intrusion. She had not, she belatedly realized, been fully ready. But David did not seem to notice. With another whispered apology, he drove himself deeper, lifting and spreading her buttocks to cradle him as his breeches slithered down his hips.

As her body again became accustomed to his, Cecilia twined her legs about his waist and drew herself against him. With her hands thrown back over her head and nothing to hold on to, she felt weightless, floundering and floating in the softness of his bed as he stood, loomed over her, shadowing her body, his face as savage and as hard as his erection. Beneath her, the edge of the mattress rocked with the power of his thrusts.

"You are mine, Cecilia," he whispered, staring down at her. "Mine forever this time."

A little frightened by the intensity in his eyes, she slackened her legs about his hips. In response, David lifted her higher, tighter, pressing himself into her softness. "Don't pull away again, Cecilia," he demanded harshly. "Not now."

Strangely, she knew he spoke not of the recent past but of one distant—almost six years distant—when she had instinctively opened her mouth beneath his, and answered, ever so fleetingly, David's need for her. Before fear and logic had overcome her. But logic clearly had no place in his bed tonight, and her fear was fast fading. Still, David was driven by something she could not understand.

Again, he deepened his thrusts, and she gasped, struggling backward. Sliding his hands to her shoulders, he pressed her down, deep into the mattress, willing her not to move. And then he raised one knee, crawling onto the bed, dragging himself fully over her, bracing his legs between her thighs, forcing her wide, giving her no quarter, no place to hide.

"Oh, yes, Cecilia," he whispered thickly. "This time, I mean to have all of you."

But it was too powerful, too new. "No, David!" she whispered, as he pounded himself inside her. "Not like—I can't—not like . . . *Oh! Oh! My God!*"

Cecilia's whole body surged toward him, and she felt release edge shockingly near. David's deep, rocking rhythm went on and on, merciless, seemingly without beginning or end. Cecilia felt herself quiver as her hips and shoulders were borne down by the weight of his body, the power of his thrusts.

"*Please . . .*" she whispered. But there was no answer. And what did she want? For him to fill her with

hot seed and passion, leaving her soul intact? Only
the creaking of the bed and the rhythmic rasping of
David's breath answered.

On and on he went—stroking, plunging, coaxing
with his cock and hands and tongue—the intensity
too much to bear. Cecilia felt disembodied, his relentless, rhythmic thrusts driving her to a level of awareness—a place inside herself—which she did not know.

Suddenly, David's hands left her shoulders, sliding
over her breasts and up her inner arm until his fingers entwined with hers. His eyes were closed, she realized, as her fingers curled slackly into his. David's
head was turned slightly to one side, his jaw clenched
tightly as he moved inside her. Flesh met flesh, sliding
silkily in the falling darkness. She rose to meet him
thrust for thrust. No candles had been lit, no fire
burned in the hearth. And yet, sweat beaded on his
forehead, trailed down his cheeks, and pooled in the
hard-boned valley below his throat.

Cecilia quivered as he slid through her, pounding
her. In the face of such furious need, she felt another
shaft of uncertainty. And yet, she wanted to pitch herself into his flame.

He must have felt her hesitation, for David lifted
himself, forcing his hardness high against her center.
Wildly, Cecilia began to pant. "Please . . ." she
breathed against the dampness of his throat.

"Not yet, Cecilia," she heard him murmur into her
hair. "Beg if you must, but not yet."

Despite his words, Cecilia felt her own response
take her, dragging her traitorous hips higher against
him. When the shudder began in earnest, it absorbed
her completely, pulsing through her thighs, her
womb, her belly, dragging the breath from her body.
She felt her head go back. As if her very nerve endings

were exposed, she felt the dampness of David's brow brush against hers even as she shook beneath him.

"Yes!" she heard herself cry. "Oh, David—*yes!*"

Still, he pushed her beyond need, beyond pain, and into a release so intense, she heard her own scream ringing through the room. Through the entire house, no doubt.

"Oh, Cecilia," he whispered. "You are mine. I won't make the same mistake twice."

He released her hands, his palms smoothing over her nipples, lightly stroking them as her trembling subsided. And then, she opened her mouth to breathe, and he took her again—with his tongue, thrusting inside, plumbing the depths of her mouth. He filled her in every possible way, as if he meant their bodies—no, their souls—to meld and become one.

To her shock, she felt her body rise to his again, and the sensation drew her down once more. As the flame of her passion rekindled from the ash, burning with his, she felt David's teeth bite into the tender skin of her shoulder, felt his fingers claw into the flesh of her buttocks as he opened her. Cecilia cried out in the darkness, and his voice mingled with hers, low and guttural, as he thrust and pounded and poured himself inside her.

In the quiet aftermath, Cecilia could feel the stillness of David's body weighing down the mattress beside her. Slowly, she rolled onto her side, inviting him to curl his body about hers, to lock his arms unassailably about her, as he had done two nights earlier.

It was full dark now, and she could hear his breath still rasping in and out of his chest. She could smell a day's worth of male sweat on his body, and the scent of horse and road dust in his hair. It was a good, earthy aroma, very unlike the expensive cologne David usually wore. And yet, Cecilia found it just as enticing. Suggestively, she reached back with one foot, curling it about his ankle.

Still, he lay at her side, staring up at the ceiling, barely touching her.

"I love you," she murmured into the coverlet.

As if in response, he rose smoothly from the bed and padded silently across the carpet to his desk. She heard the rattle of metal, the scratch of a tinderbox in the darkness, the sound of glass on glass. And then, the lamp on his desk sputtered to life. The soft *chink* of porcelain punctuated his movements, and finally, David's weight settled back onto the mattress, and he rolled against her.

With a deep groan of satisfaction, she nestled her buttocks against his pelvis. David's hand came about her then, and she felt the cold sensation of metal brushing her bare flesh.

"Cecilia," he whispered, his lips pressed to the back of her ear. "Do you love me? Do you love . . . *me?*"

She rolled over and into him then, suddenly aware of what he had brought to the bed. "Yes," she answered, her voice unsteady but certain.

"I know . . ." For a moment, his voice choked again. "I know I've asked before, Cecilia, and you have rightly refused me. But tonight, I put my heart into your hands. And I trust you, without reservation."

Confused, she stared across the coverlet into his eyes, letting her fingers come up to smooth across his cheek. "I don't understand."

David uncurled his fist, and the ruby ring glowed in the lamplight. "Cecilia, I would have no false pride or half-truths between us. I want you to marry me,

and this time, I'm begging. But there is something
you should know."

Cecilia closed her eyes. "That a part of you will always love her?"

"Who?" he asked simply. "Jonet?"

"She gave you that ring, did she not? I recognize
the Kildermore crest."

"Ah, yes," he said on a cynical laugh. "*Semper veritas*. Always truth! A bit of black humor, I often think.
And as for my esteem for Jonet, I love her, but as a
brother loves his sister."

"You mean platonically?"

"No, literally." He smiled wryly. "I'm sorry to say
that the nobleman you think you've fallen in love with
is little more than a Scottish rogue's by-blow."

Mystified, she stared at him. "A *what?*"

"A bastard, Cecilia," he answered, the bitter mockery falling away. "That's what I am, you see. In the literal sense, not just the figurative, which is so often—
and not inaccurately—applied to me."

Against the weak lamplight, Cecilia blinked. "But I
don't understand . . ." she whispered.

And so, David forced himself to tell her. He told
her everything—the sordid truth of what his mother
had suffered, the honor of the man he'd thought his
father. The perfidy of Lord Kildermore. Of the letter,
sent to him on the cusp of his manhood, which had
so deeply affected him. And then he told her about
Jonet, and of the strange and abiding affection they
had found for one another.

For a long moment, Cecilia said nothing. But she
continued smoothing her fingertips over his cheeks,
his forehead, and his lips. "I am so sorry," she finally
replied, "for your mother's pain."

And with those simple words, David realized that

Cecilia really did not give a damn about his heritage. In his heart, he had come to know that she wouldn't. And yet her answer was like the lancing of a wound, the release of something hot, horrible, and fetid inside him.

"Oh, David . . ." Cecilia held his gaze with an infinite gentleness. "Surely, you did not think that I would care?"

"I care," he said simply.

She touched him again, her hands smoothing over his brow, and David let his eyes fall shut. "There was a time," he said in the tone of quiet confession, "when I feared that all I had once believed my birthright might be stripped from me. But as the years go by, I find that I care less and less. Any challenge to my title now seems remote. And my enemies—well, I daresay I can manage them well enough."

"But what is it, then?" Cecilia asked urgently.

"My mother," David said softly, opening his eyes. "I've come to care very little what people think of me. I am wealthy enough, and the title is like a macabre joke. And yet, I would not have my mother's honor sullied by rumor or innuendo. She has suffered enough."

Uncertainly, Cecilia studied his face, bleak in the lamplight. "But David," she said stridently, "surely you don't believe that I would ever speak out of turn?"

He shook his head, his heavy hair sliding across the coverlet. "Ah, Cecilia," he said softly. "I trust rarely. And slowly. But I would trust you with my life."

Cecilia's delicate brows drew together. "What, then?"

"I want to marry you, my love. I want to give you my children, watch you bear them and raise them. But I find I cannot do it without honesty, though I was once rather desperately willing to try."

At that, Cecilia blushed deeply, apparently recalling the anger and intensity of his courtship so many years ago. "I accept your proposal," she said demurely—or as demurely as a naked and obviously well-pleasured woman could.

He felt a wry half-smile crook up one corner of his mouth. "You have the right, Cecilia, to understand whose blood you mingle with yours," he said, skimming his hand down her breast to settle on the swell of her belly. "You are a Markham-Sands—one of the oldest and most noble houses in England. Perhaps you mightn't wish . . ." His voice trailed weakly away, one brow lifting in doubt.

Cecilia stared at him, confused. And suddenly, all of his seemingly unbridled pride, the incredible arrogance, all of it made sense. Left bitter and angry, David had been playing a part, or so he believed. As his dressing room had hinted, he was one thing on the outside, another on the inside. All this time, he had been fighting for something—call it respect, perhaps even honor—which he had come to believe was not his by birthright. And yet, he had earned her respect and honor. More so than anyone she had ever known.

"But your father—was he not Jonet's sire, too?" Cecilia asked very quietly. "And does his blood not run through Lord Mercer and Lord Robert? They seem fine people to me. I cannot think that being a product of rape says anything about who you are."

"But there is . . . madness as well as dissolution in the Cameron line, Cecilia," he said in a soft, warning tone. "Most recently, my cousin, who was quite insane, committed suicide."

Levering herself onto one elbow, Cecilia looked down at him, shaking her head. "It means nothing to *us*," she said gently. "Really, David! I should sooner discuss the weather."

And she meant it, very deeply. Good God, of what

worth were a man's bloodlines? A horse, now—to
Cecilia's way of thinking, that was another thing alto-
gether. But people? She snorted softly in the darkness.
She, of all women, should know what a joke that was.

Oh, yes. As David had said so gently, her line was
old and pure. And neither attribute had done the earldom of Sands one whit of good. Perhaps an infusion of
new blood was precisely what the family had needed.
Indeed, it might well have kept them from sinking into
their mire of lethargy, stupidity, and aimlessness.

Cecilia saw no point in discussing it further. "Are
you going to marry me, then?" she challenged, boldly
crawling on top of him. "For though I'd prefer you to
make an honest woman of me, I'd like to have just another taste of sin before you do."

The seemingly incessant knocking on his bedchamber door roused David from the most blissful
sleep he'd had in years. With a muttered curse, he
dragged Cecilia's body against his, molding himself
around her fine, full hips and sliding one hand up to
caress her breast.

The knocking was at once forgotten when Cecilia
made one of her sweet little noises, easing her hips up
and down his rapidly hardening shaft.

"Open your legs, my love," he whispered wickedly,
"and I'll show you another of those positions you're
so curious about."

Cecilia sucked in her breath on a gasp, sounding
shocked and aroused.

But the damnable knocking came again, and this
time, a pleading whisper came with it. "My lord—?"
said a voice he vaguely recognized as Hanes, his second footman. "A messenger, sir. He says it's most urgent, and that he must speak with you personally."

With a sorrowful sigh, David brushed his finger-tips once more over the hardening bud of Cecilia's left breast. "Sweet Peaches," he whispered into the un-ruly pile of flame-gold hair. "Don't move an inch. I'll be right back."

Hastily, David dressed and went out, locking the door behind him and pocketing the key. Downstairs, much to his consternation, he found a small, bedrag-gled boy of some twelve years standing on his doorstep, a carefully sealed letter clutched in his fist.

"You'd be 'is lordship?" said the boy, assessing him with one narrow eye.

"I would," agreed David, looking down at the frail figure.

The boy nodded succinctly. "Then I'm ter give yer this," he said solemnly, pressing the letter into David's hand. "And I'm ter give a message, too."

"By all means," agreed David.

The boy dragged in a deep breath and let it out again. "I'm to tell you: *Pelican Stairs. Two o'clock. Tomorrow night.*" Then he nodded as if satisfied that he'd repeated the whole of it without stumbling.

David felt his eyes widen in surprise. Quickly, he glanced down to the spidery address scrawled on the letter. *Mother Derbin.* He recognized the strange pen-manship from the paper she'd given de Rohan this morning. And had it been only this morning?

Wearily, he ran a hand through his tousled hair. But the lad was still staring up at him, awaiting a well-deserved reward, no doubt. "Look here," he said to the boy. "How long since you've eaten?"

"Yesterday," the boy admitted, rubbing a soiled coat sleeve across his nose.

David laid a light hand on the boy's shoulder. Given the information the lad had just conveyed, he was not at all comfortable with the idea of releasing him—not when there was a killer running loose. It would seem Mother Derbin considered children expendable.

"Tell me, lad, have you a home?" he asked gently, realizing as he did so that a month earlier, such a question would not have occurred to him.

As he had feared, the boy shook his head.

"Your name?"

"Joseph."

David turned to the footman who stood impassively in the shadows. "Have Mrs. Kent give Joseph a sovereign for his trouble, Hanes. Ask her to feed him well, then put him to work with Strickham tomorrow." He looked down at the boy, tightening his grip on the thin shoulder. "Just for a few days, lad. It will be . . . best if you stay here."

Joseph shrugged indifferently, but David thought that he was pleased. As the footman departed with the boy in tow, David broke the letter's seal and read it standing beneath the light of a wall sconce. The words were carefully veiled, yet the essence was perfectly clear:

> *My dear Lord Delacourt—*
> *I regret that my humble establishment was unable to accommodate your particular need this morning. Since you mentioned you might do us the honor of calling again, I wished to inform you that urgent business has taken me from town. Alas, a sick relative—whose recuperation I am confident will be very, very lengthy.*
> *Kindly give my regards to your veiled lady-friend. And tell her, if you will, that when next she seeks discretion, she should take*

care to cover her distinctively colored hair as well as her face.

Yr. faithful servant—
M.D.

"Who was it?" asked Cecilia softly the moment he reentered his bedchamber. Still lying almost on her stomach, she had levered up onto her elbow, her head crooked back to stare toward the door.

David's mouth went dry as the sheet slithered off her shoulder to reveal the luscious ivory globe of her breast. Beneath the covers, her right hip swelled invitingly. Good God, was there no such thing as satiation where Cecilia was concerned?

Apparently not. Crossing the room in some haste, David tossed the letter onto his night table and began to strip off his clothes. "It was nothing," he muttered. "Nothing which cannot wait."

Smoothly, he slid between the sheets, covering Cecilia's body with his own, pressing her cheek down into the softness of the bed. He felt the sculpted angle of her shoulder blades hard against his chest. Seductively, he nuzzled at the back of her neck, drawing her scent into his nostrils.

"Slide your legs open, Peaches," he murmured, pressing his cock insistently against her buttocks. "Yes, just like—oh, *God!*" he breathed, sliding inside her warm, wet passage. "Just like that."

Flat on her belly, her wild mane streaming across the bed, Cecilia was the very picture of sensual decadence. Bending his head to suckle the skin of her alabaster neck, David slipped one hand beneath her, lifting her pelvis ever so slightly and easing two fingers inside her damp petals to stroke and to tease.

He rode her hard then, pumping himself inex-

orably back and forth, forcing her down, holding her
prisoner between his greedy cock and searching fingers. Cecilia's nails clawed at the bed linen, and in
mere moments, she was writhing beneath him, urging herself down onto his hand, rising against him as
he mounted her.

She began to shatter quickly, her hips alternately
bucking then grinding, as if she fought to throw him
off. "Oh, no, my pretty filly," he rasped, his voice thick
and foreign. "I mean to ride you until the end."

His words had been calculated to torment, and
they did. Cecilia heaved beneath him once more, and
then her mouth came open in a soft moan of pleasure. David lost himself inside her then, reveling in
the throbbing wetness which pulled at him, spurting
his seed against her womb. And hoping. Yes, this
time, hoping . . .

She had said yes at last, and he meant to hold her
to it. She was stuck with him.

Hours later, as the clock struck eleven, David
found himself standing before his dressing table, reluctantly tucking Cecilia back into her riding coat.
"Stay with me the night," he softly pleaded as he gave
a neatening tug on her collar.

"Oh, David, I can't," she whined miserably. "Giles,
Etta, all my servants! Everyone is suspicious."

David bent to brush his lips across her brow.
"But it's all right, love," he soothed, his breath
warm against her ear. "We're to be married, you'll
recall."

Cecilia tilted her chin to look up at him, her eyes
suddenly pooling with tears. A sudden shaft of fear
knifed through him. "You have not, I hope, changed
your mind?"

"Oh, my," said Cecilia with an unsteady laugh. "Just name the date, if you think that."

David lifted one brow. "Oh, I think there is no question but what it must be May Day . . . if not sooner," he said dryly, his eyes drifting down to her belly as he secured her last coat button. "After all, I should hate there to be any question of Sir Lester's losing his fifty-guinea wager."

Tenderly, Cecilia leaned into him, wrapping her arms around his neck and opening her mouth over his. She was a bright pupil, his pretty Peaches. David's knees went weak when she slid her tongue between his lips, but at that most inopportune moment, another urgent knock sounded on the door.

David jerked his mouth from hers. "My God, what now?" he snapped, glaring at the offending door.

After pausing for a heartbeat, David's footman spoke through the heavy oak panels. "Another caller, my lord?" he said tentatively. "And I'm afraid this one, too, is urgent."

"Damn it all, Hanes!" he roared. "Must *everything* in this house be suddenly urgent? Perhaps there's something *urgent* going on in here! Do people never think of that?"

Another long pause ensued, during which Cecilia was compelled to smother a giggle in his shirtfront.

"Shall I send him away, then, my lord?" whispered the unfortunate Hanes. "It's that policeman again."

As if she'd forgotten the delightful thing she'd just been doing with her tongue moments earlier, Cecilia dropped her arms from his neck. "De Rohan," she hissed, giving a sharp tug on David's coat sleeve. "We must go down at once!"

Quickly, David snatched the note from his night table just as Cecilia seized his hand. "Yes, well, as you

say—*there goes the romance of the thing!*" he said
gruffly. And then, he graciously permitted himself to
be dragged from the room.

"It is certainly the same penmanship," agreed de
Rohan moments later. They sat before a newly kindled fire in the blue and gold drawing room, David
pouring out cognac into the Venetian crystal goblets.
The police officer sat upon the brocade sofa, elbows
propped on his knees and one of Mother Derbin's
notes held loosely in each hand.

"What did you discover in Leadenhall Street?"
David asked, setting the decanter down on the tea table
between them. "The counting house is still closed?"

Darkly, de Rohan shook his head. "Bloody place is
like a tomb," he grumbled. "If anyone has been in or
out in the last three days, they've not been seen by
anyone in the neighboring offices, and I questioned
them aggressively."

"So you learned nothing?"

"Nothing *much*," clarified the inspector. "I did get
a good description of the businessman who keeps his
office there. He has a large staff of clerks, and I managed to run one of them to ground at the George and
Vulture."

"And would he talk?"

De Rohan made an ambiguous gesture. "Unfortunately, he was just a junior copyist, and he swore he
didn't have a key to the offices. But he thought he
knew the property off Black Horse Lane, and said
that it—and several like it—are owned by a wealthy
gentleman who lives in Mayfair. A sort of absentee
landlord, which is common amongst the *ton* since
they'd rather not sully their hands by giving a damn
about the people to whom they rent."

No longer disconcerted by de Rohan's pointed social barbs, David pressed forward. "And what of his employer? Did he say?"

"He claims the fellow had been taken severely ill, and had gone down to Brighton to take the air."

"Did you get a name?"

"Weinstein," said de Rohan tersely. "And a good description—tall, balding fellow of some fifty years. A bad limp, too, or so the clerk said."

Suddenly, Cecilia jerked upright in her chair. "A limp, did you say? And Weinstein—that's a Jewish name, isn't it?"

De Rohan's eyes narrowed coldly as he turned to face her. "Yes, what of it?"

David watched as Cecilia's finely arched brows knitted into a puzzled frown. "I'm sure it means nothing, but . . ."

"Go on, Lady Walrafen," de Rohan urged.

Cecilia shifted her gaze back and forth between them. "Well, it's just that I saw a man like that once," she said quietly. "At Edmund Rowland's house. And again last Thursday, when I ran into Edmund in Hyde Park. The man left in some haste, and Edmund said . . ." She paused as if in thought, then nodded swiftly. "Yes, he mentioned that the man was his broker in Leadenhall Street. A Jew, he said. And now that I think on it, the fellow looked very weak, perhaps unwell. But why would they meet in Hyde Park at midday?"

"A very good question indeed," remarked David. "Perhaps he was on his way out of town?"

"And you're sure he limped?" pressed de Rohan.

Swiftly, Cecilia nodded. "Indeed, he carried a beautiful walking stick inlaid with silver. The limp was quite pronounced."

De Rohan scratched his chin pensively. "It seems a remarkable coincidence," he mused.

"Ah, yes," said David. "And we've already heard your theory of coincidence." He paused then, just long enough to tell de Rohan what they had learned from Bentham Rutledge.

"Amazing," said de Rohan when David had concluded his story, discreetly omitting Cecilia's role.

"So Rutledge's involvement was not, just as you predicted, a coincidence," David added. "And yet, I do not believe he's mixed up in this opium ring."

Slowly, de Rohan nodded. "So if we rule out Rutledge, it leaves us with the Weinstein-Rowland theory. And Weinstein may be—*probably is*—just an unwitting accomplice." Swiftly, he glanced at David. "What do you know of this Rowland fellow, Delacourt?"

David sipped from his glass, then set it aside. "Well, he was once so near Queer Street as made little difference. Then his wealthy father died. Still, he and his wife have expensive taste, and he enjoys a lifestyle which would appear to exceed his income."

"A rotter, then?"

David paused thoughtfully. "It is widely believed he is doing *something* which is less than wholesome. But then, he is a notorious gamester."

"And yet you are surprised he might be involved," remarked de Rohan intuitively.

Slowly, David nodded. "It's just that I shouldn't have thought Edmund had the ballocks—your pardon, my dear—to smuggle a keg of cheap brandy, let alone a boatload of untaxed opium."

De Rohan gave a sardonic chuckle. "My lord, the really good criminals never appear to be what they are. That's the beauty of the thing, for catching a clever crook is like an intricate dance—with many partners swirling all about you."

Suddenly, Cecilia's hand flew to her mouth. "Oh!" she gasped. "The dance! Lady Kirton's ball! It's tomorrow night."

David looked at her in mild censure. "Cecilia, I'm sorry, but I think this must take precedence."

Cecilia thrust out a hand. "No, you don't understand," she protested. "Edmund and his wife mean to attend. *Tomorrow night.* He told me so last Thursday, and he cannot very well be in two places at once."

De Rohan leaned back, carefully steepling his fingers together. "It may signify nothing," he warned.

David frowned. "But remember—Grimes told Mother Derbin that the night of the offloading had not been determined," he interjected. "Perhaps it wasn't settled until the last minute?"

"You're right, blast it," said de Rohan. "It must be Rowland. But at least we have the information we need, and with it we will catch him. Depend upon it, he and his minions will be offloading the opium tomorrow night in the alley beside the Prospect of Whitby. Either that, or Mother Derbin has helped him lay a very clever trap."

David gave a disdainful grunt. "More likely she's simply disappeared to save her own skin," he said. "The letter was carefully worded such that should it fall into the wrong hands, there'd be no way Grimes could claim she'd peached on the operation. The important part of the message was conveyed verbally. Were it a trap, she'd hardly have taken such care."

Grimly, de Rohan shook his head. "I disagree, Delacourt. You do not know these people as I do. They are far cleverer—and more ruthless—than you give them credit for."

Cecilia sat forward in her chair clutching a glass of sherry. "What will you do now, Mr. de Rohan?"

"We'll set our own trap," said de Rohan, his voice hard yet pensive. "But that passageway is very narrow. So we'll need men in a boat on the river as well."

"I want to be there," said David firmly.

De Rohan rolled back his shoulders and sat erect in the chair. "This is smuggling," he said firmly. "A dangerous business—the business of the River Thames Police, to be precise. We don't even know what sort of situation we will be walking into. Civilians have no business there."

David leaned back in his armchair, aimlessly rolling the goblet between his hands, swishing the golden liquid. "But . . . you will not stop me?" It was more of a statement than a question.

De Rohan's mouth drew taut. "I can't think how such a miracle could be accomplished," he said caustically.

David cupped his mouth and nose over the goblet and inhaled with satisfaction. "Good," he said softly, lifting his gaze to capture de Rohan's. "Where shall we meet?"

The inspector shrugged in surrender. "Midnight tomorrow at the Wapping station house. Since they're allegedly approaching from Blackwall through the Limehouse Reach, I'll put two boats with two men each in the shadows just upriver. And one man on the street in addition to ourselves. We can risk no more, for there's no place to hide."

19

The last Waltz

$\mathcal{L}$eaning over the balustrade which ringed Lady Kirton's ballroom, David lifted his glass to his eye, carefully skimming the swirling crowd of dancers. To his frustration, he could find no sign of Cecilia. He had had a devil of a time persuading her to attend as planned, while explaining to her that he certainly could not. And yet, here he was.

David had already given up trying to understand his behavior where Cecilia was concerned. Even as Kemble was dressing him in his best evening attire, David had kept telling himself that he merely wished to reassure himself that she was accounted for. That she hadn't gone haring off on another dangerous undertaking. That she was *safe*.

And so he had come to Lady Kirton's affair after all, stuffing a change of clothing inside his carriage and telling himself that so long as he dashed out the door by eleven, all would be well. Oh, he would make his midnight appointment with de Rohan. But first, he meant to have a waltz with Cecilia. Just in case.

And he was going to hold her most shockingly close, perhaps even allow his hand to drift just a bit lower than was thought proper. If neither his conduct toward her in Lufton's nor his driving her down Oxford Street had publicly staked his claim, a few moments of blatantly proprietary behavior tonight would certainly do the trick. And as soon as this dreadful mess with de Rohan was resolved, he meant to personally deliver the announcement of their betrothal to the *Times*, and to every other rag in town, before she had time to change her mind. It wouldn't be the first time he'd run such an errand—but it would damn sure be the last.

Just then, he caught sight of her, attired in a dress of shimmering gold satin, her long, burnished tresses swept up elegantly. And she was already waltzing. With Giles Lorimer.

As the sound of the violins resonated sweetly through the ballroom, Cecilia felt Giles's fingers dig into the small of her back. His face had gone white with anger, his eyes glittering and more narrow than she'd ever imagined possible. *Good heavens!* Giles looked as if he wished to strike her.

And why had she chosen to break the news here, of all places? Because in truth, she'd had little choice. Though it was none of his business, Giles had already begun to question her long absences from home, and following David's overprotective actions at Lufton's, rumor had run rampant—with Sir Clifton Ward waving the flag before it, most likely. So the secret was out.

But it was her secret. And damn it, she was tired of always arguing with Giles over what was or was not proper. Now, however, the whirling dancers about them, the rhythm of the music, even the oppressive heat of the ballroom seemed to fade from her awareness in the face of Giles's shocking wrath.

"Surely you cannot mean this, Cecilia," Giles hissed, his voice cold and bitter. "You jilted him years ago. Why would you now wish to wed him? *Delacourt!* My God, Cecilia, you must know what he is!"

With great effort, Cecilia steadied the smile on her face. "Giles, your fingers are hurting me," she whispered through clenched teeth. "And yes, I do know what he is. A good and honorable man."

"Honorable?" Giles sneered.

"And *good,*" she firmly repeated.

Without missing a step, Giles whipped her into the next turn. To all but the most careful of observers, they doubtless appeared to be enjoying themselves.

"Cecilia, my dear," Giles finally said, his tone conciliatory, "you are still very innocent. My father protected you—or perhaps *neglected* you—to the point that you have not been exposed to the ways of Lord Delacourt's sort. It won't do. Believe me when I say you simply cannot marry such a man."

"When *you say?*" Cecilia echoed, no longer able to maintain her amiable façade. "Indeed, Giles, I do not think it is your place to *say* anything at all."

"Damn it, Cecilia, we are—" Giles gritted out the words, slowing his pace as if searching for just the right phrase. "We are *family.*"

"I think we are a little more than that," she retorted. "We are dear friends. Which is why I've shared my joy with you. But if you persist in maligning my choice of husband, I fear that our friendship will be in some jeopardy."

At her words, so coolly spoken, Giles simply jerked to a halt in the middle of the dance floor. "Your pardon, then, ma'am," he said bitterly. "I am obviously *de trop.* And since pressing business calls me elsewhere, I must go."

And then, Giles dropped her hands, spun on one heel, and stalked away. Cecilia stared after him in mute amazement, dreading the tittering gossip which was sure to follow such a cut. But suddenly, warm fingers encircled hers, and another man's hand slid about her waist.

"How kind of Walrafen to surrender you with such good grace," whispered David, sweeping her so flawlessly onto the floor, it seemed as if Giles had done precisely that. "I shouldn't have thought him so generous."

"David!" Warmth flooded her body, but Cecilia's mind snapped to attention, overriding it. "Oh, but listen! Did you get a good look at Edmund Rowland?" she urgently whispered. "He's in the card room. Half in his cups, too, by the smell of him."

"Ah, the romance!" David sighed. "Yes, love, I saw him. It may simply be an act. Perhaps he means to feign intoxication as an excuse to leave early."

Uncertainly, Cecilia shook her head. "I don't know . . ." she mused. And then, her gaze slid back to David's. "And as to that, what are you doing here? I thought you did not mean to attend."

Deliberately, David pulled her close. And then closer still, scandalously so, until they were no more than six inches apart. "I'm making a statement," he said, his lips pressed fervently against her ear. "I feared it could not wait, and from the look on Walrafen's face, I came not a moment too soon."

Lightly, Cecilia laughed and pulled incrementally away. "Oh, Giles and I were just arguing. He could not possibly be interested in me."

David stared down at her, lifting his brows. "Could he not?" he softly remarked. "Very well, then. But I *am* interested in you. And I wish everyone to know it."

Demurely, Cecilia lowered her lashes and stared into his shirtfront. "Then I daresay you've achieved your objective, my lord," she chided. "For half the ballroom is now staring at your hand—the one which has worked its way well past my waist."

Softly, David chuckled, his breath warm and comforting on her ear. Her argument with Giles forgotten, Cecilia felt suddenly at peace. Just then, the music stopped.

With obvious reluctance, David released her, stepped away, and made her a neat half-bow. "I thank you for the pleasure, my lady," he said with an unexpected wink. "My hand looks forward to completing its journey in the near future."

His mission accomplished, David returned her to the edge of the dance floor. Oblivious to the crowd, Cecilia turned to press one hand against his chest, feeling his heartbeat, strong and steady beneath her palm.

"You're leaving, then?" she asked uneasily. "You really do mean to go through with this?"

David did not bother to ask what *this* was. "Yes."

Impulsively, she seized one of his hands. "You do not need to go, David," she whispered urgently. "Indeed, I beg you not to do so. You have nothing more to prove to me."

Again, he looked at her with that maddeningly nonchalant expression, his brows lightly lifted, his face devoid of fear. "But perhaps, my dear," he said very quietly, "I have something to prove to myself?"

And with that, David strolled calmly toward the door.

"My dear girl!" said a soft, unsteady voice from the knot of people at her elbow. "You seem to dispatch your waltzing partners with an alarming alacrity!

That's the second in the space of five minutes, and both of them headed for the door as if bent upon some life-or-death mission."

Despite the prickles of unease which ran up her spine, Cecilia turned and flashed Edmund Rowland her most blinding smile. "It really is most disheartening, Mr. Rowland," she agreed with spurious despair. "Do you think perhaps I trod upon their toes unknowingly?"

Delicately, Rowland laughed. "Perhaps you've simply accepted the wrong partners, my lady," he replied, thrusting out his elbow. "Might I have the pleasure of the next?"

Already, the violins had recommenced. Glancing quickly about the room, Cecilia forced a self-deprecating expression. "I think I dare not risk it," she whispered. "Perhaps you might fetch me a glass of punch instead?"

With a civil nod, Edmund was off. But Cecilia's hope of escaping in order to observe him at a distance was quickly dashed, for soon he returned, not with punch but with two glasses of champagne. "I know this is your favorite," he simpered, giving her a silly little wink. "I saw you drink it with some relish at our February soiree."

With another lame smile, Cecilia took the stem from his hand. Discreetly, and with no small measure of alarm, she observed his condition. If Edmund Rowland were faking inebriation, he deserved a private dressing room at the Theatre Royale. Already there was a slight stagger to his walk, and his eyes were barely focused.

Unsteadily, he offered her his arm, and for the next half-hour, she was forced to endure his company. When at last she managed to rid herself of him by murmuring something about the ladies' retiring room, her freedom was short-lived. By the time the clock struck midnight, he was again at her elbow, and showing no sign that he remembered having spoken with her earlier.

By then, his eyes were bloodshot, his cravat slightly askew. Again, she was subjected to recitation of his holiday plans at Brighton. His wife's dreadful headache which had sent her to bed betimes. The sorrel hunter he'd sold for a small fortune. And then Edmund spent another quarter-hour crowing about his recent good luck at hazard. Soon, it was apparent that the man did not mean to leave her side, never mind the room.

By now, they stood near the door to Lady Kirton's entrance hall. In the distance, Cecilia could hear a clock strike the hour. *One o'clock!* There was no way, Cecilia weakly realized, that Edmund Rowland was the man de Rohan and David sought. Or, if he was, he plainly did not mean to attend the offloading tonight.

What if de Rohan and David were simply walking into a trap? It was quite possible. De Rohan had said as much. Indeed, he had tried very hard to keep David away. The realization sent a shaft of fear into the pit of her belly.

Suddenly, Cecilia knew she had no choice. She must make her way to the river in all haste. Someone had to warn them. "Your pardon, Mr. Rowland," she said abruptly. "I find that I, too, am suddenly stricken with the headache. I believe I must call for my carriage and go home at once."

Without waiting for Rowland's response, she pushed her way through the crowd and into the entrance hall, hastily retrieving her black velvet cloak from the liveried footman who stood stiffly waiting. Through the door, she could see another servant pacing up and down the pavement as he expertly dispatched the departing carriages into the night's thick fog.

With a sinking sensation, Cecilia realized that

the line was quite long. There was no way on earth she could summon her carriage and make it to Wapping in time to stop them! Not in this weather. Panic almost choked her, but she fought back with logic. Perhaps a hackney might be had in Piccadilly? Cecilia drew tight her cloak and rushed out the door. In her haste, however, she collided with a tall, broad-shouldered man who stood in the shadows. Her arm caught him squarely in his rock-hard chest.

"Good God," muttered an all-too-familiar voice as the man stumbled against the stair rail.

"Giles!" Cecilia leapt awkwardly aside. "I thought you'd gone."

Giles studied her for a moment. "And so I meant to," he coolly replied, his gaze drifting down her length. "But my leader came up short a shoe and had to be taken to the livery in Mount Street. But look here, Cecilia—what the deuce is the matter? You look as though you've seen a ghost."

Desperately, Cecilia cut a glance up and down the street, mentally counting off the carriages. Giles's equipage stood third in line for departure. "I may as well have," she said weakly, "for I have the most dreadful emergency!"

"An emergency?" Giles looked faintly alarmed. "Are you unwell?"

"Oh, Giles!" Cecilia looked up at him in desperation. "I know you are very put out with me just now, but would you—oh, please, *could* you take me to Wapping this very minute?"

"Wapping?" he responded, his voice soft. "Whyever would you wish to go to Wapping, my dear?"

On the pavement, the footman motioned away the next carriage, and Giles's rolled nearer the door. Hastily,

Cecilia grabbed him by the arm. "Just come on," she insisted. "I shall tell you all about it once we're inside."

David had arrived at the Wapping station house a quarter-hour early to find de Rohan, as grim-faced and implacable as ever, awaiting him in the entryway. At once, de Rohan had snapped his fingers, and an eager young constable by the name of Otts had leapt forward to assist.

With military efficiency, David's attire was inspected, his weapons—two pistols and a knife—extracted and examined, and, finally, his face wiped down with boot blacking. A second officer had rushed in to tell de Rohan that the police launches were now in position on the water.

After a few quick words of strategy, they set off on foot, making their way through a fog so thick David simply prayed they didn't step off an embankment and into the Thames. Yet, de Rohan moved confidently through the night, as if he possessed the vision of a cat and the tenacity of a mule. After a few minutes of walking, they had reached their destination, and Constable Otts had vanished into the night, while he, de Rohan, and the dog had settled down for a long wait.

They were huddled now behind a half-dozen empty barrels which had been conveniently stacked across the street from the Prospect of Whitby. From such a vantage point, they were able to watch the entrance of the narrow passageway which ran alongside the tavern and back to the river. They could also observe the last of the night's revelers as they staggered out the front door and into the main thoroughfare.

The pub closed early on Sunday, and, like clockwork, Mr. Pratt came out at midnight to sweep the doorstep and bolt the door. Then, one by one, the flickering candles upstairs, already muted into yellow smudges by the fog, began to die away. And as they vanished, the night's chill set in with a vengeance.

David had harbored some faint hope that the warm memories of his waltz with Cecilia would sustain him through the night, but by half past one, the river's damp had seeped through his heavy woolen overcoat to permeate every layer of clothing beneath. He was rapidly developing a deep appreciation for de Rohan's devotion to duty, not to mention his bloody fortitude. David now felt as though he mightn't be able to rise from his crouched position if his very life depended upon it—which it just might, he wryly considered.

To ease the pain in his joints, he shifted slightly to the left and rose just an inch. At once, a hard, determined hand came down upon his shoulder. "Damn it, keep still," hissed de Rohan from the shadows.

Behind him, the mastiff gave a grunt of canine displeasure, as if he, too, were annoyed by David's inexperience. But the tension was driving David wild. "God, I'd kill for a good cheroot just now," he muttered under his breath.

De Rohan rose up to peer over one of the casks. "I shouldn't, if I were you," he whispered out of one side of his mouth. "Ages the skin, you know."

David sighed and massaged one knee. "I've heard."

"Of course," the inspector added, "if you mean to rush into that alley and do something brave enough or foolish enough to get yourself killed, I daresay it won't much matter."

"Why, Max!" said David dryly. "I didn't know you cared."

"Paperwork," muttered de Rohan in the dark. "Don't want the bloody paperwork. Peers killed on my watch. It won't do, that's all." At that moment, however, a candle in a third-story window wavered, then went out.

"That's the last of them," whispered de Rohan confidently.

As if on cue, a hired hackney rolled up the street, and David felt a surge of excitement. The jangling harnesses and heavy hooves sounded muffled and strangely distant in the dampness, but the carriage had drawn up before the tavern. Silently, a slender figure in a long black cloak dropped to the ground and vanished into the murk of the alley.

"Edmund Rowland?" asked de Rohan out of the side of his mouth.

In the darkness, David drew his coat a little closer. "Yes . . ." he responded uncertainly. "I think."

Suddenly, he felt de Rohan jerk fully upright, as if he'd heard something. Carefully, David listened. And then, he heard it, too. The faint slice of oars through the water. Followed by the gentle thump of wood against stone.

Down the alley, something which looked like a huge lantern or torch flared briefly, vanished, then flashed again. Obviously, a signal of some sort. At once, de Rohan jerked to his feet, tugged his shirttails partially loose, then began to fumble at the close of his trousers.

"What the devil are you doing?" hissed David.

"Staggering drunkenly into the alley to piss," he answered, running a disordering hand through his hair. "No magistrate will convict a man of Rowland's background without a reputable eyewitness. I want no doubts on this one."

Before David could protest, de Rohan quietly commanded the dog to stay and then darted across the street. He had no sooner vanished into the passageway beside the Prospect than the rumble of a heavy cart could be heard echoing in the distance—summoned by the lantern, perhaps?

The heavy dray loomed out of the fog, drawing up in front of David's hiding place, blocking his view of the alley entrance. Only one man—but a big one—sat upon the driver's seat, his face shadowed by a broad-brimmed hat. With amazing stealth, he climbed down and strolled into the alley with a familiar, rolling gait. A seaman's gait, David thought. And then a name sprang to mind.

Grimes!

David was almost sure of it. And now de Rohan was trapped between Grimes, who was entering the alley, and the landing lightermen on the river beyond. And the cart, David suddenly realized, was the means of transporting the chests back to the brothel. De Rohan had explained that under cover of night, the goods would have been offloaded onto a lighter and rowed up-river. That boat was undoubtedly the one now moored at the base of the stairs. In the second phase, the mangowood chests would be brought up Pelican Stairs and carried to the street through the alley, which was so narrow two men abreast could scarcely pass down it.

And de Rohan had no way out. Quietly, David rose and withdrew one of his two loaded pistols. Glancing up and down the murky street, he made his way around the dray toward the alley entrance.

Though the moon was nearly full, and the alley made almost a straight shot down to Pelican Stairs, David could still see little through the fog. With a quick prayer, he stepped into the alley and pressed himself against the wall opposite the Prospect, leading with his armed right hand. He could feel the damp wall behind him, the thick, wet air before him, and he could hear the soft crunch of sand and gravel beneath his boots.

It felt disconcerting to make his way blindly into a situation which was dangerous. But surprisingly, he felt no fear, only cold certainty. He could not leave de Rohan without his back covered. A few feet ahead, he heard the rattle of a loose stone beneath someone's feet. Grimes, he hoped. But would the man, by some small miracle, make his way past de Rohan without seeing him?

Good God, he thought, how many of Rowland's people were in the alley now? Mentally, he tried to count. Certainly, there was Rowland himself—or the man who had dismounted from the hackney. Grimes. At least two lightermen coming ashore. So, four at a minimum.

Of de Rohan's men, there were more. But four of them were on the water, and would only now begin to close in. De Rohan's assistant, Otts, had been told to place himself on the other side of the Prospect. All of them were to await de Rohan's signal—save David, who'd been told to stay on the street. Yet, it seemed obvious he could not now do that. They had the smugglers trapped, yes. But de Rohan was caught in the middle.

But then, just a few yards deeper into the alley, something went horribly wrong. David heard an authoritative voice carry inland from the water. "Halt in the name of the Crown!" came the booming cry. "River Police! Secure your cargo and stand!"

Too soon!

Damn it, the police launches had moved in too soon! A gunshot rang out. De Rohan's? Almost certainly. David's blood ran cold, then froze.

At once, Grimes burst out of the fog, plowing past David in his haste to escape. Ruthlessly, David blocked him with a low blow to the left shoulder,

then caught him quickly across the ankle with his
boot. Grimes almost sprawled facedown into the
alley. But he somehow recovered and scrabbled
away.

"Otts!" shouted David, praying the constable stood
in the darkness behind him. "Take him!"

"Right, m'lord!" Otts's voice rang out, then David
heard the thud of human bodies colliding. With a
loud series of grunts and curses, the two men went
down, boots thumping and scraping against the
walls. And then, Grimes cried out in pain—his voice
unmistakable.

Hoping Grimes was seriously injured, David continued to feel his way down the alley. Confusion
rang through the narrow passage now, echoing off
the damp walls and carrying across the water. In the
darkness, he heard a splash, followed by the sound
of wood striking wood. The boats in the water, no
doubt. A loud *crack!* like an oar striking water rang
out.

Another few feet, and still no de Rohan. A second
muttered curse, the thud of a man's skull against
stone. The sound of a body smacking the water.
David could see nothing. But at the embankment
beyond, all hell could be heard breaking loose.
Somewhere, a window shattered. Another gunshot
boomed off the walls. Glass tinkled down upon the
cobblestones.

Suddenly, a flying black mass of muscle and bone
came hurling out of the darkness behind David,
launching itself at something in the depths of the
alley. With a surprisingly steady hand, David jerked
up his weapon, thrusting it into the murk. A horrific,
bloodcurdling snarl brought him to his senses in the
nick of time.

Lucifer!

And then, through the gloom, he could see the writhing and snarling black mass rise up onto its hind legs. In the fog, two men fell apart, the first throwing himself against the wall, the second collapsing to the ground beneath the thrashing bulk of the huge mastiff, arms and legs flailing as the dog mauled him into submission.

Roughly, de Rohan shoved himself away from the wall. "Let's go," whispered David, jerking his head toward the river. "Otts has the entrance. We have them trapped like rats in a drain pipe."

They neared the opening which gave onto the water. A distant lamp reflected weakly off the river, casting a hint of light at the end of the passageway. Behind them, the sound of Lucifer's gnashing teeth fading in the thick fog. Suddenly, David could see the stone stairs. They loomed up from the water rising some three feet above the alley. Cursing, splashing, and shouting still rang through the air.

At the top, the man in the black cloak stood, staring down into the fray in the water below.

"De Rohan!" someone shouted up. "Got one!"

At once, the man in black spun toward de Rohan. He lifted his arm, a hint of moonlight reflecting off the pistol in his hand. De Rohan stepped forward and aimed his gun. In that moment, a second man burst from the shadows, taking David down with a bone-shattering blow.

David's weapon flew from his hand. It struck the wall, discharging with a deafening roar. Ruthlessly, the two men thrashed. But David was both heavier and quicker—and probably more desperate, for it suddenly occurred to him just how much he had to live for.

With one last blow, he jabbed an elbow beneath the lighterman's chin, driving his head backward into a stone abutment. The resulting crack of bone was horrific. A twitch, and the man lay still.

Staggering to his feet, David was dimly aware of de Rohan still pointing his weapon up at the cloaked figure. But it was empty—wasn't it? Certainly, someone's gun had fired first.

But de Rohan meant to bluff it out. "River Police," he shouted up for the second time, his voice rock-steady. "Drop your weapon and stand down!"

"No," came a surprisingly soft voice from atop the stairs. "I don't think I shall have to do that."

Just then, another figure slid from the alley into the light. David blinked to clear his vision. In amazement, he stared at the newcomer. *Walrafen?* What the hell?

"You cannot very well shoot three of us," Lord Walrafen shouted up, lifting his hand to reveal the pistol he carried. "Drop your weapon, whoever you are."

In that moment, David was seized with a swift certainty. Remembering, he slid one hand into the pocket of his greatcoat and drew out his second weapon, primed by the efficient Otts. The man in the hooded cloak was not watching David but, instead, was desperately jerking his aim from de Rohan to Walrafen and back. Apparently deciding that Walrafen presented the greater threat, the man shifted again and yanked the trigger—but not before David fired.

The echo of his pistol shattered the darkness. With an awkward, collapsing motion, the man crumbled, falling headlong off the platform and onto the cobbled alley, returning fire with a deafening roar.

Walrafen stumbled back, one leg collapsing beneath him. De Rohan came swiftly forward, catching him under one arm, easing him to the ground.

"Walrafen, you are hit?" demanded David, rushing forward.

De Rohan's hand went to his cravat, yanking it free to bind the leg. "Only nicked, thanks to you," said Lord Walrafen, jerking his head toward the wounded man. "Who is he? Is he dead?"

Swiftly, David closed the distance to the man on the ground, rolling him over to feel for a pulse. With a soft, draping motion, the loose hood of the cloak slithered back to reveal the wide, bitter eyes which stared up at him.

"Just my . . . bloody luck," rasped Anne Rowland weakly. "For once in your useless life . . . you had to do the . . . right thing." Then her body heaved once more, arched back against his arm, and went limp.

Kneeling there in the mud and sand, David stared into her eyes, which were open yet horrifically sightless. *Good God! Anne.* Never would he have guessed . . . and yet, it made perfect sense. He could hear de Rohan's words of warning echoing in his head.

The really good criminals never appear to be what they are . . .

Cold water was soaking through the knees of his trousers now. Behind him, he was dimly aware of de Rohan hefting Walrafen to his feet while shouting orders to his men. He heard Grimes spewing obscenities at Constable Otts as the latter marched him back down the alley. Two sodden Chinese sailors were cuffed and dragged past. And still, David could not tear his eyes from Anne's.

After seemingly interminable minutes, a gentle hand came to rest lightly on his shoulder as a puddle of gold satin and black velvet settled about his feet.

"David . . . ?" Cecilia whispered as she knelt in the filth and the blood beside him. And then the warm, comforting scent of her flooded his senses, bringing back sanity with it.

EPILOGUE

In which a Joker deals the Final hand

"All Fools' Day!" muttered the Reverend Mr. Amherst as his eyes drifted over the ebullient throng which spilled from his withdrawing room and into the parlor. "Really, Jonet! What sort of people get married on All Fools' Day?"

From her chaise beside him, Jonet reached up and clasped her husband's hand, lightly pressing her lips to his knuckles. "The sort who cannot wait, I daresay," she slyly murmured, her lips warm against his skin.

The new Lady Delacourt chose precisely that moment to rise unsteadily from her seat by the hearth, and make a surreptitious dash for the ladies' retiring room.

Critically observing her retreat, Cole entwined his fingers with Jonet's and sank down into the chair by her chaise. "She seems rather more nervous than I would have expected."

Jonet leaned a little nearer and grinned mischievously. "Oh, Cecilia's problem isn't *nerves*, my love—it's *nausea!*" she whispered. "Really, darling, sometimes you are still shockingly naïve."

"And how I have remained so whilst wed to you is quite beyond me," Cole grumbled good-naturedly.

"Do you mean to say we can expect yet another happy event in our not-too-distant future?"

But his wife was no longer listening. Instead, she had pulled her fingers from his grasp and was extending both hands forward in a gesture of welcome. An elegantly dressed middle-aged man had crossed the room toward them.

"Mr. Kemble!" Jonet exclaimed. "At last! May I introduce my husband, Mr. Amherst?"

The man drew himself up proudly. "A pleasure, my lady. And Mr. Amherst, what a lovely service you conducted! Most inspiring! Almost enough to make *me* contemplate matrimonial bliss!"

"You're very kind, Mr. Kemble," murmured Cole, rising from his chair. "Now, if you will excuse me, I must have a word with Lord Walrafen."

Jonet cut a glance in that direction. Lord Walrafen looked rather wan, and bore much of his weight on a crutch. He was accompanied by a tall, striking stranger, and as Cole approached, the three men fell at once into a deep discussion. Returning her gaze to Kemble, she patted Cole's empty chair.

"Come, Mr. Kemble, do sit down. Such excitement! And you in the midst of it. You must tell me all, for no one else will. I believe they make an excuse of my condition, but the truth is, I am perfectly bloodthirsty."

Mr. Kemble looked flattered. "I confess, my lady, I was not there to see Lord Walrafen shot," he whispered. "However, the tall, very angular-looking gentleman at his elbow—that is Chief Inspector de Rohan. I have recently made his close acquaintance through Lord Delacourt, and he has told me the whole of it."

"Really?" said Jonet appreciatively. "And what does the inspector believe will happen to that horrible man—Grimes, the one who murdered the two girls from my husband's mission? Will he hang?"

"Oh, from a very high tree, de Rohan says!" confirmed Kemble ghoulishly. "Moreover, the fellow has obligingly revealed everything about Anne Rowland's smuggling operation."

Lightly, Jonet lifted her brows. "So do you think it is true, then? About Cousin Edmund? He really knew nothing of his wife's activities?"

Kemble hesitated. "Nothing de Rohan can prove."

"Perhaps the inspector is being circumspect." Jonet smiled grimly. "Of course, we'd all known that Anne kept Edmund under her thumb. The mission is fortunate that Anne did not succeed in worming her way inside, or poor Kitty O'Gavin would likely be dead, too. I think Anne wanted very desperately to find her."

Kemble cut a quick glance toward Lord Walrafen. "Well, there is a vast deal of wicked gossip floating about the Home Office, you know," he said. "I have heard it whispered that Anne Rowland was also possessed of some rather shocking habits—habits which she privately indulged at the house in Black Horse Lane."

Jonet was quiet for moment. "Tell me, Mr. Kemble, the madam who kept the house—did she know Anne after all?"

Kemble lifted his elegant shoulders. "De Rohan thinks that only Grimes knew Mrs. Rowland's identity. From all indications, Mrs. Rowland visited the house without revealing precisely who she was. Perhaps she found it interesting to spy on her own behalf. Or perhaps she merely sought a discreet place in which to indulge her—" He jerked to a halt, glancing again at Jonet. "Her personal inclinations," he tactfully finished.

"And so Edmund either did not know of her illegal activities," mused Jonet, "or he simply did not care. They both craved wealth and status—so much so that she greedily resorted to smuggling. Still, one wonders that he did not guess the truth."

"From time to time, I collect that Mrs. Rowland asked her husband to make business arrangements which perhaps a wiser man might have found suspicious. But it seems he did not question her activities too closely."

"I daresay you're right." Jonet laughed rather bitterly, then surrendered to her usual good humor. "So, what now, Mr. Kemble? My friend Lord Delacourt clearly means to get on with his life at last. But now that this dreadful matter has ended, what of everyone else?"

"Well, Edmund Rowland has gone abroad, but I daresay you knew that." Discreetly, Kemble lifted his glass in the direction of Lord Walrafen. "And as a political ally of Mr. Peel, Walrafen has persuaded Mr. de Rohan to accept a post within the Home Office—a very *discreet* sort of post, I might add."

"Oh?" Jonet drew back incrementally. "It all sounds perfectly thrilling."

"Oh, it is!" whispered Kemble knowingly. "He's to hold something of a special office, I understand. It all has to do with the Parliamentary Committee on police reform, which everyone believes will be resurrected."

Jonet was intrigued. "I thought the House had finished with that issue."

"Eventually, Peel will have his way," Kemble said confidently. "Still, there is a vast amount of corruption to be ferreted out. And de Rohan is said to be eminently qualified. Indeed, I hear that he's worked not just for the River Police but at Bow Street and in

Queen Square as well. It should all prove most inter-esting."

"Most interesting!" agreed Jonet. "And what of yourself, Mr. Kemble? Will you relent, and join Rannoch in the country after all? Or will you accept Delacourt's generous offer?"

"Oh, that." Kemble looked suddenly far away. "I am thinking," he said slowly, "of giving it up altogether."

Apparently noting Jonet's shocked expression, he swiftly added, "Of course, I'm exceptionally fond of Rannoch. And of Delacourt, too. Unfortunately, all my gentlemen do seem to marry, and then vanish at once into the dull depths of rural greenery and marital bliss. But I should much prefer the excitement of town, and so I am thinking that a little shop would suit me."

"As in a haberdashery?"

Kemble shook his head. "Porcelain, I think. Antique bits of glass and pottery, perhaps old jewelry—that sort of thing. But only the very best, of course. In the Strand, I think. Lots of traffic, reasonable rent."

"The Strand?" echoed Jonet. "You are seriously looking—"

But suddenly, her attention was distracted by some sort of activity within the crowd. She glanced swiftly toward David, who still stood by the hearth chatting with a stream of well-wishers. Cecilia had not returned to his side.

And then Jonet saw him. *Robin*. His expression impish, he had pressed his way through the crowd and paused before his uncle. With a grand flourish, he presented David with an elegantly wrapped package.

David stared down at the box which he'd just been given, feeling vaguely amused at Lord Robin's behavior. The boy had hardly spoken to him since their rather heated argument a fortnight earlier. But in the end, it had been settled. David had made good Robin's gaming debts—including every farthing the boy owed Rutledge—but at a somewhat painful interest rate. And Robin was repaying him in quarterly installments which left him essentially poverty-stricken. The boy had liked it very little, but he'd liked the alternative— flinging himself on his mother's mercy—even less.

David lifted his gaze to study Robin's face. "What is this?"

"A wedding gift, my lord," said his nephew with a wink. "Something I trust you will find deeply and personally meaningful."

"I'd never thought you the sentimental sort, Robin," he dryly remarked. "Shall I wait until my blushing bride returns before I open it?"

Chuckling, Robin shook his head. "No, I think not," he whispered. "This is more of a gesture of sympathy—a little tribute to mark the passing of a truly glorious bachelorhood."

Sportingly, David untied the silk cord and unwrapped the package, to find that it held nothing but an old pack of cards which were significantly the worse for wear. Sharply lifting one brow, he cut a dubious glance up at his nephew. "Looks like the aftermath of a hard night, my boy," he remarked. "What the deuce did you soak them in? Cheap brandy?"

Robin threw back his head and laughed. "Hardly! It was the finest French cognac money can buy— Charlie's best stock, specifically."

"*Bloody hell,*" whispered an almost inaudible voice at David's elbow.

David glanced around to see that Cole had joined them. Jonet, too, had somehow managed to cross the room on Kemble's arm. Stuart stood behind his mother. Anxiously, David glanced back and forth between them all. "Charlie's brandy—?" he muttered, feeling very much as if he had missed something. Something important, perhaps.

But Robin was still laughing. "Oh, come on, Delacourt! Do they not look the least bit familiar? When was the last time you played a hand?"

David shook his head and stared at the cards. "Why, one pack looks very like another, Robin. And I've been quite busy of late, what with the mission and . . . other things." With a strange sense of unease, David turned the pack over. Immediately, his gaze fell upon the top card, the queen of spades, its corners curled and stained from damp.

David's mouth turned up into an involuntary grin. "I say—this is the pack we played with in the book room, is it not? The very one Cole trounced me with?"

Robin lifted his brows and opened his hands in an uncharacteristically innocent gesture. "It is *one* of the packs we played with that night, yes. But not, specifically speaking, the one with which you were beaten— or not all of it, at any rate."

David caught sight of Cole, slinking from the crowd. "Not all of it?" David's brow furrowed in thought. "But I remember . . . I remember someone spilt the brandy—"

"Papa did," Robin quickly interjected.

"And then—why, we stopped the play and wiped it up. But the cards weren't harmed. I distinctly remember that. Because Cole had the queen of spades. He tossed it up to set trumps." As he spoke, David kept staring at his nephew, willing him to say something.

Robin merely grinned.

"And his queen was dry when he played it," insisted David. "I remember. He used it to trump my ace of diamonds."

Robin kept grinning. For a long, long moment.

Finally, David swallowed hard. "I was *cheated—?*" he whispered weakly. "You mean to tell me I was *sharped—?* By a bloody village parson?"

Suddenly, David felt a warm, somewhat tremulous hand slide around his elbow, and he looked down into the bottomless blue depths of his bride's eyes.

"Who was cheated?" asked Cecilia curiously. "And what did they lose? Given your expressions, it must have been something precious indeed."

"It was nothing," interjected David, scarcely considering the words before he spoke. "Nothing of value." For after one look at Cecilia's pale, perfect face, all thought of what had gone before fled his mind. And in that one blindingly sweet moment, he thought not of what he had lost—a life of wretched excess—but of what he had won. The knowledge left him weak in the knees.

HISTORICAL NOTE

~

It is commonly believed that other than the sometimes-corrupt Bow Street Runners, no organized police force existed in England prior to Parliament's passage of the Metropolitan Police Act. Strictly speaking, this was far from true, and by the time Peel centralized London's police force in 1829, the so-called river police had already been safeguarding the city's major artery—the River Thames and its environs—for over thirty years.

This intrepid band of constables and surveyors (or what would later be called inspectors) was so successful in saving lives and protecting cargo that after its first six months of operation, two thousand East End criminals rioted, and attempted to burn the River Thames Police Station to the ground.

They were not successful. And today, after two centuries of hard work, the River Police still report for duty in Wapping High Street, just as they always have.

Here is a sneak peek at Liz Carlyle's sexy new novel, *ONE LITTLE SIN*

Coming From Pocket Star Books in October 2005

MacLachlan nodded, then turned to Esmée as if she were next on his list of Catastrophes to be Dealt With. "You," he said decisively. "Come with me into the study. We've a little something to settle, you and I."

Esmée must have faltered.

MacLachlan's eyes narrowed. "Oh, come now, Miss Hamilton!"

The doctor had already vanished. MacLachlan seized Esmée by the arm, and steered her almost roughly down the corridor. He pushed open the door, urged her inside, and slammed it shut.

"Good God" he said, exhaling sharply. "What a bloody awful nightmare this day has turned out to be!"

"Oh, aye, d' ye think so?" asked Esmée, her voice tart. "Then how would you like to have your womb up tied in knots like poor Mrs. Crosby, with your life's blood leaching out, and your child all but lost? *That*, MacLachlan, is what a nightmare feels like."

The muscle in MacLachlan's too-perfect jaw began to twitch. "I am not insensible to Julia's anguish," he gritted. "I would bear it for her if I could, but I cannot. All I can do is to try to be a good friend."

"Oh, would that every woman had such a friend!" she returned. "You are off gallivanting about town with a brandy bottle as your boon companion, whilst she is all but miscarrying your next child!"

Esmée had not sat down, a circumstance which MacLachlan either did not notice, or did not care about. He had begun to pace the floor between the windows, one hand set at the back of his neck, the other on his hip. His jaw was growing tighter and tighter as he paced, and his temple was beginning to visibly throb, too.

"Well?" she challenged. "Have you nothing to say, man?"

Suddenly, he whirled on her. "Now you listen to me, you spite-tongued little witch," he said. "And listen well, for I mean to say this but once: Julia Crosby's child is none of your business—nor any of mine, either, come to that."

"Aye, 'tis none of my business if you sire a bastard in every parish," Esmée returned.

"You're bloody well right it's not," he retorted. "And perhaps I have! But whilst I'm defending myself from your hot-headed notions, let me say that I have *not* spent the day idly drinking, either."

"Oh, faith! You reek of it!"

"Yes, and yesterday I reeked of coffee," he snapped. "Neither you nor Lord Devellyn possess a modicum of grace, it seems. He slopped brandy down my trousers."

Esmée didn't believe him. "Oh, aye, you've been gone all day, and when at last you come home, you smell as if you spent the afternoon in the gutter. What's anyone to think?"

He stabbed his finger in her face. "Miss Hamilton, had I any wish to be nagged, insulted, or upbraided, I would get myself a wife, not a goddamned governess!" he roared. "And besides that, you do not get paid to *think!*"

Esmée felt her temper implode. "Oh, no, I get

paid to . . . to *what?*" she shrilly demanded as he resumed his pacing. "Satisfy the master's base instincts when his itch wants scratching? Remind me again. I somehow got muddled up over my duties."

He spun about, and grabbed her by the shoulders, shoving her against the door. "Shut up, Esmée," he growled. "For once, just shut the hell up." And then he was kissing her, brutishly and relentlessly.

She tried to squirm away, but he held her prisoner between his hands. The harsh stubble of his beard raked across her face as he slanted his lips over hers, again and again, his powerful hands clenched upon her shoulders.

She tried to twist her face away. His nostrils were wide now, his mouth hot and demanding. Something inside her sagged, gave way, and she opened her mouth to him. He surged inside, thrusting deep. Her shoulder blades pressed against the wood, she began to shudder. There was no tenderness to his touch now, just a black, demanding hunger. Esmée began to shove at his shoulders, and then to pummel them with the heels of her hands.

As abruptly as it had begun, he tore his mouth from hers, and stared her in the eyes, his nostrils still wide, his breathing still rough and quick. And then, his eyes dropped shut. "Damn it all," he whispered. "No, damn *me*."

For a moment there was an awful silence. Then Esmée broke it. "I ought to slap the breath of life from you," she gritted. "Don't ever touch me again, MacLachlan. I am *not* Mrs. Crosby. I am not even my mother, lest you be confused. Now take your lecherous hands off me, or I'll be kneeing you in the knackers so hard you heave."